Both Your Houses

SARAH HARRISON

WARNER BOOKS

A *Warner* Book

First published in Great Britain in 1995
by Little, Brown and Company

This edition published by Warner Books in 1996
Reprinted 1996, 1997

A CIP catalogue record for this book
is available from the British Library.

ISBN 0 7515 1583 3

Typeset by Palimpsest Book Production Limited
Printed and bound in Great Britain by Clays Ltd, St Ives plc

Warner Books
A Division of
Little, Brown and Company (UK)
Brettenham House
Lancaster Place
London WC2E 7EN

For the family

CHAPTER ONE

I n June 1978 Hester Blake and her two younger children, Giselle, four, and one-year-old Daniel, drove to London to the Holland Park home of Ann Armitage, so that Hester could hear a talk by a wise woman of the day on the subject of 'A Woman's Right to Choose'.

'I'm taking a day unpaid. Much the best,' Ann had pointed out, 'with the menfolk out of the way. Do come,' she urged, 'it's so vital to combat all this anti-abortion hysteria, and I guarantee you'll find Merle Shaw a stimulating speaker.'

'What about the kids?' Hester demurred. 'Rose will be at school, but Giselle's still mornings only and Daniel's clingy.'

'Bring them,' said Ann. 'Lots of other people are. I'm laying on a light lunch, and it's half term for our lot so at least two of the boys will be about.' (The Armitages were of a leftish persuasion, and Ann's husband Byron toiled at the educational coalface of a north London comprehensive, but Ann had opted for private schools for her three sons from the age of eleven.) 'Sebastian,' Ann added proudly, speaking of her eldest, 'is in Thailand.'

In the car, while the baby slept, Hester issued a stern injunction to her daughter.

'Darling, you must be a very good girl. I'm going to be sitting with the other mummies, listening to a lady talk—'

'What about?'

'About babies.'

'Can I come?'

'I think you'll be able to play in the garden.'

'I want to listen about babies.'

'No darling, it's a grown-up thing. You'll have a much better time with the other children.'

'I hate the other children,' said Giselle.

Hester was afraid it might be mutual.

But when they arrived, Ann took charge. With the relaxed authority of one whose own offspring have reached young adulthood without mishap, she took Giselle by the hand and led her out into the garden where her youngest son, Julian, fourteen, and a friend, Rupert, were presiding over half a dozen small children.

'She'll be fine,' Ann reassured Hester. She followed her friend's still-doubtful gaze, and chuckled. 'Those two are experienced babysitters, it's quite a cottage industry with them. And I've left some small-people's lunch in the playroom. Now you come along in, and bring his lordship – ' she tickled Daniel's cheek with her finger – 'with you.'

Hester was left with no option but to be led away to the drawing room where Merle Shaw, vibrantly kaftaned, was already enthroned in a basket chair, a glass of Soave in her hand, pregnant with pronouncements for her eager audience of some fifteen or sixteen women.

Only Ann, thought Hester, sitting down at the end of a row and jiggling the restless Daniel, could have persuaded all these young mothers to surrender their offspring to the care of two teenage boys, to assemble indoors in the height of summer, and to listen to this fat, childless woman expound the desirability of abortion on demand. Still, reflected Hester, who was pursuing a stuttering freelance career at the time, it might make a women's page piece for someone . . .

Having formally introduced the speaker, Ann returned to her seat, which was just behind Hester's, and leaned forward to whisper:

'I can see you're still worried – if there's the slightest problem with the youngsters, Gavin's upstairs studying for As, and will step into the breach at a moment's notice.'

Gavin was the Armitages' middle son, nearly eighteen. Hester nodded, and slipped Daniel a biscuit from her bag.

'Fine!' she said. 'I'm not worried.'

It did not take Giselle long to size up the situation in the garden and give it a zero-rating. There were three pretty little girls in Laura Ashley frocks, a small boy with ringlets and a couple of toddlers squatting pensively in the flowerbed. Rupert, the bigger of the two big boys in charge, lay on his back on the grass with his shirt off and his eyes shut. Julian, the other one, was trying to make everyone play properly.

'What's your name?' he asked her.

'Giselle.'

'That's pretty. It's a French name, isn't it?'

She stared at him.

'Would you like a game of catch?'

She didn't reply so he picked up a foam rubber ball and tossed it gently in her direction. She put her hands behind her back and it bounced harmlessly off the bib of her denim dungarees.

'Whoops, bad luck!' he exclaimed.

Giselle stared.

After a couple more throws he gave up.

'It'll be lunch soon,' he said. 'Do you like egg sandwiches?'

'They smell pooey,' Giselle told him. Rebuffed, Julian went to reclaim the toddlers from the flowerbed.

Egg sandwiches notwithstanding, Giselle was interested in the idea of lunch. She wandered back into the house. The main french window was closed, and the door she went through led her into the playroom where Ann's selection of little sausages, bridge rolls, sandwiches, carrot sticks and individual jellies lay on a paper cloth, with Tom and Jerry cardboard plates and cups stacked at one end. Giselle took a sausage roll and moved on. She left the playroom, took in the downstairs lavatory with its framed map of the world and pile of National Geographicals, and eventually turned a large, round handle and entered the kitchen/dining room. It was cool and dim, because the curtains were half-drawn across the french windows.

On the table was an array of food such as Giselle had never seen before. She was not familiar with spinach and ricotta terrine, salmon mousse, savoury jelly mould, nut roast, quiche lorraine and couscous, but her eyes gobbled up the smooth striped bricks with their medallions of green and red, the glossy pink fish frilled with watercress, the cool glint of the jelly, the savoury golden crusts and intriguing little grains in their earthenware dish. On a side table was a huge bowl of strawberries, more than she had ever seen in one place before, and two jugs of cream. She pulled a chair over and helped herself to a few, leaving the well-sucked, star-shaped hulls floating on the surface of the cream.

She walked along a high-ceilinged corridor to the front of the house. She recognised the door by which her mother and she had entered earlier, and from behind another she could hear the murmur of a voice, rising and falling. She went up the stairs, drawn by the urge to explore. On the next floor there was another lavatory, a big bathroom, and some large, tidy bedrooms. There were also more stairs, and she thought she could hear someone up at the top.

She continued upward until she reached a smaller landing. It was hot up here beneath the eaves of the house, and Giselle was tired with her long climb. She stood panting for a second. It was then that she heard sounds again, and went across to the nearest door to investigate.

The door wasn't locked, or even closed, and she pushed it wide open. The room was big, with a sloping ceiling that had two windows in it. All the furniture was very low, right down at Giselle's eye-level, so she had no difficulty seeing the big boy and girl, who were on the bed with no clothes on. The boy was lying down with his hands behind his head and the girl, who had long stringy hair, was kneeling between his legs, hunched over as if she was being sick. Which she probably would be, thought Giselle, if she went on eating the boy's bottom like that.

'Yee-uk,' she said loudly. 'You are *yukky*.'

'Jesus H. Christ!' said Gavin. 'Where did that little turd spring from?'

'One of your mum's ladies, I should think,' said Tanya.

'Do you think she cottoned on?'

'I doubt it.'

'I fucking hope not.'

'She won't even know what she saw.'

'I thought Jules and Rupert were supposed to be in charge of that rabble,' grumbled Gavin, pulling on his jeans and T-shirt.

'Like you were supposed to be in charge of Jules and Rupert . . .?'

'I'm studying. I was only a fall-back position.'

'Tell me about it,' said Tanya, her eyes narrowing.

'Get off. You'd better go now, anyway.'

'I'll go in and sit at the back, shall I?'

'Get lost.'

Giselle went back down to the food. On the way through the hall she heard the voices of lots of women all talking at once and, rising above it, the piping tones of Daniel.

In the kitchen she gave in to temptation and tasted a bit of everything, using her hands. Time spent in Creative Play at the village hall had not been wasted on Giselle. She kneaded and moulded, and squeezed and spread, and crumbled and squelched. It was better fun than sand, water, finger-painting or playdough and had the advantage of tasting nice as well.

The sound of the lavatory flushing heralded the arrival of the boy with ringlets.

'What you doing?'

'This,' said Giselle, throwing a strawberry at him.

The strawberries were warm and ripe; they went splat. When they'd used about a third of them, Giselle got bored. She went into the lavatory, ran the tap and washed her face and hands. Then she went into the playroom and joined the other children round the table. Rupert was stubbing out a cigarette on the patio, Julian was pouring orange squash into the Tom and Jerry cups. She heard footsteps coming along the corridor, and held her breath in terror.

'Bloody hell—!'

It was the big boy from upstairs. Giselle let her breath go. A moment later, as the drawing room door opened and the women's chatter became louder and more shrill, he came into the playroom, carrying the boy with ringlets out in front of him, the way her father carried the cat when it had a dead mouse in its mouth.

'So much for supervising!' he shouted. 'What have you two been doing? You've never seen anything like the frigging disaster next door. Mother'll go spare!'

'That's Jasper,' said Julian. 'Give him here, I'll go and get him cleaned up. I want to take a look anyway.'

'What did he do?' asked Rupert, over the silently munching children. 'He only went a moment ago, to the bog.'

'Then he must be a fast worker. Their lunch is completely bloody wrecked.'

Giselle chewed, but the hinges of her jaw felt stiff.

Gavin heard the women approaching. He could imagine the guilt trip that would be handed out later on, when his mother had done her loaves and fishes number and saved the day with something out of the freezer. Scanning the party distractedly he noticed the dark kid who'd burst in on him and Tanya. Her face and hands looked clean but there were suspicious-looking coloured deposits all over her dungarees.

'Hang on,' said Gavin, stepping forward and pinning her arms to her sides. 'What's this?'

She didn't speak, but twisted her head and looked up at him. She had an extremely decided face for a kid of her age, with a fierce scowl and unblinking dark eyes. He found himself wondering if it were possible . . . whether she just might . . . It wasn't worth the risk.

He released her roughly. 'Get on and eat.'

'Never mind,' said Ann, in the soft, bell-like voice she used when things were at their worst. 'My fault for leaving it all so accessible. A mother of my experience should know better! Please, no recriminations now, it simply is not worth it.' She gave a light laugh. 'Why doesn't everyone have another drink in the drawing room? I'll salvage what I can and send one of the boys out for French bread.'

'I'll tell them, shall I?' said Hester, struck by a terrible surmise.

The women filed out obediently, exchanging looks, and agreeing mutedly that Ann was absolutely wonderful.

Hester, full of dread, peeled off and opened the playroom door. The children were sitting round the table, and the two Armitage boys and Rupert were in attendance.

'Your poor, poor Mum,' she said to the eldest. 'If it was me I'd be having hysterics and berserking with a meat cleaver.'

'Not her style,' said Gavin.

'Anyway, she wants one of you to go to the shops,' said Hester. Julian nodded and she stood aside to let him pass. 'Which is the culprit?' she asked, as lightly as she could manage. Gavin made a jabbing downward movement at Jasper's ringleted head.

'Really?'

'Caught red-handed, literally.'

'Giselle—?'

Her daughter looked up at her, her lips encrusted with pastry crumbs.

'You weren't playing about with the food, were you?'

Giselle did not reply. 'Because,' said Hester tensely, 'your dungers are in an awful state.'

Gavin came up close to Hester, with his back to the rest of the room. 'No, she's in the clear. Only a spot of joining in.'

His manner, though curiously urgent, was credible. Relieved, Hester withdrew.

On the way home, Hester began to shape her amusing little article based on the events of the day. With hindsight there were a lot of possibilities. For instance, there was something poetic in the way the awful disaster with the food had probably done more to advance Merle Shaw's cause than all the well-turned phrases in her overlong speech . . .

She felt giggles rise up in her like champagne bubbles. As she began to laugh she looked in the rear-view mirror at the children. Daniel was asleep, his head lolling sideways in his safety seat.

Giselle returned her look with one of quelling and impenetrable seriousness.

'What are you laughing at?'

'Nothing. So, did you enjoy it, darling? Nice lunch?'

'Yes,' said Giselle, 'the lunch was nice. But those big boys were yukky.'

CHAPTER TWO

Friendship, Hester told herself one evening in early May 1992, is a wonderful thing. She gazed benignly on her dinner guests, Ann and Byron Armitage, who had driven all the way from London to The Old Clink, Chuffington, to eat Hester's undistinguished artichoke soup and her workmanlike pork with Calvados, and who had been polite enough not to ask the provenance of the chocolate roulade (a special from Freezerworld).

The rewarding thing about friendship, she mused, especially one as long-standing as this, was that it could embrace change. It was fluid, flexible and forgiving. Where there was real liking, trust and – she glanced at Ann – respect, your paths might diverge, but this mutually enriching relationship could survive and even grow. It was not diminished but enhanced by differences . . .

She passed coffee cups down the table, waved a hand at sugar, milk and cream, gave the handmade chocolates (brought by Ann and Byron) an inviting nudge. Hester's husband Jonathan, Jonty to his intimates, was talking about Earthtrust, the environmental organisation of which he was Publicity Director.

'. . . and of course there is a problem of perception, of the public's perception, of what exactly it is we do. They picture a lot of people in tanktops hand-knitted from organic muesli' (here Ann smiled with quiet appreciation and Byron chuckled – Jonty looked gratified as he continued) 'staging sit-ins in areas of outstanding natural beauty and asking for millions to help preserve some South American tree frog about which the man on the Clapham omnibus knows little and cares less.'

Ann was still smiling her appreciative smile as she poured a thin trickle of cream into her coffee and said: 'Of course, this is your area of expertise, Jonty. How would you choose to be perceived?

And how would you set about changing existing perceptions?'

'It's actually very simple . . .' began Jonty. Hester feared he was about to become boring – she always feared that if either of them spoke at their own dinner parties for more than a couple of minutes at a time they were being boring – but the Armitages appeared enthralled. Ann sat with her hands linked around her coffee cup, watching Jonty's face and listening to him with the unblinking concentration for which she was famous. She was a compact, pleasant-looking woman in her early fifties, with deep-set eyes and a mouth which looked always slightly pursed, as if she were considering matters. Her greying hair was well cut, in a style which might in the seventies have passed muster as a 'Purdy' but these days could only be described as a pudding basin. If Hester had had to come up with a single adjective to describe her old friend it would have been 'collected'.

Hester admired collectedness because it was the quality she herself most lacked. This was not false modesty – she knew her strengths. The column she wrote for one of the more respectable tabloids, for instance, was an object lesson in how to imbue trivia with a universal resonance. In the village she had something of a reputation as a galvanic fundraising force, mistress of the inspired impulse – 'from nought to sixty in five seconds' was how the vicar had once put it. On a good day she could do a passable impersonation of a woman successfully juggling her life. On a less good one she could feel the Indian clubs raining down all round her, out of reach and out of control. The floor of her study disappeared beneath a rustling carpet of loose paper. There were more clothes on the ironing board than in the cupboards. Her freezer (and 'by their freezers shall ye know them', as she had once pronounced in print) had the telltale substratum of loose chips, rattling peas, and samosas petrified into flint axeheads . . .

'No-one could fail to applaud the concept,' Ann said to Jonty, 'but how do you envisage implementing it?'

A well-rounded question, thought Hester, from a well-rounded person. Ann had a degree in economics, and a Dip. Ed., and her CV bristled with vigorous voluntary involvements. Substantial private means had allowed her the luxury of changing course in her middle years, from educational administration to counselling. Hester was sure she was excellent at her job: firm but approachable; the high-achieving mother of three sons and as such a shining example of self-motivation; rigorous herself but patient and understanding with others; aspirational but non-judgmental . . . Hester could have gone on, but found it too demoralising.

'And what about funding?' asked Byron.

It was Byron they'd known first, when he and Jonty had met at Lords, the high temple of a shared passion. Unlike Jonty, who still turned out at Number Six for the Chuffington XI, Byron was not a cricketer himself. He was a gangling, unco-ordinated man, with a thick shock of mad professor's hair, whose keen intelligence lay largely concealed beneath an assumed and charming bufferishness. The intelligence had never been put to any sustained productive use. Now retired, he had wandered unhappily through various teaching jobs, unable either to keep order or to transmit anything of what he knew and believed to his pupils. Hester had always liked Byron. She and Jonty decided that the Armitages were a classic case of the attraction of opposites, and that the same could be said of their friendship with them.

An initial standoffishness on Ann's part had in retrospect turned out to be simply a period of appraisal, as a result of which the Blakes found themselves admitted to the Armitage circle. For it was not just herself and her very considerable wits that Ann collected, but people of an appropriate kind. It was impossible not to feel flattered.

Hester laughed, a knee-jerk reaction to another of Jonty's familiar verbal grace notes. She stretched out a hand and selected a fat white chocolate swirled with brown, like a sultan's turban. That chosen-ness was the thing about friendship. Your family demanded, and occasionally gave back, an obligatory devotion, but one's friends were chosen. Especially in London, where there was so much choice. Here in Chuffington, on the Essex-Hertfordshire border, friendships were to a large extent dictated by the environment. With only six or seven hundred souls in the village it was advisable to at least try and get on with everyone. To opt out was to be toffee-nosed and Hester would have died rather than appear toffee-nosed. In the wee small hours she sometimes wondered whether she might not have been a superior writer if she had been able to cut herself off from the community in which she lived. Perhaps if she spent less time attending home sales parties and school barn dances she would spend less time writing about them . . . But that way madness lay. After all, the HB Page, with its wry view of everyday life, was one of the *Post*'s chief selling points.

Byron's coffee cup swam into view.

'May I . . .?'

'Of course.' She poured.

'Not a word to Bessy,' said Byron confidentially as he stirred in three spoonfuls of demerara. He smiled his sweet, *distrait* smile. 'Something tells me you weren't paying awfully close attention to the old man's discourse.'

'No . . . I was, actually. But I have heard it before.'

'That's what Ann says about me. Tell me, are we husbands turning into a couple of old farts?'

Hester was nonplussed. After all, Byron was at least ten years older than Jonty, and looked it. It didn't seem altogether fair to lump the two of them together in this way.

'Certainly not.'

'Actually,' said Byron obligingly, 'that's not altogether fair. How old's Jonty, if it's not a rude question? Forty-five? Forty-six?'

'Something like that,' said Hester, sounding coy because she couldn't offhand remember exactly how old her husband was.

'And I'll be sixty next birthday. So in his case I withdraw the "old".'

Ann, always alive to social nuance, used Hester's laugh as a segue into a change of focus and of subject. She turned in Hester's direction and Byron, well-trained, instinctively swung towards Jonty.

'Tell me,' said Ann, 'how are the family?'

'They're well.' This was a part of the conversation Hester never relished.

'And what are they all up to?'

'At this very moment?'

'I really meant more widely. But—' Ann rolled her eyes upwards – 'it sounds as if someone's at home.'

The fierce, insistent pulse of Boyz R Wild (though fortunately not the obscene lyric) could be heard through the dining room ceiling.

'Yes, Daniel's in.'

'And he's what, now . . .? Refresh my memory.'

'Fifteen.'

'GCSEs this summer?'

'Yes.' Horribly soon, thought Hester. 'He's the youngest in his class.'

'And does he intend taking A Levels?'

Hester recalled dejectedly her most recent altercation with Daniel on this subject. 'Possibly.'

'And Rose . . . She's at Bristol, I believe you said?'

'Yes, she's in her second year.' Hester was on more solid ground with Rose. 'She loves it there. And she's got an exceptionally nice boyfriend at the moment.'

'Something in your voice,' said Ann sagely, 'tells me that has not always been the case.'

'As a matter of fact, Rose has never brought home anything too frightful,' said Hester. 'But with teenage girls you're always prepared for the worst . . . something you don't have to worry about, Ann.' She calculated that Sebastian and Gavin must be around thirty and Julian in his late twenties.

'Oh I don't know,' said Ann, 'you'd be surprised the strange things our boys spring on us. But we take the view that their friends are our friends. Everyone's welcome at Raglan Road.'

'In principle, we feel the same,' agreed Hester. 'But it's not always easy. I mean, Giselle—'

She stopped abruptly, not having intended to mention her middle child, but Ann was on to it in a trice.

'Yes, Giselle – how *is* Giselle?'

'She's fine.' Byron was outlining some point in the air with his hand, but through the circling gesture Hester fleetingly caught Jonty's eye. 'Fine,' she repeated, with as great an air of finality as she could manage.

'I've always been fond of Giselle,' mused Ann, 'I don't know why . . .'

Hester didn't know why either. She supposed it must have something to do with Ann's being a counsellor, compulsively drawn to problem people.

'How does she fill her days?' Ann asked, offering the chocolates round and taking one herself.

'She does this and that, odd jobs, you know . . .' Hester ducked down, pretending to look for something on the ground at her feet. It wasn't the days that Giselle needed to fill, since she spent a large part of each one in bed. Hester slithered her napkin to the floor, picked it up again and made a production of resetting it on her lap. She smiled gaily. 'She's not exactly an advertisement for the Protestant work ethic.'

'So I understand. From your column,' explained Ann. 'But I don't think you need read too much into it at her age.'

This was too much for Jonty, who had only been half-listening to Byron anyway.

'Ann, what's this? You're not telling us you read the *Post*!'

Ann laughed indulgently. 'Er – no, Jonty. But our cleaning lady does, and I occasionally sneak a look at what Hester has to say.'

'I'll believe you, thousands wouldn't.' Jonty pushed his chair back. 'Anyone like a drink? Cognac? Sloe gin? Or I've got rather a decent malt I picked up in duty-free?'

Ann lifted a hand. 'I'm the chauffeur. But Byron is extremely partial to malt whisky.'

'Byron? A tot?'

'Sounds as if I'm allowed – yes, why not.'

'Really, Byron, these people all think you lead a life of misery and deprivation,' said Ann. She shook her head at Hester in a 'men-they're-all-the-same' manner.

'Have we got any Amaretto?' asked Hester. 'If so, I'll have one.'

Ann furrowed her brow. 'You like Amaretto . . ? It always reminds me of Chanel No. 5.'

'I love it,' said Hester. 'Anything with almonds. I always buy too much marzipan for the Christmas cake so I can eat the leftovers.'

'Ready-made almond paste is marvellous these days,' agreed Ann. 'I really don't know why I soldier on, making my own.'

There were times, and this was one of them, when Hester wished she did not cannibalise her own experience quite so freely in her column. The minutiae of family and village life were her stock in trade, as was a swingeing disregard for domestic drudgery – the making of marzipan would have got short shrift on the HB Page, but she felt on shakier ground discussing it with Ann. Similarly, writing about her children's misdemeanours was both purging and therapeutic, but when they were the subject of discussion with an exemplary parent such as her friend she wondered whether she had given too much away. By and large one hoped that readers would realise one exercised a bit of journalistic licence in the interests of being amusing. But one's friends were in a position to judge if that were actually the case . . .

'One Amaretto,' said Jonty, putting it in front of her.

'*Vis-à-vis* Giselle,' said Ann, 'I think the girl needs full marks for doing any work at all. These days there is a tendency for all the young to continue in full-time education for as long as possible, accumulating mediocre passes in a host of soft-option subjects, and emerging into the real world as neither use nor ornament.'

'That is one way of looking at it,' conceded Hester.

Ann fixed her with an intent look. 'Tell me what Giselle would *like* to be doing.' She settled her shoulders in a small gesture of anticipation.

'Heavens . . . I don't know. That's the trouble, we've none of us got the least idea . . .'

'Oh but I have,' broke in Jonty, betraying once more his basic lack of interest in Byron's discourse. 'Giselle is in training to be a bump on a log.'

'That is a calumny, I'm sure,' said Ann.

'Not at all.'

'But she works, Hester was just telling me.'

'Ah!' Jonty raised a finger. 'Correction. Various unsuspecting people in the area have had the misfortune to employ her over recent months. None for more than a few weeks, nor was any of them willing to provide a reference. She's so far failed to make the grade as a washer-up, a shelf-stacker, a hander-out of free leaflets and a potato-picker.'

'Potato-picker?' queried Byron. 'What can go wrong with potato-picking?'

'You can fail to pick any potatoes.'

Ann chuckled. 'Surely she picked *some*?'

'Not enough to earn the minimum wage.'

Byron raised his eyebrows. 'So what was she doing?'

'Arguing the toss about pay and conditions with the woman in charge.'

'I'm delighted to hear it,' said Ann, tapping the edge of the table in approval. 'No-one should meekly accept sweated labour.'

'Come on,' said Jonty, with an edge of genuine exasperation, 'you accept that the day you turn up in the potato field. We aren't talking Jardine Matheson here. We're not talking General Motors or the Hong Kong and Shanghai Bank, we're talking spud-heaving, okay?'

'I hear what you're saying, Jonty, but surely all work, however menial, should be subject to the same basic rules of fairness.'

'It's perfectly fair. It's a bum job with bum wages. And no job security. QED.'

Byron smacked his lips. 'Delightful malt.'

'Not bad, is it?' agreed Jonty.

Ann turned back to Hester. 'But she's not in tonight, I take it?'

'No . . .'

'Out clubbing?' Ann asked, with the slight over-projection of someone who has but recently added this term to their vocabulary.

Hester executed a brief mental survey of Giselle's likely whereabouts, and was uneasy. 'I'm not sure.'

'It's nothing but worry, is it,' agreed Ann.

'But yours are all safely off your hands, surely?'

Ann shook her head, rueful but not displeased. 'In theory, yes. The reality is somewhat different. The problems don't go away, they just change. And get bigger, like the perpetrators.'

She began to enlarge on recent difficulties with Sebastian, who was involved with youth work in the Paddington area. He was, apparently, being sexually harassed by one of the youngsters in his charge, a black girl named Patsy.

'I make light of it,' said Ann, 'but in reality it's a nightmare. The girl is unhinged. She's obsessed with him.'

'Like *Fatal Attraction*.'

This meant nothing to Ann, who continued without breaking stride. 'She locked him in the unit one night and disappeared with the key. They had to break the door down. But obviously he has to be extremely careful. It's a very sensitive situation. And now, with the Children Act, it's like walking on eggshells.'

'It sounds horrific. Poor Sebastian.'

'It was a traumatic experience,' agreed Ann. 'But he's surprised us all by showing considerable maturity.'

Hester considered this. When she had last encountered Sebastian, in the hall at Raglan Road, with his spiky thatch of bleached hair, stained pinstripe waistcoat and donkey jacket, he had struck her as a young man for whom maturity was still patiently waiting.

'So it's an ill wind,' she said. 'And Julian?'

'He's in France, teaching English and coaching rugby, would you believe, at a little private school near Arles. He's adoring it, and there have been frequent mentions of a certain Lisette . . . but we say nothing. Something tells me he's not ready to settle down. And as for Gavin,' she added happily, 'we despair!'

'Despair?'

'Abandoned the idea of seeing him in any kind of long-term

relationship. Without wishing to be simplistic, he's always been the archetypal middle child – overcompetitive, striving for attention . . . and now every ounce of that super-energy' (Ann always spoke of her sons as though profiling them in a Sunday supplement) 'is being poured into his work.'

'Remind me what it is he does,' mumured Hester, mellow now with Amaretto and glad that Giselle as a topic had been dropped.

Ann bridled with obvious pride. 'He is the proprietor of a highly successful restaurant. Well, co-proprietor, but there's little doubt that Gavin is the moving spirit behind the enterprise.'

'Really? Which one? I probably know it.'

'You may well have heard of it,' agreed Ann. 'It's more of a large brasserie – "Schmooze", in Maida Vale. For the uninitiated, to schmooze is—'

'Yes, I know what it means.'

'Of course, I forget that as a journalist you're more abreast of the trends than most people.'

'I have heard of Schmooze, as a matter of fact. We wrote it up in the *Post*. I gather it's made rather an impression in a short time.'

'It has indeed. I've amassed quite an album of cuttings.'

Hester exclaimed admiringly, 'Isn't it rather intimidating to have a son who's an expert on food?'

'Not really,' said Ann, 'because the culinary side of it is not Gavin's preserve. Naturally, he aspires to excellence in that department – they have an extremely gifted young chef, and a Michelin star – but Gavin came to the job from the world of commerce. He is both the business manager, and responsible for the whole *style* of the operation.'

'And is business booming?' asked Hester.

'Mmm . . . hard to tell . . .' Ann sipped her Buxton Water. 'Gavin has always ridden an emotional roller coaster, and catering is a fiercely competitive field. One day business is booming, the next, if he is to be believed, they're staring bankruptcy in the face. But the impression I get is that Schmooze is making the competition *pre-tty* nervous.'

Ann went on to expound enthusiastically on the triumphs and disasters encountered by Gavin and his co-investor on their way to the top. Hester listened attentively, but she was not surprised at the meteoric rise of Gavin's brasserie. Success was something Ann's boys, as she was wont to call them, had been raised to expect. Reflecting on the recent passage of arms with Daniel concerning A Levels ('I don't wonnoo! Wossa point?') she was sure that no such exchange had ever taken place in the Armitage household, where aspiration and self-fulfilment had been ingested with the sieved carrot and baby rice. Even Sebastian's vexed career in youth work, following as it did assorted attempts at vocational training, and an unpleasantness (summarily dispelled by Ann) with the DSS, was seen as a process of learning and self-discovery, healthy and not to be condemned.

Of Hester's own children only Rose displayed the kind of drive and focus one could justifiably vaunt, and this was combined with a worrying tendency to colour code socks and underwear, and arrange books in order of height. Daniel's was, she supposed, the fairly standard charmlessness of the pubescent male. And Giselle was a real worry.

When Hester announced, as she often did, that she was a failure as a parent, Jonty's was the robust line that is easier taken in conversation than in practice.

'That's what parenthood is about, Hes – failure. When you assess someone as a parent you don't measure success, but the extent of the failure.'

'You're just saying that to placate the gods.'

'Okay, let's be sternly practical. You turn a very useful buck through claiming to be an indifferent parent.'

'Gee, thanks. So you admit I'm indifferent?'

'Come on, Hes, that's not what I said – besides, if you're indifferent where the devil does that leave me? We do our best, for God's sake.'

'Do we? I'm not sure that we do.'

'You speak for yourself.'

'Oh God . . !'

This was the point at which Jonty would begin extolling the children's virtues, another activity more readily undertaken in their absence.

'Anyway, what exactly are you complaining about? We have three delightful kids.'

'You think so?'

'I do, yes. Rose is excelling herself down in Bristol. Daniel is managing to fit work around his social life as much as could possibly be expected of a boy of his age and temperament. And Grizzle—'

'Yes?' Hester challenged. 'Yes?'

'Grizzle is interesting.'

'That's mealy-mouthed, even from her father.'

'No, she is. She's an intelligent, imaginative girl who hasn't yet found a niche.'

'You hope.'

'How d'you mean, "I hope"?'

'I mean that this may *be* her niche. She may already have found it. She may be going to be a burden on the state, a martyr to rough trade and a monument to sloth her entire life!'

'I give up.'

'That's what I'm afraid of!' Hester would wail. 'That we've given up! And one of these days we may discover that our children have gone to the dogs while we slept.'

'She was at the dogs the other night, I gather. Squandering her allowance on a series of three-legged no-hopers.'

'I didn't know that. Why on earth didn't you tell me?'

'Didn't think it was important.'

'Good grief, our eighteen-year-old daughter placing bets at a dog track!'

'We should thank our lucky stars she didn't decide to buy one . . .'

These exchanges usually ended with Hester feeling better, if only because Jonty had persuaded her that her standards were somehow too high for the average family to live up to. Her conscience murmured that this was not in fact the case, but the murmur was very faint, and she allowed herself to be soothed.

Now, the Armitages were making departing noises. 'I was sitting up with the women's group until one this morning,' explained Ann, rising from the table and putting her chair neatly back in place. 'So if anything's to get done tomorrow I'd better get my five hours.'

'It's Sunday tomorrow,' Hester pointed out.

'A good day, I find, to do some catching up. I don't know if you remember, Hester, a good many years ago when you'd not long moved out of London, coming to Raglan Road to hear Merle Shaw speak . . .?'

'I do, yes,' said Hester, with a prickle of anxiety, but Ann was all happy reminiscence.

'I can pinpoint that day as the moment the group began. That talk created so much interest, so much *energy* – I knew I couldn't simply let it go to waste.'

Byron pointed at his wife. 'She's got Ava Lawrence coming – when, Ann?'

'In July,' said Ann modestly. 'We always try to have something special before the summer break.'

'Who's she?' asked Jonty, still sitting down as though he hadn't noticed his guests were leaving.

Hester overrode her husband's mild cussedness. 'That's amazing! There are chat-show hosts and features editors all over London who'd kill their grannies to get her. How did you do it?'

'Who is she?' repeated Jonty, still sitting.

Ann smiled self-deprecatingly. 'I wrote a simple, straightforward, polite letter inviting her to address us. She responded positively almost at once.'

'Quite a feather in her cap,' commented Byron.

'Nothing short of a personal triumph, I'd have thought,' said Hester, leading the way into the hall and picking up Ann's grey, fringed throw from the chair.

Jonty finally got up. 'Yes, but – excuse my ignorance – why?'

Ann, very slightly nettled, pretended not to have heard and advanced on Hester with a smile of appreciation and a murmur of thanks. It was left to Byron to say: 'As a matter of fact, I wasn't too well acquainted myself, but since Ann told me about her I've seen her name everywhere. She's a sort of post-feminist guru. American, of course.' He lowered his voice slightly. 'Rather glamorous.'

Without looking at him, Ann said: 'You wouldn't make a remark of that kind if she were a man.'

'If Ava Lawrence were a man,' retorted Byron, with an asperity for which he would pay, Hester thought, on the drive home, 'I'd be extremely surprised.'

'I'll have to look out for her,' said Jonty. He opened the door. 'Oh.'

Giselle was on the doorstep. She was a big girl, eye-to-eye with her father and not far off his weight, dressed in a style that Rose, out of earshot, called salvage sadist – in this case a moth-eaten 1940s taffeta cocktail frock worn with a T-shirt beneath and a leather jacket on top, thick black tights, oiled wool slouch socks, and boots with soles that would not have disgraced a combine harvester.

'Look out for who?' she asked.

'Ava Lawrence,' supplied Hester automatically.

'Never heard of her,' said Giselle.

Jonty betrayed a glimmer of satisfaction. But as his daughter stepped inside he peered out suspiciously – another figure hovered in the dark, just beyond the reach of the porch light.

'Hallo, my dear,' said Ann. 'We were only talking about you earlier.'

'No kidding.'

'Who's that?' asked Jonty, with a jerk of the head.

Giselle peered, checking. 'Ark.'

Jonty pushed the door to. 'What's he doing here?'

'Waiting to come in.'

'For crying out loud – ' Jonty tapped his watch – 'it's half past midnight.'

'That's not what your father meant,' said Hester.

'Perhaps we should withdraw,' suggested Ann.

'Got any more of that malt?' asked Byron. 'Or would you like us to clear off?'

'No, no, no,' Hester gave a brittle laugh. 'Or at least, only insofar as you were going anyway, and you've got a long drive . . .' She opened the door again. The figure was still there, though a little farther off. 'Hallo!' she called.

''Evening,' came a non-committal voice from the dark.

'We're just seeing some friends off . . . they're driving back to London!'

'What are you doing explaining our actions to him?' asked Jonty loudly.

'Goodnight, Hester,' said Ann with the warm, unruffled neutrality of the true friend. 'A delightful evening. I shall be in touch. Goodnight, Jonty.' She patted her host's biceps forgivingly. 'Come along Byron, we must be on our way.'

'Many thanks.' Byron planted a kiss on both of Hester's cheeks. 'We must play the return match very soon.'

'Give our love to the family,' said Hester.

'Oh, them—!' called Ann gaily from the drive as she unlocked the Toyota, 'they're a law unto themselves. Good evening,' she added to Ark, who was standing nearby. 'Bye-bye, Giselle! Drop in on us if you're in town!'

She got in and leaned across to unlock the passenger door. Byron turned to give a last wave and then felt obliged, out of politeness, and notwithstanding a certain solidarity with Jonty, to include the outcast in his farewell.

'Goodnight.'

''Night.'

The Armitages sped off, paused at the gate, and turned with a cheery double-blip of the horn towards the London road. The Blakes and Ark stood there for a moment, watching the dark space where the car had been.

'You want to come in?' Giselle called to Ark.

'It's awfully late . . .' demurred Hester.

'Why not? Let him come in! Liberty Hall . . !' Jonty left the door open wide and retired into the dining room, where he began to stack dishes noisily. Ark loomed out of the night, stepped sideways over the threshold and wiped his feet on the mat with slow, repetitive movements reminiscent of Michael Jackson's moon-walk. Hester smiled faintly as she closed the door.

'Come on then,' said Giselle, disappearing up the stairs.

'Excuse me,' said Ark. He took another couple of sideways steps, and then followed Giselle more briskly up to her room. Hester listened to the heavy tread of two pairs of boots across the landing, and the obligatory passage of arms as Giselle pounded on her brother's door and instructed him, with much use of the copulative adjective, to keep his music down. The boots then continued into Giselle's room, the door banged shut and there was the click of the bolt being shot. Almost at once a backbeat far louder than anything Daniel's puny speakers could produce surged forth, sending a shudder through the upper storey and creating a curious whine in the ill-fitting window in the kitchen below.

She went into the dining room. Jonty was sitting at the table in the chair vacated by Ann, munching a chocolate and unwrapping another. Plates and cups stood stacked to his left. The lamp was off, the overhead light on, and the candles doused: their dead smoke drifted above the dinner debris and filled the air with an acrid smell.

Without turning, he said: 'At times like this I wish we still had old Gus.'

'Don't be ridiculous, what could he have done?'

'It doesn't much matter. That type doesn't like dogs.'

'Gus wasn't dogs.' Jonty, knowing this to be true, didn't answer. The Blakes' black Labrador had been a canine clown, all floppy friendliness and gangling charm. A welcome mat for intruders, as

Jonty had himself remarked on many occasions. It was barely six weeks since Hester had taken the thirteen-year-old Gus to the vet in Forbridge, thence to be despatched to the great kennel in the skies. She had been practical – it had to be done – but Jonty's wounds were still raw.

'Well,' said Hester in a different voice. 'I think they enjoyed it.'

'Mmm.'

'It's always good to see them. They're so appreciative.'

'They are, yes.'

'Byron doesn't change.'

'No.'

'Ann interrogates a bit, but I honestly believe that's because she's genuinely interested.'

Jonty looked sceptical. 'Honestly . . . genuinely . . .'

'You know what I mean. She's someone who likes to keep abreast of developments.'

'M-hm.'

'What's the matter?'

'Nothing.'

'Come on. Have they started to get on your nerves?'

'Not at all. Of course not. I always like seeing them, you know that.'

'What then?' Hester began assembling the unused cutlery.

'Okay.' Jonty swept crumbs into his cupped hand and poured them back on to the table. 'It's nothing new. Are we really happy with that bozo up in our daughter's room?'

'You as good as invited him in.'

'I gave way to the inevitable.'

Confronted with the disobliging realities of family life Jonty was far less philosophical than when discussing the theory. Hester rattled a drawer open and began putting the cutlery away. 'No, I'm not particularly happy,' she conceded, 'but what can we do? This is the nineteen-nineties, she is over eighteen—'

'Just.'

'—which makes her an adult—'

'In the eyes of the law maybe, but that doesn't mean I care for them doing – whatever they do – under my roof.'

Hester slammed the drawer shut. 'Then you'd better ban it, hadn't you? Or him.'

'I can scarcely do that *now*, can I?'

'You can do what you like, it's your house.' Hester took the chocolates from beneath his hovering hand and closed the lid.

'It would seem so arbitrary at this stage.' Jonty picked crossly at the nodules of cold wax on the candlesticks. 'I suppose what I hoped was that Grizzle would simply *feel* that it wasn't right – the whole situation. That she'd somehow have been imbued with our values and get a sense that this – this—'

'Bozo.'

'—well, whatever – that he didn't fit in. And that it certainly wasn't on to usher him up to her bedroom every time he breaks the horizon. I mean, what does she think we think they're doing up there? Playing Pelmanism?'

'Listening to music,' offered Hester, gathering up the table napkins and dropping them in a heap by the door.

'You don't listen to that racket, you disappear into it,' said Jonty. As if to lend credence to this observation the thirties brass electrolier which was such hell to clean jiggled slightly. 'Jesus H. Christ, they're at it already!'

'I'm sorry, but I don't know what you want me to say.' Hester picked up a stack of side plates and pudding bowls and dumped them on the hatch. 'I mean, you have to allow your children their privacy and, God knows, we're only too glad when they all troop off to their rooms instead of hogging the TV and smoking down here. So at what point do you start accusing them of nooky and saying they can't do it? It's absurd! If you don't like the thought of Giselle associating with Ark under this roof then you'd better come clean and say so, and risk looking like a mastodon, or Edward Moulton Barrett or whatever it is you're afraid of!'

'I'm not—'

'It's a case of put up or shut up,' added Hester, and dropped a cut-glass whisky tumbler (a second, but good for all that) to the floor with a crash. 'Bugger.'

'What a pity,' remarked Jonty, calmed by his wife's outburst. 'That was the last one of those.'

If pressed, Hester and Jonty would have admitted that they were confused. Ann Armitage was rarely confused, and would never have admitted to it. Now, having taken the short cut she had worked out for herself on the road map, she joined the southbound motorway and moved into the middle lane, there to maintain a steady 75 mph. She glanced at her husband

'Are you awake?'

'Certainly,' replied Byron, who had almost not been.

'Make a note for me, would you?'

Byron opened the glove compartment and took out a spiral notebook with a biro clipped to the cover. 'Fire away.'

'Just put J and H . . . roulade . . . Giselle.'

'Got it,' said Byron.'

'Thank you,' said Ann. 'You can go back to sleep now.'

Upstairs in The Old Clink, tossed on a tidal wave of sound from The Cure, Giselle lay back on her musty sheets and clutched Ark's ponytail as he rooted between her thighs with the uninhibited relish of a lion at a kill.

'Go, Ark . . .' she sighed, transported. 'Go, Ark, go . . .!'

CHAPTER THREE

The Blakes were reckoned by most of their friends in Chuffington, London and elsewhere to have got the business of marriage about right. They were not smug. They did not call each other 'darling' all the time. They did not make telling little references to wet Sunday afternoons or weekend breaks in the Cotswolds. Most crucially they did not brag about their children. This would have been more or less impossible anyway, since Hester spilled the beans on a regular basis in the *Post*, which was the Chuffington set's, if not the London crowd's, favourite paper. On a local level Mrs Carson, the Blakes' cleaning lady these two years, was not noted for reticence or discretion . . .

The Blakes didn't make you feel uneasy. Dear old Hester was a bit scatty, a creative type, the sort who might at any time tumble-dry the cat or drive to Aberdeen with the handbrake on. You had to like her. And everyone performed a bit for Hester, there was covert competition for some sort of exposure, however oblique, on the HB Page.

Jonty was a great bloke, too – his batting average for Chuffington last season had been thirty-two, no less. He was also a high-flier who had done what most people only talked about, and packed in the fat salary and company BMW in favour of quality of life and job satisfaction. Mind you, he could afford to, after raking it in at Ruggles Ryder for years, but he'd still gone ahead and done it. The village had benefited in a tangential way because Hester organised incredible dos in aid of Earthtrust – everyone still talked about the twelve-hour street party a couple of summers ago, and of course people *would* make the effort and join in if it was in a good cause and there was some local connection . . .

As for the children, it was comforting to know that the Blakes had their problems like everyone else. One of the great strengths of the HB Page was that it gave the *Post's* readers a warm, all-in-the-same-boat feeling. It made the women, especially those who were married with children, identify with Hester – droll, dry, and engagingly inconsistent.

Rose Blake, of course, was utterly delightful. She was clever and personable and had developed in the approved manner from a gawky and myopic ugly duckling into a tall, slender swan with tinted contact lenses and sleek plumage. In short, she had become what other mothers respectfully referred to as 'a lovely girl'. Not only was she pretty but she remembered people's names, and said 'It's nice to see you' and took telephone messages in a way that made her parents' colleagues' hearts beat faster. From the local mixed primary Rose had gone to the girls' high school twenty miles away, emerged *summa cum laude* and was now at university, returning from time to time to fill the village store and the saloon bar of the Axe and Compass with her delectable fragrance and her winning smile. Rose had no obvious vices.

A few years later there had been Daniel – the only one of the Blakes' children to have been born in the village. Or at least born at the cottage hospital, where the bed in the delivery room bore a plaque with the mystifying inscription: '*Donated by the boy soldiers of Chuffington Barracks, 1966*'. If Rose was a Lovely Girl, then Daniel was a Grand Lad. In other words, he did not stand out from his peers and contemporaries in any way. He was averagely idle, averagely scruffy, averagely lippy and more than averagely nice-looking, with fair hair and dark eyes. Daniel smoked whenever funds and circumstances allowed, like all the boys of his age. Hester had written that there was no point in forbidding your children to smoke in the house, because they'd only do it somewhere else. And everyone absolutely agreed with her. The line of least resistance was also the healthiest one.

In between Rose and Daniel there was Giselle. Ah, Giselle – the daughter from Hell . . . Giselle, who made everyone feel *so* much better about their own offspring. Although of course everyone was quick to say that she wasn't a bad girl at heart, and would almost certainly find her niche in time. Giselle was five-feet-eleven and twelve stone. Her hair was dyed black and red, and was cropped close at the back and sides, with little whorls like crop circles carved into it. The top, which was longer, sprouted from her scalp in strange, stiff fronds. She was never to be seen without a *maquillage* which would not have looked out of place in a video nasty. Not only did she always have a cigarette between her fingers, but she carried with her the musky odour of raves, and squats, and bus shelters late at night. She was a creature of darkness, a loner, to be spotted leaving her lair at twilight, and returning to it in the small hours or at dawn. And, like the scientific definition of matter, she took up space but did no work.

At primary school Giselle, though never as bright as her older sister, had been neither more stupid nor more difficult than most others. School photos showed a heavy, dark girl with a ponytail and strikingly winged black eyebrows. In nativity plays and harvest festival celebrations she was generally among the rank-and-file, and placed on the end of a row so that her stolidly averted head and lifeless tambourine would attract the least possible attention. On the sports field she lurked on the periphery, slow but fearsomely strong.

But there were omens. At Leavers' Assembly in the final week of her final term, when the chairman of governors walked to the table to present the Cecil Bultitude Memorial Cup for social skills and personal development, he found it filled with water. Floating therein was a tampon, swollen to several times its normal size . . . a crime directly traceable to the physically precocious Giselle.

In secondary school, this shot across the bows developed into outright war. Only Hester's widespread popularity and both parents' input on the PTG prevented Giselle from achieving her unmistakable aim of being cast into educational outer darkness. As it was, she emerged at sixteen with two GCSEs in English and Art, a sheaf of spoiled papers and accompanied by a sigh of relief from teachers and governors alike.

There had been no question of troubling the education system any further on Giselle's behalf, and the received view, gratefully adhered to by the Blakes, was that non-academic youngsters such as their daughter, for whom school had not been a positive or productive experience, were probably better off out in the workplace, boosting their self-esteem with a bit of hard cash. Hester and Jonty, concerned that this state of affairs should come about as soon as possible, pulled strings and exercised influence on her behalf. Giselle, however, wanted to cut out the middle man and proceed directly to the cash without the delay and inconvenience of work. Given her lack of interpersonal skills, this wasn't difficult to bring about. It followed as the night the day that she and her duties were soon parted.

Now, at just turned eighteen, *le tout Chuffington* noted that she was a fully-fledged layabout (in more senses than one) and it was simply *marvellous* how philosophical the Blakes were.

For Jonty and Hester there was no alternative to marvellousness. In the same way that chronic invalids are described as wonderfully brave simply for being chronic invalids, Jonty and Hester had no option but to make the best of it. Besides, they loved Giselle. They could remember a different time. They both knew, though they often had to remind themselves, that the present Giselle was a deliberately contrived and assiduously maintained façade, a protective colouring designed to show how little the wearer cared for the world's opinion. They knew that sheltering behind it was the original Giselle – wilful but also serious, determined, loyal and affectionate. They knew, as today's parents must, that no matter what the difficulties it was essential to keep the lines of communication open – but communication is a two-way process and no-one told you how to communicate with a young woman who was determined to ignore you.

For a long time Giselle, like Rose before her, showed no interest whatever in the opposite sex. But whereas in Rose's case the lack of interest was a flirtatious hauteur in the face of universal longing, Giselle's (everyone thought but only Daniel was honest enough to say) was because no boy was going to have anything to do with her. They might have deduced from her attitude that they were wrong. For Giselle was unperturbed. She strode on her way with massive self-possession, a post-punk amazon queen, her confidence undented. A largely automatic 'fuck off' was all that was needed to convey this unconcern to Daniel.

Of her two daughters, Hester often said: 'Actually, they're more alike than you might imagine.' But it convinced no-one, least of all those who, on venturing upstairs to the bathroom of The Old Clink at dinner parties, had been vouchsafed a view, through half-open doors, of the girls' respective bedrooms.

Rose's room, even when not completely tidy, conveyed an air of sweetly feminine disarray – a kimono trailed on the floor; make-up scattered (but never spilt) before a mirror framed by dryads; a book open and face-down on the frilled pillow; all somehow charming, evidence of a pleasant life of ordered self-indulgence. Rose collected things – one wall was thick with miniature, flower-bedecked straw hats, a shelf was crowded with whimsical pigs, another with seashells. Her clothes, if anyone had cared to look, were perfectly organised. She was the only person Hester knew who actually used (and replaced) those sheets of scented paper to line her chest of drawers. And the only one who folded knickers, and threw away laddered tights, and employed something called a soap-saver, and replaced her toothbrush every three months, and had a Liberty-print diary with a padlock, to which she had not lost the key . . . Hester sometimes worried that Rose was anally-fixated – had she potty-trained too early? – but Jonty's response was that if this were anal-fixation they could all do with some spread on their toast.

Giselle's room was disgusting. Along with the oven, it constituted one of Mrs Carson's no-go areas. (In common with the rest of her kind she preferred cleaning rooms which were already essentially clean.) It was a good job the scorched and tattered curtains were normally closed – to exclude light rather than from any sense of shame – or the unwarily snooping visitor would have been exposed to the full horror of the room's dirt, disorder and neglect. They would have seen yellowing newspaper cuttings – more properly 'tearings' – Sellotaped layer on layer to the walls like the magnification of some unpleasant skin disease; an unshaded light bulb painted battleship grey and further degraded by a film of sticky dust; a large and ornate birdcage, empty a twelvemonth but not cleaned out since the death of its occupant; a dull-eyed and malodorous stuffed stoat; one or two posters (Sellotaped over the newsaper) depicting ravening humanoids in various stages of lively decay; a hardy yucca, trailing, Miss Havisham-like; a fine netting of gummed-together hair-clippings, cobwebs and ancient fluff; a coverless duvet piebald with sinister stains; and (the unwitting centrepiece) sprawled on the rumpled bed with its flaccid limbs in macabre disarray and its fixed, sunken face staring into the dark, an inflatable man, collared, tied and pinstriped, caught in interminable creeping detumescence amid the squalor. And emanating from it all there was a smell . . . musky, rancid, suggestive. The odour not of sanctity, but of sex.

Sex undertaken with a surly, casual zeal. Sex on demand. Zipless,
zit-stained sex.

For, in common with many a lost soul, Giselle had had considerable sexual experience before she even left school. Her
style may have been forbidding but her physique was strikingly
Junoesque. She permitted, with scowling contempt, such squeez-
ings, palpatings and suckings as her first year schoolfellows were
capable of, lost her virginity in the third year, and by the time GCSEs
came round was enjoying a full-blown liaison with a peripatetic
pottery master in his Sierra Estate. All this unknown to the rest of
her family.

After school there had been a succession of short-lived relationships – a heavily tattooed roofer, a sad student in a parka,
a Lebanese chef – but until Ark came on the scene none of the
followers had a name. They were shadowy loiterers – a flip of the
letter box, a swift footstep on the gravel, a series of stuttering revs
in the lane beyond the gate. They came under the general heading:
'Out . . . none of your business . . . dunno . . .', as in: 'Where are
you going? Who with? When will you be back?' They were merely
the unseen agents of Giselle's comings and goings.

Ark had broken the horizon quite recently, on Giselle's eighteenth
birthday. This occasion was seen by Jonty in particular as one which,
handled correctly, might see their second duckling metamorphose
into a swan.

'I don't somehow think so,' said Hester doubtfully.

'You never know. If we fork out for a do – we did for Rosie,
after all.'

'That was completely different. Rose wanted nothing more than
to get poured into black lycra and stilettos, and away the lads.'

'Grizzle might, when she sees the colour of our money.'

'She's not the same. Come *on*. Her idea of a good time is – well,
the fact is I don't know, we neither of us do, exactly what it is.'

They were to find out. Jonty made his approach one early evening,
that brief period of the day when both Giselle and her parents were
simultaneously awake, dressed, and functioning. It was a Sunday
in late March. They were in the kitchen. Jonty had made his special
stuffed peppers – tasty, if a tad leathery – and Hester had finished
a column and had been out in the garden for an hour, grubbing
about in soil that was still too heavy to do much with. At half past

six the air was cool and still and watery, but full of the delicious delayed promise of long, leisurely evenings to come. Bright shocks of daffodils burst pluckily from the damp, tussocky grass that couldn't yet be mowed, and from the dark flowerbeds where the perennials were just beginning to make their presence felt, reaching upward and outwards from their tidy winter separateness, yearning for the jumbled intimacy of summer.

The garden of The Old Clink was partly ancient orchard, partly a straggling ribbon of common land snipped off by the Enclosures. When the village lock-up had become a private dwelling at the turn of the century, the owners had commandeered the ground and used it for keeping pigs and growing robust everyday vegetables, and the ground had acceded with amiable rustic tolerance, without ever entirely giving up its independence. It had no pretensions to neatness: no raised beds, sharp edges, tramlines or artful artlessness. It was shaggy and uneven, with too many arthritic old fruit trees for the good of Hester's herbaceous border, and battalions of couch grass ever-threatening at the end furthest from the house.

Hester sat at the table with a glass of dry cider. Her hands, though washed under the cold tap, were still seamed with black earth, because she had not yet been and bought the annual pair of new gardening gloves which traditionally preceded the finding of the existing pair. Jonty leaned back against the sink, drinking Budweiser out of a can. He was a lifelong beer man, and had always been happy with a bottle of the local Dobbey's light ale until Daniel had introduced him to the idea of designer beer. It was a secret weakness of Jonty's that he was susceptible to trends.

'Where is everyone?' he asked. 'I cooked for an indeterminate number.'

'Daniel's round at Spike's. Rose has gone to the pictures with Sophie.'

'What's on?'

'Woody Allen.'

'Funny, isn't it,' observed Jonty comfortably, 'how perceptions change. Not so long ago, when one heard the name Woody Allen one felt a good warm tribal feeling, that here was a chap discerning people recognised as funny, perceptive, sympathetic. Now, that's all changed.'

'I don't see why,' said Hester, not thinking about it much. 'I like his films.'

'You're not listening to me. *I* like his films. I just don't feel so good about liking them any more.'

'That's an extremely Woody-Allenish remark.'

There was the bang of a door in the upper reaches, a heavy tread across the landing and down the stairs.

'Ah,' said Jonty, 'a taker for my peppers, perhaps?'

'In your dreams.'

Giselle came into the kitchen. She wore her habitual black and grey tatters, but this evening there was a warlike red bandanna round her head. 'Hallo, love,' said Hester.

'Hi there,' said Jonty to Giselle's backside as she peered in the fridge. 'Sleep well?'

'Where's that hummus that was in here?'

'Gone,' said Hester.

'It was here a few days ago.'

'Exactly.'

'You have no need of it,' said Jonty. 'I've cooked.'

Giselle swung the fridge door shut. She opened the cupboard above it and subjected the shelves to a withering survey.

'Stuffed peppers,' went on Jonty. 'Can I tempt you?'

She closed the cupboard and opened the outer oven door. 'Is that them?'

'Are those they?' corrected Hester automatically.

'I just asked him that.'

'Yes,' replied Jonty. 'Want some?'

'No.' Giselle closed the oven. 'I'm going out.'

'Just before you do, Grizzle,' said Jonty, 'there was something we wanted to ask you.'

Giselle stood with her back to him, looking over her shoulder like someone hearing out a pollster before telling them to drop dead.

'With your eighteenth coming up, we wondered if you'd like to celebrate it in some way.'

'Sure,' Giselle said, indulging them brusquely. 'Okay if I go now?'

'We'd like to throw a party for you – here – or anywhere, within reason – if that's something you'd like.'

Giselle shrugged patiently. 'Could do.'

'So you're basically in favour of the idea?' asked Hester.

Giselle looked over her other shoulder at her mother. 'What sort of party?'

'Well—' began Jonty, putting down his Budweiser.

'I don't want anything like that thing of Rose's.'

'No, well—'

'I don't want it here.'

'Fine, it doesn't have to be—'

'I'd want to go out.'

'Of course,' said Hester, trying to be firm and agreeable but sounding shrill, 'it's your birthday and it should be your choice.'

'I want to go out.'

'Yes, but on the other hand, if your father and I are paying—'

'You offered.' She laid a bludgeoning emphasis on the first word.

'I did,' Jonty agreed. 'And I meant it—'

'But now you don't.'

'Did I say that?'

'You didn't have to. You want to give me what you want, not what I want.'

Fleetingly, guiltily, Jonty caught his wife's eye. 'That's not true.'

Giselle gave him a look of searing contempt.

'Okay. Okay.' Jonty folded his arms and crossed his ankles. His tone said right-young-lady, thought Hester, but his body language whimpered be-gentle-with-me. 'Okay. Be specific. What would you like?'

'I need to think about it.'

'Now come on, Grizzle, that's silly. You've got a pretty fair idea or you wouldn't have said what you said.'

'Yes!' said Hester, and then added rather tamely: 'Absolutely.'

'I told you. Go out for the night. Have a blast. Enjoy myself.'

'Who with?'

'Who cares?'

'We do – what about other members of the family?'

'You, you mean?'

'Well – no – not necessarily. But an eighteenth birthday is a family occasion, don't you think?'

'No,' replied Giselle. 'It's about the person growing up and being separate, isn't it?'

This time Hester looked at Jonty.

Giselle looked from one parent to the other. 'So?'

'We'll consider it,' said Jonty.

'Oh yeah . . .' Giselle made for the front door. 'I know.'

'There's no reason—' began Jonty, as the door slammed.

'Hey-ho . . .' Hester got up heavily and put her glass in the sink. 'Another triumph for family unity.'

'She's right, in a way, you know,' Rose had observed, later that night.

'*Et tu*, Rosie?' said Jonty.

'No, I mean it isn't altogether fair to offer something and then expect to dictate the terms. I know you didn't mean it like that, but that's how she was bound to see it.'

'I'm not looking for Brownie points here,' put in Jonty, who was. 'But you had a smashing party, didn't you?'

'Yes, I did. But then it was exactly what I wanted. You could hardly expect Griz to enjoy something like that.'

'That's what I said,' remarked Hester.

'So what am I supposed to do?' asked Jonty. 'Fork out so that Grizzle and assorted low-lifes can get plastered in some warehouse off the M5?'

'People don't get drunk at raves,' Rose reminded him.

'No,' said Hester, 'they take drugs.'

'Some of them do.'

'And we're supposed to feel better about that?'

'If you want my opinion,' said Rose reasonably, pulling her long, slender legs into the lotus position, 'she'll go into town to listen to heavy metal. She's a bit of a Curehead. I tell you one thing, it'll be a lot cheaper than holding a bash here.'

'We've thought about it,' said Jonty to Giselle at the end of the week. 'And we accept your argument.'

'What was that?'

'If you want to celebrate your birthday in your own way, you can. But keep it legal and decent, eh, Grizzle?'

'Smart,' said Daniel. 'I'm on for that.'

'No,' said Hester, 'you're not.'

'I'll ask her.'

'No, Daniel.'

'It's nothing to do with you.'

'Excuse me, but it is. It would be quite different if she were

having a party here, under this roof, but she wants to go out –
on the town.'

'Is that what it's called? It's her eighteenth birthday, can't her own
brother go along?' His voice became both sneering and plaintive.

'Daniel.'

'What?'

'You're not invited – one. And two – even if you were, you
wouldn't be allowed.'

'Christ! You!' Hester flinched. She knew what was coming. 'If
your bloody readers knew what you were really like they'd hang
your bloody page up in the karsy and wipe their arses on it!'

At 4.30 a.m., the morning after Giselle's birthday, the phone rang.
It was on Hester's side of the bed.

'Yes?'

'It's me.'

'Yes? Where are you?' Hester struggled to cover as much essential
ground as possible. 'Have you – are you having a good time?'

'It's been okay.' There were different grades of 'okay', and Hester
recognised this one as being distinctly positive.

'Good. Where did you say you were?'

'I didn't. I'm in hospital.'

'What?' Alerted by her shrill blast of panic Jonty rolled on to his
back with his arms over his face.

'Jesus wept, what?'

'Why are you in there?'

'She's not in the cells . . .?'

'Shut up, Jonty, I can't hear her—!'

'Mum? I had a fight with this girl.'

'A fight! What on earth did you do that for?'

'You don't want to know.'

'Did she win?'

'I heard that. Tell him I did.'

'I'll do no such thing. What's the matter with you? Are you
all right?'

'I'm fine. I've got a few stitches in my eyebrow.'

'My God! What about the others – the other people you went
with?'

'They've gone home.'

'That was nice of them. In the taxis we funded, I suppose.'

'Sure. What were they supposed to do, walk?'

Hester told Jonty: 'She's in hospital. She had a fight. The others have gone home.'

'I see.' Jonty clapped his hands over his eyes and lurched into a sitting position on the side of the bed. 'So, a good time had by all.'

'Yes, thanks,' said Giselle into Hester's ear.

'She says yes, th—'

'Give that to me.' Jonty reached across and took the receiver from Hester. The phone fell off Hester's bedside table with a crash. 'Giselle! Are you there?' Hester rescued the phone and lay back, holding it on her stomach. She noticed idly that Jonty was developing a spare tyre. Actually, not one spare tyre but several small ones.

'Give me some information, please,' he said, a touch too pompously for the spare tyres. 'Which hospital are you in?' He paused. 'And I take it you're in A and E? What? Accident and Emergency. Right. So you're able to come home now?' He paused again. 'Right. I'll come and pick you up. Just stay where I'll be able to spot you, and don't, for God's sake, get into any more arguments.'

He passed the receiver back to Hester, stood up and began dragging on clothes.

'Darling?' said Hester. 'Dad's on his way.'

'He doesn't have to bother, Ark could bring me back.'

'Ark?'

'He's here with me.'

'She says Ark is there with her,' Hester told Jonty, 'and he could bring her back.'

'Who the devil's Ark?'

'I don't know, but he's there with her.'

'Just tell her I'm coming, will you?'

'Don't worry, your father's coming.'

'Right,' said Giselle. There was a fraction of a second's pause. 'What about you?'

'Don't worry,' Hester replied, her heart leaping. 'I'll come too.'

They had to assume that Rose, a sweet-smelling dormouse in a nest of sprigged duvet, had absorbed the information on a subliminal level and would convey it to Daniel.

'Anyway, we shan't be all that long, shall we?' asked Hester as the Range Rover barrelled along the bypass in the direction of the hospital.

'Depends if it's a police matter,' said Jonty annoyingly.

There had been only four people sitting on the hard chairs in A and E: a little old lady wrapped in a green hospital blanket in a wheelchair; a man with a tracksuit on over his pyjamas; and Giselle, with Ark.

'Christ,' muttered Jonty as they walked across.

'He is at least *here*,' Hester reminded him. 'We should be grateful.'

Giselle got up and her companion, more slowly, perhaps reluctantly, did likewise. He was of average height but bulky, with brown hair scraped back from a receding hairline into a ponytail. He wore the cracked leathers, zipped boots and neckerchief of a Hell's Angel but to be fair, thought Hester, he didn't look hellish, just rather wary. Giselle had a large dressing over her left eye. Hester remembered, piercingly, an occasion when Giselle had fallen off the scramble-net in the school playground and she had been summoned to collect her from the secretary's office. Then, as now, Giselle had worn an expression of threatening stoicism. It said, unequivocally, that they sympathised at their peril.

Hester knew better, now as then, than to take too much notice of the threat. Fearlessly cutting through the laser beam of mutual suspicion between Jonty and Ark, she went and put her arms round her daughter.

'Darling – are you okay?'

Giselle made a minute reciprocal movement behind Hester's back. 'Fine. Can we go?'

'I'd like to talk to a doctor,' said Jonty.

'Why? They said I could go.'

'Head injuries can be nasty.'

'This one isn't.'

'I shan't be long.' Jonty strode purposefully to the reception desk. Giselle sat down. Ark took a step backwards as though realising that with their arrival he had gone down several places in the pecking order. Hester smiled encouragingly.

'Aren't you going to introduce us?'

'This is Ark.'

'How do you do.' Hester held out her hand and after a moment's consideration, or it might have been consternation, Ark placed his own in it.

'How you doing.'

'Thanks for keeping her company,' said Hester.

'No hassle.'

Hester sat down next to Giselle. 'How are you feeling?'

'I told you, fine.'

'What on earth happened – what were you doing?'

'Mind if I slip outside for a smoke . . .?' asked Ark, going.

'Of course not,' said Hester.

Giselle folded her arms. Hester kissed her cheek and she flinched sideways as though she'd been struck. Normal service, Hester thought wistfully, had been resumed.

'We've been so worried. We thought you were having a really good evening, and then this—! You have to see it from our point of view.'

'I don't have to see anything.'

Hester sighed. Jonty, who had been talking to a frazzled-looking young woman in a white coat, came back.

'We can take you home. But you have to ring and fix a follow-up appointment for a couple of weeks' time. Wait there and I'll go and bring the car up to the door.'

'I can walk,' said Giselle.

'I dare say, but there's no need to walk more than you have to.'

'Ark's out there. Don't go asking him about what happened, will you.'

'I've no intention of asking him anything.'

Jonty headed for the swing doors.

'Why? What did happen?' asked Hester.

'It was this woman he was going out with.'

'She was the one you were fighting with?'

'Donna, yeah.'

'And you won, you said.'

'Yeah.'

Hester permitted herself a smile. 'Oh, well. Only the brave deserve the fair.'

Ark was squatting on the edge of the kerb near the ambulance bay, a flattened roll-up dangling from his fingers. Jonty went up to him, jingling his keys.

'There's no need to hang about. I'm just going to fetch the car, and we'll take her back with us.'

'Okay.' Ark looked up at him, taking a drag. His relaxed air unsettled Jonty.

'Thanks for bringing her in.'

'My pleasure.' Ark tapped ash into the road. Jonty caught a poignant, half-forgotten smell. 'What did the doctor say?'

'There's no serious damage. God knows what she thought she was playing at,' said Jonty, adding pointedly: 'It'll be some time before she's out and about again.'

'Don't bet on it,' said Ark, rising. 'She's tough.'

'We'll see.' Jonty was aware of a hidden agenda: Who knew Giselle best?

'Anyway – I take it you have transport?'

'I'll be all right.'

'Goodnight.'

As he pushed open the swing door Jonty glanced over his shoulder to see Ark dropping his roach carefully between the bars of a drain.

'What does that chap do?' asked Jonty on the way back.

'What do you mean, what does he do?' The immediate danger over, Giselle's temper was worsening by the minute.

'I mean, how does he live?'

'He's a therapist.'

'No!' Hester was surprised and impressed, in spite of herself. 'Really?'

'An alternative therapist,' expounded Giselle less grudgingly.

'I might have guessed it would be something alternative,' said Jonty.

'What's that supposed to mean?'

'Yes,' agreed Hester, 'it was a bit curmudgeonly.'

'It wasn't meant to be.' Jonty flipped the lights on to beam and accelerated as they hit the dual carriageway. 'So tell us about the therapy.'

'He's a Reiki Master.'

'Er – give us a clue.'

'His hands get very hot. He can make people relax. Sort of centre them. Focus their energies.'

'I see,' said Jonty. He stretched his neck slightly, to catch Hester's eye in the mirror, but she was looking out of the back window, smiling.

It struck Hester as a sign of the times, that the closest thing the Blakes had had to a family meal in months was breakfast that morning. Was this what it took, she asked herself, to get everyone round the table at the same time?

'Wicked,' said Daniel, scrutinising the injury. 'You look like shit.'

Rose sipped herbal tea and glanced up from the *Post*. 'You do, actually.'

Hester placed a fried egg sandwich in front of Daniel and another in front of Giselle. 'Eat.'

'I don't suppose she feels too jolly either,' said Jonty, who had showered, dressed and was considering how the night's events might most amusingly be summarised for the benefit of his colleagues at work.

'I feel okay,' said Giselle, through egg, 'but I'm buggered.'

'Tired, I believe, is the word.'

Rose turned to the horoscopes.

'Aries. "The feeling that you're beating your head against a brick wall is one you should take note of today." There you are, Griz. "Perhaps it's time you stopped causing yourself all that pain and frustration and looked around for a door. Courage and perseverance can all too easily become pugnacity and pigheadedness."' Rose shook her head. 'How true.'

'Piss off,' said Giselle. 'I'm going up.'

'Have you opened my present yet?' asked Daniel.

'Yeah. Thanks.'

'Can I borrow it some time?'

'Sure,' said Giselle. 'That's why you bought it, right?'

A little later, as Hester was making a start on her column, the phone rang.

'Hester Blake.'

'It's me,' said Jonty. 'How's Grizzle?'

'Asleep.'

'Good. Look – I'm sorry, but it's been preying on my mind – what did you think of that fellow last night?'

'Ark?'

'Whatever his bloody silly name was.'

'I thought he was quite nice,' said Hester.

'He was smoking pot outside A and E last night, did I say?'

'Something you never did, of course . . .'

'It was the sheer blatancy of it – the assumption that I wouldn't mind.'

'You're on record as saying—'

'And what was all that "Reiki Master" baloney?'

Hester pressed 'Save'. 'I've heard of that somewhere . . . or read about it. I think the *Post* did something about it a year or so ago . . . It works for a lot of people.'

'I can't pretend I'm happy about it,' grumbled Jonty. 'What the devil can he and Grizzle have in common anyway?' Hester opened her mouth. 'Don't answer that.'

'I thought he was fine,' persisted Hester. 'He's obviously fond of Giselle—'

'*That* much I don't doubt.'

'As long as he's not married or anything.'

'Hang out the flags! So he's a crackpot but not an adulterous one – as far as we know. Your trouble, Hes,' added Jonty generously, 'is that you're absolutely incapable of not seeing everybody else's point of view.'

'I know,' Hester had said humbly.

Six weeks later, as she lay in bed after the dinner party, too tired and overfull to sleep, she listened to the clunk of the front door as Ark left, and thought: ain't that the truth.

CHAPTER FOUR

A nn was in her large, airy study at Raglan Road this Sunday morning, the morning immediately after the Blakes' dinner party. In the middle distance church bells rang not too intrusively, reminding those who cared to listen (and in this particular parish there were not many) that it was time for their weekly observance of Rite A. The top of the long sash window was open, and the bells were plainly audible over the Poulenc on Classic FM, but that didn't trouble Ann. She prided herself on a steady, intelligent liberalism which allowed everyone their devices and desires, provided they also acknowledged their responsibilities.

She took up a sheet of headed notepaper and her Mont Blanc pen.

Dear Hester, she wrote, *That was such a pleasant evening you gave us the other night. As always, there was far too much catching up to do – we must make a real effort to see more of each other. I find it quite frightening how the years slip by: seeing Giselle really brought that home to me. I don't think you should worry about that daughter of yours. From all Jonty was saying she is clearly a young woman of character. Tell her if she is ever in Town she must feel free to come and ring our bell – I should be delighted to see her. It often helps to unload some emotional baggage on to an older woman who is not one's mother . . . and I have the additional advantage of having a trained ear . . .*

We were so sorry to hear about your dog. I well remember when you first got him, and what a bundle of energy he always was – my Jaeger skirt never fully recovered! Not being pet owners ourselves we can only imagine what a loss it must be.

Thank you again for a delightful dinner. Byron has not forgotten the malt, and if you have a moment in your hectic schedule I'd welcome the recipe for that chocolate roulade . . .

We hope to see you down here in the very near future.

   Best regards,

Ann

This was Ann's third draft – she always found that spontaneous little effusions required the most careful attention – and it was a relief to seal it into the envelope and put it not into, but beneath, her wire 'Out' tray, because she did not intend posting it until first thing Tuesday. Over-prompt thank-you notes were crass, and conveyed the false impression that one was simply getting the task out of the way.

She studied her list. She often took clients on a Sunday (one had to be sensitive to other people's work schedules). Today she had none, but one or two outstanding tasks remained before she could leave her desk and see how Byron was getting on with the cork tiling in the top bathroom. Assuming all was going well, she would then start preparing Sunday lunch. Gavin had been persuaded to trust his employees with the brasserie for once, and was bringing along a girlfriend, Katie Hogan. Ann entertained only modest expectations of this relationship. Katie was young, pretty and personable and (at the last count, anyway) thought the world of Gavin. She would come bearing a bunch of flowers. She would converse attentively, and offer to help with the clearing away. But whether she had the necessary resources to stay the course with Gavin, Ann took leave to doubt.

Doubts notwithstanding, Ann was nothing if not welcoming and hospitable toward her sons' girlfriends. For lunch she was going to serve her famous Moroccan leg of lamb with a stuffing of herbs, apricots and raisins, accompanied by saffron rice and a salad of mixed leaves with a walnut oil dressing. Next, in the French manner, there would be Camembert, goat's cheese and grapes. And finally, caramelised oranges with slivered, toasted almonds and crème fraîche. Ann and Byron had eaten at Schmooze on their wedding anniversary and she knew she was the equal of the starred Glaswegian chef. Where cooking was concerned, she was quietly confident. It was a state she aspired to in all that she did.

She glanced at her watch: ten-fifty. She dialled Sebastian's Notting Hill number, and sat composedly, letting it ring. She had made it her business to find out how long it generally took Sebastian to free himself from the trammels of sleep, and whatever woman was currently sharing it with him, stagger to the phone in the next room, light a cigarette – or one of last night's joints, whichever was the closer – and lift the receiver. In this calculation she had sensibly allowed for an initial resistance to answering at all. The timing and persistence of the call would indicate to Sebastian that it was she, his mother, who was ringing, and he would eventually respond.

Twenty-two rings was the boundary line, after which she permitted herself either to become annoyed, or to give up and move on to the next thing. Twenty-two complete, double rings, that was, not single blasts amounting to eleven double rings . . .

On the twentieth, Sebastian answered.

'Hallo.' His voice was throaty and slurred with sleep. It was also very surly, but Ann discounted that. If he was grumpy, she told herself with an inward smile, it would be because of some woman. He was a charmer. It did not surprise her that her eldest son had wound up in one of the caring professions.

'Seb – it's Mum.'

'Who else could it be at this time on a Sunday . . ?'

Ann heard the flump and creak of the ancient settee as he flopped down on it and took a drag. Some time before Christmas she was going to have to get Sebastian to choose a couple of essential items of furniture at Peter Jones.

She chuckled. 'I know. But it's a good time to catch you, before you go out and I start on other things. By the way, I am cooking a joint today, Gavin and Katie are coming . . . are you at all interested?'

'Pass,' said Sebastian. He coughed noisily, and then added: 'But I might pop over later and snaffle a plateful for the microwave.'

'If there's any left,' admonished Ann playfully, making a jotting to the effect that she would carve a helping for Sebastian first.

He yawned. 'So, what's new?'

'I was going to ask the same thing of you. Are you alone?'

'More or less.'

'I mean, can you be overheard?'

'No.'

'I wondered if you'd succeeded in shaking off that wretched girl . . ?' enquired Ann, in a tone both casual and concerned.

'Who?' asked Sebastian.

'The one whose attentions you were finding so unwelcome. The one who locked you in the Unit.'

'Patsy.'

'Was that her name? I don't recall.'

'Forget it,' said Sebastian, 'that's history.'

'I'm so glad,' said Ann, stifling a certain disappointment. 'Your father and I have been quite concerned. I actually made a few preliminary enquiries as to the legal position.'

'No, no,' said Sebastian affably. 'You have to expect a bit of aggravation from time to time in this line of work. It goes with the territory. It's all sorted now.'

'Good. And you're keeping well otherwise?'

'Picture of health, thanks.'

'Well . . .' Ann could tell by the escalating geniality of Sebastian's tone that she was being dismissed. 'I'd better go and let you get on. So we might see you later on? Raiding the fridge?'

'You never know,' agreed Sebastian.

Back in the bedroom he dabbed his half-smoked joint into the saucer on the floor, and crashed back on to the futon. A plump black shoulder rose from the folds of candy-striped bedding like some exotic dessert, *nègres en chemises* . . .

Sebastian hiked across the mattress and burrowed convulsively into the warm, yielding wall of flesh.

'Patsy . . .' he growled. 'O-o-o-oh, Patsy . . . Show us the legal position . . .'

The second item on Ann's piece of paper was a sub-list of the things she wished to ask Gavin, and the information she hoped to elicit from Katie without alerting Gavin – or indeed, Katie herself if it were possible. Ann made some cryptic jottings. She was an experienced gleaner of unconsidered trifles and interpreter of same. By the time they left, which would be at around half past three if no walk were mooted, she would have a fair idea of which way the wind blew.

The third item was a reminder to herself to prime Byron about Katie. He was often a touch too flirtatious for these politically correct times, and there was no need to antagonise the girl or frighten her off unnecessarily . . . Ann straightened her desk and slipped the list inside the cover of her spiral notebook. As the peal

of church bells slowed to a measured single chime she switched off
Classic FM, left the study and went upstairs to have a word with
her husband.

Raglan Road ran at right angles to Holland Park, and anyone
walking briskly – as Ann often did – could be in the park itself
in five minutes. Number 7 was a double-fronted detached house,
white with battleship grey woodwork, situated almost on the corner
– on still summer nights you could hear the unearthly screams of
the peacocks. The Armitages had been sensible of what a shrewd
investment the house was when they'd bought it twenty-five years
ago with a substantial inheritance from Byron's mother. It had
been one of several such investments made at the time (Ann was
a keen student of the financial pages) and they regarded it as a
property kept in trust for the boys. The house was scrupulously
maintained, and even the most impulsive casual callers rarely
found it disordered. The paintwork inside and out was regularly
freshened by a firm from Shepherd's Bush, aided in the fiddlier
areas by the painstaking Byron. Fixtures, fittings and furnishings
were in plain and unruffled good taste, and purchased without
regard to cost, on the understanding that quality endures. Unlike
The Old Clink, where every room testified to impulse buying
and the good-natured adoption of ancestral junk, 7 Raglan Road
spoke of sensible, far-sighted expenditure and a polite ruthlessness
of execution. Colours were plain, materials were good, pictures
were few and arresting, books were legion but confined to the
walls of the study, and exhaustively catalogued. Outside the
back door, alongside her dustbins, Ann and her cleaning woman,
Josette Devine, an Afro-Caribbean single mother, had established
a platoon of secondary bins for recyclable materials – tins, bottles,
newspaper, cloth. Being financially secure did not in Ann's view
excuse profligacy or waste.

  Before his departure for France, Julian had been living at Raglan
Road, and it was not unknown for the other boys to 'touch base'
for short periods in order to recharge their batteries with Ann's
cooking and other home comforts. But when the house was empty
for any length of time Ann would take in the occasional carefully
vetted lodger. At the moment she had a Mr We-We Sun from Hong
Kong, on secondment to the Paediatrics Department at St Mary's
Paddington. Though he spoke fluent American-English, Ann had

made a point of learning a few phrases of Cantonese to make him feel at home.

Today Mr We-We Sun was out having Sunday lunch with a colleague's family in Elstree, which was why Ann had set Byron to doing the cork tiles. She ran up the stairs and paused momentarily to catch her breath (a sign of the times) before calling out:

'Byron!'

'In here . . .'

'I want a quick word,' said Ann, putting her head round the bathroom door, 'about Katie.'

Byron sat back on his haunches. His bushy hair was more than usually wild and his face was red. 'Katie?'

'Yes,' said Ann. 'Remember to treat her like a member of the human race, and not a dolly bird.'

'Dolly bird?' Even to Byron this phrase had an archaic ring.

'Young women notice these things.'

'I like Katie.'

'Precisely,' said Ann.

Gavin turned his red Vauxhall Cabriolet into a residents' parking space and put his 'Doctor On Call' card on the dashboard. Katie clicked her tongue.

'You are hopeless.'

'It's not to be taken seriously. I'm making a statement. It's Sunday, for Christ's sake.'

'They weren't born yesterday, you know.'

'If they were that bright they wouldn't be traffic wardens.'

'Honestly . . .' Katie shook her head. 'You talk about them as if they were marsupials or something.'

'Marsupials . . .' Gavin cocked his head to one side. 'I like it.'

Katie folded down the sun visor and studied herself in the mirror. 'How do I look?'

Gavin surveyed her. He himself was tiring of Katie and her Home Counties niceness, but she was the business for a Sunday lunch with the olds – fair-haired, clear-skinned, bright, but not bright enough to seriously discombobulate anyone. She was also versed from infancy in all those token politenesses which went down so well – the pot plant, the offers of help, the capacity, nurtured at countless Sunday morning cocktail parties, to ask formulaic questions and appear interested in the answers.

Today she wore the cream suit and white blouse he'd always considered matronly.

'You look great,' he said. 'I've always liked that.'

'Fibber.'

'I have.'

'Last time out you said it made me look like a provincial mayoress.'

'Well, hush my mouth.'

'I thought it was appropriate.'

'It is.' Gavin ducked to look in the wing mirror and run his hand over his own curly mop. 'Maddeningly appropriate. It'll go down a storm with my father, he has a penchant for smart little suits.'

'I like your father,' said Katie. 'He's good fun.'

'Now then Katie,' said Ann, 'have more salad with that. Dig in, don't wait to be asked.'

'There's no doubt we're ahead of the field in almost every area,' Gavin explained to Byron, 'which is why we're attracting so much jealousy.'

'Does that matter?' asked Byron, his brow furrowed. 'After all, business is business. Not that I know anything about it . . .'

'Business is business, yet,' agreed Gavin testily, 'but any public service operation is to some extent at the mercy of the critics. We have a packed place, a hundred covers, six days a week, but it doesn't help when all these splenetic old queens in the glossies look down their noses at us.'

'More lamb?' asked Ann.

'It's the tall poppy syndrome,' went on Gavin, who had not noticed the offer. 'Something this country's very good at.'

'I suppose so,' said Byron, passing his own plate via Katie. 'May I . . .?'

Ann gave him a small slice and a reproving look.

'Any show of enterprise, or initiative or innovation is seen by the old guard as threatening, and stifled at birth or patronised to death.'

'More meat?' asked Ann again.

'Thanks.' Gavin pushed his plate sideways. 'It's bloody frustrating. We're forging ahead, there's nothing else like us north of the river, we've already achieved beyond our backers' wildest dreams, and what do we get from the Establishment?' They waited respectfully for the answer. Gavin ran the side of his hand across his throat before reclaiming his plate from Ann.

'And why do you think that is?' asked Ann, sitting back with her wine glass held between laced fingers.

'Two words,' said Gavin, helping himself to the last of the rice. 'Youth. And brilliance.'

'That's three,' said Katie.

Byron snorted and poked his fork at her. 'Right, it is.'

Ann ignored both these remarks. All her attention, her concern, her potential resources, were for Gavin.

'Della Carteret's not especially young, surely.' She referred to Gavin's co-proprietor.

'No, she's not,' agreed Gavin. 'But neither is she the creative powerhouse. She's just a rich bitch. Modesty forbids, *capice*?'

'One of your problems, darling,' said Ann, 'is that you have never been a team player.'

'I'm not ashamed of that. Quite the reverse.'

'Good. But you must accept that if you are the cat that walks by itself, others will stand back.'

'They'd better,' said Gavin. 'They can watch my dust.'

He ate voraciously and without apparent relish, his knife and fork clattering on the plate.

Ann gave Katie a confiding smile.

'Thank God I'm not a thrusting young entrepreneur in the last decade of this century,' said Byron, wielding the wine bottle.

'Darling,' said Ann with a kind of comfortable malice, 'there was never any danger of that.'

'True.'

'What exactly did you used to do?' asked Katie brightly, and then realised how this sounded and blushed fierily. 'Oh God, did that sound terribly rude . . .?'

'Yes,' said Gavin, 'but he won't mind.'

'You're quite right, I don't,' said Byron. 'I was a schoolmaster.'

'I bet you were wonderful at that.'

'To be honest with you,' put in Ann, 'I think his time is far fuller now than it ever was when he was teaching.'

'She's a slave driver,' Byron told Katie behind his hand.

'You love it,' said Gavin. 'Admit it.' He put his knife and fork down with a bang. 'It's all of less than minimal significance anyway, since no-one in this country gives a shit about education.'

'That's rather a sweeping statement, Gavin,' said Ann, captivated by the sort of opening gambit she found most stimulating. 'Would you care to justify that?'

'With pleasure . . .'

Byron caught Katie's expression of gathering despond. He leaned sideways.

'Shall you and I do the honours?'

She smiled in polite bafflement. 'Sorry?'

'Shall we clear the plates?'

'Oh – of course.'

Gavin was now in full flight. Ann, torn between the total attention she owed her son and her duties as a hostess, glanced up and frowned meaningfully, but Byron took no notice.

Out in the kitchen he said gently to Katie: 'Our hero seems a bit down.'

'He was absolutely fine before we arrived.'

'Maybe it's us.'

'Oh, I'm sure not,' said Katie at once. 'You know what it is, he gets wound up about his work.'

'I do know it,' said Byron. 'I do indeed.'

'. . . I'm sorry if I sound cynical,' concluded Gavin with no hint of remorse, 'but my whole experience in setting up Schmooze has contributed to that cynicism.'

'You're coming round for the second time,' said Katie.

'I apologise if I'm boring everyone,' snapped Gavin unapologetically.

'You're not boring anyone. On the contrary,' Ann assured him, but Katie was encouraged by her exchange of confidences with Byron.

'You were going on a bit.'

'More coffee anyone?' asked Ann, holding the pot aloft.

'You're saying I'm bitter and twisted?' asked Gavin.

'No!'

'Don't be daft,' said Byron.

'If I am, it's scarcely surprising.'

'You're not, my love,' soothed Ann. 'I for one found everything you had to say most interesting.'

'Well, I'm glad someone did,' said Gavin, and left the table.

'Oh dear,' said Katie. 'I am sorry. I can be such a fathead sometimes.'

Byron stretched out and patted her arm. 'Not at all.'

'Gavin's is a quicksilver temperament,' mused Ann. 'It'll blow over.'

In the drawing room they found Gavin sitting in the window seat smoking a cigarette and reading the *Sunday Times* Culture supplement.

'Ah, the Sundays,' said Byron. 'Might I be allowed fifteen minutes' immersion in newsprint before getting back to that infernal bathroom?'

Gavin, apparently quite restored, nodded towards the pile on the coffee table. 'You want to look at Food and Drink, we're in it.'

'Paper, Katie?' asked Ann.

Katie picked up the nearest one and stared sightlessly at a profile of a revered Hungarian film director. From the window seat Gavin, good humour apparently restored, began pointing out inaccuracies in the restaurant column to his father.

Ann, who had sat down next to Katie on the chesterfield, said: 'It's very rude of me, I haven't yet asked how your work is going?'

Katie lowered the Hungarian film director, not without a sense of relief.

'Actually, I've just landed a new job.'

'Splendid, congratulations! May one ask . . .?'

'It's nothing grand, but it is a step up in terms of . . . I'm going to be on the diary staff of the *Post*.'

'You must be delighted,' said Ann.

Katie blushed. 'I know it's a bit right-wing, but it does have a huge circulation, and the highest proportion of women readers of any national newspaper.'

'So I understand,' said Ann.

'And the diary will be good because of all the contacts. I'll wind up with an amazing address book.'

'Of course.' Ann nodded sagaciously. 'When does all this start?'

'In a couple of weeks. I'm terribly nervous.'

'You shouldn't be. As a matter of fact, it may surprise you to learn that we know someone else who works on the *Post*.'

'No! Who?'

'Hester Blake.'

'Wow,' exclaimed Katie, 'I am truly impressed.'

'She's an extremely nice woman,' said Ann. 'And a very old and dear friend.'

On the doorstep, three quarters of an hour later, Ann said: 'Good-bye, my dear, it was nice to see you again. And the cyclamen is a delight.'

'Thank you for the gorgeous lunch. Bye-bye—' Katie held out her hand to Byron, who took it, and placed a kiss on her cheek. Ann smiled indulgently.

'I shall tell Hester to look out for you. She's not there every day, but I know she'd wish to introduce herself.'

'Oh, good Lord, she's far too important, please don't even—'

'It's as good as done.' Ann turned from Katie to Gavin and patted his lapel. 'Now listen to me.' She gazed intently into his face. 'Learn a little diplomacy, yes? It isn't demeaning to know the value of public relations. If you can do it with customers you can do it with the critics. Shall we have lunch next week?'

'Shafted!' snapped Gavin, screwing up his parking ticket and dropping it in the gutter. 'Bloody little jobsworths!'

Ann put the kettle on for a cup of tea in the kitchen.

'Well?' asked Byron. 'How did I do?'

'How did you do what?'

'Was I too forward? Too nudge-nudge, wink-wink?'

'Don't be silly, Byron.'

Byron looked crestfallen. 'She's a nice girl.'

'Hmm,' said Ann. 'I wonder if she might not be a little too nice.'

'You really know how to bolster a man's morale, don't you?' said Gavin, executing a screeching U-turn at the top of Raglan Road.

'Careful—! Sorry?'

'Accusing me of boring everyone to death the moment I try to steer the conversation towards something that really concerns me.'

'I didn't accuse you of anything.'

'And all that sickening eyelash-batting with my father.'

'Your father's sweet.'

'I'm sure he's very flattered.' Gavin darted out ungraciously in

front of an Espace packed with women and children and sped down
Holland Park towards the lights. 'My father has about as much idea
about the real world as Muffin the Mule.'

'Who?'

'My mother, with all her faults, does at least have a reasonable
appreciation of the problems I have to face.'

'Calm down.'

'No.'

'Anyway, I do—'

'Have you not yet learnt that the surest way to infuriate someone
is to tell them to calm down?'

'Okay!' Katie put her hands to the sides of her face, like blinkers.
'Okay.'

'It's so fucking patronising.'

'Both your parents are nice. Lunch was delicious.' Katie was
turning pink. 'I honestly have no idea what all this is about.'

'In *that* case,' said Gavin, 'you're even stupider than I thought.'

They were at the lights on the Bayswater Road.

'In *that* case,' there was a catch in Katie's voice, 'perhaps you'd
like me to catch a taxi.'

'Good idea.'

'Gavin – this is silly—'

He leaned roughly across her, opened the door and gave it a
push. 'Damn right.'

She clambered out and stood holding the door. 'Gavin—'

The lights turned amber.

'Chop-chop!'

'God, this is awful – I don't believe this is happening!' said Katie.
She wasn't used to scenes, let alone causing them. Her eyes were
bright and her mouth trembled. The Espace, which had since pulled
up behind them, beeped its horn. 'Sorry!'

'Please don't apologise,' said Gavin. 'Just rack off.'

The car was already moving as Katie swung the door shut.
Tears oozed down her face. She mouthed another 'Sorry' at the
stony-faced woman at the wheel of the Espace. The children
gawped at her. Another fusillade of horns sounded. Katie leapt
back on to the kerb as the traffic surged forward. Her last sight of
Gavin was his hand raised to head height, the middle finger tautly
and obscenely raised.

*   *   *

Gavin made an unscheduled detour via the brasserie and reduced his newest waiter to tears before getting back to his flat in George Street, Paddington, in a towering rage. For a full half hour his surroundings lacked their usual power to soothe. He slammed doors, kicked his cat, Mensa, swore aloud, and broke his favourite mug by banging it down too vigorously in the sink.

The rage was soon replaced by deep gloom. He was alone. No-one understood the pressures he faced. To whom could he turn for comfort? For support? He sat on the side of his bed with his head in his hands and told himself that he was desolate.

'I had our Gavin on the phone,' said Sebastian, putting a plateful of Moroccan lamb in the microwave and pushing buttons. 'Going apeshit, as only he knows how.'

'*Oh* dear.' Ann looked up from loading Sebastian's bedlinen (tactfully scrunched up) into the machine. 'I feared the worst at lunchtime.'

'All standard stuff,' said Sebastian, sitting down at the kitchen table and lighting a Marlboro. 'He's mentally wrecked and physically shattered, he's creatively blocked in his work, and his current woman's an undermining cow without two brain cells to rub together.'

'She's a sweet girl.'

'There you go then.'

'But,' Ann sighed, 'she has no idea how to handle Gavin.'

'Who does?'

'Now that's not fair, Seb.' The microwave bleeped and Ann took out Sebastian's plate and handed it to him, together with a kitchen fork from the cutlery tree and a napkin. 'Your brother may not be easy, but that is not, so far as I know, a crime. He's also very gifted and fiercely ambitious and doesn't suffer fools gladly.'

'He's fucking paranoid.' Sebastian shovelled down the lamb. 'This is okay.'

Ann sat down opposite him as the washing machine began to trundle and splosh in the background.

'What else did he say?'

'Nothing much. That lot took the best part of an hour. I watched the whole of *Masterchef* while he was banging on about it.'

'I must say,' said Ann, 'I think there is the potential for a lot of damage in this latest relationship of his. You will keep an eye out for him, won't you? I worry about him.'

'You're wasting your time. Tell you what though,' said Sebastian, scraping up the last grains of rice with the side of his fork, 'I feel sorry for that woman. He's a bastard when he gets on his high horse.'

Ann allowed a small reproachful pause to elapse, before saying: 'There is a tiny spot more. Your father's better off without it. Would you like it?'

By later that evening, when he'd had a chat with his brother, Gavin was much restored. The incident at the traffic lights had been bad news. He'd fucked up, but perhaps not irreparably. It might be possible to salvage something while keeping clear water between himself and Katie. After all, she was off to work for Orde's Diary, which could be bloody useful.

For this exercise it was necessary to create a mood. First he removed his shoes and put a Joan Armatrading on the CD player. Next, he poured himself a Jack Daniels with plenty of ice, and stuffed a piece of pitta bread with peanut butter, lettuce and salad cream. Finally, with both of these at his elbow, he sat down with pen and paper and prepared to open a vein.

Katie was taking a two-week break before starting at the *Post*, and her flatmate Jackie was at work, so she was on her own in the Islington flat. There was a sad irony in this, because she often dreamed of quiet, leisurely Monday mornings at home, but now that she had one it was sheer hell.

Last night had been ghastly. She'd drunk too much and cried a lot on Jackie's shoulder and Jackie had told her that she had to take charge of her life and her self-esteem and tell the creep to drop dead. Katie had pointed out, through sobs, that there had been error on both sides, and Gavin was under so much stress . . . and Jackie had said stress be buggered, he was a verbal bully with an emotional age of two-and-a-half and if Katie couldn't see that then she deserved everything she got. And Katie said she supposed so . . . and Jackie said she knew so, have another one . . .

And so it had gone on. Katie wasn't proud of herself. This morning she had a copybook hangover – headache, sweats, nausea, weak knees – and still the persistent feeling that she had mishandled things. She thought about lunch yesterday, and how nice most of it had been – how kind and hospitable Ann and Byron were, and how well they treated her. And Gavin *was* different, one of London's most successful restaurateurs and only just turned thirty, a 'tall poppy', as he put it. His mother knew how to handle him. Katie should have taken a few tips out of her book, but it was too late now.

At midday she was lying on the bed trying without much success to face up to a mug of hot Marmite. She would have quite liked to ring her mother in Hampshire, except that she wasn't sure she could take her mother's 'plenty-more-fish-in-the-sea-darling' style of comfort. At the moment she couldn't face the thought of the other fish. They were all going to be boring. Gavin was special, and she had failed the Gavin test . . .

When the front door bell rang she tottered to the intercom with a swimming head, and it was a full five seconds before she could speak.

'Yes . . .?'

'Interflora for a Miss Hogarth.'

'Miss who—? Oh, Hogan actually . . . come on up.'

There were a dozen white roses, with a letter pinned to the Cellophane.

'*My lovely Katie,*' he had written. '*No – you mustn't shoot the messenger. Please take these out of the bin again – they don't deserve to be punished for the way I behaved yesterday. Put them in water and try to enjoy them for themselves. They're not red, because red's for love and I realise I've forfeited the right to say "I love you" and to hear you say it back. They're white for peace – peace between us, now that it's over, and peace that I hope you will enjoy without me in your life to screw it up for you.*'

Here Katie, who had been standing just inside the front door with the roses in one hand and the letter in the other, slid slowly down the wall till she was sitting on the floor. The letter was so *sweet*. The rest of the words shimmered through her tears.

'*Because it is over. I accept that. I'm not even going to insult your intelligence by apologising. An apology demands forgiveness and that's something I don't deserve. You're way too good for me, Katie. But you were good for me. You showed me what a really decent, unselfish person is like, and I shan't forget that.*

'You must forget as quickly as you can, though. Please. And as for me — you will always be gentle on my mind. Gavin.'

'Very nice,' said Jackie drily. 'Must've cost a king's ransom. I sincerely hope you're not going to do anything rash?'

It was the following evening at half past eight, and Jackie was out at step-aerobics when Katie called George Street to speak to Gavin's answering machine. She knew she was being feeble, but she wasn't quite ready to talk to him in person yet. She felt better today, no longer ill, and not weepy and maudlin, either. She was not crawling back, or saying sorry, or any of those demeaning things that Jackie warned against. She was simply being mature; trying to renegotiate the terms of her relationship with this difficult, rewarding man.

'This is Gavin Armitage.' His voice always sounded lower on the machine. Katie was forcibly reminded that this was a man of sorrows, and acquainted with grief. 'I'm sorry I'm not in right now, but leave your message after the long tone and I'll get back to you as soon as it's possible to do so.'

Katie hung up the first time. Then she collected herself, dialled again, listened to the message and waited, tensely, for the long tone.

'Gavin? It's Katie. I wanted to say thank you for the roses. They're not in the bin, and I am enjoying them. Do call if you feel like a talk. You know where I am. Bye.'

Her voice was as she wanted it to be. But she was all of a quiver when she'd replaced the receiver.

Gavin got back from Schmooze at half past one, in high good spirits. It had been a classic night. Classic. He had a bath before playing his messages, then reset the machine, and went to bed with his book. It was a Booker-shortlisted novel, but he didn't rate it.

The phone woke Katie, with horrid images of crashes, and deaths, and police. She glanced at the digital display on the clock-radio: 02.47. Jackie stirred and groaned.

Katie answered it.

'It's Gavin.' He sounded exhausted, she thought. Drained.

'I left a message, did you . . .?'

'I just got it, that's why I'm ringing . . . Christ, is that the time?

Look, you get back to bed, I didn't have anything to say worth
disturbing you for.'

'I'm here now,' said Katie. There was silence at the other end.
She sat down on the sofa, bunching her knees up inside her nightie.
She was prepared to be endlessly patient. 'I'm awake. Do please say
whatever you were going to say.'

'It's . . . look, Katie. I almost cried when I heard your voice. It
was so lovely – such a relief, somehow.'

'I know – I felt the same.'

'I can't tell you how I'm missing you. If ever I needed showing
the error of my ways . . .'

'Don't be silly. And anyway—' she took a deep breath. 'It doesn't
have to be like this.'

'Oh . . .' His voice broke, and she felt as though her heart might
do the same. 'Katie, you're so good.'

'I miss you, too.'

'How can you say that? After those things I said . . .'

'We all say bad things when we lose our temper. And you were
right, I was being insensitive. I'm sorry.'

'Katie . . . oh God, Katie . . .' He was weeping now, she could
hear the great racking sobs, the shuddering intakes of breath . . .
she stood up, frantic with compassion and remorse.

'Gavin, darling – please! Please don't! Let me come over, now –
Gavin?'

'No.' His voice was surprisingly strong. 'You mustn't.'

'But I can't bear to hear you like this—'

'I'll be all right. Don't come over, Katie. Not now, not ever. I'm
bad news, Katie. The best thing I can do is stay out of your life.'
The bleakness of his words appalled her.

'No, honestly – that's not true.'

'It is. And that's exactly what I'm going to do.'

'We can be friends, at least—'

'I should never have made this call. Goodbye, Katie.'

'Gavin!'

'Take care of you . . .'

His voice was breaking again as he rang off.

'It's all over with that woman,' said Sebastian, when he came to
collect his washing at the end of the week. 'She gave him the
bum's rush.'

'I find that so hard to imagine,' said Byron, who was laying the table – Mr We-We Sun was in for dinner.

'Did he say why?' asked Ann, cutting up vegetables for a stir-fry.

Sebastian took a piece of carrot and munched on it. 'He did try to apologise, apparently, on the way home last Sunday, for being crabby over lunch or something—'

'Quite right, too,' said Byron.

'I'm glad he did,' said Ann, 'though I'm less certain about the need for it.'

'Anyway, she wasn't having any. He didn't mention it at the time, but it was one of the reasons he was in such a god-awful nark that evening on the phone. She just jumped out of the car at the lights, and buggered off.'

'PMT perhaps . . .?' suggested Byron innocently.

'Byron!'

'Sorry . . .'

Sebastian started on some strands of white cabbage. 'Then he had another bash – sent round some roses and a letter. That didn't work either. She left some curt message on his answering machine and when he returned her call she as good as told him to go play with a loaded gun.'

'Poor Gavin.' Ann's brow furrowed as she turned the heat up under the wok. 'Did he sound very down?'

'On a scale of one to ten,' said Sebastian, 'four? Four and a half?'

'Thank God,' said Ann. 'Byron – shall we have a glass of wine?'

Ann couldn't sleep. When she was sure that Byron had well and truly gone off, she permitted herself the luxury of a little self-pity. What she had always most wanted to be was a sound, supportive, understanding parent. It was something she consciously worked at and prided herself on having gone some way to achieving. Her sons could never say that she had no time for them, that she belittled them or was not interested in their lives. She was scrupulously fair, and she expected nothing in return – being a mother was nothing to do with amassing credits. Still, there were times when she felt utterly drained by all of it – the boys, their wants and needs and problems – and this was one of them. She thought despairingly of Gavin, who in spite of all he had going for him had had such rotten luck in relationships. The departure of Katie (and she took the Gavin/Sebastian version of events with a grain or two of salt) would not prevent her from contacting Hester on the girl's behalf, nor from greeting Katie warmly should she happen to bump into her in the street. It was important to separate things out. A person did not become the devil incarnate simply because she had behaved in a way that adversely affected some member of one's family: Katie was still the nice, pretty, cheerful girl she had been last Sunday even if she had walked out on Gavin . . .

After a few minutes she pulled herself together, put on her dressing gown and slippers and went down to the kitchen. There was still a faint aroma of prawns and oyster sauce. She made herself a camomile tea and stood looking out into the garden – broad and churchlike with its high wall and tall trees. She felt keenly all the threads which led from her to those she loved: to Byron, snoring gently upstairs; to Julian in his warm, shuttered apartment in Montaigle; to Sebastian, entwined with some girl under the bare duvet (she knew he wouldn't have replaced the clean cover yet); and to Gavin who would probably be wide awake, like her, still high from an evening at the brasserie. Despite the enforced gregariousness of his job Ann perceived him as the most alone of all her boys. He, more than any of them, needed the love and support of a strong yet undemanding woman. But where was such a woman to be found?

She looked at her watch. It was tomorrow already. Ann straightened her back, washed and dried her mug, and pulled down the hanging light low over the table, before sitting down with her kitchen notebook to make a list.

CHAPTER FIVE

The time Hester spent at the *Post* wasn't strictly necessary. By Tuesday lunchtime at the latest she'd written her page, consulted with the cartoonist about the illustration and could without difficulty have filed the whole thing from home. Quite simply, she enjoyed going to the office. It reminded her that there was life outside Chuffington, and concerns beyond those of Rose's accommodation, Daniel's GCSEs, and Giselle.

She liked the gregariousness of it. There was her secretary, Mary Chitty, with whom she shared the task of going through the mail. It wasn't all fan mail by a long chalk, but there was always masses of it, and that in itself was gratifying. There were various old chums to talk shop and gossip with: the cartoonist, Mick; Bill, the Pictures Editor; Anthea from Features; Derek, the TV critic. As often as not the Editor, Robert Walton, would invite her in to discuss future ideas, and flirt with her a bit. He was a dark, consumptive-looking Scot, in appearance more like a radical poet than the editor of a hugely popular tabloid newspaper, with a melancholy, ironic manner which Hester found charming. He alone of all her acquaintance called her Hetty.

And then there was lunch, occasionally with Robert, more often with assorted others. With Robert it would be at one of the two small, recherché restaurants he favoured in the Drury Lane area. With the others it was usually at The Huntsman, a barn of a pub with blackboards crammed with supposedly home-made dishes which it would have taken an army of trained chefs to prepare.

The *Post* occupied the third and fourth floors of a glittering glass tower off Holborn. Editorial was on the fourth floor, and Hester's office was on the corner of the building. It was light and bright – so much so that on summer afternoons they had to have the blinds drawn – and Mary took a housewifely pride in making it nice. The room was filled with pleasing bits and pieces bought by Hester at her secretary's instigation: flowering plants, pictures, cups and saucers from the Neal Street Shop, a humidifier, a mini-fridge, a cookie jar regularly replenished, and a blow-up of Hester's by-line photograph in which she looked – as Mary said, and Hester had blushingly to admit – fantastic. Hester had got used to this huge, idealised image of herself smiling confidingly down from the wall. She was only embarrassed when first-time visitors caught sight of it and asked: 'Is that you?' or with rather more frankness: 'When was that taken?'

Mary Chitty was the same age as Hester (and the same star sign, they had established that) but she seemed older. She was the sort of woman who still saw her job as an enjoyable bonus, paying for the little extras in life and getting her out of the semi in Bexleyheath. This in spite of the fact that she had been at the *Post* for twenty-five years, and was regarded as one of its great institutions. Mary had one son, Stephen, who was doing Engineering in Manchester and whom she spoke of with unconscious sexism as being the sole bearer of the Chitty family standard. It was well known that Mary had turned down preferment and a move to Editorial in order to work for Hester whom she admired as a real person, not just a 'journo'.

This week's page was about the appropriateness or otherwise of letting your children conduct their sex lives beneath the family roof. Hester's line had been to accept the inevitable. Like smoking, if you banned it it would only take place somewhere else.

'*Even more vivid in the memory than Kennedy's death, and still more traumatic,*' she'd written, '*is the moment when as children we realise that our parents "do it". That fell night when we get out of bed to go to the loo and hear the muted voices, the creak of bedsprings, the gasps and grunts of horribly old people enjoying themselves . . . But worse even than that is the point at which the wheel comes full circle and our own children, the fruit of our loins, the little innocents to whom we read Babar the Elephant and forbade sweets (at least for a year or two), fall victim to their hormones. Suddenly we're sure of only one thing: WE DON'T WANT THEM TO DO IT. On the other hand, we'd quite like them to be good at it . . . especially the boys. BUT WE DON'T WANT OUR DAUGHTERS DOING IT WITH THE SORT OF BOYS WHO ARE AS WE SECRETLY WANT OUR SONS TO BE.*

'*Sooner or later we have to accept that they're doing it, and then another dilemma presents itself. Are you going to stop them doing it under your roof? Are you going to interpose your body, like some monstrous seaside landlady, between your child's bedroom door and anyone who isn't your child? Are you really prepared to burst in, rolling pin in hand, in the small hours, and sunder the young lovers? Do you even have the will or the gumption to ask: "What's going on in there?" If the answer to any of these is "yes", then all I can say is, you're a better man than I am, Gunga Din . . .*'

Hester had gone on to regale her audience with a selection of more-or-less-true but amusingly enhanced anecdotes based on personal experience. She had ended with a direct appeal to the readers, something she resorted to from time to time, mainly to provide the material for some later page.

'*It's all horribly confusing. Oh, for the dear dead days when all was repression and hypocrisy! What do you think? Do write in and tell me. A bottle of champagne goes to the writer of the letter which best sums up our modern predicament.*'

'You could live to regret that,' said Mary, who liked to read Hester's copy before it went any further.

'We'll cope.' Hester caught Mary's eye, which was sceptical. 'I promise faithfully I'll help you sort the stuff out.'

'Seven maids with seven mops . . .' said Mary. 'Remember facelifts?'

'But it shows they're reading the page,' pointed out Hester. 'And it keeps me in touch with what people think and feel.'

'It keeps you in touch with what the people think and feel who can be bothered to write in to a newspaper,' declared Mary irrefutably. 'Not civilians.' This was the name given by Mary to The Millions of Ordinary People who did not engage with the media in any way but carried on with their lives, long-suffering, blameless and in the main cheerful, without ever rocking the communal boat. The main reason she liked Hester was because she was the closest thing the *Post* had to a civilian.

'You're right there,' said Hester. 'But there isn't much we can do about that.'

She considered that the page was a good one. It was funny and personal, but it raised a genuine issue, one with which all parents could identify. She was not an issues writer, but if one came along as the by-product of a particular topic it was no bad thing. It made her feel less frivolous and exploitative – more the sort of writer of whom Ann, say, would approve.

Ann had rung her up at the weekend.

'Hester, I think we've known each other long enough for me to ask you a small favour.'

It was a preamble generally calculated to make the heart sink; on the other hand there was something pleasing about being asked a favour by Ann, a woman more used to granting them.

'Of course, if I can.'

'I have a young friend, Katie Hogan, who is going to be working at the *Post* as from Monday.'

'Oh yes . . .?'

'On the diary page, I believe.'

'She'll enjoy that.'

'Katie's a very bright, personable lass, but she's understandably nervous about her first job on a national newspaper.'

'There's no need, Larry Orde's a poppet.'

Ann gave no credence to poppets. 'She is also a great admirer of yours.'

'How sweet of her,' said Hester. 'Would it be helpful if I said hallo?' She wondered why people in general thought it such an imposition to ask you to be nice to someone.

'*Would* you?' replied Ann warmly. 'I think it would be a tremendous boost to her confidence in those anxious early days.'

'I'll take her out to lunch,' went on Hester. 'She can come round the corner to the pub with the rest of us.'

'That would be above and beyond the call of duty. If you would only introduce yourself, I know that would give her a tremendous boost.'

'Of course, it'd be my pleasure,' insisted Hester. 'And by the way – that roulade you asked about. I'm sorry to say I bought it.'

'You didn't!' exclaimed Ann. 'I'd never in a million years have guessed.'

Katie considered that although Hester Blake was not as glamorous as her photograph, her face had more character and humour than the camera conveyed. Her fair hair was permed and highlighted but both curls and streaks were beginning to grow out, and a button on her long black Joseph cardigan was hanging by a thread. She had blue eyes and a generous mouth, but there was a touch of anxiety in her ready smile and a self-deprecating note in her laugh. Katie was predisposed to like anyone who paraded their foibles and failings so engagingly in print, and in the flesh she warmed instantly to Hester.

They went round to the Huntsman at 1.30 with Bill and Anthea but Hester very sweetly made a point of sitting between Katie and the other two so she could talk to her separately. Katie ordered a Weightwatchers' salad, but rather regretted it when everyone else tucked into things like battered bangers and lamb curry, accompanied by bowls piled with jumbo chips.

Hester shunted her own bowl of chips in Katie's direction. 'I'll never get through all those.'

'Are you sure? I feel a bit of a fraud ordering this and then . . .'

'You did absolutely right, Katie. And look at you, you don't even need to worry. I'm a martyr to diets as a rule, but this is my day off the leash.'

'Well, thanks.' Katie picked a chip. 'This is nice of you.'

'It's fun, isn't it?' agreed Hester. 'Now tell me how you know the Armitages.'

'It's slightly embarrassing actually,' admitted Katie. 'I've been going out with their son for about six months.'

Hester speared a piece of sausage and dunked it in ketchup. 'That would be – Sebastian? Or Gavin?'

'Gavin, yes.' Katie's cheeks felt hot. 'Do you know him?'

'We've known Ann and Byron for donkey's years, we've come across all the boys from time to time, but I wouldn't say I *know* any of them particularly. Gavin's the whizz kid, isn't he?'

'Yes.'

'He runs the brasserie.'

'Schmooze. Have you ever been there?' Hester shook her head. 'It's brilliant. It's really huge, and they have zither music, and a table with books and magazines and newspapers, and a place to play chess – it's just amazing.'

'It sounds it.' Hester smiled. 'So you and he are what's known as an item?'

Katie thought it best to be absolutely straight about the situation. 'Not any more. Unfortunately.'

'Poor you, I'm sorry.'

'Not at all. How could you possibly know, anyway? But it is sad, especially when Ann and Byron have been so good to me, and Ann got in touch with you.'

Hester nodded. 'She's like that.'

'It's so decent of her not to bear a grudge.'

'Why on earth should she?'

'I don't know . . .' To her acute embarrassment Katie could feel her mouth beginning to tremble. 'Poor Gavin, I did let him down rather.'

'He's not easy, from what I can gather.'

'No, but then I knew that at the outset. I can't help feeling guilty—'

Hester scrunched up her paper napkin and dropped it on the plate. 'The female disease.'

'Tell me about it . . .' Katie laughed shakily. 'And it makes such a bore of a person, too.'

'Not if you don't let it.'

'That's true.' Katie couldn't get over how sweet Hester was – she'd have to let Ann know.

'Let's drink to resolve.' Hester drained her wine glass and held it out to Bill. 'Your round, William.' The loose button on her cardigan fell to the ground and she leaned under the table to pick it up. 'Damn,' she said, pink-faced. 'Look at me, I'm falling apart.'

Giselle and Ark sat on the steps of City Hall, sharing a can of Four-X. Next to them, folded flat, was the A-frame board advertising Ark's services as an exponent of Reiki and, in a plastic carrier bag, a stack of printed fliers on the same subject. Contrary to Jonty's analysis, Ark was a dog-lover. His own pet, Dolly, a registered pit bull, lay on the pavement at his feet, muzzled and comatose (having lunched on leftover Spud-U-Likes), but still ensuring that the steps did not become crowded.

'How many do you reckon we've got rid of?' said Giselle.

Ark peered in the bag. 'A few. Could be worse.'

'People are awful, aren't they? Brain dead.'

'You can't blame them, what do they know? They can't be interested in something they don't understand. This lot – ' he tapped the bag – 'is about consciousness-raising. Educating them.'

Giselle passed the can back to him and took a packet of Silk Cut out of the pocket of her leather jacket. 'It's going to take forever.'

'Patience,' said Ark. 'Patience.'

'Bor-ing.' said Giselle.

'It won't be so bad this arvo,' pointed out Ark, 'the old one man band'll be here. That's good for us on two counts. One, we can listen to the old chap playing *The Floral Dance* while we're dishing them out, and two, people will congregate and he'll soften them up for us.'

Giselle took a puff on her cigarette and squinted at Ark through the smoke. He grinned at her. She made a face at him. He put his arm round her shoulders and pulled her towards him. A woman in a three-quarter mac paused to glare.

'Think you're hard, don't you?' he said, slipping his hand down between her thighs to where her leggings were split and the flesh – soft, smooth and womanly – peeped through. 'Think you're really hard . . .'

'No, but I bet you are . . . Let's go somewhere and I'll show you.'

'Later.' Ark released her reluctantly and stood up. Dolly immediately did the same, getting rid of the woman in the mac.

'We got work to do.' He carried the A-frame down the steps and set it up, tethering Dolly to one corner.

Docilely Giselle picked up the bag of leaflets and joined Ark on the pavement.

It would have surprised Giselle's parents to learn that she and Ark had a plan. It was only a plan in broad outline, somewhat lacking in detail or a specific time-frame, but a plan for all that.

Ark had a healthy regard for the work ethic. The idea was that when local consciousness had been raised to a high enough level he would rent a room in the community centre for a few hours a week – Saturday mornings only, perhaps, to begin with, followed by an evening mid-week – to practise and purvey Reiki. Giselle's role was to be a help and support to Ark. She was going to try and get some sort of job to help finance the venture through its first faltering steps. When the practice was established she intended to learn Reiki as well, on Ark's optimistic assumption that the area would yield an ever-expanding market. She had as yet little idea of what the science, or art, involved, and there was a considerable shift in mind-set required first, as Ark pointed out. For starters, beating up on people was out, whatever the provocation. All forms of deliberate confrontation were also proscribed. The important thing, he told Giselle, was to be centred: to know your own worth and be confident in it. Like all enthusiasts Ark was persuasive on his subject.

He was also a tender and commanding lover. Giselle had not had a lover before. She'd had rides, lays, bonks, screws and good seeing-to's, usually involving a cut-off point somewhere before the brain. This had less to do with age – the peripatetic pottery teacher had been the worst of the lot – than with attitude. Ark was the first man who had seen something in her other than her tits to like and admire. He teased her and told her she was a hard woman, and an old slag and somehow she felt flattered because of the note of irony in his voice. He could say those things to her because his tone implied he knew they were not true.

There were other things, harder to express. Ark didn't throw his weight about or raise his voice but he was protective of her. Giselle relished her buccaneering persona but she discovered that it was not unpleasant to feel safe with someone. In bed he took charge of her, called her 'Zelda', which she liked, and brought her to climax with a calm, almost studious generosity.

From time to time Giselle wondered if she was in love with Ark.

So it was tricky, her parents not liking him. Not that she gave a toss what they thought, but considering the long line of geeks and spasmoes she'd been with and they'd never turned a hair, it was a bit much, them objecting to Ark. This line of thought, crystalline in its logic to Giselle, overlooked the fact that her parents had scarcely met any of the others. Most of her admirers since the pottery master and the chef had been between sixteen and twenty, nice middle-class youths wearing hundred-pound trainers and out of their skulls on dance music and what went with it. In other circumstances and in daylight many of them would be considered Grand Lads, not least by Hester and Jonty. Giselle, baleful and androgynous in her weird clothes and hairdo, had nothing but contempt for them. She permitted intimacy as and when she felt inclined. It was all right at the time. It was powerful.

But Ark, from that evening when he'd sat so patiently next to her in the Accident and Emergency Department, had shown her another side of herself, and one that increasingly she liked. One evening recently she'd bolted her bedroom door, wedged a chair under the handle for good measure, and done a bit of an experiment with her hair, brushing the long part down. It wasn't a success. The effect had been comical, like the feather hat worn by Helen Mirren in *The Cook, The Thief, His Wife and Her Lover*. Only she wasn't Helen Mirren, and this wasn't a hat. Frantically, with tears in her eyes, she had brushed it all up again and fixed it in place with gel and spray. The incident brought home to her how difficult it was to alter one's image overnight. Her present one had evolved over some months. The haircut had been the final flourish, the *pièce de résistance,* and modifying it would be seen by everyone as a public climb-down. She wasn't yet ready for that.

Ark wanted her to move in with him. He had a room in a friend's house in town. The room was neither as large nor anything like as well appointed as Giselle's at home, but Ark had made the best of it. She really liked the room, and the idea of being free, and with Ark all the time, but was a bit concerned about money. The great thing about home was that everything was there, on tap. Even skint, you could get by. It was not impossible that if she moved out her allowance would be stopped, and she would be totally dependent on Ark. Until he started getting clients for the Reiki practice, that left her basically with her dole giro, which she was used to treating as pocket money. This was why she felt she should ask her parents rather than simply walk out.

'You're an adult, you don't have to ask,' said Ark.

'I know that.'

'Not so hard, are you?'

They were lying supine on Ark's bed, side by side and hand in hand like a couple in effigy. It was six o'clock and they'd succeeded in getting rid of about a quarter of the leaflets, which wasn't bad. Dolly was chewing a bone, a rhythmic grating and slurping in the gathering darkness.

'That's not it,' said Giselle. 'Give us a smoke.'

Ark felt in his jacket for his tin, took out a roll-up, lit it and handed it to her.

'Thanks. I don't want to have a row.'

'I buy that. They're nice people.'

This unsettled Giselle, because it was true. 'Crap.'

Ark shrugged. 'Don't ask me then . . .'

'I wasn't.'

'You don't have to give them a hard time or anything.'

'I know.'

'So when?'

'Soon.'

*   *   *

Intent on keeping a weather eye open, Ann had persuaded Gavin
to drop in for an early bite at Raglan Road before going on to
Schmooze. He looked exhausted, but supper was going quite well.
She was dishing up pudding for Mr We-We Sun when the phone
rang. She put his bowl of apple amber in front of him and said,
'Excuse me, would you. Byron, cream.'

The voice on the other end said: 'Is that Ann?'

'Yes.'

'Ann, it's Katie.'

'Hallo there!' Ann cast an anxious glance over her shoulder at Gavin,
who was helping himself and Byron to pudding. 'How are you?'

'Fine, thanks. Is this a bad moment?'

'We're eating dinner, but that doesn't matter, the others are
getting on very well without me.'

'I wanted to say thank you for contacting Hester Blake for me.
She was great, I really liked her.'

'I'm so glad.'

'That was all, really.'

'It was nice of you to ring. Keep in touch, won't you?'

'I will if that's okay. I mean, if it's not awkward, under the
circumstances . . .'

'Not at all. Life goes on.'

'Thanks for being a brick.'

'Goodbye for now, then.'

'Bye, Ann.'

Ann returned to the table. Gavin had started his pudding, Byron
sat with spoon hovering, Mr We-We Sun was waiting politely,
hands in lap.

'Please, do carry on,' said Ann, glancing at Gavin as she helped
herself. Mr We-We Sun lifted his spoon.

'Who was that?' asked Byron.

'Only a client.'

'Satisfied, I trust?'

'Perfectly.' Ann was curt because she hated to lie. She prided
herself on being able to conduct all aspects of her life freely, fairly
and openly. There was no reason why she should feel guilty about
maintaining friendly relations with Katie. She tried to do the same
with all her sons' ex-girlfriends. But this particular falling-out was
very recent, and the wounds still fresh. 'Yes,' she added, with an
air of finality, 'I'm happy to say.'

'You lead such a busy life,' observed Mr We-We Sun admiringly.

'That's like calling Genghis Khan boisterous,' said Gavin, scraping his bowl. 'She's an adrenaline junkie.'

Byron took another quick dash of cream. 'Hark who's talking.'

'No, I shall take that as a compliment,' said Ann. 'I couldn't bear it any other way.'

'Do you get time for leisure?' enquired Mr We-We Sun.

'Hmm . . .' Ann thought about this.

'You'll have to bear with her on that one,' Gavin told him. 'It's not a concept she's familiar with.'

'I wouldn't mind, only she expects the rest of us to keep pace,' said Byron, smiling respectfully at his wife.

Mr We-We Sun leaned towards him. 'Do we have another Iron Lady here?'

Byron's smile broadened. 'In a way, yes. Isn't she, Gavin?'

'Jesus, yes! Like Margaret Thatcher? I should say so!'

Ann bridled. 'Be quiet, you two. I'll admit to a comparable energy level, and that is all. Take no notice of them, Mr Sun, you should know that I have never been a Tory supporter, and I regard Mrs Thatcher as having been a pernicious influence and a thoroughly dangerous woman. Can I give you some more?'

'Thank you.' Mr We-We Sun passed his bowl. He had not yet quite got his landlady's weight. If he had, he would not have added, impishly: 'I think you are like Maggie in another way too – you like to care for everyone and mind their business for them.'

It was simply, Ann told herself, an understandable misuse of English idiom.

'Possibly,' she said.

After dinner, when Mr We-We Sun had gone up to his room and while Byron loaded the dishwasher and made coffee, Ann was able to enjoy a brief moment alone in the drawing room with Gavin.

'So how are you, darling?' she asked. 'You look tired.'

Gavin rubbed his eyes. 'Yeah . . . Work, you know . . . It's a bloody madhouse.'

'But all going well?' she asked cautiously.

'Not bad.'

That was as good as she was going to get, and Ann had no intention of pushing it any further. There were other areas to cover.

'I am sorry about you and Katie.'

'Can't be helped.' Gavin lit a cigarette, and Ann put an ashtray on the arm of the sofa. She was a non-smoker herself, and disapproved on principle, but she was secretly susceptible to the habit's discredited glamour.

'Sebastian indicated that she gave you rather a rough ride.'

'I don't want to talk about it.'

'Of course. That was insensitive of me – I apologise.'

'Katie was a great girl. It was fine while it lasted.'

'It's good that you can reflect on it in such a positive light, darling.'

Gavin frowned down at the cigarette between his fingers, exhaling deeply. 'I can't pretend I'm proud of the way I handled things.'

Ann, gazing at her son's mop of boyish curls, felt her heart contract with love and sympathy, as it always did when one of the boys showed real character. But she was careful to keep her expression calm. It was important, as a mother, not to be simply reactive in one's relationships with one's children – to maintain a measure of distance in order to be of use.

'I'm sure,' she said quietly, 'you have nothing to reproach yourself with. It's fruitless to apportion blame. These things happen.'

'I can be a real bastard sometimes, I know that,' went on Gavin, warming to his theme. 'I may simply have pushed her too far.'

'If, and I only say if,' replied Ann, 'that was the case, then clearly she gave back as good as she got.'

'That's true.' Gavin stubbed out his cigarette. 'But it takes two. I may not have deserved all the things she said to me, but I sure as hell deserved some of them.'

Ann leant across and placed her hand on his. 'Maybe. But you have to let it go now.'

'Why do I always screw up?' Gavin looked at her with tears in his eyes. 'Why?'

Ann patted and stroked. 'Let it go . . . Let it go . . .'

Byron entered, carrying a tray with the cafetière and mugs. 'Here we are!' He put the tray down and glanced doubtfully at the two of them. 'Everything okay?'

Ann, her hand still on Gavin's, gave her husband a speaking look. 'We were talking about Katie.'

Byron plumped down in an armchair. 'Oh yes, Katie – what on earth did you do to her?'

'You see?' Gavin stood up, shrugging on his jacket, thrusting his shirt down into his waistband, combing his fingers through his hair. 'I'm out of here.'

Ann directed another even more meaningful look at her husband before beseeching Gavin: 'Darling, don't go – stay and have a cup of coffee at least.'

'Sorry, can't. I've got a mountain of figures and several hundred punters to attend to.'

'Be gentle with them,' joshed Byron gamely, rising once more out of the armchair.

Taut-faced, Gavin gave Ann a peck on the cheek. 'Thanks for dinner.'

'Any time at all,' said Ann, 'you know that. I'll come and see you out.' She gave Byron another scorching look as she escorted Gavin into the hall. There were murmurs. The door closed quietly.

When she came back, Byron lifted a hand, palm outwards. 'Okay, okay. I'm sorry. I put my size nines smack in it, didn't I?'

'Yes.'

'He's so jolly touchy.'

'He is your son, Byron. You've known him all his life. Surely you've learnt something about him in that time.'

Byron poured two coffees. 'Yes. But one sort of hopes that they will grow out of these amateur dramatics. Grow *up*, if that isn't an outdated concept.'

Ann's voice became so soft and measured that it was barely audible. 'Gavin lives with unusual stresses. He is committed to nothing short of total success in what is currently an extremely harsh economic climate, he has a considerable workforce to think of—'

'God help them . . .'

Ann's brows drew together in a look of disapproval. 'Byron, that was unworthy.'

'I know. I know.' The inevitable remorse caused Byron's shoulders to slump. 'All right, I take it back.'

Victory within her grasp, Ann sat down with her coffee and assumed a gentler expression.

'You must think before you speak.'

'I intended no slight, believe me—'

'And I must say,' went on Ann firmly, but with quelling restraint, 'I was impressed and moved – yes, moved – by his attitude.'

'Really?'

'He was taking a good deal of the responsibility. Admitting fault. Conceding the problems. It was a great pity you couldn't have heard him.'

'It was, yes,' said Byron glumly.

Ann leaned forward, looking into his face. 'He deserves all our sympathy and our support. Not cheap cracks.'

Byron was taken aback. 'Is that what it sounded like?'

'Yes. I know it wasn't meant as such, but yes.'

'I'm sorry. I'll give him a bell tomorrow and make my peace.'

'I think that would be very much appreciated.'

They sipped their coffee. Byron regained his composure sufficiently to ask: 'Shall I fetch those truffles? Do you fancy one?'

He was barely out of his chair when he caught his wife's eye. 'No, you didn't – what, all of them?' He sank back. 'Oh well . . . It'll give us something to talk about when I ring.'

Jonty and Byron met up in town about once every couple of months. It wasn't an organised thing, that was simply how it worked out. They were old friends, after all. Seven or eight weeks would go by and one of them would experience the urge to see that particular view of themselves which only the other could provide. If there was a test at Lords, they met there, or sometimes at the Oval if there was a real draw like the Windies or Australia. If cricket wasn't on the menu then Byron, as the freer agent, would take the tube to Leicester Square (Earthtrust was based, improbably, in Greek Street), and they would eat something ethnic in Soho.

On this occasion it was Byron who contacted Jonty.

'My treat for a change.'

'Well, if you're sure.'

'Any objection to The Old Hat?'

'Not if you're paying, squire.'

The Old Hat was a place off Windmill Street which specialised in old-fashioned, unfashionable food. Whenever he went there – usually with Byron – Jonty was sharply reminded why such fare had gone out of fashion. And today was unmistakably the first true day of summer, all tender blue and caressing sunshine, a day for salad *niçoise* and sitting out of doors. But when Byron craved The

Old Hat he craved it as an infant craves the breast and there was no arguing with him, expecially if he was footing the bill.

The restaurant's décor was by Boarding School out of Home Counties Teashop. The cruets were Sheffield plate – not a pepper mill in sight – and jugs of tap water came as standard. The waitresses were strikingly pretty and fresh-faced, in dark blue dresses with matching tights, and white aprons and frilly caps, like nurses. They gave the impression of having been sprung overnight from the senior dorm, and they served at table with a cavalier amateurism which defied complaint.

Sitting down at their table near the sideboard, Jonty and Byron presented an intriguing contrast. The uninformed observer would have taken Byron, in his out-at-bottom cords, shapeless woollen waistcoat and safari jacket, as the country bumpkin, and Jonty, tall and *dégagé* in Hugo Boss and Tommy Nutter (a habit from his Ruggles Ryder days that he was unable to kick) as the quintessentially urbane Londoner.

They ordered. Byron had Squire's Pâté, followed by silverside with dumplings, carrots, cabbage and mashed potato. The choice was more difficult for Jonty. The Old Hat, like other specialist restaurants, was surly about those who did not toe the line. Those dishes which were not old-fashioned were outstandingly disgusting. In the end Jonty skipped the starter and opted for Lancashire hotpot.

'I shall be horribly torn,' said Byron.

'Feel free to send raiding parties.'

Under the influence of a comforting Côte du Rhône they ranged, through the pâté and most of the main course, over compassion fatigue, property prices, the latest classic serial on BBC2 and the folly of the England selectors. By the time Jonty was beginning to pick the inevitable small shards of scrag end bone from his mouth, and Byron was slurping up his beef liquor with a pudding spoon, they had come, as it were, right down to the wire.

'I tell you one thing,' said Byron, 'I envy you your daughters.'

'Good God, why's that?'

'Girls – they seem so much easier.' Byron gazed lugubriously about him at the bouncy waitresses in their black lace-ups.

Jonty tried a bracing line. 'You have met Giselle, haven't you?'

Byron shook his head. 'That doesn't matter. You don't have to be a *role model* to girls.'

'That weighs heavy on you, does it?'

'It weighs . . . it weighs.'

'We've got Daniel,' mused Jonty. 'But I confess I haven't really thought about what sort of role model I am.'

'When you've got a whole rake of them it's impossible not to feel inadequate,' complained Byron. 'I've led such a sheltered life. Groves of academe, first one side then the other, early retirement . . . a litany of nearlys . . .'

'For crying out loud—'

'Married,' added Byron gloomily, 'from time immemorial.'

Jonty entertained a shocking but titillating surmise. 'Byron, you're okay, are you? You and Ann . . .?'

'Oh, yes!' Byron waved a dismissive hand. 'We went on automatic pilot yonks ago. And anyway, Ann's one in a million. I'm devoted.'

Jonty, looking at his friend, believed him. 'What then?'

'It's just as I say . . . I suppose I half expected them, or at least one of them, to be like me, you know, taking it pretty easy, cultured but not pushy, setting up house, blamelessly hitched to a good woman . . .' Byron sat back as the waitress cleared their plates. He sighed heavily. 'Instead of which they tear about like blue-arsed flies, starting things up and dropping them again, drinking like fish and smoking like chimneys, tossing wobblers all over the place, getting through women like there was no tomorrow—'

'Really?'

'You wouldn't believe the way they carry on. Sebastian claims to have been sexually harassed at work – and that's another thing, why does harass have to rhyme with amass these days instead of with arras?' Jonty shrugged. 'Nor me. Arras was good enough for us. At any rate, Sebastian's being threatened by this big black lady with a crush on him or something – you'd have thought it would've turned him off sex for the duration but no, whenever you ring or call round there he's on the nest, and this man is supposed to be a *youth worker*, Jonty, whatever that may mean. It makes my blood freeze.'

Jonty couldn't help laughing. 'The lad's but young himself.'

'He's over thirty. Come to years of discretion, one would hope.'

'They're all different.'

'Telling me. And none of them like cricket,' Byron added, as though that put the tin hat on it. He took the pudding menu and handed it straight back. 'I'll have the bread-and-butter pud. With evaporated milk.'

'I'll pass. Coffee? Coffee twice.'

'You're telling me,' repeated Byron. 'And then there's Gavin.'

'Indeed,' said Jonty. 'You and I ought to try that place of his some time.'

Byron shuddered. 'Heaven forfend! A great barn full of yammering media types and students, people reading papers like a station waiting room, raw vegetables and no side plates.'

'A great success, for all that.'

'Yes, yes,' agreed Byron in a tone which made it perfectly clear he was sick of being told. 'But try getting Gavin to admit that. It's all bloody doom and gloom.'

'This is a queasy time for new ventures. He's probably wise not to be too optimistic.'

'No fear of that, I assure you. And then he takes up with a series of females – the last one was a dear, a really enchanting girl – but none of them last—'

'You're being a shade old-fashioned, aren't you?'

'I don't know . . .' Byron gazed down at the bread-and-butter pudding as it was set before him. 'It's not that I necessarily expect him to tie the knot, but some sign of stability would be a comfort. And he doesn't treat them all that well, in my view.' He tucked in.

Jonty watched him. The pudding looked quite appetising, but seeing Byron wolf it down made him feel virtuous. 'I assume he has to work unsocial hours,' he suggested diplomatically. 'Besides, these are spartan times we live in. It's not all a rose and a glove.'

'Mm – mm – mm – ' Byron waved his spoon, indicating that he wished to speak but had a mouthful to swallow first. 'Yes, I do appreciate that. You hear them talk about their "relationship" as though it were a Jacobean sideboard or something, but at the first sign of trouble they consign it to the skip.'

Jonty was laughing like a drain. He found Byron in this vein vastly entertaining.

'If it's any comfort to you,' he said, 'Giselle wants to move in with some ponytailed witch doctor or other.'

'Ponytail, you say?' Byron wiped his mouth on his napkin. 'Fancy. So what did you do?'

'We said we wanted time to think about it.'

'A perfectly respectable position.'

'We hope so.'

'Mind you, she's over eighteen, isn't she – she doesn't need your permission. Based on my own experience with our lot I call it pretty damn civil of her to mention it at all.'

'She didn't exactly ask our permission. It was a sounding-out exercise. I've a shrewd suspicion she's checking the financial position.'

'Aha . . . she thinks you might cut her off without a penny. And would you?'

'Probably not. No, of course not. This character she wants to shack up with is the very model of a waste of space – how would she survive?'

'What you should do,' advised Byron, leaning back to welcome the coffee, which came in big cups, saucered and blown, 'is learn from the Ancients. Test her resolve. And his, come to that.'

'How?'

'Send her abroad for a bit.'

'Grizzle's hardly nanny material.' Jonty, stirring his coffee, looked doubtful. 'Still less finishing school.'

'A murrain on those places,' said Byron, 'I once attempted to fondle a girl from a finishing school . . . With a quart of *glühwein* inside her she still kneed me.'

'Byron – and you're always saying what a sheltered life you've led.'

'It was the exception that proves the rule. Anyway, there's my advice. Bribe her with foreign parts for a bit. Put some cash in her back pocket and tell her to bugger off and seek her fortune, for a few weeks anyway. See how she does.'

'I remain unconvinced,' said Jonty. 'She's nobody's fool, Grizzle, in spite of appearances.'

'I rather like her appearance,' said Byron, who Jonty could now see was sozzled. 'She's a handsome girl. Not a beauty like Roz—'

'Rose.'

'—but extremely striking. Take my word for it.'

'How's Julian?' asked Jonty, signalling for the bill. 'Better not leave him out.'

'Julian? Ah, Julian!' Byron pointed a finger across the table. 'There's a case in point. Ann found him a place in the Gallic equivalent of Dotheboys Hall, and not a bit of trouble since. I can't recommend it too highly.'

'Message received and understood.' Jonty passed him the bill. 'Yours, I believe.'

By the time Byron had gone in the taxi to King's Cross with Jonty, for the ride, and then caught the tube home, taking the wrong line once, it was nearly six o'clock. He encountered Mr We-We Sun in the hall.

'My dear chap – do you have time for a drink?'

Mr We-We Sun was demurring but wavering when Ann's voice floated along the corridor.

'Byron! Byron – Sebastian and I are in here!'

'A summons . . .!' said Byron *sotto voce*, and the two of them tiptoed in opposite directions with exaggerated care.

Ann and Sebastian were sitting at the kitchen table.

'Did you have an enjoyable lunch?' asked Ann.

'Delightful, thanks.'

'I can smell it from here,' said Sebastian, waving his cigarette like a fumigator. A bit steep, coming from him, thought Byron.

'I'm sorry to be the harbinger of bad news,' went on Ann with that hint of tranquil self-importance which got on Byron's tit rather. 'But I've had a call from Julian's school. In France.'

'Yes?'

'He's got mumps. Or at least a mump – the side he didn't get as a child, do you remember that holiday near Tintagel? Anyway, he's very poorly and in hospital in Arles.'

'Oh God,' said Byron. Deflated, he sat down next to Sebastian. 'Poor old Jules. Mumps can be a bit nasty.'

'That'll wipe the silly smile off Lisette's face,' said Sebastian. 'So who's for visiting the sick?'

CHAPTER SIX

Giselle removed her T-shirt, spread it out and lay down on her back on the grass, using her rucksack as a pillow. The sun beat with splendid intensity on her closed eyelids and bare breasts. The place where she lay was on the edge of a field of maize, and the tall stems gave off a gentle, confidential murmuring, as though they were talking about her. She felt protected. Only a few yards away on the other side of the hedge was the car park of the *routier* – she could smell the faint whiff of the toilets, and hear the bang and chatter of the kitchen through the open transom window. A lorry started up with a roar and a hot blast of diesel, but here she was in complete seclusion, sweating wine and belching gently on her *haché* and *frites*.

Giselle was not in the habit of actively seeking happiness, or positively identifying it when it showed up. Life was almost invariably a bitch, with the odd compensation. But at this moment she could definitely call herself happy. All you needed, she discovered, was plenty of the basics – heat, food, drink – and the most basic thing of all, no hassle. She was really grateful to her parents for suggesting this trip. She'd hated them at the time for being so pathetically transparent – trying to bribe her into going away so that they could have a bit of peace – but it had turned out brilliantly. Four weeks into the allotted six and home had assumed its proper place in her life: on the sidelines. At this distance she was able to feel a much greater sympathy and affection for her family: her parents and their pathetic shilly-shallying, Rose with her brilliant, boring future in some poxy TV studio, Daniel (poor little sod) grafting right now over his GCSEs – what did they know? She, Giselle, was the star of her life, and it had taken this holiday to show her.

It wasn't the first time she'd been off on her own, far from it.

There had been Cornwall, and Wales, both shrouded in rain and the bilious fog of a permanent hangover, and a camp site in Spain from which she and another girl had been summarily ejected for rowdy behaviour. There had been weekends in Brighton and London – with the Lebanese chef and the pottery master respectively – both of which had required an elaborate (and expensive) back-up of disinformation by Daniel and Rose. But none of them had had the lazy, greedy, hedonistic magic of these weeks in *la France profonde* . . . Giselle undid the top button of her sawn-off Levi's.

Nor had her parents strictly intended this as a holiday. 'We'd like to give you some basic cash,' was how her father had put it, in his 'we've-always-tried-to-be-both-fair-and-businesslike' voice. 'But it won't be enough for more than a couple of weeks unless you pick up some work. So that's up to you. Keep in touch, you know where we are. Otherwise you're on your own.'

When you got down to it, they were innocents. Eyes still closed, Giselle smiled to herself and slipped her hand inside her waistband . . .

Gavin, speeding south to visit his younger brother, felt his spirits at last begin to lift. It was good to be on the open road, a free agent, untrammelled by business, family or women. And although the pretext for this week's jaunt was to check on Julian – who anyway declared himself to be fully recovered – he was long overdue a holiday. He wouldn't hang about long in Montaigle, which was a dead-and-alive hole. Once he'd delivered his mother's box of provisions – he'd sampled the walnut bread and it was well up to standard – and revived himself with some quality kip, he'd be off.

He put Marvin Gaye on the tape deck. The window was open, and he rested his elbow on it and drummed his fingers on the roof. At present he could still feel the tensile threads of responsibility tethering him to Schmooze, its turbulent battalions, the threat posed to it by the vicissitudes of fashion. Gavin was a notoriously poor delegator – but what choice was there when the standard of numeracy, literacy, social skills and basic competence among the rank and file was so bloody lamentable?

He slowed down for a *péage*. In the queue for the neighbouring tollbooth an attractive blonde woman sat at the wheel of a Peugeot estate. She took one hand from the wheel and the front windows hummed down to their fullest extent. In the back of the car were two tanned children in safety seats; in the rear, an old English sheepdog, its panting pink tongue quivering amongst the long hair.

As the two cars crept forward, Gavin noticed the woman's hand tapping the steering wheel in time with *Dock of the Bay*. He turned it up a little. She glanced across, impassive behind hornrimmed dark glasses. Gavin smiled. She pushed the glasses down with one manicured finger and smiled back, lips curved but closed, the suggestion of a dimple on the left cheek.

'*Bonjour*,' said Gavin. '*Vous aimez ça?*'

'Oh yes. Very much.' Her accent alone was a turn-on.

They inched forward again. The air over and around the *péage* vibrated with noise and heat. Somewhere behind and to their left there was an irate volley of horns. Gavin ejected the tape and held it out at arm's length towards the woman.

'*Pardon?*'

'*Prenez-ça, s'il vous plaît, madame.*'

'No, no, thank you—' She shook her head and laughed flirtatiously. The dog let out a single, booming bark. The children, stunned by heat, stared.

The cars moved forward again. The Cabriolet and the Peugeot were now only one away from the booths, they would soon be separated. Gavin opened his door, got out, and dropped the tape through the Peugeot's window on to the woman's lap. The children continued to stare. The dog gave two barks.

The woman opened one hand in a charming gesture of helpless surrender.

'*M'sieur . . . vous êtes trop gentil. Merci.*'

Gavin caught her hand and kissed it. A horn sounded. Somebody whistled. He was enjoying himself.

'*De rien, madame* . . . The world needs futile gestures.'

For a few kilometres after the *péage* he stayed within sight of the Peugeot and its driver, but then she turned off in the direction of a small town that boasted a castle. Gavin wondered if she would tell her husband about the eccentric young Englishman and his charming, futile gesture . . . He liked that kind of glancing encounter, brief but intense – it was a way of snaring a tiny stake in another person's life. The woman might forget phone numbers and anniversaries and dentist's appointments and the name of her husband's boss, but she would always remember him. He put his foot down and moved into the fast lane as he headed for the ton.

It was two-thirty and he'd been off the *autoroute* for more than an hour when hunger and thirst suddenly hit him. The brasserie, open from 8 a.m. till midnight, had aggravated his natural tendency not to plan for food and drink. The result was that he could go for long periods without either until he was suddenly poleaxed with the need for both, at once and in large quantities.

He wasn't particularly fussy. He pulled into the first *routier* he came to and stoked up on pork chop and chips accompanied by a can of Stella Artois. He toyed with the idea of ringing Julian and telling him he wouldn't be there till tomorrow – it would be nice to have a night in a hotel on his own – but there was some character – English, needless to say – camping out on the payphone, so he shelved the idea and went outside.

He didn't go back to the car at once, but lit a cigarette and strolled across the car park. It was bordered at the back by an untidy hedge, beyond which the 'vasty fields' – Gavin congratulated himself on his eclectic frame of reference – rolled away into the haze. In contrast to the yammer and bustle of his over-populated, hyper-stressful existence at home, he felt cast adrift here, a dot on the map. He was not sufficiently unwound yet, the sensation still hovered between pleasure and panic.

He dropped his half-smoked cigarette and ground it beneath his foot. He wanted a pee, but the toilet didn't smell too good. There was a gap in the hedge a little way to his left and he went and stood in it and opened his fly.

It wasn't till he'd finished, and took a step forward to survey the view, that he almost tripped over the girl, who was lying supine on the ground between the corn and the hedge. She had her eyes shut, so for a moment he was able to stare unobserved.

She was a Fellini fantasy . . . unfashionably statuesque, with broad shoulders and big breasts which stood up like a couple of upturned funnels. Her black hair was cut skinhead short. There were several earrings in each ear, and a thin silver hoop in her right nostril. Her eyebrows and lashes were sooty black and luxurious, her skin – and there was a lot of it on view – deeply tanned. Her large, sultry mouth bore the vestiges of plum-coloured lipstick, most of which had been eaten off.

The waist of her shorts was undone and below her navel the merest fine feathering of hair ran down into the darkness. One hand, a pewter ring on the thumb, was behind her head, but the other was inside her shorts, moving in the unmistakable rhythm of self-gratification.

Gavin was riveted.

She opened her eyes. At once, she ceased to be a sight and became a disconcertingly unabashed presence.

Unused to being disconcerted, Gavin was steadied only by the knowledge that she had to be more embarrassed than him. Her hand stopped moving, but as if to call his bluff she did not at once remove it from her shorts.

'Excuse me,' she said, meaning 'push off'.

'I do apologise. I was admiring the view.'

'Oh yeah.' She nodded her head. 'Is that why your flies are undone?'

Gavin glanced down and hurriedly adjusted his zip. 'I took a pee.'

'Gimme a break.' She raised her pelvis in order to do up the button on her shorts. The movement revealed the strong, pronounced muscles in her legs. Her feet were bare, and dirty.

'No, really,' said Gavin. 'And I hadn't been staring. I almost tripped over you.'

She ignored him. With perfect composure she sat up, her breasts rolling forward in a way that Gavin found almost painful. A generous tyre of smooth brown flesh bulged over the top of her shorts. She pulled her T-shirt out from beneath her and shook it vigorously with even more disturbing effect. Then she pulled it on, and scrubbed her hands over her stubble of hair, freeing it of grit and wisps of grass.

'Incredible heat,' said Gavin.

'Yup.' She stood up, and hoisted her rucksack on to her back. She was fractionally taller than him. You could get lost in a body like that.

'Excuse me.' This time it was a request, though only very perfunctory.

'Sorry.' Gavin stood aside. But as she trudged away he fell in behind her. 'Are you heading south?'

She stopped, but did not look at him.

Gavin caught up with her. 'I wondered if I could give you a lift?'

Slowly, she turned and looked him up and down. Her left eyebrow was split by a small scar.

'Drop dead.'

Back on the road, Gavin reflected on this, his second chance encounter of the day, and found it pleasing but a little uncomfortable. In this instance he was not sure that he wished to be remembered.

'No worries,' said Ark. 'Dolly's okay.'

He pocketed the piece of paper with Jonty's telephone credit card number, given to Giselle in case of emergencies. It had come in handy for checking on the dog.

'And I got us a lift in an HGV.'

It was a squeeze in the cab of the lorry, but Ark took the short straw and sat in the middle – he was funny about things like that. The driver was a taciturn Belgian whose conversation extended only to naming the point at which he would drop them off, but that was fine with them. They preferred lorries for that reason. In a car there was usually some attempt at conversation, which was a pain in the arse, especially with Giselle's minimal and Ark's non-existent French. And they could smoke.

'Who was that guy you were talking to?' asked Ark.

'No-one.'

'English.'

'Yeah. Bit of a Barry.'

'What did he want?'

'Nothing.'

'Right . . .'

Impulsively, Giselle squeezed Ark's arm. 'Nothing, honestly.'

He smiled at her. 'Settle down, Zelda, I believe you.'

For some reason she was disinclined to enlarge on the exchange. To find some bloke staring at you when you'd got your hand in your knickers . . ! He was quite a bit older, which didn't make it any less embarrassing. She retained an impression of a thin face, its indoor pallor smudged by overnight stubble . . . sharply focused grey eyes, red-rimmed . . . brown curly hair worn longer than was fashionable . . . an educated voice with a sarcastic glint . . . He reminded her of someone – either that or she'd met him before. As it happened she believed him when he said he'd been taking a slash, but he'd definitely been staring. And she'd been turned on.

'Shit,' she muttered.

'Don't let it get to you,' advised Ark.

Hester's page this week was about living with exams.

'A Levels and degrees may be tougher on the student,' she wrote, *'but GCSEs are hardest on the parents. The child is not only living at home, but at a stage in his development when he is at his most unlovable. These exams, which anyway he suspects he is only taking to get you off his back, and which will (in his opinion) fit him for none of the work he might conceivably want to do, aren't calculated to enhance your relationship. And the Catch-22 is that if you don't want to go through the whole thing again in a year's time you'd better wise-up. Become a doormat. Remember those bonsmots of St Francis which Margaret Thatcher quoted to such good effect?'*

Hester stopped here, because although she could recall the gist of it, she couldn't come up with the exact words. She put a check mark in and went on:

'All sorts of interpersonal skills need brushing up. Servility; self-abasement; a grovelling humility that would shame Uriah Heep. I know it sticks in your gullet, but it has to be done. Stop thinking of your child as a foul-mouthed idle clod with the sensibilities of cold toast, and try to picture him in a new light: as a proud, sensitive being, finely tuned as a racehorse and with a comparable appetite. That way you will at least be beginning to get it right . . .'

Hester wondered how Daniel was getting on with RE, a subject in which, rather surprisingly, he was expected to do well.

Rose put her head round the door. 'Okay, so who's getting it in the neck this time?'

'I'm doing exams. Effects and repercussions of same on the family of the examinee.'

'With particular reference to the mother.'

'Of course.'

'You've done that before, surely.'

'There's nothing new in this game.'

Rose came in and perched on the edge of the desk. She wore a duck-egg blue kimono and her head was swathed in a towel.

'It's money for old rope really, isn't it. Be honest.'

'It's harder than it looks,' protested Hester. 'You smell nice.'

'Amérique . . . Jez gave it to me.' Jeremy was Rose's boyfriend down in Bristol, with whom she was due to go to Italy in a

week's time. Rose sniffed her own wrist. 'I'm not so sure. It's a bit overpowering.'

'No, it's nice.'

Rose peered at the screen. 'Have you finished that?'

'No,' said Hester pointedly, 'not yet.'

'Sorry – I'm sorry!' cried Rose. She waved a manicured hand at the screen. 'It looks good. Your usual witty and perceptive stuff.'

'Are you patronising me, Rosie?'

'Would I?'

'You with your eddication, taking the piss out of your poor old hack of a mother.'

'I was not taking the piss. In common with millions of others, I like what you write.'

'Hmm . . .' Hester rubbed her face and thrust her fingers into her hair. 'It's not exactly Pulitzer Prize material.'

'Neither's Jilly Cooper, so?'

'I suppose.'

'And what's more,' said Rose, wagging an emphatic finger, 'it serves a useful purpose.'

Hester raised an eyebrow. 'It does?'

'Sure – you're like a one-woman support group, you make other women feel that they are not alone in their failures.' Hester lowered her face into her hands at this, laughing silently, but Rose pressed on. 'No, you know what I mean. Loads of people I know who are my age and don't have husbands or children or anything read your page because they sort of *feel* it's true. And it makes them laugh. So there!' She gave her mother's shoulder a push and went out of the room. Then she put her turbaned head back in and delivered a parting shot.

'Mind you, you're lucky to have such a damned interesting family . . .'

'I don't think I'm so depressed now,' said Mrs Ramilies to Ann, adding, in case her counsellor should be lulled into a false sense of security: 'but some days it still comes over me.' To emphasise her point she took a bunch of tissues from the box which Ann always left tactfully on the sofa next to her clients.

'That's not surprising,' said Ann. 'Behavioural changes are bound to cause turbulence. You can't expect to be a different person overnight. You're working on it, and that's what counts.'

Mrs Ramilies swiped vigorously at her nose and cheeks. 'I am, but it feels so pointless sometimes, now that he's gone, and it's not as if the kids notice anything, the moon and stars circle round them and their friends as far as they're concerned . . .' She wavered, and then took a grip. 'And the sun shines out of that bastard's backside!'

She began absent-mindedly to shred the tissues. The pieces floated to the floor. Glancing where they fell, Ann couldn't help noticing that Josette had not moved the sofa when she last hoovered. There was a tideline of fluff distinctly visible behind Mrs Ramilies' feet. A quiet word was needed in that quarter.

'Are you sure,' mused Ann, 'that they think so highly of him?'

'Of course they do!' snorted Mrs Ramilies. 'And I'm the wicked witch who threw him out.'

'Children absorb a good deal of information on a subliminal level,' said Ann. 'And their conclusions are often more sophisticated than we give them credit for.'

'It makes me sick,' Mrs Ramilies stormed on, 'that someone can behave the way he has and his kids still think he's some kind of knight on a white charger.'

'You're angry,' said Ann.

'You're darn tootin' I'm angry!'

'That's good. Feel that anger. Use it. Anger is heat, and heat is energy. Make the anger work for you.'

'How?' asked Mrs Ramilies reasonably enough.

Ann shook her head. 'That is a question you must ask yourself. Finding the answer is part of the healing process.' She glanced at her watch. 'Now we only have a couple of minutes left, is there anything you would particularly like to talk about next time?'

'Maybe,' said Mrs Ramilies darkly, 'there won't be a next time.'

'You're feeling that much more confident, are you?'

'I don't know that I can manage another twenty-four quid.'

'It would be sad,' said Ann calmly, 'if this were all to come down to a question of economics, when we both know that it's the real value to you of these sessions, in terms of personal growth, that counts.'

'We'll see.' Mrs Ramilies got up. Little bits of tissue puffed away from her high-heeled sandals.

Ann did not at once rise herself. Mrs Ramilies was still a very confused and disturbed woman. It was up to her as the counsellor to dictate the pace and mood of her client's departure, so that she left feeling she had derived something positive from the encounter and would consider it worth coming back.

'My instinct tells me,' she said in her measured way, in a voice so soft that Mrs Ramilies would have to concentrate to hear it, 'that there remain several avenues we could productively explore . . . Promise me that you won't simply dismiss the idea of another visit here. I ask no more than that.'

'Don't worry,' said Mrs Ramilies. 'I'll think about it.'

When she had gone, Ann went back into the drawing room – she preferred to see clients in the formality of this room rather than in her study, which was somehow too full of personal touches. She sat down in the chair she had just vacated. The large house was very still. Byron was out at the library; Mr We-We Sun was at the hospital. It was mid-morning, and even the road outside was quiet. The silence had a dense, hypnotic quality.

Ann sat.

It was extremely rare for her to be like this, motionless and unoccupied, at any time, especially in the middle of the day. It wasn't that she didn't have things to do – the list was endless – but that she couldn't for a moment summon the mental and physical resources to make a start.

She looked down at herself, checking to see what she had put on this morning. She was without vanity and hated shopping, but she liked to be clean and neat. Her underclothes were changed daily and her top clothes every second day unless she had been engaged in some messy activity like gardening, or there was a sudden change in the weather. Now she observed that she was wearing her loden green needlecord skirt, with the green and white striped blouse and brown Hush Puppies. Her hands were resting on her lap and she spread the fingers: they were small hands, short-nailed for convenience and practicality. There was a shiny patch of scar tissue on the back of the left thumb where she had scalded herself years ago, rushing to prepare home-made soup for the boys' firework party. She wore no rings other than her wedding ring, which was narrow and plain. She thought of Mrs Ramilies' hands – large and freckled with chipped red nail varnish and two clusters of glittering diamonds. Her own seemed like a child's by comparison.

Mrs Ramilies had been married twice before her union with the philandering Mr Ramilies, and made no bones about her need for 'a passionate relationship', whereas Ann had been faithfully married to Byron for thirty-five years, and while passion was not exactly spent, it was no longer a major issue. She recalled an expression of Sebastian's: 'Been there, done that, got the T-shirt'.

Some weeks ago she had picked up Josette's copy of the *Post* and read the Hester Blake Page. It was about one's children's sexuality and how to deal with it. All treated very lightly and superficially, of course. One of the points raised was the supposed contradiction in parents' attitudes towards the boys they wished their daughters to go out with, and their own sons. The gist of what Hester had written – and Ann could only suppose that it was her personal view – was that whereas people wanted their daughters to associate with New Men, and be treated with sensitivity and respect, they wished their sons to be cavalier Lotharios, flitting from flower to flower.

Ann considered this highly contentious. She herself had no daughter, but she was a staunch feminist, and hoped and believed that her own boys, although sensibly not yet settled and with a few wild oats still to sow, were capable of serious emotional commitment. She knew all too well from Mrs Ramilies and others of that kidney what the congenital philanderer could do to a woman's self-esteem. In a straightforward conflict between the sexes Ann would, she told herself, always be on the side of the woman.

It might make an interesting topic for discussion at the Women's Group . . . She had better make a note. A little stiffly she rose, picked up the box of tissues and replaced it on top of the bookcase, and went through to her study.

Gavin and Julian were coming back from the *Mammouth* hypermarket. Ann had sent cash, but her advice as to how it might be spent had been largely ignored, and the boot of the Cabriolet groaned with local wine, *Gitanes*, and tinned cassoulet. Gavin intended to conduct exhaustive tax-deductible research into local restaurants, and his humanitarian purpose did not extend to cooking for his brother.

'So when do I meet Lisette?' asked Gavin, flicking ash out of the window at traffic lights.

'Never, if I have anything to do with it.'

'All washed up?'

'As far as I'm concerned. The trouble is I've been taken up in a big way by *maman et papa*. He's the mayor and a bit of a cheese, so you see my predicament.'

Julian put his feet up on the dashboard. Gavin swiped at them with the back of his hand. 'Off!'

'I think,' went on Julian, 'that they actually thought we were going to get spliced.'

'I take it that wasn't on the cards?'

'Christ almighty, you're joking.'

'I don't know, do I – I haven't met the lady.'

'Lisette's all right – touch of Isabella Rosellini – but not for life, oh no.'

'I know what you mean,' agreed Gavin. 'And the French are like that, petty bourgeois, every last one of them.'

'You said it . . .'

Content to have made his point, Julian put his plimsolls back on the dashboard and turned on the radio. He looked young for his age and could have passed for a student of nineteen. This, combined with a sportsman's physique and the breathless, floppy-haired charm of an *ingénu* in a Merchant-Ivory film may have accounted for his popularity at school where he was fawned on by boys and staff alike. This afternoon Gavin and he had been swimming at the open-air pool in Montaigle, and he wore a crumpled beige linen jacket over his bare chest, with a school tie through the belt-loops of frayed white jeans, and a striped towel still draped round his neck. Neither he nor Gavin was tanned – the Armitage skin was notoriously pale and the boys had all learnt early on to make a virtue of necessity.

Julian glanced at his older brother. 'What about you? Getting it regularly?'

'You're coarse, do you know that?'

'Are you?'

'I've finished with Katie, if that's what you mean, but I'd hardly have called it regular even then. She was a nice enough kid but chronically immature, and it was becoming a pain having to pander to her all the time.'

'A free agent, then.'

'You could say that. Although – ' Gavin rested his wrists on the wheel as he undid another packet of cigarettes – 'that presupposes I'm in the market for another mauling. Which I most emphatically am not. Apart from anything else Schmooze takes up eight days a week, and I'm running on the reserve tank as far as energy's concerned.'

'You're a glutton for punishment if you ask me,' said Julian.

'If by that you mean that I'm the only one in this family who knows about work, then you're right.'

'Steady on, *I* work.'

'Correction: you're paid to play.'

'That's true.' Julian was quite satisfied with this analysis.

'No-one seems to understand,' went on Gavin, his voice rising along with the speedometer, 'that when you're the owner-operator in an outfit like mine you can't ever let up. You drive the show and it drives you. The competition's snapping at your heels the whole time. You can never switch off.'

'Fucking horrible,' said Julian. 'You've got to be a headcase to do it.'

Gavin slapped Julian's feet for the second time, but without rancour. 'I'll take that as a compliment.'

'Attaboy,' said Julian. 'Fancy a *boisson*?'

Giselle and Ark walked along the grass verge, in and out of the shadows of the trees, in the direction of Arles. It was eight in the evening, but at the end of June, with the days at their longest, the air was still hot.

They were so into this walking now, they had a rhythm that they fell into, and once in it they felt they could go on for ever. It was nice to get the lifts to cover ground here and there, but the walking was no trouble. They took turns taking the lead and kept going till they got hungry or tired, when they bought something to eat. They had Ark's small ridge-tent with them, but often they hadn't even bothered to use that, and just rolled up in their sleeping bags under the sky. They'd made love with the zoom of traffic only metres away, and at other times in a landscape so deserted it was as though they were the only people in it. Once, they'd looked up to find a hare sitting up like a kangaroo staring at them, front feet and nostrils quivering with what looked like fastidious distaste.

At the moment, Giselle was behind Ark. He walked a touch slower than her, she always had to adjust to that. Each time she followed him she noticed the split in the heel of his right canvas baseball boot getting bigger. And there was a frayed patch below the pocket of his jeans which would start to go soon, too. He wouldn't wear shorts, and he'd only swim if it was in a river or a lake where he could go in naked. At a swimming pool he'd sit on the grass and smoke, and watch her, looking slightly out of sorts, like a girl crying off with her period.

The balance of their relationship had altered during this holiday, and they both knew it. It wasn't so much that either of them had changed, as that certain characteristics which had always been there had begun to appear, like buds opening in the sun. Away from her one-woman resistance movement against the parents, Giselle felt much more in control. If anything it was she who held the cards (including her father's telephone credit card).

And Ark himself seemed – smaller, somehow. She found herself thinking a lot more critically about him, and wishing he'd cut his hair short. As far as sex went they were still good together, but she got fed up with his worries about the dog, and his slowness, and a slight pickiness about food which she hadn't noticed before. Although it was nice to have the sex and the company, Giselle would not have been brokenhearted if he'd decided to go home the next day and left her on her own. She wondered, as they walked along, whether this growing detachment meant that it was all over between them. If that was the case, she could see the irony of it – her parents would think separation had done the trick when it had been just the opposite.

She smiled to herself and Ark, glancing over his shoulder at that moment, thought the smile was for him and returned it. They hadn't rowed or anything. It was impossible to have a fight with Ark, because he was non-confrontational: it was part of his Reiki training.

They were coming into a village.

Ark asked, still walking: 'What d' you reckon, shall we doss here for a bit?'

'If you want.'

'Let's see what gives.'

It was more of a small town, really. Round the *place* there were plenty of shops still open in the relative cool of the evening, and three cafés. They dumped their stuff by a table and Giselle left Ark to order cold beers while she went into the chemist to buy Tampax. It wasn't like Boots. More like some sort of shrine, cool and pale and rather empty, with a woman in a white coat and gold-rimmed glasses behind the counter at the far end. Giselle scanned the shelves, scowlingly aware of her travel-stained appearance and the fact that there were no tampons on display so she was going

to have to ask for them. The assistant did not look as if she
had any truck with bodily juices, let alone anything as messy
as menstruation.

Giselle advanced on the counter. '*Excusez-mois* – Tampax? *Vous
avez?*'

The woman shook her head. '*Non.*'

'*Ou* Lil-lets?' Another head-shake. '*Pas du tout?*'

'*Pas du tout.*'

'Fine!' Giselle was buggered if she was going to give the
ice-matron cause for further high-handedness. She turned and
almost bumped into someone who had been standing behind her,
a bottle of Factor 9 sun cream in his hand.

'They have them in the supermarket.'

It was the man from earlier, the one who'd caught her with her
hand in her knickers.

'Hi,' he added, 'again.'

The woman's attitude changed. '*Oui, madame – au supermarché, en
face—*' She pointed gaily.

'Thanks,' said Giselle, not to her but to the man.

'Glad to be of service.' He handed over the sun lotion and some
cash. 'Just as well I didn't drop dead.'

'Sorry, but—'

He grinned as he pocketed his change. 'Don't apologise. You did
what any well-brought-up girl should do when offered a lift by a
stranger.'

She wondered if he realised how much that annoyed her, and
decided that he almost certainly did.

'That's not it,' she said brusquely. 'We're hitching anyway.'

'So it was personal,' he said. 'Darn.' She left and he followed her
out on to the pavement. 'How about a drink?'

'I've got to go and—'

'Yes, but that only takes a couple of shakes.'

'—meet someone,' said Giselle.

'Okay, I know when I'm licked.' He seemed quite unconcerned.
'*Au revoir* . . .' He sauntered off, tossing the bottle of sun cream
lightly in one hand.

Giselle felt ruffled.

She felt even more ruffled when she joined Ark five minutes
later, only to find the same man, with another bloke, sitting only
two tables away. She was busy trying to fix her features into an

expression which would indicate the pressing need to go elsewhere, when she realised she'd been spotted.

'Hey – come and join us, why don't you?'

Ark looked up at her, then over his shoulder. 'Excuse me . . .?'

The man got up and came over. He held out his hand to Ark. 'Sorry, I'm Gavin Armitage.' Giselle frowned. 'I bumped into your friend at the *routier*, miles back, and by an extraordinary coincidence we washed up together again by the counter in the chemist.'

'Ark,' said Ark, allowing his hand to be shaken. 'Zelda you've met.'

'Zelda . . .' Gavin looked at her with narrowed eyes. 'That's nice.' He addressed himself to Ark again: 'Won't you let me buy you both a drink?'

Ark glanced at Giselle, whose face was hewn from granite. 'Sure, okay – why not?'

Giselle's baleful glare should have conveyed reason enough, but the matter was decided now. With heavy reluctance she leant down to pick up her rucksack, but Gavin was there before her.

'Here, let me.'

She shrugged gracelessly. At his table the other young man rose to his feet as they approached, and pulled out a chair for Giselle.

'Jules, this is Ark, and Zelda. This is my brother, Julian.'

'Hi, nice to meet you,' said Julian. He proffered a hand to Giselle, which she ignored, and then to Ark, who shook it.

'Smoke, anyone?' Gavin offered a packet round. Ark took one but Giselle said, 'No thanks', and took her own out of the back pocket of her shorts.

The waiter hovered with his tin tray.

'Let's get another round in, shall we. How about a bottle of wine?'

'Sounds good,' said Ark. His laid-back affability was annoying Giselle more and more.

'I'll stick with beer, thanks.'

'Okey-dokey . . .' Gavin ordered the wine, and another beer, and at once began asking Ark questions about their itinerary.

Julian turned to Giselle. 'On holiday?'

'Kind of.'

'Lucky you.'

She glanced at him. 'You're not?'

'I work here, would you believe.'

'You're a waiter?'

He laughed good-naturedly. 'I teach at a local private school.'

'What?'

'Rugby, and a spot of English. And you?'

'Nothing much.'

'Still making your mind up,' he suggested chivalrously.

'You could say that.'

Julian looked up at the sky and smiled contentedly. 'Nice way to do it.'

The drinks arrived, and Gavin handed Giselle her beer and poured wine for the rest of them.

'Cheers,' said Ark.

'So how did you two meet?' asked Julian.

'Yes,' said Ark unexpectedly, 'how *did* you two meet?'

'Aha . . .' Gavin shot Giselle a swift, playful grin. 'That's for us to know and you guys to find out, eh, Zelda?'

Giselle felt her face getting hot.

Julian laughed. 'You are a rotten sod, Gavin.'

'Sorry,' said Gavin, 'I couldn't resist telling him.'

'Telling him what?' asked Ark.

'You've got poor old Ark shitting himself,' said Julian. 'Don't worry, he's winding you up.'

'She's a free agent,' said Ark, looking across at Giselle. She was aware of being majorly embarrassed.

Gavin blew smoke from the side of a narrow smile. 'No, it was nothing. I went to pee behind a hedge, privately like, and there was Zelda sunbathing topless.' Giselle felt the heat drain from her face. 'It made my day, I can tell you.'

Ark gave a small, mirthless laugh. 'Glad to hear it.'

'It was the surprise factor,' said Gavin. 'You expect to see that on more or less every beach and poolside south of Bordeaux, but not behind the hedge in a lorry park. Sorry, Zelda—' he reached across and touched the back of her hand, 'that was naughty of me, not to say sexist.'

'It's okay.' She was so relieved she didn't care about anything else. She had honestly thought for a moment there that he was going to describe exactly what he'd seen. She caught his eye, and he raised his eyebrows slightly as if acknowledging the secret between them.

'So you two are hitching around . . .?' asked Julian pleasantly.

'Till the money runs out,' said Ark.

Giselle thought that he was making it sound as if it were his money. Usually she couldn't have cared less but this evening that nettled her.

'My parents packed me off to find work,' she explained, not catching Ark's eye. 'But we thought, stuff that – ' Julian and Gavin laughed appreciatively – 'and you can live on next to nothing, specially if it's hot.'

'That's true,' agreed Gavin. 'God, this makes me realise how dysfunctional a bad climate makes you.'

'He likes the sun,' mouthed Julian, interpreting. Giselle smiled.

'England has a great climate,' put in Ark. Everyone looked at him. 'A great climate, but bad weather.'

Gavin wagged acknowledgement with his cigarette. 'Good distinction, yes. But this, come on, admit it, this is the business. It's the light as much as anything. I mean, to *have* light. You've heard of SAD? Seasonal Affective Disorder? Well, I reckon I suffer from it.'

'Don't play the old soldier,' said Julian. 'Everyone prefers the summer.'

'No, no, SAD's a well-documented phenomenon,' said Ark. 'But your depression might not have anything to do with it. I practise Reiki,' he added modestly.

'I've read about that,' said Gavin. 'It's a laying-on-of-hands, isn't it?'

'Not so much a laying—'

'No,' cut in Julian, 'your hands get hot. You don't necessarily touch the person.'

'That's right.'

'Reiki's great,' said Gavin, 'but I mean, look here.' He leaned across and pulled a rolled-up newspaper out of his brother's jacket pocket. He opened it and gave it a snap to uncrease the pages. It was yesterday's *Post*. 'Yes . . . here. Temperature in London – seventeen degrees. Fifty-one – in mid-summer – it's pathetic. Bordeaux – twenty-seven. Now *that's* more like it. You could put up with the miserable bloody winters if the summer was reliable. It's no exaggeration. There must be thousands of people in England who will go their whole lives not knowing what it is to fire on both cylinders, simply because of the climate.'

He closed the paper and surveyed the front page. 'Jules, what are you doing buying this fascist comic?'

'You forget,' said Julian, 'it's high season. You've got to be bloody quick off the mark to pick up a quality paper in Montaigle in June.'

'Careful,' said Ark. 'Zelda's mum writes in that.'

'She doesn't, does she?' Gavin fastened a sharp, intrigued look on Giselle. 'Does she really?'

'Only once a week,' muttered Giselle.

'*Only* once a week – you mean she's a columnist?'

'Watch it, he's on the scent of a name,' said Julian.

'What is her name?' asked Gavin.

Ark picked up the paper and began turning the pages.

'Forget it,' said Giselle, 'it's not her day.'

'She's not Hester Blake, is she?' asked Gavin.

'Yes.'

'Jesus!' He blew a stream of smoke straight up into the air. 'That's so interesting.'

Ark folded and replaced the paper. 'She's not in, you're right.'

'No,' said Julian, 'it's such an incredible coincidence. We must already know each other.'

Giselle looked at him blankly. 'Must we?'

'If your parents are Hester and Jonty Blake, then they're very old friends of our parents – Ann and Byron Armitage.'

'That's right,' Gavin turned to Giselle and repeated more slowly, 'That's right.'

At that moment Giselle remembered where and when she had met Gavin before. And saw in his eyes that he remembered, too.

Suddenly good-humoured, she said: 'What a small world, and stuff.'

'We should have taken them up on their offer,' she said a couple of hours later as they pitched the tent in the corner of a field, watched by two large, mild-eyed horses.

'We're better off independent.'

'A bathroom would have been nice.'

'You haven't missed one so far.'

'No, but when someone's got one it makes you realise you might like it.'

Ark looked across the top of the tent at her. '*Have* you met them before?'

'When I was a kid. It's funny, I thought I knew Gavin's name when he first mentioned it.'

'They're prats,' said Ark equably, banging in the final peg.

'I thought so at first,' agreed Giselle. 'But in the end they were okay.'

'Tribal recognition.'

'What's that supposed to mean?'

He plucked speculatively at a guyrope. 'The middle classes sniffing each other's backsides.'

'Fuck off, they bought us dinner.'

'Why wouldn't they?' mumbled Ark, not looking at her. 'He got a good eyeful of your tits earlier on, he was probably hoping for another as you came out of their bathroom—'

This flash of jealousy was not altogether unjustified, which was probably why Giselle took such violent exception to it. She fetched Ark a straight-armed blow to the shoulder which made him stumble, trip over the rope and crash to the ground. The two horses wheeled sharply and thundered away, tails flying.

'Steady on! What was that for?'

She didn't bother to answer.

Ark rubbed his shoulder reproachfully. 'I don't care if you've been exchanging Christmas cards for fifty years – they're still prats, Zelda.'

CHAPTER SEVEN

A nn had invited Hester to drop in on her way home from work for either a cup of tea or a drink, whichever was best.

'Oh, whenever your day finishes,' Ann had said airily in response to a question about the time. But then added: 'It'd be best if it wasn't before six, because I have clients till five-thirty and I'd welcome a few minutes to turn myself round . . .'

This invitation was unprecedented in the annals of their friendship. The usual form was for the two couples to have dinner, or occasionally Sunday lunch, at one another's houses several times a year, and for the men to meet separately in town now and again. Between Hester and Ann there had always existed, along with a high mutual regard, a trace of awkwardness. They did not quite understand each other. Theirs had never been the sort of relationship which involved sitting over the kitchen table, sharing a bottle of red wine and chewing the fat. Hester could not help wondering, therefore, what this summons might mean.

She concluded that about six-fifteen would be right. Right for Ann, that is. For her it involved a frightful rush-hour drive, and then the desperate business of finding somewhere to park in or near Raglan Road. By the time she rang the bell she was hot and bothered to a degree.

'Bless you for making this effort!' cried Ann, opening wide the door.

'But it's such a nice idea,' insisted Hester. Entering, she was struck as usual by the spacious orderliness of the Armitages' house. It exerted a soothing influence on her disgruntlement.

'Byron has taken the PG to an exhibition,' explained Ann, leading the way through to the kitchen, 'and I suggested they have a bar snack or something afterwards, so we've got the place to ourselves for a change.'

'Yes, we're quiet at the moment too,' replied Hester. 'Rose is in Tuscany with her chap, Giselle's still at large in France, and now that exams are over Daniel's either in bed or out of the house.'

'Peace, perfect peace,' agreed Ann.

In the kitchen, the french windows stood open, and a white iron table and two chairs were set out on the grass. Ann steered Hester by the shoulder.

'You go and sit yourself down. I shall be right with you.'

Hester sat down and slipped her shoes off. The grass felt lush and cool beneath her tired feet. The back of the house looked more informal than the front, with windows standing open, and here and there something on a windowsill – a plant, some books, an ornament. Hester felt privileged to be vouchsafed this intimate perspective on the Armitages.

Ann came out of the kitchen carrying a tray with two jugs – one Thermos, one cut-glass – and two tall tumblers. When she put the tray on the table Hester saw that there was also a shallow dish containing a constellation of delicately scalloped bite-size quiches, hot – she could smell them – and fresh.

'Now then,' said Ann. 'What can I tempt you with – I have iced tea, or sangria?'

Hester was overwhelmed. 'Ann, you are good. Sangria, please. This is lovely – don't tell me you made these specially?'

'I'm afraid not,' said Ann, but not in the tone of someone but lately returned from Marks and Spencer. 'I turn out a batch once a month and pop them in the freezer. They're rather good but *extremely* simple.'

'Mm . . .' Hester popped one in her mouth, where it melted deliciously. 'Absolutely yummy.'

'Have another . . . just help yourself.'

'I will, thanks.' She took a second and gazed about her. 'Isn't your garden looking nice?'

'It's all basic stuff which will keep on coming up reliably with a minimum of fuss,' admitted Ann. 'But this is its good time, I grant you.'

They surveyed it together for a few moments, until Ann asked lightly:

'You say Giselle is still on the continent . . .?'

'In France, yes.'

'Do you have any idea when she's likely to return?'

'Well,' said Hester, 'we've scarcely heard from her in five weeks, but she did call the other night, and I gather she'll be back at the weekend.'

'M-hm.' Ann nodded, a little *Giaconda* smile on her lips. 'And did she sound as if she was enjoying herself?'

Hester tried to remember. 'I think that might be overstating the case rather, but she certainly seemed quite okay.'

'I have something I must tell you,' said Ann. She picked up the jug of sangria and replenished both their glasses. 'One of those extraordinary coincidences which make even an agnostic like myself believe in some higher power.'

'Heavens.' Hester took out a slice of orange and sucked it. 'Go on, the suspense is killing me.'

'I don't know whether we told you, but Julian had mumps a few weeks ago, and was extremely unwell.'

'No, you didn't – I am sorry.'

'He's quite recovered and no unpleasant side effects, I'm happy to say.'

'Oh good,' said Hester, wondering whether perhaps Julian had had a sudden conversion, or out-of-body experience.

'However,' went on Ann, 'it has been a worry. And though one doesn't like to be a fussy parent I was anxious for a rather more objective view of his general health, if you follow me.'

'They don't have much clue, do they?' agreed Hester. 'My lot have nothing between "okay" and "sod off".'

Ann smoothed her denim skirt. 'Even had I the time I didn't want to go haring over there myself. But it struck me that Gavin was in crying need of a holiday – quite apart from work he's been through a very trying time emotionally – so we persuaded him, with difficulty I might add, to take a week and check up on his brother.'

'What a good idea,' said Hester, increasingly mystified.

'It's quite an achievement to prise him away from that baby of his these days, but Byron felt – quite rightly as it turned out – ' Ann said this with a faint note of surprise – 'that the way to do it was to give him a task. Gavin likes to feel purposeful and, I believe, needed.' She looked intently at Hester.

'I'm sure you're right.'

'In any event, it appears to have done him the world of good. And

the other day we had this . . .' She lifted the dish of little quiches
to reveal a postcard lying on the table beneath. She picked it up.
'Shall I read it to you?'

'By all means.'

Hester was at a disadvantage. Ann had something in store for
her, but she had no idea what. She was being played like a fish
on a line. With any other female friend she might have yelled at
them to get on with it, but such behaviour was out of the question
with Ann.

Ann held the postcard in one hand, at eye level and rather
to one side, like someone about to embark on '*The Hallelujah
Chorus*'.

'It's postmarked Montaigle,' she explained. 'That is the small
town near Arles where Julian lives and works.'

'I see.'

Ann cleared her throat. 'He writes: "A wasted journey – Julian's
fine and appreciated the provisions. I supervised disposal of cash
as instructed. Met Giselle Blake here last night, an absolute stunner.
We hit it off. Back soon, G."

Ann lowered the postcard.

'How extraordinary,' said Hester, 'it must be a chance in a
million.'

'He's obviously smitten,' said Ann.

'Yes, and that's even more extraordinary.' Hester took another
quiche. 'I mean Giselle – stunning? How could you tell under
all that?'

'I dare say she has opted for a more natural look under the rigours
of the road. And Byron and I have always thought her essentially
very handsome.'

'She certainly used to be . . .'

'Exactly. And don't you think there is a certain poetic harmony
in these two meeting at this particular moment – Gavin recovering
from a broken relationship, Giselle sent abroad – forgive me, but I
believe this is the case – to forget . . .?'

'That makes it sound terribly heavy. We were simply trying to
broaden her horizons a bit—'

'Without her follower.'

'Her—? Well, yes. Obviously.'

'Quite.' Ann put the postcard on the table and beamed. Hester
had rarely seen her so animated. 'I have to tell you, it is almost

unprecedented for any of our boys, and especially Gavin, to announce a woman at first meeting in this way.'

Hester smiled and shook her head. 'I'm sorry, it's that word woman . . .'

Ann looked stern. 'You have a problem with it?'

'Not as such, but I admit I find it hard to apply it to Giselle.'

'But, Hester, she is most emphatically a woman – physically, emotionally, legally – what more do you want?'

'I accept that, it's only a natural maternal tendency not to take one's offspring seriously.'

'I think you should begin to do so,' suggested Ann reprovingly.

'I suppose . . .' said Hester, irked that she was falling into the usual trap of letting Ann dictate to her. There wasn't time to explain the complexities of her feelings for her daughter. As for Gavin, her memory from some long-past fork supper was of a tousled, restless young man, attractive but caustic, with both brain and mouth in overdrive. She tried to imagine this person and her daughter 'getting it together', as the phrase went, and failed.

'I'm saying nothing,' Ann was saying. 'One can't live their lives for them. Eyes wide open and mouth shut shall be my maxim . . . but I can't pretend I shan't be watching with the greatest interest as events unfold.'

This was too much for Hester. 'I wouldn't hold your breath, Ann – the chances of your son contacting my daughter once they're back here and out of holiday mode are practically nil.'

'You're very sure about that . . .'

'I'm ninety-nine point nine per cent certain. Quite apart from the age difference, which is considerable—'

'I don't believe that matters where emotional commonality can be established.'

'Okay, if you like, but the fact is that they don't have a single thing in common. Not one. Gavin is a bright metropolitan spark wedded to what is by all accounts a twenty-four-hour-a-day job and Giselle is – well, not.'

Ann pinned Hester with a penetrating gaze. 'There is much in the old adage about opposites agreeing.'

'In terms of temperament, perhaps. But I can't help feeling there has to be some level of shared experience.'

Ann put down her glass and settled her shoulders. Hester resigned herself to being counselled.

'Let me put my cards on the table. I confess nothing would please me more than that some kind of relationship should develop between these two. Gavin is, as you rightly point out, a workaholic, and highly – perhaps over – ambitious. I believe that Giselle, still a rough diamond whom, if I may say so, you are rather too ready to disparage, might be exactly what he needs. Are you saying that you and Jonty would not welcome such a development?'

Hester saw that it was time to wrest back the initiative, and without the benefit of further sangria if she was to drive back to Chuffington with a clear conscience and a clean licence.

'Please, Ann, you've got me all wrong. Of course it would be fun if something happened between them, but we should try to be realistic here. It's not that I wouldn't welcome it – God knows, after some of the Neanderthals Giselle's knocked about with it would be a miracle – but I honestly don't think it's going to happen.'

Hester stopped. Ann was still gazing at her. She felt her own fervent expression cool and become rigid, fixing her features in a grotesque mask.

'Do you?' she added, to fill the void.

'Only time will tell,' replied Ann.

'Speaking of which, I ought to hit the road.'

'Must you?' asked Ann, rising.

At the door, they brushed cheeks. Hester was one of nature's kissers, Ann was not. Hester got the impression that her friend had developed a self-adjusting mechanism which regulated skin contact to a minimum. She thought fleetingly of Byron.

'Thank you,' she said, 'for a very pleasant interlude.'

'We should do it more often,' agreed Ann. 'You know tomorrow is the day we have Ava Lawrence coming to speak to the group – would you care to join us?'

In fact, Hester would have liked to – the occasion might even have made a column – but she shied away from the possibility of more notes and queries on the subject of Giselle.

'How maddening, I'm tied up tomorrow evening. Never mind,' she added, 'I'll keep you posted if there are any developments.'

Ground had been given. Ann smiled appreciatively. 'Thank you, Hester. I should welcome that.'

'I mean,' exclaimed Hester to Jonty over corned beef and baked potatoes. 'Can you see it?'

'Only with the greatest difficulty, I admit. But nothing's impossible.'

'Take it from me, this is.'

'Cupid's dart, and so forth. Who knows?'

'Good grief,' said Hester, 'you're as big a fantasist as she is!'

Jonty put his knife and fork together. 'And speaking of fantasy, I must totter down to the pub and firm up my availability for Codgers at home on Saturday.'

Sitting alone at the table, Hester began to formulate next week's column under the heading 'A Knavish Lad' . . .

Ann had made coffee, but only she was drinking it. Byron had been treated to an authentic Chinese meal by Mr We-We Sun and something in it had disagreed with him. He lay back with his eyes closed, a glass of Alka-Seltzer resting between clasped hands on his solar plexus.

'I'm enormously fond of the Blakes,' admitted Ann, 'but Hester does have a propensity to run her children down.'

'I can't say I've noticed,' murmured Byron. 'If she does, she doesn't mean it.'

'I'm not so sure . . . Giselle is a case in point. She is obviously a girl with many and considerable strengths and yet Hester will characterise her as first and foremost a problem.'

'Oh, Ann,' groaned Byron, opening one eye. 'You're not still on about the postcard?'

'I hope you didn't mention Ark on that card,' said Giselle to Gavin, 'because he's not supposed to be here.'

They were sitting at their usual table in the *Café de Place* in Montaigle, drinking cold beers and doing some damage to *assiettes de campagne*.

'Don't worry,' said Gavin. 'Your secret is safe with me.' He glanced around. 'Where is Ark today, by the way?'

'Search me.'

'Is that an offer?'

By way of reply Giselle gave him the slightly threatening smile which sent a shiver down his spine.

'Where is he?'

She shrugged, and turned the shrug into a stretch which did

interesting things to her torso. When she spoke, it was round an exaggerated yawn:

'Buggered off somewhere.'

'How sporting of him,' said Gavin.

Rose and Jez lay prone and shoulder to shoulder beside the pool. The villa was a farmhouse of honey-coloured Tuscan stone, now sympathetically converted into half a dozen holiday lets of varying sizes. Beyond the pool bronze hills studded with dark, sentinel cypresses buzzed with high-summer heat. Pink and white dog roses and purple bougainvillaea rioted around the house. Towels and bathing costumes festooned the shutters. Most of the other apartments were occupied by families, and at this time in the evening Rose and Jez were alone at the poolside except for one die-hard German mother, her hair in a scarf, her skin conker-brown against her white one-piece.

'She's going to be such a wizened old crone in ten years' time.' whispered Rose.

'She's okay now though.' Jez slid his eyes in the woman's direction.

Rose nudged him. 'Don't, it's rude.'

'Why not? She can't see me.'

'Not rude to her, nobber, rude to me!'

'You're okay now, too.' He put out a hand and rubbed her bare back. 'Better than okay . . . Your skin is so hot . . .'

'I'm not burnt, am I?'

'Don't think so.'

They lay for a while in heat-stupefied silence, Jez's hand still resting in the hollow of her back.

'You know something?' Rose murmured.

'No, but I think you're going to tell me . . .'

'I couldn't go to bed with someone who wasn't good-looking.'

Jez moved his hand. 'Flatterer.'

'No, I couldn't, honestly. You look at some couples and you wonder what on earth is going on.'

'Monroe and Miller?'

'He wasn't so bad . . . and there is something about a towering intellect . . . like money or power . . .'

'Loren and Ponti . . . Bancroft and Brookes . . . Jackie and Ari—'

'Actually I was thinking more of my sister.'

Jez rolled on to his back with a snort. 'Your sister?'

'What's so funny?'

'She's no daisy herself.'

'That's not kind. She may wear weird stuff—'

'And the rest.'

Rose leaned up on her elbow. 'No, Grizzle's basically a nice-looking girl—'

'Grizzle!'

'She is! She's got a cleavage to die for. But you should see this guy she's going out with at the moment.'

'Why, what's he like?'

'He's all right, he's not a bad bloke I suppose, but he looks exactly like Animal out of the Muppets.'

Jez cupped his hands round his eyes and rolled his head to look at her. 'Sounds like they deserve each other.'

'I couldn't do it. It makes my flesh creep to contemplate it.' She shivered fastidiously and reached out for her bikini top. 'Let's go in. I bet I have burnt.'

Daniel, with his friends Spike and Muffer, sat in the pool bar of The Needle's Eye, each with a half of best. Unlike the Axe and Compass in Chuffington, the Needle, hard by the barrack gate, served underage drinkers on a no-questions-asked basis, because it was the landlord's view that the younger the lads the less likely they were to get into a ruck with the squaddies.

'So what we gonna do then?' asked Daniel. 'If we don't fix something pretty soon they'll be on at me to go to Greece with them.'

'Greece, eh?' Spike said. 'Smart.'

'Fucking hell,' protested Daniel, 'they'll say "bring a friend" – nightmare.'

Muffer said: 'I'll come.'

'You just don't get it, do you? I've had it with holidaying with them. My mum feels if we're not all doing something together all the time we're a problem family; my dad says, "Let everyone do their thing, we're on holiday", and then they fight about it.'

'I don't mind doing something together with your mother,' admitted Spike.

'Nor me,' said Muffer. 'She's all right, your dot.'

'Not on holiday she's not,' Daniel assured him. 'Get her on holiday and she's a total fruit.'

They sipped their beers thoughtfully.

'Does she still wear a bikini?' asked Spike.

'Yeah . . . mega-cringe.'

They thought some more.

'Tell you what,' said Daniel, 'Cornwall's supposed to be good.'

'We used to go there,' said Muffer, 'it's smart.'

Spike shrugged. 'Suits me.'

'We could go to a camp site . . .' Daniel warmed to his theme. 'Do a bit of surfing . . .'

'Bar-bar-bar! Bar-barbra-ann!' barked Spike.

'When shall we go?' Daniel glanced at his watch. 'Coupla weeks?'

'Go for it!'

Daniel wondered why people made such a thing of organising holidays. 'Sorted,' he said.

Julian returned from dinner at Lisette's house – it was hellish difficult to extricate oneself from these family set-ups once they took a hold – to find Gavin lying naked on the bed, smoking and reading the *Post*.

'Hi,' said Gavin. 'Caught in the act.'

'Which one?'

'Reading the Hester Blake page.'

'Oh.' Julian undid his tie, pulled his shirt out of his waistband, and went to lean out of the unshuttered window on his folded arms. 'I get you.'

'Why, what did you think I meant?'

'Come on, where is she?'

Gavin shrugged. 'Under canvas with the Missing Link.'

Julian turned and leaned back against the windowsill. 'What exactly are you playing at?'

'Who, *moi*?'

'She's not exactly your type, and the parents knowing each other could be a hell of an aggravation.'

Gavin lowered the newspaper. 'One, don't tell me what my type is. And two,' he leaned over the side of the bed and dropped his fag end in the chamber pot he was using as an ashtray, 'who gives a flying fart about the parents?'

Julian shrugged. 'You know how excited the old girl gets – and you've actually told her about this. You must be off your trolley.'

'You underestimate them,' said Gavin peaceably. 'They'll be cool. And Hester Blake's always looking for something to write about.' He slapped the paper with the back of his hand. 'Talk about living in the glare of publicity. Zelda said her brother was doing GCSEs and sure enough, here it is, Exams and How to Survive Them.' He let the paper drop. 'She's a good-looking woman for her age. I wouldn't push her out.'

Julian shook his head admiringly. 'You're unbelievable.'

'Only joking. For some reason I'm really interested in that crazy daughter of hers,' said Gavin modestly. He caught his brother's eye, and added, 'And you can take that look off your face, because it may surprise you to know I haven't yet done a single thing unbecoming of a gentleman.'

'Not here, Pats,' said Sebastian, glancing around nervously. 'It's more than my job's worth, you know that.'

It was nearly midnight and they were standing outside the Hayes Road Youth Club in Notting Hill. Nearby a group of boys muttered and sniggered, rustling a plastic bag.

'What about tomorrow?'

'Tomorrow's out, I'm in court as an appropriate adult for Denny and Rhona.'

'Next day?' Patsy's large, bright eyes, the colour of treacle toffee, fixed on Sebastian's, which held for a second and then wavered and slid sideways.

'Not good. I said I'd help out with something my mother's organising near her place.'

'Oh, *well*,' said Patsy loudly, putting her hands on her hips. 'Oh, *well*, in that case, sorry I even mentioned it, pardon me while I crawl right back under a stone and disappear up my own arse—!'

'Steady on, Pats—'

'No, no, if Mummy has spoken then Mummy must be obeyed!'

'Come on, she asked me this one small favour—'

'You're crap, you are, Seb-ars-tian Smarmy-army-tidge!'

There were snorts of muffled laughter from the boys.

'You lot!' bellowed Sebastian. 'Clear off home!'

'Hang on,' said Patsy, running after them. 'I'm coming too!'

Although it was late, Sebastian took a bus from Hayes Road to Paddington. He didn't own a car – apart from the expense it was a liability in this area, and in his job, where the little bastards saw any unattended vehicle as an open invitation to loot. He was going to George Street to feed Mensa. He'd missed a couple of days and had an idea Gavin might be back soon and wouldn't be too chuffed if the mog had wasted away in his absence. It was certainly peckish – it came through the cat-flap like a bog-brush on speed, and twined and writhed round his ankles in a frenzy as he opened a tin of Whiskas and emptied it into one of Gavin's Lalique glass bonbon dishes.

He didn't leave right away, but had a quiet crap while reading Gavin's latest *Viz*, and then rolled himself a spliff. He lay on the sofa with his Timberlands up on the arm, puffing contentedly in the half-light. As far as Patsy went, he'd decided it was all for the best. She was bad news. The whole thing could have lost him his job. The only reason he'd hung on to it was that the supervisor (poor benighted sod) thought he'd made a big, selfless effort to get along with Patsy after her weird behaviour earlier.

The cat came in, flanks bulging, and sat down in the middle of the carpet to wash itself, purring loudly. Sebastian began to feel mellow. He slid off the chesterfield and went across to the television on all fours. He collected the remote control and crawled back again. Stretched out once more he channel-surfed idly until he stumbled on a colourful techno-splatter set in post-nuclear Chicago.

Ann was touched that Sebastian had agreed so readily to help out on the night of the Ava Lawrence visit. She offered him remuneration but he had declined, and even said that it was a pleasure. Ann was devoted to all her boys, but her first-born had always had that little bit of charm which oiled the wheels and made him so much easier to deal with.

His presence tonight would be invaluable. Because they were expecting an audience swelled by guests and visitors for this special speaker, she had booked the church hall instead of their usual annexe to the library. This meant that chairs had to be assembled and set out, a couple of tables hefted into position, and the refreshments she had prepared unloaded from the car. She also wanted someone to keep an eye on the parking – the hall had a parallelogram of tarmac for the vehicles of 'worshippers only' (Ann supposed that's what they were for the purposes of this evening), but the difference between organised

and disorganised parking could mean space for as many as half
a dozen cars.

The audience was in place and buzzing by a quarter to eight.
Ava Lawrence was arriving by taxi. Ann had invited her to come
at seven-thirty so that she could enjoy a glass of wine and a
home-made samosa before speaking, but she had explained that
that would be impossible because of commitments elsewhere
beforehand. Her new book, *The Politics of Pressure*, an investigation
into conflicting aspirations in women, was due out later that week,
and she was caught up in a hectic promotional schedule.

Ann, on her way to look out for Ava Lawrence, encountered
Sebastian in the lobby, consuming the wine and smoked salmon
sandwiches which had been set aside for him.

'There's no need to stay, Seb,' she said. 'Do go whenever you
want. I'm most grateful for your help.'

'Cheers,' said Sebastian. 'I might as well hang about for a bit –
will I get my balls bust if I stand at the back?'

Ann laughed. 'Don't be silly.'

'I won't be unconstitutional or anything?'

'Certainly not. Our whole animus is towards open-mindedness.'

'Glad to hear it – hey, is this her?'

Ann switched to alert, then switched off again. 'No, it's Josette.
You've met Josette, surely?'

'I don't know . . .' Sebastian smiled at Josette. 'I'm sure if I had
I would have remembered.'

Josette dumped the three supermarket bags she was carrying,
and blew upwards to cool her face.

'We've met,' she said perfunctorily, and then to Ann: 'I hope
I'm not late, I thought I'd shop first and there were queues at the
checkout like you wouldn't believe.'

'You're not late,' Ann told her. 'And it's lovely that you could
come. I know you won't regret it. Why don't you leave those at the
back of the hall – Sebastian will keep an eye on them for you.'

'Sure,' said Sebastian.

'And make sure you have something to eat and drink,' went on
Ann. 'Vidyut's on refreshments.'

'Thanks,' said Josette, picking up her bags and heading for the
hall. 'I could do with some.'

Sebastian put his glass on his empty plate and looked round for
somewhere to put them.

'Here,' said Ann, 'let me park those for you.'

As soon as she'd gone, a taxi pulled up in the road outside. Sebastian walked to the doorway and watched with interest as a tall woman dressed in a long, lean, cream knitted shift got out, paid and looked about her. She had a mass of tumbling red hair, and her face and arms were lightly burnished by the sun. When she raised a hand to lift her hair from her neck a cluster of gleaming wooden bracelets fell down her slender forearm.

'Excuse me! Is this St Xavier's hall?'

Sebastian realised she was addressing him. He ambled forward. 'That's right.'

'The women's group meeting?'

'Right again.'

'My, oh my,' she laughed and looked him up and down. 'Things are looking up.' The taxi was still thrumming behind her. 'Say, could you give me a hand? I have one or two books here . . .' She opened the back door of the cab to reveal four sturdy cardboard cartons.

'Ava Lawrence?' It was Ann, walking briskly (she never ran) from the hall. 'I do apologise that I wasn't here to greet you.' She held out her hand and Ava shook it. 'Ann Armitage.'

'Nice to meet you, Ann. I guess I'm a little late.'

'Not at all.' Ann looked at her watch. 'Precisely punctual.'

'Oftentimes that is late.'

'Not here, I do assure you. I see you've met my son, Sebastian.'

Ava Lawrence smiled at Sebastian, a wide, strong-jawed American smile, a tribute to expensive orthodontics. She exuded a glossy, intelligent charm.

'Sebastian's a hero – he offered to help me with these books.'

'Good idea,' said Ann. She glanced fleetingly at the cartons. 'Sebastian, if I take Ava into the hall, perhaps you could put the books at the back, and we'll organise a table for them.'

'Leave it with me.'

'This is really good of you,' said Ava, bestowing another ravishing grin on Sebastian. 'I appreciate it.'

'My pleasure.' Sebastian reached for the first carton and pulled it towards him. It weighed a ton. A touch grudgingly, the cabbie got out to help.

As they walked towards the hall, Ava said: 'A certain poetic irony, don't you think, Ann, that one comes trailing clouds of feminist glory and winds up asking a nice young guy to carry one's books . . ?'

Ann laughed happily.

Sebastian, following them rather unsteadily beneath the combined weight of two cartons, was transfixed by Ava Lawrence's swaying backside . . . high, wide and handsome. And unless he was very much mistaken (and he was a judge of such things) she was naked as a sausage inside that tube.

It had been a tremendous success.

Ann was exhausted, but flushed with triumph. The women were coming up to her in droves, telling her what a wonderful evening it had been, how refreshing, how stimulating, how *inspiring*. The books had all gone – not everyone had bought one, they were a touch pricey for people like Josette, but several people had bought two, and Ava Lawrence had taken orders for more. Her talk had been intellectually rigorous, but not lacking in humour, and afterwards she had mixed and mingled like a trouper, and complimented Ann not just on the work she was doing, but on the quality of the refreshments.

'These hors d'oeuvres are to die for!' she exclaimed, licking her fingers and smacking her lips with robust relish. 'They remind me of kids' parties. Problem is you tell yourself you're not really eating, whereas in reality you're pigging out!'

They'd all laughed a touch enviously because Ava Lawrence had the physique of a goddess – tall, toned and glowing with health – and they suspected that when she wasn't pigging out in church halls she was eating macrobiotic foods and flushing out her system with eight pints of filtered water a day.

Sebastian put the tables away, stacked the chairs, pushed the big broom around a bit and folded down the empty cartons. Josette, collecting her carrier bags, nodded at him.

'That's what I like to see!'

'I'm not proud,' said Sebastian. 'Enjoy it?'

'Fantastic,' said Josette, putting her thumb and forefinger together. 'Tops. I got her autograph. What a woman!'

When everyone had gone except Ann and Vidyut, who had to tidy up the leftovers, Ava said:

'Ann – time I was gone. It's been a great evening.'

'We can't thank you enough,' said Ann. 'And you will let us know your expenses?'

Ava waved her long hands before her face with a soft click of bracelets. 'I wouldn't dream of it. This is *me*. This is what I *am*. And let me tell you it beats working.'

She was a smooth operator, thought Sebastian. You had to make a real effort to remind yourself that she had just shifted several hundred quids' worth of hardback books.

'Now,' she went on, 'what are my chances of picking up a cab outside here?'

Ann looked doubtful.

'Not all that good,' said Vidyut. 'We can call you a minicab, though.'

Sebastian came over, carrying the folded boxes. 'I've got a better idea, why don't I give you a lift? My car's right outside the door.'

Ava looked hesitant. 'I'm at the Inn on the Park, Sebastian . . .'

'That's only up the road, it'll be a doddle this time in the evening.'

'Seb, my dear,' said Ann fondly, 'that would be kind.'

'It would be – *too* kind,' agreed Ava.

'Oh well, if you think it's *too* kind . . .' said Sebastian.

Ava laughed. 'No, no, I retract – I give in. Let me go and do what a girl's gotta do and I'll be right back.'

Ann kissed Sebastian's cheek in tender appreciation. It was moments like this which made the struggle worthwhile – moments when you saw that the training had paid off. 'Thank you, darling, this is good of you.'

'Not at all,' said Sebastian. 'I aim to please.'

On Saturday morning Hester and Jonty were waiting for Giselle to return. She'd said she'd be on the overnight ferry, but was sure she'd be able to get a lift up from Dover, and would only call if she was desperate. Since it was now nine o'clock and they hadn't heard anything they had to assume she was on her way.

'I hope she hasn't been hitchhiking all the time,' said Jonty, pressing down the plunger on the cafetière.

'Well, we did rather turn her loose,' Hester reminded him.

'She had a railcard.'

'She went, she did it, and she's coming back, unscathed so far as we know,' said Hester. 'Mission accomplished. We owe it to her not to interrogate her.'

'I'm rather looking forward to seeing her,' admitted Jonty, with a note of mystification.

'Me too.'

'I wonder what changes six weeks on the road will have wrought . . ?'

Jonty needn't have worried. When, about twenty minutes later, there was the sound of tyres on gravel and they went to the front door, it was a sleeker, browner, luminous Giselle who stood there with a fine gold chain undulating over her collar bones and a white muslin shirt knotted at what was now discernibly her waist. Hester beamed.

'Darling – you look smashing!'

'Hallo, Grizzle – welcome home.'

Giselle stepped back to reveal a scarlet car standing in the drive. A Byronic young man in black was leaning (on his hands), on the bonnet but straightened up and began strolling towards them.

'Mum, Dad,' said Giselle, her tone a mixture of caution and defiance, 'this is Gavin. He brought me back.'

CHAPTER EIGHT

G avin stayed for coffee, and then Giselle walked with him back to the car. Hester left the front door open for Giselle's return, but her tactfully retreating voice spoke loudly of popping into the garden to deadhead the shrubs.

'Your parents are great,' said Gavin.

'Yours are all right too,' conceded Giselle. 'Last time they were out here your mother was really friendly.'

'Was she.' It was a comment, not a question.

'She said I could call in on her any time I was in town.'

'Then you must. There are always cookies in the jar down there.'

'You're so sarcastic.'

'I'm not.'

'I like her.'

'Good. But bear in mind,' said Gavin, lowering his voice, 'that my mother never stops thinking.'

They were standing next to the car now. He placed a finger on Giselle's cheek and turned her face to his.

'She doesn't have a spontaneous bone in her body . . . Unlike you.' His voice and look intensified as if he were about to kiss her on the lips, but instead he opened the car door briskly. 'I must be off.'

'Thanks for the lift – and everything.'

'Don't thank me. Let's hope you don't get any grief from Ark.'

'He's cool.'

Gavin got in behind the wheel and looked up at her. 'May I call you?'

'If you want.'

'Does the Pope kiss tarmac. I'll give you a bell.'

'See you.'

Giselle watched the car turn out of the drive. Gavin waved out of the window as he disappeared. She folded her arms.

Gavin put on Bob Marley and lit a cigarette. He was feeling really, really good. He'd hooked her for sure.

Up the garden Hester stood absentmindedly plucking at a purple buddleia. Jonty leaned against an apple tree with his third cup of coffee. He was there under orders because Hester did not think they ought to be hovering expectantly when Giselle came back into the house.

'We should at least appear to be taking this in our stride,' she explained urgently.

'I am taking it in my stride.'

'Really? Well I'm not – you could have knocked me down with a feather.'

'I don't see why – steady on, that was a perfectly good flower.'

'I'm completely staggered. He used to go out with Katie Hogan who works on our diary page.'

'I fail to see the connection.'

'She's a nice, fresh, well-educated girl with boarding school vowels and hair that moves about.'

'He obviously has catholic tastes,' suggested Jonty.

Hester shook her head in wonderment. 'I take it all back. Your fell scheme worked.'

'It wasn't a fell scheme, it was a perfectly straightforward attempt to let some light in on the proceedings.'

'I can't understand why you're not gloating.'

'You shouldn't judge others by your own standards,' admonished Jonty.

'What do you think of him, anyway?'

'He seems fine. Bit of a bullshitter, but that may be nerves.'

'Is that it?'

'Come on, Hes, I've only just met him.'

'No, we have met him before,' corrected Hester, 'but not to observe properly.'

'He could talk for Britain,' said Jonty dourly.

'Yes, and what a pleasant change that makes – it's so long since Giselle produced anyone who wasn't practically catatonic. Only think, we'll all be able to have conversations together!'

Jonty laughed. He put out a hand and brushed a scattering of tiny purple petals from Hester's threadbare grey T-shirt, an old one of his. Her cheeks were pink, her eyes bright and excited, her fuzz of fair hair caught up in a scrunch band on top of her head. She looked young and pretty: he felt a pulse of intense pleasure because she was his wife, and they had come this far together. Still crazy after all these years.

Hester laughed back, uncertainly. 'What's so funny?'

'Don't get too carried away, will you?'

'I shan't.'

'They bumped into one another and she cadged a lift home with him, that's all. I hate to say this, but you need to revive a little of your earlier healthy scepticism. In order to avoid disappointment.'

'You can be so ruddy patronising,' said Hester without rancour.

'I didn't—'

'*And* you move the goalposts all the time!'

'I—'

'Ssh – hallo, darling!'

Giselle had appeared at the french window.

'Okay if I have a bath?'

'Go ahead, there's plenty of hot water!'

Giselle disappeared again.

Hester pointed in the direction of the house. 'Hear that? She asked if she could have a bath.'

'Better yet,' added Jonty, emptying his coffee dregs on to the grass, 'she doesn't even look as if she needs one.'

Hester watched her husband walk back to the house. He was right – Giselle looked wonderful. Her heart was pattering and she felt ridiculously elated. Was this, she wondered, how the prodigal son's father felt? A flurry of images, unbidden and wholly unjustified, swirled around in her head like confetti: Giselle dancing in a long ball dress . . . Giselle bewitching guests at a cocktail party . . . Giselle receiving roses at the door . . . Giselle in white lace, her dark hair spangled with white flowers . . .

An upstairs window, unlatched, banged back against the wall.

'Mum!'

It was Daniel.

'Mum! Give us a lift to Muffer's!'

'Why?' called Hester.

'Now!' replied Daniel.

*   *   *

Giselle had emptied the hot water tank.

Now she lay back in a steaming nimbus of foam with her knees slightly bent, and her feet braced beneath the taps at the far end. Back here in the soft English light her body looked insolently dark and exotic.

Someone had been into her room while she was away and cleaned it up – the yucca was green and glossy, there was a shade on the overhead light, the sheets were changed and the carpet hoovered. The inflatable man had been tucked up cosily beneath the duvet. It was all right. Restful, somehow.

She tried, in a spirit of fair play, to spare a thought for Ark who was still, as far as she knew, in France. But she found it difficult to visualise him. Ark, Dolly, his room, the Reiki practice, were like those little black and white snaps in the older family albums – small, quaint and faded, time viewed through the wrong end of a telescope.

She then considered Gavin, who was about as different from Ark as it was possible to be – sharp, a motormouth and full of shit much of the time. But – well, charming. Giselle had never been susceptible to charm – it was something from the world of suits. But Gavin had a foot in both camps: he worked his rocks off (according to him) in the sort of place she couldn't stand the thought of, but he knew all the good bands and had an off-the-wall sense of humour. She was also more pleased than she would have cared to admit that her parents liked him. It was nice to know there would be no hassle. She felt she had come home in more senses than one.

They hadn't slept together yet. They were playing a game with each other: who would crack first. Giselle was confident she could outlast him. His poncey café cut no ice with her. Underneath he was just like all the others – a great big gland on legs. Smiling to herself, she closed her eyes, and submerged . . .

The party to launch *The Politics of Pressure* was held in the Delett art gallery in Mayfair. This was partly because Mark Fein, the owner of the gallery, was a friend of Ava's from way back when, and partly because the Delett was a large, light, elegant space which would display Ava to advantage. Her publisher, Clarion, very properly put fine writing at the top of their list of criteria, but they accepted that pulchritude in the writer did no harm either. Looks sold books. Ava's cover photograph was the most talked about in London –

the head and bare shoulders without a scrap of jewellery, cloth or make-up; full-face, unsmiling and back-lit so that the lion's mane of hair appeared aglow with electric energy.

This photograph, blown up to billboard proportions, was displayed in the gallery's foyer, and here and there on the upper level so that wherever you were the author's spine-tingling image was never far away. The gallery was the perfect backdrop. Mark Fein specialised in contemporary work – huge, stark paintings comprising geometric blocks of dense colour and smooth, pale, rounded sculptures like rocks eroded by aeons of wind and water. It was impossible to escape the impression that these artefacts too were in some strange way the product of Ava Lawrence's fecund intellect, astounding thoughts and precepts waiting, in solid but inanimate form, to be given life by her words.

Katie was in danger of feeling overwhelmed. There must have been over a hundred people at the bash, all apparently familiar with Lawrence's work, all confident in their right to be there and to pass an opinion. These were guests with attitude. Katie was deafened and disorientated by the massed bat-squeaks of their circling egos.

Her brief was to trawl for gossip – to spot names and faces, pick up on any new pairings or separations, and most importantly to speak to Ava Lawrence herself.

'It won't be a problem,' Larry Orde had assured her. 'She's a great Anglophile and an arch self-promoter. This is the woman who posed topless for a male camera club so that she could write about it afterwards, and who used the pictures in the article, hm?'

'I haven't managed to finish the book,' Katie told him.

'Book, schmook. It'll be the same old stuff shot from a different angle, and it'll get the lion's share of the books page anyway. Tell her we hear she's thinking of buying a place in London—'

'Is she?'

'Tell her that's what we hear. See who she's with and make something of it. Oh, and give her my love. She's a cinch, you'll be fine.'

It was very hot. Katie stood near the window with her glass of orange juice growing tepid in her hand. She had been here for half an hour and hadn't done too badly on the secondary stuff. She had spotted, tracked down and talked to a famously stroppy female rock star who had recently come out as gay; and a dashing Indian cricketer who squired the brightest and best-looking daughters of the nobility about town but who planned to return to his country for an arranged marriage; she had also overheard a conversation between a Tory spin-doctor and a senior civil servant which might prove to be the seed corn for a future story. But Ava Lawrence had so far evaded her.

Katie could see her – it was impossible not to, given her great height, big hair and five-inch heels – but like the goal of some mythical hero she remained always just out of reach. She was hedged about by acolytes and admirers, turning the vivacious concentration of her gaze on this person and that, constantly focused, fascinated and attentive in a way which appeared completely genuine but realistically could not be. Katie appreciated that she was watching a consummate professional at the peak of her powers. If she was to imprint her own presence on the proceedings she was going to need a proper drink. She worked her way round to the bar, doing her best not to be jostled by everyone en route, nor to apologise for being in their way, but to look like a woman with a purpose.

The bar was manned by a brace of sylphlike black youths in robes and beaded skullcaps. They were serving American cocktails, champagne or fruit juice. Furnished with champagne, Katie gathered herself for the assault on Ava Lawrence.

'It's Katie, isn't it?'

It was Gavin's brother, Sebastian. 'Good heavens, hallo!'

He was drinking Coke from a classic, grooved bottle. His hair was seraphically blond, but his T-shirt had the words 'New Laid' over the left nipple. Katie liked Sebastian – he was so relaxed. She did not anticipate any awkwardness.

'What brings you here?' she asked.

'Purely social, you know.'

'What an exciting life you must lead.'

'Not really. What about you?'

'I'm here for the *Post* – I work on the diary page. For Larry Orde . . .?'

'Blimey.' Sebastian drained the Coke and put the bottle down on the bar. 'That wanker.'

'You know him?'

'Don't need to. I've read his page.'

Katie felt a little miffed. 'What do you expect of a diary?'

'Yeah, you're right,' said Sebastian. He gave her a sudden,

disarming grin, fished out a crumpled packet of Marlboros from his jeans and when she refused, took a cigarette from the packet with his lips, and accepted a light from one of the barmen.

'You split with Gavin, then.'

'Yes . . . a shame – but one of those things . . .'

'He can be a right bastard.' Katie thought she detected something admiring in Sebastian's tone. 'All he cares about is that pretentious chophouse of his. You're better off out of it.'

'We had some good times,' she said stoutly. 'I don't regret anything.'

'*Non, rien de rien* . . .!' warbled Sebastian.

Katie was not sure whose side he was on. 'How is he, anyway?'

'Fine so far as I know. Just got back from France, visiting Julian.'

'I'm glad to hear it, he needed a holiday.'

Sebastian blew a couple of smoke rings. 'Rumour has it there's a new woman.'

Katie rode the punch. 'I'm so pleased,' she said, and hoped that her eyes weren't watering. 'He deserves someone nice.'

'Do me a favour,' said Sebastian, amiably enough. 'He deserves shit.'

'Oh well . . .' Katie gulped at her drink. 'So who do you know here?'

'Apart from Ava, only you.'

'You know Ava Lawrence?'

'I wouldn't be here otherwise, take my word for it.' Sebastian dropped his half-smoked cigarette into an empty glass. 'Do you want to speak to her?'

'It's my main objective. I was psyching myself up for the approach when you said hallo.'

'Come on then, I'll introduce you.'

Larry was tickled pink.

'Good girl. She really played ball.'

'I was lucky, we got on.'

'Obviously,' said Larry. 'And who's this "mutual friend" who said she'd be spending more time this side of the pond?'

'Trade secret,' said Katie.

'Petal, I am trade.'

She shook her head. Larry laughed.

'Fair dos, why should a girl reveal her sources? Anyway, it's a nice little piece.'

The following day Katie met Hester Blake in the corridor. Hester stopped to chat in her usual friendly way.

'I gather you did great things with Ava Lawrence.'

'Oh, I don't know about that . . .'

. 'Larry does. He thinks you're a smart cookie.'

Katie glowed with pride.

'I was invited to go and hear her speak the other night,' Hester went on, and then hesitated. 'But I couldn't make it. Is she as gorgeous as everybody says?'

'Unfortunately, yes.'

'How sickening.' Hester touched her arm confidentially. 'We must have a drink very soon so we can commiserate, woman to woman.'

Continuing on her way to Robert Walton's office, Hester was acutely relieved that Katie had not mentioned Ann. Gavin had been on the phone to Giselle until 1 a.m. that morning, and the last thing she wanted to do was to say anything which might inadvertently hurt Katie, who was a poppet.

She and Robert were going out to lunch. She tapped on the door and put her head round. Robert was on the phone. He lifted his eyebrows and one hand at her, to indicate he wouldn't be long. His secretary Di ushered Hester to a seat.

'Would you like a drink, Mrs Blake?' she whispered. Di was a class act, always the soul of discretion and formality. She brought Hester a gin and tonic the way she liked it – long, with a twist of lime, and brimming with ice – and then retreated to her desk, with downcast eyes, and put on headphones.

It was another ten minutes before Robert finished his conversation, but Hester was perfectly happy sitting in one of his cream calfskin armchairs, sipping her drink and savouring the sense of wellbeing and general optimism which had overtaken her recently.

'Thank the Lord.' He put down the receiver and came to stand before her. 'I'm so sorry. Shall we?'

Robert was a son of the manse, *douce* and grave, whose soft voice and level look could bring hardboiled heads of department slinking to heel like whipped pups.

He took Hester to L'Hibou, where they sat at his usual table in the corner next to the window. While they studied the menus he had a scotch, Hester another gin and tonic. They ordered *quenelles* of salmon trout, with new potatoes and fresh vegetables, and a bottle of Pouilly Fumée. They looked at one another with quiet pleasure.

'Two gins,' said Hester. 'How decadent.'

'You think so?'

'Don't you read the foodie writers? Spirits are supposed to bludgeon your taste buds into insensibility, especially before fish.'

Robert gave a small, silent laugh.

'But then again who cares?' added Hester.

'Not I.'

There was often a moment near the beginning of these lunches with Robert when Hester wondered what it was all about, and why she had been invited. Indeed there had been times in the past when she had spent the whole lunch waiting for Robert to get to the point – to come out and say whatever he wanted to say. It had only recently begun to dawn on her that he asked her simply because he wished to be in her company. And she was now sufficiently attuned to his behaviour to suspect that his reticence spoke volumes. It was as if he took for granted that there was something between them, something mutually acknowledged but left unexplored.

His wife, Fiona, was one of the great and the good, trustee of numerous charities, tireless fundraiser, and a prominent member of the Howard League. Both Robert and Fiona had appeared on *Question Time* but Fiona was reckoned to have done better. She was a big, fresh-faced woman who looked a little older than her husband, ample but elegant, exuding a shrewd warmth and enlightened common sense. She was one of very few women who could wear a plaid stole and get away with it.

Hester had great respect for both Robert and Fiona. And she had a healthy personal morality which she would have been the first to admit was based on self-preservation – she would never do anything damaging or rash. But there was something captivating about these long, reflective lunches. They left her in no doubt that in the field of mature and circumscribed flirtation, less was definitely more. Had anything been made overt through word, look or gesture the spell would have been broken. She had learned that Robert was entertained by her, that he was charmed by a loucheness in her nature of which she was generally a little ashamed. And she had learned, too, that he kept his counsel. He would talk about work, and about her and about generalities, but very little about himself. He was profoundly reserved. Very occasionally this imbalance made her feel foolish and exposed, as if she were guilelessly giving too much away with nothing in return. She had to remind herself that there was no plot – this was just the way the two of them were. Robert was quiet and close. She was garrulous and open – 'a rattle' he had once called her. It was the secret of their success.

The food was now in front of them, and the wine poured. He raised his glass.

'Hetty – you look marvellous today.'

'Thank you! Must be the gin – or the company, of course.'

'I liked your last piece,' he said, 'concerning Cupid's dart.'

'Oh, that old thing—' she waved a hand airily. 'But I did have a pretext at least.' She told him about Giselle and Gavin. What the story so far lacked in length it made up for in colour and Hester's own speculative angle.

'It's funny,' said Robert, when she'd finished talking and he was politely presiding over the last couple of mouthfuls of his *quenelles*, 'I didn't have you down for a matchmaker.'

'I'm not.'

'You entertain hopes.'

'Not really. If I do they're pretty faint. But our daughter, who was lost to us, is found.'

'To what do you attribute this epiphany?'

'To this new relationship, directly. I mean, let's invert it. Did you ever as a child have a best, best friend, a soulmate, who you were always going to be friends with – when the two of you were destitute you would share your last crust, and when you were rich and famous you'd attend each other's premières, and all that kind of thing—?' Robert favoured her with his close, amused smile. 'Well, maybe you didn't, maybe it's more common among girls, but at the time you think you're going to stay friends till hell freezes over, you stand in the corner of the playground and try terribly hard to prick your fingers so that you can become blood brothers, and you say the most appalling things about other perfectly innocent children because that's all part of the bonding process. And rather surprisingly the friendship *does* continue. It bumps along, sometimes in the background, sometimes coming to the fore, but still there until – wham!'

'Wham . . .' echoed Robert thoughtfully, filling Hester's glass.

'Your friend takes up with, and ultimately marries, the most god-awful creep it has ever been your misfortune to encounter. So now they're a couple, an item, and you find yourself looking at this man and wondering what in the name of all that's holy she sees in him. And the worm of doubt enters your heart. It's the beginning of the end. Because if she can harbour such tender feelings for this nerd, or bastard, or wimp or brute, such incandescent passion that she wants to spend the rest of her life with him, then it follows that there was a part of her you never knew. She has become a stranger overnight. Do you see?'

'I do,' said Robert. 'But I also recall that you said this was an inversion.'

'Yes, because the opposite is true, too. With my daughter and her new bloke it's as if a part of her I was sure was there somewhere, underneath all the grunge and the hostility, has suddenly burst through and restored my faith in human nature. Like the desert blossoming as the rose . . .'

Robert glanced up from under his eyebrows at Hester. 'I hope you're not making the mistake of expecting her to be like you.'

'I don't *think* I am. But it's nice that she can be attracted to a fully paid-up member of the human race – a charming man – and he to her.'

'M-hm. . .' Robert considered this as Hester renewed her attack on the cooling *quenelles*. 'My own daughter's husband was a charming man. So charming in fact that he was able to keep two marriages alive simultaneously. Beware charm, Hetty – it can be a poison chalice.'

Hester looked at him in astonishment. It was the closest thing to a confidence Robert had ever uttered. And for once his eyes did not meet hers but fixed themselves on some point outside the window.

'As to friendships,' he went on, 'I'm not one of those who feel they can't live without them. But it seems to me one can set greater store by those forged in adulthood. There's less of the journey remaining, if you follow me.'

Hester laid down her knife and fork. 'You mean there's less time left for things to go wrong.'

'No. Fewer changes to be encompassed.'

'That's true,' said Hester. Their eyes met, and held for a few seconds, until the swift hands of the waiter intervened.

Gavin conducted a regular meeting with the senior staff of Schmooze at 8 a.m. on alternate Monday mornings, the only day of the week when the brasserie was not open till lunchtime. At today's meeting he intended being a pussycat – that would take the ground out from under the feet of the whingers. He liked to keep his colleagues on their toes. If there was one thing he couldn't stand it was complacency.

He got in early – the Schmooze premises were only a five-minute car journey from Paddington, and there was adequate parking for selected personnel at the back of the building. He could have walked, but Gavin's mind was of the cast which discounted healthy, prudent alternatives on principle, and readily acknowledged the role of the car as a testosterone fix. He drove fast and aggressively and parked with an antisocial disregard for the needs of others in an overcrowded city. Displayed in the kitchen at George Street was a spaghetti jar stuffed to capacity with parking tickets.

The side street where Schmooze had its premises was in Maida Vale, off Warwick Avenue, an enclave which retained, amid the solidly upward aspirations of its surroundings, a raffishness in keeping with the area's past, when no streetlamp was without its attendant group of tarts, and dusk brought out the kerb-crawling cars with sidelights only. The brasserie occupied the broad frontage of what had once been an 'art' cinema, with on one side an employment agency and on the other an Indian clothes mart. With these neighbours Gavin maintained the coolest relations allowed by politeness – you never knew when you might need a favour.

Ranjit, the proprietor of Sari Select, was a surly, ambitious and tirelessly entrepreneurial Bangladeshi, whose numerous contacts in areas such as adult videos and recreational substances enabled him to drive in from St John's Wood each day in a Jaguar XRS. He was sufficiently astute to know that conspicuous wealth can be unhealthy, and would always park the Jag a little way up the road, deputing scurrying minions to feed the meter at intervals. His silk suit draped on a hanger in his office, Ranjit sat pasty and heavy-eyed, dressed in a rancid nylon vest and stained tracksuit bottoms, surrounded by sunbursts of brilliant cloth and rich embroidery – a fat spider at the centre of a web of shady deals.

The agency, Just the Job, had its uses. There was a brisk turnover among the junior staff at Schmooze. Gavin, who as owner believed that his flair and business acumen had earned him a certain licence, did not tolerate fools gladly, and there were times when he was pushed to the limit by the perceived incompetence of those around him. On these occasions he would administer a verbal pistol-whipping which few could withstand, often in front of customers. Tearstained girls and white-faced youths fled his employ at regular intervals, and Just the Job – whose elderly lady manager was susceptible to flattery and a special table at lunch – could be called on for temporary replacements at a moment's notice.

Letting himself in at the back door, Gavin walked through the gleaming, state-of-the-art kitchen and burst, John Wayne-like, through the swing doors into the brasserie itself – his undisputed domain. It never failed to give him a rush.

Gavin's background was in, first, public relations, then magazines. The impulse to start a restaurant had been born not of a passion for food, but from the restless conviction that he knew how to launch, target and promote a product. He observed the kind of restaurants his contemporaries favoured, and began there and then to formulate the idea which became Schmooze. It was a big idea, and complex – although to Gavin the whole was stunningly simple. Getting the finance together had been a sweat, because of the difficulty of persuading the bank that a restaurant could be so many different things and yet retain an organic identity, absolutely guaranteed to appeal to large numbers of A/B spenders in their twenties and thirties.

His business plan had posited a brasserie that was also a 'destination restaurant' (the argot had come naturally to him) . . . a hang-out for creatives . . . clubby in atmosphere but without a club's attendant cliquishness . . . a local drop-in with a community feel . . . and a cafe in the Vienna/Budapest tradition, where people could read the paper and drink good coffee any time, any day, all day . . . Of course, if it was to fulfil all these criteria and still turn a profit, it had to be *big*. Gavin retained a boyish fondness for railway stations: their lofty resounding spaces and purposeful clamour; the sense they gave of intense emotional interaction lent a curious privacy by noise and bustle; of a thousand different lives crossing and re-crossing at different paces and with different destinations – he was a romantic about his work.

And now that his vision – so hard to convey successfully in words – was reality, it had been proved triumphantly right. Hands in pockets, he strolled between the tables in the early, blind-shrouded half-light, and when he reached the centre of the room lit a cigarette and turned slowly, inhaling deep and long on his success.

Schmooze was several thousand cubic feet of wonderful, atmospheric space, high-ceilinged, the floor on different levels, the separate areas melting into one another with an artless, unforced ease, the achieving of which had brought a handful of top architects to breaking point. Gavin had hired and fired with reckless arrogance: he knew what he wanted, he knew it would work.

The décor was strong, plain and uncluttered. Bare wooden floors, plenty of space between the tables and chairs – but the tables were just the right height and all the chairs were padded, with arms. Paper cloths were whipped away and replaced. There were no flowers on the tables, but numerous vases of huge blooms – real and artificial – stood about, and tall plants were clustered round the soaring wooden pillars. On the walls were big mirrors, and densely grouped framed photographs – all of people, all monochrome, from all sources and periods – so that customers were confirmed not in their exclusivity, but in their awareness of belonging to a human family (a tactic which resulted, as Gavin had intended, in a warm, self-congratulatory sense of exclusivity). The bar was about three-feet above the main eating area – Gavin remembered old black and white movies where people doing deals and making trysts looked down on a vista of other heads. There were no smoking restrictions and anything on the menu could be ordered at any time of day. No-one who was not actually throwing up, mainlining or attacking a fellow diner was ever asked to leave. The impression was of a generous, practical, infinitely flexible and accommodating place, whose vast motor, working at full throttle, enabled rushed people to relax, and whose functional, uncluttered comfort let bright people shine.

Gavin considered himself passionate, a man of strong emotions and intense feelings. But the purest passion and the deepest emotion he had ever experienced had been in the conception, execution and running of this brasserie. As he went up to his first-floor office he had a hard-on.

Gavin's office décor was minimalist, but its austerity was the only quality it shared with the floor below. The disparity between his business surroundings and his product confused and intrigued people, which was how he liked it. Up here all was sleek, sparse elegance, the kind of expense which proclaims itself by conspicuous restraint. Grey leather and chrome, smoked glass, grey self-printed silk on the walls, plain ivory silk blinds, concealed lighting and, always, white tulips in a heavy glass cylindrical vase. This was where Gavin himself saw colleagues, employees and petitioners. Everything to do with the nuts and bolts of the business was in Bar's office next door.

Bar, his latest PA, had been with him for nearly three months. She was a stout, ruddy northern girl to whom sarcasm and invective were water off a duck's back. There was a possibility, faint but real, that she was up to the job.

This irritated Gavin rather, for on her own admission Bar was only slumming in his employ, doing a 'fun' job while deciding what might attract her in the long term.

This morning Gavin had made himself a second cup of espresso by ten to eight, when Bar arrived. For all her 2:1 in Modern Languages, she was an indifferent timekeeper. He glanced through the adjoining door as she came in, but forbore to say anything. This, he reminded himself, was one of his good days.

'Morning!' she called breezily, dumping her raffia holdall on her desk and rummaging in it for the bottle of Freshly Squeezed Orange Juice without which she could not begin to function. 'How's sir this morning?'

'Good, thanks – yourself?'

'Better now – aah!' Bar smacked her lips. 'So—' She swung her chair round and sat down. 'What's to do?'

Her manner was breezy. It irritated Gavin. On the other hand she was cheerful and competent and impervious to shock. He entertained an unsettling picture of Bar never finding the long-term job, and being here ad infinition gulping juice, laughing loudly, making light of the brasserie . . .

'Board,' he said.

'You will be!'

He ignored this. 'Will you chase up the plants people, and draft a press release about one year, one star, the most meteoric success in town.'

'Ay-ay,' said Bar.

'Any personal calls—' The phone rang and Bar lifted it, one hand over the mouthpiece, '—I'm not in,' he concluded in a stage whisper.

Bar nodded. 'Schmooze . . .? Oh yes, hallo. It is, yes, clever of you to remember. If you'll hang on for one minute I'll see if he's around.' She put her hand back over the mouthpiece. Gavin scowled furiously. 'I know, I know, but it's your mama.'

He hesitated only momentarily before picking up the receiver on his own desk. 'Yes?'

'I hope you'll forgive me for ringing you at work,' said Ann in her most businesslike and un-clucky voice, 'but I wanted to know whether there was anything I could pick up for you at the supermarket. I shall be going there this morning, and there's a client I have to visit near George Street on my way back. I could drop by and leave it in the kitchen for you.'

'Sure,' said Gavin. He glanced at Bar, who was busy opening the mail. 'That might be useful. Are you at home?'

'I am for the next – oh, ten minutes?'

'I'll fax you.'

'Certainly,' said Ann.

'I must dash – staff meeting.'

'I'll await your instructions.'

Gavin put the phone down and scribbled a list. His mother's custom was to leave not a till receipt but a handwritten note with a generously rounded-down sum, so it was worth adding a few little extras. Besides which, he was doing her a favour. He knew her game. She was eaten up with curiosity about Giselle, and this was the first tentative probe in the post-France investigation. A snoop round the flat was what she was after.

He added frozen king prawns to the list and went into Bar's office, standing with his back to her as it stuttered through the fax. Della opened the door on his side.

'Hi, Brains – ready for us?' Ewan, the head chef and assorted others were at her shoulder.

'I'll be right with you,' said Gavin. Ignoring the sunnily smiling Bar he took the used sheet from the fax, tore it into four and returned to his desk, closing the connecting door behind him.

* * *

Ann unloaded the large box from the back seat of the Honda – her own shopping was in the boot – locked the car and carried the box to the front door. Gavin's single pint of full cream milk was on the step, and she put that in the box too before unlocking the door. Then she picked up the box, pushed the door shut with her heel, and went up the stairs.

Ann had always had keys to the boys' flats. It was sensible, in case of emergency, that one spare key should be lodged with a neighbour and another with the family. Julian, before he left for France, had been sharing a rented place in Camden, and the key of that had now reverted to the landlord.

Ann would never, ever, have abused this trust. If for any reason she did wish to gain access she always contacted the son in question and sought permission. It was vitally important for each of them to feel he had his own separate and inviolable space.

Now she let herself in, and carried the box of shopping through to the kichen. Apart from being a little stuffy, the flat was respectable. Gavin had always been tidy. Even as a child he had displayed a feeling for his surroundings, and tried to make them nice (this was when he wasn't hurling toys across the room in a fury). The place only became a tip when his work was in overdrive, and then you could hardly blame him. In fact, these were the only times when Ann did take the liberty of coming over and having a little whoosh round with a hoover and a damp cloth. Today, she put the shopping away in the cupboards and the fridge, and threw away one or two things she found there which looked rather past their best. For someone in the catering business Gavin was surprisingly indifferent to, and careless with food. At the brasserie food was a concept, at home it was merely fuel. There seemed to be little real pleasure attached to it.

Mensa was dropping sinuous hints, so she put down a saucer of milk and another of Kitti-Crunch. That dealt with, she tore a sheet from Gavin's apple-shaped memo-block and wrote a brief note telling him the approximate cost of the shopping. Remembering that tomorrow was rubbish day in this area, she removed the contents of the overflowing swing bin, and put the bag – tied at the top – near the door to take down with her when she left.

She allowed herself a brief glance at the cork pin-board by the wall-phone in the hall. Katie's picture had gone. The only photograph was a postcard reproduction of a Cartier-Bresson couple kissing in the street. The remaining items on the noticeboard were a sheaf of bills about to burst free of their drawing pin, an outdated Labour election address, a cutting from *Time Out* about a new alternative comedy club, and a list of useful telephone numbers put there some time ago by herself.

She went to the sitting room, taking a peep into the bedroom and bathroom on the way. Neither vouchsafed any startling revelations, although she noticed more evidence than was acceptable of smoking in bed, a habit which worried her in someone like Gavin, who was often so exhausted he could drop off in mid-sentence. It might be advisable to have a quiet word. And a smoke alarm would be in order as well. She could not imagine why she had not thought of it before.

In the sitting room she opened the windows, and collected up the old newspapers, putting them by the binbag in the hall. She filled a milk jug with cold water and watered the plants, being careful not to repeat her famous mistake of soaking the silk fig tree in the corner. It was a beautiful piece, the leaves a tremulous silvery green, and the trunk and branches coated with real bark. She plumped up the cushions, briskly stacked the scattered videos and debated with herself whether to hoover. She opened the door of the little room off the hall and switched the light on. Gavin was always going on about how he was going to make this room into a work centre, but for the past three years it had been no more than a glory hole, filled to capacity with spare bits of furniture, a broken bicycle, boxes of old files and books, and domestic paraphernalia. The hoover was there, but Ann considered that would be overdoing it. She turned the light off and closed the door.

In spite of herself, she felt a pang of disappointment. She had come here to deliver Gavin's shopping, and for that reason only. But it would have been nice to stumble across some evidence of a new relationship – a snapshot, a message, a phone number pinned to the board: Chuffington 720311 . . . That reminded her that Hester had not been in touch, which frankly surprised her. Did that mean there was no news, or had she simply not got round to it? Gavin had said nothing, and she would not lower herself to ask directly – his personal life was his own, after all. It had been very unlike him to mention the meeting with Giselle in the first place . . . Ann craved information.

She was closing the sitting room windows again, preparatory to leaving, when the phone rang.

It gave three rings, and then the answering machine cut in, with Gavin's slightly lowered voice explaining that he wasn't there at present (Ann shook her head, she had warned him several times about that) and asking the caller to leave their message after the long tone.

Ann wasn't listening, she was adjusting the strap of her shoulder bag so that it would be easier to carry the rubbish. But the fact remained she was still standing in the hall when Giselle spoke:

'Hi. It's me, returning your call. You didn't give me your work number, dickhead – speak to you soon. Bye.'

Ann went out of the flat and down the stairs with wings on her feet. If the girl was calling Gavin a dickhead they must be fairly intimate. She was halfway to Raglan Road before she remembered she'd left the rubbish bag in the hall.

CHAPTER NINE

Schmooze Inc.
Fax transmission from Gavin Armitage

TO: Zelda
FROM: Gavin
DATE: August 3rd.
TIME: 8 a.m.
NO. OF PAGES INCLUDING THIS ONE: Who knows . . ?

My darling . . . yes, I know you'll still be stewing in that pit of yours, but I had to make contact with you. I wonder if you have any idea how hopelessly, desperately besotted I am? You're so good for me, Zelda, I feel as if at long last I may get my emotional act together, if you'll help me. What are your plans for the autumn? May I dare to hope that you might come down and be with me in London? You say you have no qualifications, but I'm certain you could find work down here, and we could be together, as I'm sure we're meant to be. Hell, am I being obsessive? If so, it's only because I find it so hard to think of anything else. God knows what I'll do when your parents get back from Greece and I can't send you these letters whenever I feel like it – your mother's great, but I wouldn't want to end up as column-fodder. Will you come down at the weekend? I need to see you – did I mention that sex with you has been a revelation? I must have done, but it bears repeating. I get horny just writing it. I'd better change the subject before my stout secretary gets here and thinks she's in with a chance . . . If you were to come, I'd make time, I promise. We could go to The Joke Shop and hear that foul-mouthed woman you liked so much last time. There are supplies of beer in the fridge. We can eat pizza for breakfast if you like. I'll watch Mask *for the umpteenth time. I miss you like crazy—*

G.

P.S. I'll try and ring you from work tonight, after eight. If you're not going to be there – why not? – then please, please, call me first.

Fax transmission from Hester Blake

TO: GA
FROM: GB
DATE:
TIME:
NO. OF PAGES:

I'll come at the weekend if I can. I could just fancy a couple of days away from this lot. Ditto, ditto, don't know what to say, I'm not good at this sort of thing. Speak to you tonight. G4G. XXX

Thursday a.m.

Bar—

1. Mail. Use your initiative but do <u>not</u> respond to invoices pro tem.
2. Send flowers to usual person/address. Check last time and make sure they're different, but same approx. price. Card just 'G'.
3. Formal note to Ranjit – wording up to you, message that we're not his personal answering service. His wide boys turned up at kitchen entrance night before last. Not appreciated.

Cheers. Gavin.

30/7/92

Girls – hate to tell you, but it's heavenly here. The heat would be unbearable, but up here in the hills we're laughing. At the beach in ten minutes, early till eleven, then four till six. We're so brown it's obscene, and I've put on weight – it's a tough job but somebody's got to do it . . . Hope Daniel's okay. Look after selves and house – M & D X

7 Raglan Road
London W11

August 8th

Dear Hester,

I know how hectic it is when one is first returned from holiday and getting back into harness, so rather than telephone I thought I'd drop you a brief line to keep you abreast of events at this end. It would appear that the Grand Passion has well and truly taken off – Gavin is typically playing things very close to his chest, but I have it on good authority (Sebastian) that this relationship is the light of his life. My feeling – and I know Byron agrees with me on this – is that whatever the outcome it can only be beneficial to both of them. The disparities in age and experience, about which I know you have perfectly valid concerns, can only be of mutual benefit to them, and the various personal difficulties they have both encountered in their short lives have undoubtedly given them insights into the difficulties of others. I am sure that Gavin derives much that is positive from Giselle, and that he in his turn has much to offer her. You and I have – dare I say it – successful marriages, and so we know that the secret of an enduring relationship is growth. These two young people, because of their differences, have a special opportunity to grow and change together. Gavin, though a high achiever in other spheres, has found personal happiness elusive. I honestly believe that in Giselle – of whom you know I have always been fond – he may have found the means of attaining it.

Don't think for one moment that I am loading this youthful romance with too great a burden of maternal expectation. Gavin and Giselle must have their freedom above all else, but I can't deny that this happy coincidence is a source of considerable quiet pleasure to both myself and Byron.

Now then – what chance that you and Jonty could come down to pot-luck at Raglan Road, say the first Saturday in September, when you should have a reasonable journey in. I'm taking Byron on a cycling tour in Denmark at the end of September – not our most adventurous holiday but one which we both hope will get us back in trim before the winter. It would be so nice to see you both before then. I shan't invite anyone else, so if we want *to discuss family matters we shall be free to do so.*

I hope you had a marvellous holiday. We remember our own idyll in the Peloponnese as being a uniquely rewarding experience.

                              Yours,
                              Ann

Monday

Mum said be in touch, so I am. Pissing down but having a great time. Talent not all that, but Muffer's scored. The place on here's not where we are, so don't come looking.

                              Daniel.

The Old Clink, Chuffington, Near Forbridge, Essex

10/8/92

Dear Ann

Thanks for your nice letter – I'm actually breaking with precedent and replying in kind, because what with clients and your lodger I never know what will be a good time to get you. Yes, we'd love to come to dinner that Saturday, and will look forward to it.

As to our very own Abelard and Eloise, Giselle certainly seems very taken up with the whole thing, and her appearance has altered out of all recognition, so there is a God! We haven't seen that much of Gavin because they quite understandably prefer to get together in London due to his pressure of work and where they have some privacy, but he's been out for the odd Sunday lunch – flowers for the cook, already! I agree that it's very good for Giselle, but I'm also afraid it may all end in tears, and the tears are likely to be hers. No criticism of Gavin – just the most probable scenario.

Still, everyone's happy at the moment, so we're not about to rock the boat. Look forward to seeing you soon,

Love,
Hester

Came round but you weren't answering. Saw the car outside – so what were you doing, you dirty little bugger? If you're really good I'll let you buy me a drink some other time.
                          Sebastian.

RELAX . . .
          ESCAPE
                    INTO
                         KNOWLEDGE
                                   INTERNAL . . .

You're lucky – you live in an area where it's possible to find peace through REIKI.

REIKI is an alternative form of healing therapy.

REIKI will help you to know your other self – the other self that is tense, frightened, angry or depressed. Learn to take your other self by the hand and lead it back into the warmth and the light. Leonard Arkwright is a Senior REIKI Master, and from the beginning of September he will be available for consultation in the Morris Room at the Barlow Community Centre from 10 a.m. to 4 p.m. on Saturdays, and from 6-8 p.m. on Wednesdays.

To book a consultation, or if you simply want to know more about

REIKI, call Leonard Arkwright on Forbridge 910375.

THROW AWAY THE PILLS, AND CALL – IT COULD CHANGE YOUR LIFE.

The Old Clink, Chuffington, Near Forbridge, Essex

Sept. 2nd

Dear Ann,

Just a line to say many thanks to you both for a lovely evening. I must have enjoyed myself – I had a head like a bucket on Sunday! It was nice to see Julian again after so many years, and you must be pleased to have him back for a while, even if he is nursing a broken heart.

You might be interested to know that Giselle has got an interview for a part-time job (!) at a health food shop (!!) somewhere near Gavin's flat (!!!) So even if the course of true love doesn't run smooth, it may be the means of getting her back into salaried employ – wonders will never cease.

Thanks again, and good pedalling if we don't speak again before you go,

> Love,
>> Hester

September 6th

Dearest Sebby,

You and I have known for a while that I could not stay for ever. I love England and I adore being with you, but I have commitments in New York which I can no longer ignore. Please forgive this note – I wasn't sure my resolve would hold up if I had to say this to your face. We had fun, didn't we? Don't forget if you're ever in the States to look me up, and I hope I may always do the same. We shouldn't let a good thing go to waste.

Here's to you, my own little Roger Rabbit. Have a great life.

Ava

THE HESTER BLAKE PAGE

Summer's over. The leaves aren't actually falling yet, but the swallows are massing and jabbering like kids in a bus shelter. The goal posts are in position alongside the cricket square. Most of us have got the exacting ritual of the annual holiday safely out of the way for another year. The light is becoming a lot kinder to those parts of the house which have needed painting for years. And it's impossible to get hold of the chimney sweep because half the county have suddenly realised they'd better book him quick or risk self-immolation. (The other half had their chimneys swept in June – they presumably are the same people who bought their Christmas cards in the January sales and made two fruit cakes in August, just in case.)

But I like the autumn. Those 'Back to School' signs in the shop windows which spread so much gloom among the young give parental spirits a real lift. Even now that I don't have one child left at school (yes, I lost the battle over A levels) there is a buzz to be had from the knowledge that things are getting back to normal. I experience the urge to straighten my desk and sharpen my pencils. After the social wasteland of August the village is humming again – committees meet, dates are set, bookings are made. My resolve never, but ever, to sit on another such committee, begins to waver. In autumn, it's nice to be part of things.

Forget the spring, pale and insipid and usually freezing. Autumn's the time for tidying up and making resolutions, and lighting the fire, and falling in love . . .

Pats –

Read this somewhere quiet, will you? I've been thinking about you – and about us – such a lot lately. It's quite simple: I miss you. You were right, as always, we did have something special. You were also right to be tough on me – I like a woman with a firm hand . . . You're a great girl, Pats, and we were good together. We shouldn't let a good thing go to waste.

You know where to get hold of me. You always did . . . and how!
                                        X Sebastian

4 Rue Mairie
Montaigle
Tarn et Lotte
14 Septembre

My dear Julian,

I shall write a very short letter, because there is only a little to say. Why did you go and not to say anything to me? I was very sad, but now I am very mad. I should like to kill you, and so would my father. You are a pig and a bastard,

Yours faithfully,
Lisette

13/9/92

Dear Mrs Armitage,

I have written this note instead of speaking to you in person because I am rather embarrassed about what I have to say. For a long time I have wanted to further my education, as you know, because we have talked about it. Working for you has made me realise that I could do a lot more. I thought Ava Lawrence's talk in the summer was really interesting and inspiring and it made me think seriously about doing some more studying. To cut a long story short I have begun an Open University degree course in Social Studies. The first module is called 'The Changing Family'. My tutor seems very nice and is encouraging about my work, but there is a lot to do. Would it be possible for me to alter the times that I work for you, so that I do two longer sessions on Tuesday and Thursday instead of the three shorter ones? There are also some questions I would like to ask you as part of a survey we have got to do.

I do hope this will be all right, and not be an inconvenience to you,

Yours sincerely,
Josette Devine

7 Raglan Road
London W11

Mr V. Paretska
'Good and Healthy'
Ladysmith Road
London W2   *September 13th 1992*

Dear Mr Paretska
                    Re: Miss Giselle Blake
Thank you for your letter. I have known Miss Blake for most of her life and know her to be a young woman of great character and energy. Since leaving school she has concentrated on widening her horizons with a variety of part-time jobs, and has spent the summer in France, travelling and improving her spoken French. She has always shown a keen interest in alternative therapy and diet.

Miss Blake is a direct and forceful person who can nonetheless relate well to a wide cross-section of people. I have no hesitation in recommending her for the job in question.

                    Yours faithfully,
                    Byron Armitage

The Old Clink, Chuffington, Near Forbridge, Essex

Sept.17

Dear Byron,

Thanks for playing the white man vis-à-vis the reference for Grizzle. I'm happy to say that your efforts have paid off, and she starts at the end of the week. I experienced an infinitesimal twinge of conscience over the exploitation of her previous swain under the headings of 'alternative therapy' and 'wide cross-section of people'; but you displayed a masterly deftness of touch. You must let me treat you to a spot of lunch, by way of thanks.

I trust you and yours are well – does Gavin have any idea what he's letting himself in for? Grizzle's barely housetrained, let alone conversant with the domestic arts . . . I suppose love conquers all.

Have a good holiday – tell Ann a man of your years and weight shouldn't do more than two miles a day . . .

All the best,

Jonty

P.S. What about the squad for the tour down under? They might as well send the Chuffington Brownie pack.

LEONARD ARKWRIGHT
REIKI MASTER

September 15

Dear Zelda,
How's it going? This is to say that as far as I'm concerned there's no hard feelings, and I hope if our paths crossed tomorrow we could still be friends. I'm sorry you wanted someone else more than me – that hurt. But I still want you to be happy so I hope he's good to you.

I washed up at the café for a bit to earn some bread, and got a lift with a bloke who played Jim Reeves all the way to Calais. I've started the practice, and have picked up a few regular clients. If you ever feel the need to make use of my skills, they are at your disposal, without prejudice.

I don't know if you're still living at home, but I expect your Mum will pass this on to wherever you are. There's no need to write back, but if you do, don't worry, it won't make anything heavy.

Good luck Zelda, and remember, you got a friend.

Ark

The Old Clink, Chuffington, Near Forbridge, Essex

September 16th

Darling Jez,

You have no <u>idea</u> how much I'm looking forward to seeing you again. It is a madhouse here. Daniel has got a job sticking prices on at Tesco's which appears to have given him brain fever, which in turn means he cannot so much as carry a mug from one room to another . . . Grizzle's going to live in London with her smart new bloke (have you heard of that new place 'Schmooze'? Well he owns it!) Mum is getting overwrought about the whole thing. I can't imagine why when she and Dad have done little else for ages but dream about Griz moving out. The job at Crabtree and Curwen is okay, and I have saved a bit, but LA Law it's not. I'll be down in ten days' time, and I can't wait. Get in a bottle of champagne and let's celebrate. Love you lots –

Your Rose

Fax transmission from Hester Blake

TO: GA
FROM: GB
DATE:
TIME:
NO. OF PAGES:

Gav – Mum's giving me a lift down tonight with my stuff, can you be there to give us a hand your end? I start work tomorrow.

G4G X

Schmooze Inc.
Fax transmission from Gavin Armitage

TO: *Zelda*
FROM: *Gavin*
DATE: *Sept. 16th*
TIME: *3.25 pm*
NO. OF PAGES INCLUDING THIS ONE: One

Dearest Zelda
   Got back from a tedious lunch to find your fax waiting. Aargh! I wish you'd let me know sooner about tonight – Della and I've got a meeting down in Knightsbridge with Arnold Loebl. He's insufferable, but vital to our expansion plans, so it's a three-line whip. Will you and your Mum be able to manage? If not, leave the heavy stuff in the hall and I'll get Sebastian to get his arse in gear to give me a hand tomorrow.
   Can't believe you'll actually be there when I get home tonight.
                     Love you loads,
                         G XXX

Byron – I have to attend a seminar at the Crabtree at 4.15 so this is in extreme haste. Gavin has been on the phone, distressed because Hester is bringing Giselle and her possessions down to George Street this evening and he is prevented from being there by a vital meeting. Would you very kindly pop across and assist the exercise? Julian is going to the theatre.

On the kitchen table there is a carton of vichyssoisse and some garlic bread out of the freezer, plus a short welcome note for Giselle. Please take them with you. Cold cuts and insalata tricolore for you and WWS on the side – Ann

Seventh Heaven

My dearest . . .

You looked so peaceful I couldn't bring myself to wake you. But just in case, I've set the clock-radio for seven-thirty – you don't want to be late on your first day.

My only worry is, can we keep the pace up? You're in danger of making a happy man very old . . .

Love you loads,

G XXX

Sept. 17th.

—*arrange session with Josette re: parent profiling*
—*Julian – arrange view flat Belvedere Rd*
—*Sebastian – finances*
—*Shoes – holiday*
—*Byron – Doc – pre-holiday*
—*Locate Good and Healthy for future ref.*

CHAPTER TEN

Giselle worked mornings only at Good and Healthy, from 8.30 to 1 p.m. and on those rare occasions when Mr Paretska was unable to be in the shop for whatever reason. She had survived the month's trial – it was the longest she had ever been in a job – and was earning £3 an hour, cash, and no questions asked. Once a fortnight she took a day return to Forbridge, signed on and collected her giro at Chuffington sub-post office.

She was surprised at how time had slipped by. Something perilously like a routine was emerging. Gavin woke up at six, but had a twenty-minute 'snooze' interval on the clock-radio, during which he ardently pressed his suit with the still comatose Giselle. He then got up and had a shower, made himself black coffee from the espresso machine which had been his last birthday present from Ann and Byron, and brought his cup back into the bedroom while he got dressed to the accompaniment of Capital Radio. Once dressed he had another cup of coffee, smoked a cigarette, and made Giselle a cup of strong tea with milk and sugar. This he placed by the bedside along with a plate bearing two Maryland cookies, and turned the volume of the radio up slightly to maintain her level of consciousness. He then kissed her and was out of the door by seven.

On Sundays he got up at the same time and went to buy the Sunday papers. Sometimes he made brunch, and brought it to her on a tray at 11 a.m., complete with toast in a toast rack and a flower in a tumbler. On these occasions Giselle (who was not a morning person, even on a weekday) sat up and did her best to seem appreciative.

On weekdays, the sound of the front door closing behind him and the bang of the street door as he left the house occasioned a surge of relief. With practised economy of movement she slurped her tea and munched her biscuits, and then poured the sweet, cooling dregs on to the plate for the waiting Mensa. It was a ten-minute walk to the shop, and she needed only fifteen minutes to get ready, so this interval was her own time.

Every day when she first got up she wondered where all her stuff had gone. There had seemed to be so much of it when she and Hester had brought it down, and, with Byron's help, had carted it into the flat. But somehow her things had been subsumed in Gavin's. Even left lying about as they generally were they made little impression. This place was his – his taste, his experience, his possessions, his rubbish, his food. There was a sense of everything having been carefully chosen, quite unlike the hotch-potch of accumulations in The Old Clink. Some of it she liked, some she didn't. She wouldn't have called it homely, but that was hardly surprising when he spent so little time there. He had a nice bed made of bamboo, and his bedlinen was white, patterned with bamboo in shades of green. When she spilt her tea on the duvet, she felt obliged to turn it upside down and end to end to hide the stain. Gavin had no washing machine, but used a laundry service: he put out shirts, towels, sheets, boxer shorts and socks in a box once a week and they were returned immaculately fresh and pressed two days later. When she added her own things to the pile, lo! they too were transformed, many of them looking better than they had in years.

Gavin's décor was stylish and thought-through. All the windows had rattan blinds, and the carpeting was pale green throughout. The kitchen had wriggly terracotta tiles on the floor, white scandinavian storage units with recessed handles, and an enormous number of gadgets, including a pasta-maker which actually looked as if it had been used, and a toasted-sandwich-maker (which looked as if it hadn't until Giselle got there).

The bathroom was a bower of plants and mirrors which made taking a bath feel like a dip in a tropical pool. It was small, and the shower was in the bath – she had once made the mistake of turning on the tap without checking its orientation, and had got deluged from above. In the loo there was a pile of magazines – *Viz*, *Harper's*, *Time Out* and *GQ* – and on the back of the door a cluster of photographs. These showed Gavin eating in restaurants, drinking at parties, lounging on boats, receiving certificates and awards, and shaking hands with a bespectacled politician she recognised but could not name. The girls who featured in the photographs were mostly blonde and lovely, all sparkling smiles and tossing tresses. There was also a cartoon of Gavin, drawn on the side of a Gay Hussar menu and signed illegibly by the artist. The cartoon captured something about him which the photographs did not – what a headbanger!

The sitting room had a green and white striped sofa and a plain grey chesterfield with a landslide of giant cushions in Indian prints. One wall was covered in books, mostly on business philosophy and techniques, another with tapes, CDs and videos, a third was taken up with a bay window, and the remaining one, uniquely painted a deep tobacco brown, was covered in framed photographs. These were period pieces – sepia and black and white – of people, singly and in groups, some obviously portraits, others less formal. In answer to her query he explained that the photographs were overspill from the walls of the brasserie, and this explanation was born out by the fact that they were periodically changed. She had so far avoided going to Schmooze. She'd never heard of it before she met Gavin, and the more he told her about it the more convinced she became that it would be full of pseuds and posers and that she wouldn't fit in.

She didn't really fit in here. Her yucca looked moth-eaten next to the silk fig, and her books and clothes seemed scruffy and paltry among Gavin's more numerous and substantial possessions. Only the inflatable man reclined on one of the sofas as if of right, his pinstripes and small, glazed smile utterly unchanged by his altered circumstances. Hester had not been keen on Giselle taking the man with her, and to begin with she hadn't. But she'd missed him, and had travelled all the way down by train and tube with him on her knee because he was a sod to blow up from scratch.

Gavin didn't like him.

'Why can't you have a teddy bear like everyone else?'

'He's kept me company for two years.'

'It's perverted.'

'He's my guardian angel.'

'But you're with me now.'

'Exactly,' she said.

As bosses went – and though Giselle had only scant experience of employment she had a great deal of employers – Mr Paretska scored high. He gave the impression that having decided to take her on (and here she owed much to Byron's reference) he simply assumed she was up to the job and would get on with it without bothering him. He did not trouble her with long lectures about the customer always being right, nor comment on her dress and appearance, nor betray the tiniest interest in her life outside Good and Healthy.

Victor Paretska was a second-generation London Pole, in whom his nation's characteristic romantic melancholy had curdled into a glum misanthropy under the burdens of commerce. He had an old-fashioned heavy moustache, a paunch and drooping eyes, but flashes of the handsome man he must once have been could be glimpsed as he weighed yoghurt brazils, cut wholewheat flans into wedges and turned the vegetarian cheddar good side uppermost.

Health food was not a vocation with him. It was simply a business, bought as a going concern and scarcely changed since the day of purchase. The only addition he had seen fit to make was to the fresh food counter, which now boasted several of Mrs Paretska's home-made delicacies. Ivy was not a Pole, and her most notable contribution was faggots, some of which Giselle took home for Gavin's supper one evening and they agreed were like damp tissues held together with snot.

She dawdled back to the flat after work, wandering in and out of the shops in Queensway, sometimes buying a kebab, or a T-shirt, or earrings. There was nothing to hurry for. All that usually awaited her at George Street was a message from Gavin on the answering machine, proclaiming his undying love and suggesting she drop in at the brasserie, or not bother to wait up. The lively babel in the background of these messages made her wonder how many people heard both protestations, excuses and suggestions, and what they made of them. As she whiled away the hours till his return, eating, reading and watching early-evening soap operas with Mensa enthroned on her stomach, Giselle would consider her situation.

Her removal to London had been a capricious impulse, and once installed she was not at all sure what the terms of her stay were. Gavin was all over her like a rash when he was around, but that was not very often. If she forced herself to look ahead to a few months from now, something she generally preferred not to do, she could not see herself still dividing her time between George Street and

Good and Healthy. For now it was a bit of a laugh, and it got her away from Chuffington and the beaming parents . . . She and Gavin screwed each other senseless at every opportunity, but when he said he'd love her till the end of time she had so far avoided returning the compliment. For one thing, she didn't believe him; and for another, she wouldn't say what wasn't true.

Gavin was not the only one making false assumptions about their relationship. His mother seemed to be taking an unusual interest. Giselle felt as though she had undertaken a small but amusing part in a play, only to find a few weeks into the run that the script was being rewritten to give greater prominence to her role and to accommodate certain key new scenes.

There was, for instance, the Reconnaissance Visit. Ann had called in at Good and Healthy soon after she and Byron returned from Denmark at the end of September.

'Hallo, my dear – how's it going?'

'Fine.' Giselle glanced at Mr Paretska who was re-organising the cold cabinet. 'Can I get you anything?'

Ann smiled understandingly. 'Of course. I'll have a half of three-bean salad.' She added casually: 'By the way, do call me Ann.'

'Right . . .' Giselle dolloped beans into a polystyrene tub. 'Anything else?'

'And two slices of carrot cake – it's one of Byron's favourites and he can afford to indulge after pedalling twenty miles a day for a fortnight.'

Giselle extracted two slices and laid them carefully on greaseproof paper.

'How's it going at George Street?' asked Ann.

'Okay.' Giselle slid the cake into a paper bag and twirled the corners. 'It's a really nice flat.'

'It is, isn't it?' agreed Ann, handing over a fiver. 'It was a complete wreck to begin with you know – Gavin and Byron did a lot of the work themselves.'

Giselle gave her her change. 'It's good.'

'He's looking after you, I hope?'

'I don't need looking after.'

'I dare say, but I hope he's spending some time with you. I know Gavin. As I'm sure you do, only too well,' added Ann diplomatically. 'He lives to work. He can always find pressing reasons to stay at the brasserie. Whether rightly or wrongly, he regards it as his baby, and himself as indispensable to it. But now you are in his life . . .' she paused, her eyes on Giselle's face. 'Make sure you stake your claim in no uncertain terms.'

Giselle swabbed the counter with a J-cloth. 'I'll try.'

'Would you both like to come over to Raglan Road for lunch one weekend?' asked Ann. 'We'd be very pleased to see you. Say the one after next?'

'She didn't say she had to check with Gavin,' Ann told Byron approvingly over spicy meat loaf and three-bean salad. 'She has a mind of her own.'

'That's the stuff,' said Byron. 'Not carrot cake, surely, for afters?'

'Shit!' said Gavin. 'You might have asked me.'

Then there was Sunday Lunch.

'. . . and if we can persuade Loebl to cough up for the premises in Shepherd's Market we'll be laughing,' explained Gavin. 'I reckon we're *that* close. If he comes across and we do expand I think we could soon reach the point where we're totally identified with the concept, and where the concept itself has passed into the language. That's what we want to aim for. To change the face of British eating-out . . .'

'Giselle, some more—?' Ann held the serving spoon invitingly over the chocolate roulade.

'Yes, please.' Giselle watched as a generous second helping was dealt out. 'We get one a bit like this from Freezerworld.'

Ann smiled serenely. 'Your mama is a very busy woman.'

'Isn't anyone else going to have some?'

'Not at the moment,' Ann whispered, with a knowing look at the far end of the table. 'But I might join you,' she added, taking a very small spoonful. 'I must say it's a pleasure to feed someone who enjoys their food.'

'I love it,' said Giselle, adding whipped cream.

Ann cast her an enquiring sideways look. 'Have you visited the brasserie yet?'

Giselle caught the 'yet'. 'It's not my scene really.'

'I'm not sure,' said Ann thoughtfully. 'Byron and I had a very pleasant meal there. Not that that fact in itself,' she conceded, 'necessarily commends the place to you.'

'I can't understand half of what he says when he starts going on about it.'

'I hope you tell him so.'

Giselle shrugged. 'I don't bother.'

'You should. He *ought* to be able to communicate his interest to you.'

'It doesn't matter,' said Giselle, 'I just switch off.'

Ann chuckled, but her eyes were thoughtful.

Byron had been watching the two of them as Gavin inveighed in his left ear against the British curse of food-snobbery . . . It was odd to see Giselle sitting at the table in Raglan Road. Odd, but not unpleasing. He hoped Ann, God bless her, wasn't getting too close for comfort. The girl didn't look the settling-down type to him . . . rather less so than the last one, as a matter of fact. Byron liked her a lot, but he would never dream of being flirtatious with her, not for any daft feminist reasons but because he sensed she lacked the inclination or emotional vocabulary to respond. There was something tough about Giselle. Tough, but essentially honest. Had the girl not so obviously been round the track a few times, he might even have called it innocence.

'. . . if we can get this one in the bag there'll be no holding us,' Gavin concluded. 'We'll be one of the major players and the foodie mafia will have to take us seriously.'

'Sounds good to me,' said Byron, eyeing the last slab of roulade. 'But then what do I know?'

'Take my word for it,' said Gavin. Ann put the remaining roulade on the sideboard, and then inclined her head towards Giselle. 'Julian will be back later and it's more than my life's worth not to keep some for him.'

'My brother's like that,' said Giselle.

'How is Daniel?'

'A pain.'

'He'll grow out of it,' Ann assured her. 'I've raised three of them, and I know. But Julian needs a little spoiling, he's been through an emotionally bruising time in the past few months.'

Over coffee in the drawing room, Ann asked Gavin: 'Tell me, is it time there was a washing machine over at George Street?'

Gavin looked at her in astonishment. 'I don't think so.'

'I was trying to think of something sensible your father and I could give you for Christmas this year,' went on Ann, 'and it occurred to me that with Giselle there too a machine might be useful.'

'No, thanks,' said Gavin. 'Socks will be fine.'

Byron snorted. 'Since when did we give any of you socks for Christmas?'

'Anyway, you know my kitchen, there's no room for it.'

'That need not present a problem,' said Ann.

'Take it,' said Byron, 'and we can cross it off the list.'

'Yes, go on,' said Giselle. 'Your Mum's right, it's a great idea. It's got to be cheaper than using that laundry service every week.'

'They're hopelessly unaesthetic.'

'Laundry service?' Ann raised her eyebrows.

'I don't like them, it's as simple—'

'He puts everything out in a box,' said Giselle, 'and it's delivered back again clean. I never knew you could do that. It must cost a bomb.'

'Not a brass farthing,' said Byron in a stage whisper to Giselle. 'You want a laundry service – ' he pointed at his wife ' – you're looking at it.'

Ann held up her hands. 'Guilty, I'm afraid.' She smiled in contented apology at Giselle. 'But I do feel with the two of you there—' The door opened. 'Julian! Hallo, my love. Your Death By Chocolate is under clingfilm on the sideboard.'

'Enjoy it,' Byron muttered. 'It's my seconds.'

Gavin went along to the kitchen to collect his JPs. Julian was sitting at the table eating roulade and reading the *Observer* fashion page.

'They're going to give me a bloody washing machine!'

'So? You start moving women in, that's what you get.'

'Giselle doesn't want a washing machine either.'

Julian looked up. 'That I believe. You'll never get her to play house.'

'Stay out of it, Jules,' said Gavin, scooping up his cigarettes. 'MYOB, huh?'

'My pleasure, old son,' said Julian, tranquilly returning to the paper.

Giselle was mortified. 'I'm really sorry,' she said to Ann. 'There was some stuff of mine in there last time. In the box. I didn't realise it was you who did it.'

'Oh, my dear,' Ann chuckled, 'don't give it another thought. It made a change to see a few scanties going round.'

'She loves it,' said Byron.

'I do not love it,' corrected Ann, 'but Gavin's job allows him very little time, and he should wear a properly laundered shirt.'

The Visit to Schmooze became inevitable.

Giselle held out against it as long as she could, but Gavin became plaintive.

'They won't believe you exist unless you show your face some time.'

'Who's they?'

'The team.'

She pictured 'the team' as a little flock of sheep, the sort you saw on *One Man And His Dog*, with Gavin as the sinuously alert collie, darting here and there, confusing and controlling them, occasionally snapping.

'Okay,' she said, 'if it'll make them happy.'

'It'll make *me* happy.'

'*Okay.*'

She walked from Bayswater to Maida Vale one late afternoon, which Gavin had said was the brasserie's quiet time. She went in through the restaurant, where only a few people lounged about reading, smoking and drinking tea, and took directions from the barman on how to get to Gavin's office.

For some reason she had naively imagined a group of them going to a pub, and sitting round a table with beers and crisps. Instead of which it was like a reception. There were half a dozen people in the bleak, smart, colourless office. On the white stone coffee table stood several bottles of chilled Blanc de Blanc, one of Jack Daniels and a solitary four-pack of lager. Everyone was holding a wine glass and the noise level, which dropped sharply on her entrance, indicated that they had been doing so for some time. Gavin, who was standing with his back to the door, spun round and hailed her with open arms. He wore a febrile, unfocused stare, its brightness aimed at impressing other people rather than her.

'Zelda!' he cried as she submitted guardedly to his embrace. 'Come and say hallo to everyone.'

He snapped off a can of Harp and thrust it into her hand.

She handed it back. 'I'd rather have wine, thanks.'

Gavin slapped his own wrist. There was a murmur of laughter. One of the women passed her a glass of wine.

'Thanks.'

'This is Bar,' said Gavin.

'Bar by name, bar by nature,' said Bar, wringing Giselle by the hand. 'We've spoken on the phone.'

'I remember.'

'It's me,' added Bar jovially, 'who sends you all those flowers!'

'Oh.'

Gavin hurried Giselle to the next outstretched hand.

'And this is Ewan, our head chef. We think he may be a genius.'

Ewan was in his twenties, with straight dark hair brushed back off a pale, dour, pock-marked face. 'Well, hallo at last,' he said in a rich Glaswegian accent. 'We've all heard such a lot about you.'

'Have you?' Giselle looked at Gavin, but he was already moving her on.

'You're never going to remember all these names, are you?' asked a lean, fortysomething blonde in a natty pinstripe trouser suit.

Shades of the loo photos, thought Giselle. 'Probably not.'

'Be nice to her,' whispered Gavin playfully, leaning towards Giselle but with his eyes on the blonde, and loud enough for them both to hear. 'She's Della Carteret, my partner . . .'

'Please, my dear, only financially,' said Della. 'How do you do, Zelda. Is that your real name?'

'No, it's Giselle.'

'Which do you prefer?'

'Makes no difference.'

'In that case, I'll go where the mood takes me.'

The last two were Luke, the restaurant manager and Cosmo, the book-keeper, both described by Gavin as 'shit-hot'. Luke was handsome in a wussy, Coke-commercial way. Cosmo had a damp handshake and white socks.

'Nice to meet you,' said Luke. 'How you doing.'

'Not everyone's here,' Gavin explained.

'Just the important ones!' said Bar. She had drifted closer to Giselle, as Gavin moved towards Della. Ewan joined them. Giselle found herself wondering what Ark was doing.

'Actually,' went on Bar, 'we all have a lot to thank you for.'

'Oh, why's that?'

'Sir is in a much better humour since you came on the scene.'

'Really?'

'No question,' said Ewan. 'He even trusts us enough to leave the building from time to time.'

'Does he?' Giselle pondered this.

Bar clapped her on the shoulder. 'It all goes to show that it's true what they say about the love of a good woman.'

'Je-sus.' Giselle laughed. 'It's the first time I've been called that.'

'She's taking the rise,' said Ewan.

Giselle added: 'And who said anything about love?'

Later, Gavin found fault with her performance.

'What were you trying to do back there, Zelda? Make me look a complete idiot?'

'Since when did you need my help with that?'

'Seriously. "Who said anything about love?" Was that fair?'

They were in bed. Gavin was smoking and holding an American bestseller, upside down. Giselle had been trying to go to sleep, but now she rolled on to her back and stared at him.

'Have you been thinking about that all this time?'

'It preys on my mind.'

'I wasn't even talking to you.'

'Precisely.'

She rolled away. 'I don't know what you're on about.'

There was a brief silence, followed by the sound of the book falling to the floor and the cigarette being stubbed out.

'You can be incredibly cruel, Zelda.'

She didn't reply. Gavin lay down, his back to hers. She felt a slight shudder pass through it. Then another. She turned towards him again, touching his shoulder.

'Lighten up – it's not important.'

'Not important?' Suddenly he was out of bed and standing over her. 'Not important, when you tell friends and colleagues that you don't care for me? Not important when I've told them how fundamental you are to my life—'

There were tears in his eyes. Giselle sat up, rubbing her hands over her head.

'Okay – okay. I'm sorry.'

'And then you walked out on me.'

'I didn't. I'd finished eating and you were busy—'

'I have to talk to people, I have to be seen, it's part of the job. Couldn't you have waited even five minutes?'

'You'd been gone half an hour. You'd forgotten about me—'

'Aah . . .' he was bitterly sarcastic. 'Poor little Grizzle!'

'I was pissed off, if you want to know.'

'Not half as pissed off as I was when I brought a couple of friends over and found you'd buggered off without telling me—'

'I said I was sorry, Gavin!'

'It's not enough!' He sank down on his knees and buried his face in the edge of the bed. 'I love you, Zelda! You know it – why must you be so cold?'

'Cold? What was that we were—'

'That was just sex!' He looked up at her with anguished eyes. His switch from pompous rage to injured devotion was swift and seamless. 'Can't you hear me? I love you!'

Giselle was stumped.

'I don't know what you want me to say,' she mumbled miserably.

'Christ, I don't believe I'm hearing this . . .!' He turned round and sat on the edge of the bed with his back to her, lighting a cigarette.

'I never said I loved you, did I?' Her voice rose in exasperation.

'No, you never did.' The tears had gone and he was cutting. 'You never did, because you don't know the meaning of the word.'

She feared that might be true, and he knew she feared it. Such swift, wounding verbal slashes were a speciality of his. Confused, she sought something to restore normality. 'Fancy a cup of tea?'

He drew snappishly on the cigarette. 'No!'

'I think I'll have one.'

'You do that.'

As Giselle reached for a T-shirt Gavin was already half-dressed, zipping his fly and stepping into shoes, the cigarette dangling from his lips.

'Where are you going?'

'Out.'

Sebastian cleared a space amongst the unwashed dishes, tinfoil takeaway cartons, saucers of cigarette butts, beer cans and smeared glasses.

'You want coffee?' he asked Gavin.

'No, thanks.'

'Spliff?'

'I'd rather have a decent drink.'

'Sorry, fresh out.'

'In that case I'll risk the coffee.'

Gavin watched glumly as Sebastian made two mugfuls. After a couple of sips he handed the JPs and nodded in the direction of the bedroom.

'Anybody in there?'

'No.'

'You're kidding.'

'Uh-uh. Resting.'

'Wise move.'

There was another silence.

'What's up?' asked Sebastian. Gavin shrugged. 'Woman trouble?'

'Sort of. She's demanding . . . you know?'

'And eighteen.' Sebastian smirked knowingly. 'Tell me about it. I've been there.'

'No. Emotionally.'

'Oh yeah?'

'The thing is, I care about her, I really do. I want this one to last—'

'Oh, yeah . . .'

'But I'm not eighteen. I'm working my butt off at the brasserie, and she's got no interest whatsoever in what I do.'

'That's her problem. Why worry?'

'Because I still want to make a go of this.'

''Course you do. She's the sexiest thing you ever brought back.'

'She is, isn't she?' Gavin exhaled a Niagara of smoke through his nostrils. 'I appreciate you listening, Sebastian.'

Sebastian shrugged. 'Ask me another.'

Giselle sat on one of the high, uncomfortable chairs by the kitchen breakfast bar, drinking her tea and eating a chocolate-nut spread sandwich. She sat in the dark, but the blind was up, and because it was still only 11 p.m. there were squares of light in the neighbouring houses, keeping her company. Now she was calmer she tried to think dispassionately about Gavin. She was here in his posh flat because she'd fancied him and because he was so different from anyone else she'd been out with, and – she was honest with herself –

because it was quite nice to be keeping so many other people happy. But seeing him at work had made her realise how low a priority she was in his life. The drama queen stuff was all for show. She'd been acquired, and if she wasn't careful she'd be just another scalp hanging from his belt.

Mensa sat by her mug on the table, staring at her. She scratched his ruff with her finger. For a second he acquiesced, eyelids lowered, face thrust forward. Then with swift, arbitrary spitefulness he clasped her hand with his front paws and sank his teeth into it.

Hester was stirring gravy while listening to *Desert Island Discs*. A timeless moment, she thought, picturing the battalions of other gravy-makers also listening, perhaps reckoning like her that this particular programme was not a vintage one. The guest was a politician with an image to think of, and his choice of records smacked of the midnight oil. Hester was not entirely unsympathetic. It was tough trying to be all things to all men – cultured and popular, moral but flexible, amusing yet fundamentally serious. She knew that from the HB Page. One false move, one wrong note and you were snowed under by an avalanche of letters, furious, saddened, disappointed, disaffected.

She sipped her G and T, and turned the heat off under the gravy, which was now bubbling. She was wearing a plastic apron with the body of a gorilla on it – Daniel had given it to her on her last birthday. Through the french window she could see Jonty, in an out-at-elbow army surplus sweater and black wellies, putting in bulbs.

The politician confided winsomely that as a boy he had wanted not simply to emulate but to *be* Gene Kelly, and that therefore he wished to have 'Singin' in the Rain' so that he could twirl one-handed round coconut palms during tropical downpours on his desert island. Hester performed a few tentative steps to the familiar introduction as she went to the cutlery drawer and began laying the table.

It was nice to be making Sunday lunch. With Rose back in Bristol, Giselle in London and Daniel invariably cooling his fevered brain in bed it had hardly seemed worth it in recent weeks. But Giselle had turned up, unannounced and alone, yesterday evening and declared her intention of spending Sunday at The Old Clink, so there had been a reason to disinter a shoulder of pork from the freezer. The pleasurable comfort of ritual was only slightly snagged by the question of why Giselle was here.

She came into the kitchen now, just as Hester was doing a shuffle and ball-change with the salt and pepper. Hester said 'Discovered, curses!' but Giselle appeared to have noticed nothing. She sat down at the table and began spinning a knife.

'Who's got the smelliest armpits?' suggested Hester as the knife spun. It came to rest pointing sternly out into the garden. 'Your dear father, and I shouldn't be a bit surprised.'

Giselle pressed the prongs of a fork so that the handle rose in the air, then released them so that it fell back with a clang. She did this several times.

'Would you like a drink?' asked Hester.

'No, thanks.' The fork clanged again, in slow motion. Hester studied her daughter. She'd lost the glow of summer, but she'd kept the weight off, and though she wasn't yet the vision in white lace of Hester's wilder imaginings, she was still looking good. Her hair was proper hair: short, black and silky like rook's feathers, lying in little points on the nape of her neck and her forehead. Her heavy winged eyebrows, with the white streak of scar, gave her face a sardonic cast. Without the death's head make-up her skin was admirably clear. Yes, thought Hester, her daughter looked – nice. A term only a mother would use.

She switched off the radio and sat down next to Giselle.

'Everything okay?'

'Oh . . . yeah.'

'Job all right? No problems?'

Giselle shrugged. 'No.'

'And Gavin?'

'He's fine.'

'How are you shaking down in the flat?'

'All right.'

'I think of you a lot,' said Hester. 'We miss you. Rose was asking after you the other day – she's full of admiration.'

'Admiration?' Another clang of the fork.

'Yes. Going to London, getting the job – and hanging on to it—'

'Yeah, everyone's amazed about that, aren't they?'

Hester could have kicked herself. 'It's not easy at the moment – and in a new place and everything. We were a bit worried . . . it was all rather precipitate . . . I'm glad it's working out.'

Giselle dropped the fork altogether and rocked her chair back on two legs, holding the edge of the table between finger and thumb. Her expression had changed, she looked intently at Hester.

'How do you mean, working out?'

'I don't know – that you're happy.'

'Oh.'

'You are happy, aren't you?'

Giselle appeared not to have heard this. 'I'm not staying there forever, you know.'

'Well – no – I never assumed you were,' protested Hester, suddenly aware from her own reaction that in some way she had assumed exactly that. 'I hadn't even thought about it in those terms.'

'Hadn't you? Gavin has.'

'Has he said as much?'

Giselle let the chair fall forward. 'He doesn't need to.'

'So he's very – keen, is he?'

'He says,' said Giselle acidly, 'that he loves me more than life itself.'

Hester picked up her glass and had upended it over her nose and spilled the wedge of lime down her front before she realised it was empty. Giselle gave a small sniff of laughter.

'There's nothing in that.'

'I've realised that.' Hester retrieved the lime. 'And do you feel the same?'

'How can I when I don't know how *he* feels.'

'But you said that he—'

'That's what he says, not what he feels.'

'I see,' said Hester. 'I think.' From the tail of her eye she observed Jonty straightening up, and stretching. For some reason she could not identify she did not want him to join in this conversation. But to her relief he began to push the wheelbarrow which had held the bulbs up to the end of the garden.

'How do you feel? Is everything all right between you?'

'Not really.'

Hester's heart sank, with a swoosh of sadness and disappointment, like a child deprived of a treat. 'Oh dear – I'm so sorry.'

'It's not the end of the world,' said Giselle tersely.

'I know, but—'

'He'll get over it.'

After a small pause, Hester asked: 'Get over what, exactly . . .?'

'Search me. I don't think he knows himself.'

'I believe,' Hester chose her words carefully, 'that he's always been rather temperamental.'

'He's a basket-case.'

'As a teenager he was difficult, I gather. But – well – that's not uncommon—'

'Okay, okay, point taken.' Giselle lowered her head to the table, bumped her forehead once as if to clear it, and then came up for air. 'Look, I know him, all right? Better than you. Better than anyone.'

'Except presumably his mother.'

'Ann?' Giselle gaped, then looked disdainful. 'She knows sod all about any of them.'

Jonty was advancing down the garden. Hester put her hand on Giselle's arm.

'Look, love – we're always here. You don't have to confide in me, but you can if you want.'

'I know.'

'And remember, if Gavin says he loves you, and he means it – well, difficult people often repay perseverance. Don't be in too much of a hurry to throw the whole thing over.'

'Did I say I was going to do that?'

'No, but you—'

'Don't worry.' Giselle slid Hester a look of quelling world-weariness. 'I can hack it for a bit longer.'

For some time after Giselle had left the room Hester sat at the table, oblivious to the rapidly evaporating gravy. This had been her moment to be a friend to her daughter, to say something wise and womanly, to offer, unconditionally, the space for manoeuvre which was so essential. Instead of which she had the dismaying feeling that she had sent Giselle back into the front line, unarmed and unsatisfied. Her heart ached.

'I can tell lunch is coming along,' said Jonty, entering fresh-faced from the garden. 'Where's the fire extinguisher?'

Mrs Ramilies was back. She was sitting in her usual place in the drawing room at Raglan Road, alongside the box of white mansize tissues, and she was in buoyant form.

'I've been reading this book, *The Politics of Pressure,*' she announced, 'and it's changed my life.'

'Tell me more,' suggested Ann.

Mrs Ramilies needed no second bidding. 'The scales have fallen from my eyes,' she trumpeted. 'That two-timing little prick can go and fuck himself.'

'That's the spirit,' said Ann.

'As I read that book I realised,' explained Mrs Ramilies, 'that by upsetting myself I was letting him run my life from a distance. I was! He's living with his peroxide floozie in Walthamstow; good riddance, I don't even *want* him, and no matter what the kids think they don't want to live there with her, so I'm not about to lose them – so what am I getting so upset about? He didn't hurt me, he did me a big favour – I'm free. Free of that fat pervert with his bad teeth and smelly trousers! Free!'

'It certainly sounds like it.' Ann permitted herself an indulgent smile. 'I shall have to tell Ava that her book has been instrumental in at least one notable success.'

'Oh, my God. . .!' breathed Mrs Ramilies reverently, 'you don't *know* her, do you?'

'As a matter of fact, I do.'

'Do you think she'd mind if I wrote to her myself and said what a difference her book has made to my life?'

'I'm sure she wouldn't. It would be wrong of me to hand out her address, but if you let me have the letter I can forward it.'

Mrs Ramilies leaned forward. A rush of strong scent preceded her. 'Tell me – what is she really like?'

Ann fixed her eyes on a point above her client's head as she reflected for a moment.

'Very impressive. A strong, independent woman. Confident in her social, sexual and intellectual identity. Concerned, but rigorous in the exercise of that concern—'

'Is she as gorgeous as she looks on the cover?' Mrs Ramilies wanted to know.

Ann gave a self-deprecating shake of the head. 'I'm afraid you're asking the wrong person. All my instinct, and my training, leads me to look past the surface at the person beneath.'

'I see . . .' Mrs Ramilies sat back, disappointed. 'Never mind.'

*   *   *

Josette found Byron in the kitchen fixing a plug on to an electric drill. She said good afternoon and he glanced up.

'Hallo there, Josette – Julian's found himself a flat so I think this may be called into play.'

'You're so good to your family.' Josette put her bag on a chair and removed her coat. 'Where's Mrs Armitage?'

'With a client.' He glanced at her. 'Do you want her for something?'

'No, not really. I'll catch her before I go.'

Mr Armitage pointed at her bag with his screwdriver. 'Something to do with the course?'

'That's right.'

'You're doing Social Studies, aren't you?'

Josette nodded. 'I'm doing a module on "The Changing Family" at the moment.'

'I'm sure we all feel we know a bit about that,' said Mr Armitage, in a tone which invited the laugh Josette was too polite to give.

'My degree was in sociology,' he added. 'In the days before sociology got a bad name. So let me know if there's anything I can do to help.'

Josette looked pleasantly surprised. 'Are you sure?'

'I am a man of many parts,' said Mr Armitage, getting up with the drill in his hand, and plugging it in above the work surface. 'One of which, you may be astonished to learn, has a brain.'

He switched on the drill and listened with a wan, introspective smile as the sound of its motor rose to a piercing whine.

CHAPTER ELEVEN

Jonty was on his way to have lunch with Byron when he saw Hester with Robert Walton.

Since this was his rather overdue thank-you lunch for the reference Byron had given Grizzle, he had invited him to the Joli Bateau in Floral Street – his gratitude did not extend to thick gravy and Bird's custard at The Old Hat – and it was on the short walk between Greek Street and Covent Garden that he spotted them.

They were in a second-hand bookshop in the Charing Cross Road, standing near the window absorbed in a large book which Hester was holding. Jonty paused on the pavement, other people flicking past between him and the shop window, some of them sidestepping to avoid him and sucking their teeth in irritation. If Hester had looked up, she would have seen him, but she did not. She turned the pages, smiling, occasionally pointing. Robert stood at her shoulder, peering intently. As Jonty watched he felt in his inside breast pocket for his glasses, and put them on, without taking his eyes from the book. Jonty had met Robert a couple of times at parties at the *Post* – a dour individual with a rather steely charm. A nice, brainy wife. There had been absolutely nothing in his manner, or Hester's, to suggest a relationship that was anything other than strictly professional. In fact, Jonty recalled that on the way back Hester had said Robert only kept her on because he was baffled by her popularity.

But there was something close in their shared examination of the book. Buying books was in itself an intimate business. And Robert Walton must have made time for this – he was not, Jonty imagined, a man with much space in his working day for browsing in shops . . .

He was momentarily mesmerised. Then Hester closed the book

and looked up at Robert, who in turn took off his glasses, and Jonty walked on in a rush of guilty confusion.

He drank more than usual at lunch, and ate less, which he registered as a waste because the Joli Bateau was first-rate. As a result of this uncharacteristic behaviour he found himself confiding in Byron over the brandy.

'Do you ever find yourself reacting to things in a way which you realise is irrational?'

Byron considered. 'I'm not sure that I do. You'd have to ask Ann.'

'On the way here I saw Hester and her Editor in a bookshop together and for some reason I was shocked.'

'What did she say?'

'Say?'

'When you saw her?'

'No – we didn't speak. I saw them through the window.'

'Ah.'

Jonty glanced at Byron. 'I told you it was an unreasonable reaction.'

'Not exactly grounds for divorce, no.'

'No. It's always a little strange observing someone you know when they aren't aware of you. It makes you realise how dependent you are on the one aspect of themselves they choose to show you.'

'You're getting a bit metaphysical for me,' said Byron.

'Don't come that. You know exactly what I mean.'

'You should have gone in and passed the time of day. Imprinted yourself on the proceedings – I'm surprised you didn't, frankly, you're generally rather good at that.'

'It didn't seem right,' said Jonty. 'It would have felt like butting in.'

'Then you're a fool to yourself,' said Byron. He patted his solar plexus. 'This has been a delightful lunch.'

Back at Earthtrust's overcrowded top-floor office in Greek Street Jonty surveyed his own colleagues with a wild surmise. Were there currents and connections here which he did not even recognise himself? In his salad days in advertising, before (as Hester put it) he went straight, the office of Ruggles Ryder had pulsed with sexual and emotional intrigues, but he had never got caught up.

Not, it had to be said, due to any lack of offers or opportunity. He'd had his chances and declined to take them. He was the man who danced with his wife, always had been. Appetites were the currency of advertising; titillation and temptation were its stock in trade. It was a business which did not seek to deny its own glamour. It was unashamedly all artifice and allure – such substance as there was belonged to the client. The office itself was a shrine to the ephemeral glitter of style. Here the office was as you might expect, down to earth. And the people, though by no means wearing the tanktops and thongs of unkind caricature, were certainly not fashion victims.

Jonty's boss put her head round the door. Jen O'Flinn was a handsome, wild-haired woman who shared her life and her bed with a female QC in Fulham. She winked at him.

'Cheer up, Jonno,' she said. 'It'll never happen.'

'How do you know it hasn't already?'

'Snap out of it and come along to my office. I've got some stunning pictures for you to drool over. A publicist's wet dream.'

A coarse expression that, thought Jonty as he followed Jen, and was for the first time offended by it.

'Yes, it was excellent,' Byron said again later, in response to his wife's enquiry. 'French, but not aggressively so.'

'Jonty knows his restaurants,' approved Ann. 'A legacy from his misspent youth as an adman, one supposes. We really should take the Blakes to Gavin's place some time . . . And how was he?'

'In pretty good form. At least—' Byron furrowed his brow '—he was and he wasn't.'

'Now Byron . . .'

'He claimed to have seen Hester with her Editor, Charley Farnsbarns—'

'Robert Walton.'

'Probably. Anyway, Jonty saw them together and gained the distinct impression that they were more than just friends.'

'You surely don't mean it.' Ann, who was at her desk, sat back in her chair and looked at Byron properly for the first time.

'That's what he said . . .' Byron was a little taken aback by the force of her reaction. 'Mind you, he did open the batting by admitting he was being irrational.'

'Perhaps,' mused Ann, 'it was simply instinctive.'

'I asked why he hadn't said hallo to Hester and he said it would have been like butting in. If you want my opinion he's imagining the whole thing.'

'Hmm . . .' Ann placed the tips of her forefingers together and tapped them pensively against her lips. 'One thing is certain – no-one knows what goes on inside a marriage except the people themselves.'

'Your secret is safe with me.'

'And friendship,' went on Ann, 'is a trust.'

'Don't lecture me,' said Byron, emboldened by the Joli Bateau's white Burgundy. 'I'm not about to bruit abroad some tabloid version of these reported events, I merely told you because you asked.'

Ann gazed thoughtfully at him, fingers still to lips. She lowered them to her chin and said: 'The Blakes are two old and dear friends. I don't think that something said to you in confidence, Byron, over what was clearly a two-bottle lunch, should be given house-room. We should put it from our minds.'

'Right,' said Byron. 'Absolutely.'

The first Saturday in November was Jonty's birthday, his forty-eighth. The Blakes did not usually make a song and dance over family birthdays, unless they were eighteenths, or an exuse to jeer, like fortieths. This occasion would have been no exception, but that Rose and Jez had already arranged to be at home that weekend, and Giselle had rung to ask if she could drop Jonty's present off, so Hester had invited her and Gavin to spend the night. Given Giselle's account of his working habits she had been surprised and encouraged to hear that they'd both be coming.

'So it looks like a gathering of the clans,' she told Jonty a couple of days before.

'My God,' said Jonty, 'if I don't feel old on the day, I sure as hell will after.'

'It's going to be fun,' declared Hester.

'You sound like a Butlin's redcoat.'

'You know you'll enjoy it when the time comes.'

'Is that an order?'

Daniel was even less equivocal. 'Nightmare!'

'No, it won't be. Why should it?'

'Why? With Rose and Griz and both their poncey boyfriends?'

'Stop being so jolly objectionable,' admonished Hester.

'I liked Ark,' complained Daniel, 'whatever happened to Ark?'

'I've no idea, and anyway it's Dad's birthday, okay? So it's a case of put up or shut up.'

Hester was also confronted with the problem of sleeping arrangements. She reminded herself ruefully that it was only eight months ago that she had given this dilemma an airing on the HB Page. The difficulty now was that her daughters were returning as grown women in committed relationships (she found herself thinking in the way that Ann spoke). They both spent most of their time these days well beyond the reach of parental surveillance, and it would scarcely be reasonable, or even polite, to start imposing separate beds as a matter of form. The Rubicon had been crossed, and there was no going back.

She had a further debate with herself over which room to give which couple. The Old Clink's only double bed – other than the one she and Jonty occupied – was in the spare room. In the end she decided that Gavin and Giselle should have this, in view of Gavin's seniority and the condition of Giselle's own room which was tidy but still undecorated. Rose had a three-foot pine bed, and her room was as fragrant as ever, so she and Jez, used to student lodgings, would be fine in there.

As she grappled with clean duvet covers Hester recalled the winner of the reader's letter competition she had set back in the spring. She and Mary had waded through a record postbag from the length and breadth of middle-class, middle-right Britain, ranging from lunatic-fringe liberal to bloodthirsty castrationists. They'd disposed of about two-thirds of them on the grounds of illegibility, and half of the rest as being dangerously extreme. Among those remaining there was one letter they'd kept coming back to. It was neither strenuously amusing, nor sententious, but had a direct and irrefutable truthfulness which in the end won the writer the promised magnum of champagne.

'Dear Hester Blake', it said, *'My two children are five and seven, so I haven't had to face this problem yet. But in my own heart I cannot avoid the fact that I was not married to their father, and that he did not love us enough to stay. It's hard to be honest with them about this but not to make them hate him. I have to explain that he and I did love each other once, and that I still love them. Children know if you're saying one thing and doing*

*or thinking another, and I don't believe grown-up children are any
different. The reason I respected my own parents was that I knew they
were the same all the way through. So I think parents have to do what
they feel is right and feel comfortable with in their own homes and not
try to be one thing because it's trendy or another because it's respectable.
Our children need self-respect and self-discipline in order to be happy,
and they learn that from us.*

'*This letter isn't really for the competition, it's just something I
wanted to say. I enjoy reading your page every week. Yours sincerely,
J.Devine (Mrs)*'

Introducing that letter the day they printed the winners Hester
had had the uneasy feeling that she herself was not a sensible or
grown-up person.

She banged pillows and adjusted lampshades. She bought large
flowers which did not need arranging, and thrust them into vases.
She filled the log basket. She wrapped Jonty's present and ordered
a salmon for his birthday dinner. Wishing she were tougher about
making extra demands on Mrs Carson she applied real beeswax
polish to the oak sideboard. It was nothing short of perfection that
she aspired to.

As she washed the glass wall-lamp shades in hot soapy water she
reflected on how success might be measured, and concluded that it
was in terms of harmony and unity – a sense of the family coming
together in good humour and with goodwill. And at the end of it
maybe – just maybe – there would be a chance to draw what Jonty
called a double horizontal in the back of the family Bible . . .

'Any particular reason why they get the double bed?' asked
Rose frostily on Friday evening when Jonty and Jez had gone to
the pub.

'You've seen Giselle's room,' pointed out Hester.

'That's her look-out.'

'But it's not Gavin's and it's the first time he's stayed here—'

'And I suppose the fact that he's a trendy restaurant owner's got
nothing to do with it?'

'Certainly not.'

'Nor that he's Ann and Byron's son?' Rose raised one eyebrow.
Hester reminded herself of the winning letter. She was going to be
scrupulously truthful and conceal almost nothing.

'Yes, that has got something to do with it. I wouldn't want

any reports going back about how scruffy conditions were out here.'

'You don't honestly think he's going to report back? He's a big boy, for God's sake.'

'No, of course not, but I want everyone to be comfortable. And your room is always nice, darling.'

Rose closed her eyes and shook her head. 'Honestly, Mum, you are so transparent sometimes.'

Not in the mood to go back to sleep, Hester got up early on Saturday morning and padded downstairs in her matted sheepskin slippers and red Courtelle fleece dressing gown (lovely and warm but not exactly Greta Scaachi). It was a cold, grey day, sullenly overcast. She stoked the Rayburn, put some croissants to heat in a covered dish on top, and turned on the immersion heater. Then she made a pot of Darjeeling with leaf tea, not bags, and carried it up to their bedroom.

Jonty was lying on his side watching her as she came in, pushed the door shut with her heel, and put the tray down on the chest of drawers.

'Stone me,' he mumbled comfortably, 'conjugal rights *and* tea in a pot.'

'Anyone would think,' said Hester, pouring, 'that you lived a life of ghastly deprivation.' She took him his tea, and bent to kiss him. 'Happy birthday. Again.'

'Thank you. . .' He pushed his hands inside the dressing gown and felt around with familiar relish. 'Mmm . . .'

'Come on, we've done that.'

'Is it on ration?'

'Yes.'

He craned his face up to hers, looking at her mouth. 'Even on a chap's birthday?'

'Especially.' She kissed him, an affectionate *mou* on the lips. 'A chap has a present to open.'

'Oh good.' He fell back. 'Let's see the colour of it then.'

Hester got up and fetched the parcel from the top shelf of the wardrobe.

'Ah . . .' Jonty hauled himself up against the pillows. 'So that's where you've been hiding it.'

Hester made a face. 'I suppose you've been rummaging.'

'Rummaging? *Moi*?'

He opened the card first, and studied it, still a little slow from sleep and sex, before laughing. It was a 'Far Side' design depicting wildebeest at a cocktail party. She had taken ages to choose it. Even more so the present. Her heart actually beat faster as he began pulling at the Sellotape. Men were so horribly difficult to buy for. But she reckoned she'd struck oil with this one.

He lost patience with the last bit of Sellotape and tore the remaining paper off. She tried to imagine herself being him, seeing what it was, how he would react.

He gazed at it, then at her.

'I say,' he said, 'isn't this superb?'

She smiled, and got up to pour her tea. Her excitement was tarnished. Something wasn't right.

It was incredibly awkward. Hester was watching him so intently. He felt as though his face were being displayed in enormous close-up for one of those awful reaction shots one occasionally had to do for TV. However he arranged his features it was not going to disguise his feelings.

The book was a guide to London in the early 1800s. It was exactly the sort of thing he loved, and in mint condition too, with all the beautiful old maps and illustrations shielded by tissue paper, the pages edged in gold leaf, the print wonderfully sharp and fresh.

'Where did you find it?' he asked.

'In an antiquarian bookshop in town.'

'It's perfect.'

Hester smiled briefly at him, acknowledging how imperfect it was.

'I'll treasure it.'

She shrugged, scraping her hair up into a bunch for a bath. 'As long as you enjoy it.'

'I shall . . .' He turned it, stroking the cover. It was a pleasure to handle such a book.

Or would have been, had it not been the book chosen by his wife and Robert Walton.

Rose and Jez were going into Forbridge at lunchtime to buy Jonty something.

'Don't go mad,' said Hester, 'he doesn't expect anything.'

'Oh, he *does*,' retorted Rose. 'He loves being made a fuss of. In fact he's nice to buy presents for because he's such a big kid about it.'

'Did he like that book?' asked Jez.

'Yes,' said Hester.

'What a brilliant find,' Jez enthused. 'Don't tell me you just stumbled across it?'

'Yes, I did actually.'

'Come on,' said Rose, 'or we'll never stumble across anything.'

'Didn't Daniel say he wanted a lift?' asked Jez.

'Yes, but he's not here, is he?'

'I'll give him a shout,' said Hester. As she went up to the half-landing she caught the hisses and squeaks of a tightly reined-in argument behind her.

'He's coming.'

'Great,' said Rose.

As soon as Jez had parked his white Mini Metro – one careful lady driver, only two thousand miles on the clock – in the multi-storey, Daniel was off.

'We'll be back here at two!' called Rose at his receding back view, 'and if you're not we're not waiting!'

There was some kind of response – a sound, a twitch.

'And don't forget to get something for Dad!'

Daniel disappeared through the swing doors.

Jez said: 'He ought to be able to, do you know how much he's earning at that supermarket?'

'I shudder to think.'

'It's quite indecent, actually, considering a chimp could do it.'

'Oh well,' said Rose, 'no wonder Dan finds it taxing.'

Daniel collected some dosh from Barclay's hole in the wall, bought chips with curry sauce from the van near the market and headed for the Barlow community centre. Once there he went up to the first floor. The shutter on Ark's door indicated that there was a session in progress, but there was no-one waiting outside. Some magazines lay on a wooden table, but they were mostly *Essex Quarterly* and *Anglian Life,* so he didn't bother. There was a step-aerobics class going on in the room opposite and he walked across and stared through the glass porthole at the women bobbing up and down with their faces all blotchy, until the one nearest marched over and shooed him away, and then stuck a piece of paper over the glass with Sellotape.

After about ten minutes Ark's door opened and a woman came out. She wore grey tracksuit trousers, a khaki parka with a fur-trimmed hood, and a red knitted hat with a tassel.

Daniel got up and almost bumped into Ark, who was coming out with Dolly, on her lead and muzzled.

'Hi, Ark.'

'Dan. I was going for a bite, you had something?'

'No,' said Daniel. These things were all relative.

He followed Ark downstairs and over the road to a pub, the Red Cow. They sat at a table near the window, and Dolly went under the table and lay down. They got a pint of Dobbey's each, with jumbo bangers for Daniel, a veggi-burger for Ark, and double chips in a Pyrex bowl.

'How's it going?' asked Daniel.

'Not so bad. A few regulars. You know. It takes a while to take a hold on people's consciousness, right?'

'Right.' Daniel nodded sagely. 'Making any money?'

'Not so's you'd notice.' Ark wiped foam off his moustache. 'You?'

'Not bad. Work's crap though.' Daniel offered Dolly a piece of sausage. Ark leaned down and unbuckled her muzzle so she could eat it. To a woman who was staring, he said:

'Don't worry, she's registered.' He turned back to Daniel. 'How's Zelda?'

'Still with this Gavin bloke in London.'

'Serious, is it?'

'Don't ask me. He's a right ponce.'

'He is.'

Daniel looked surprised. 'You know him?'

'I've met him.' Daniel knew there was no point in asking any more. Ark was good at keeping his counsel.

'Is she happy?'

Daniel shrugged. 'I suppose so. She's down there with him, so she must be. And she's got a job in a health food shop.'

'That's good,' said Ark. He began rolling a cigarette. Daniel took another long drag on his beer.

'I reckon my mum thinks they're going to get married or something.'

Ark licked the paper with care, his tongue forming a point. 'What do you think?'

'She won't get married!' Daniel had drunk enough to be one hundred per cent sure. 'I mean, can you see it?'

Ark shook his head. 'I care about your sister. I wrote to her back in the summer.'

This was all getting a bit iffy, but Daniel was spared having to comment because Ark picked up Dolly's lead and, in response to another hard stare from the woman, fastened her muzzle.

'I've got no-one there till three, you want to come back for a coffee?'

'Yeah, sure,' said Daniel, without giving it much thought.

By the time they were back in the Barlow he'd looked at his watch and registered that it was one-thirty, and he had to get his father a present.

'Look, I'd better split. I got shopping to do.'

Ark slapped the back of his hand against a nearby noticeboard. 'Buy yourself a session with the city's only Reiki master.'

Daniel looked at the board and saw Ark's poster there. He felt a bit bad. Ark was making no money but he'd let him buy lunch. Sod it, the guy deserved a break.

'Yeah, I'll buy one.'

'You won't regret it. Use it yourself or give it to a friend. The path of peace starts here,' intoned Ark, smoothing first one palm and then the other.

'How much?'

'Ten pounds. Eight-fifty to you.'

'Ten's okay,' said Daniel, savouring the sweets of patronage. He thrust a note at him. Ark got out a pad with 'The Path of Peace Starts Here' on each sheet, and scribbled on it.

'All paid for.' He tore off a sheet and handed it to Daniel. 'Call and book any time.'

'Cheers.'

'Give my love to your sister.'

'Yeah.'

Daniel went to HMV where he was sure he'd find Muffer or Spike, and sure enough there they both were, leaning up in the doorway watching the Gloria Estefan promo on the overhead TV. They greeted one another.

'Hey, right, what can I get my Dad for his birthday?'

'Sharon Stone?'

'Yeah . . .' They all laughed appreciatively. 'No, any ideas?'

'What's he into?'

'He thinks he's a bit of a styler.'

'How old?'

'Dunno – forty-five?'

'They got black silk boxer shorts in Tie Rack, they're well-cool.'

In the end Daniel plumped for these, throwing in a Garfield posing pouch for good measure. Conspicuous expense tempered with humour. He reckoned he'd done well, and even more so when he got back to the car to find he was there first.

Gavin came looking for Hester as she was laying the table for Jonty's birthday dinner. She wanted to make it look special. The oval beechwood dining table was one of their better pieces of furniture; they had actually chosen and bid successfully for it at a country house sale. Hester had washed the best glasses and dried them with a hair dryer (a trick she'd learned from Ann), ironed damask napkins and bought handsome ivory church candles to put in the newly cleaned silver candlesticks.

When Gavin came in she was arranging some of the chincherin-chis that he and Giselle had brought as a centrepiece.

'You're very busy,' he said, coming in and leaning against the windowsill.

'Not really. But I'm not particularly interested in the soccer and I like doing this sort of thing.'

'Me too,' agreed Gavin. He and Giselle had arrived at two-thirty. They had brought Jonty a pair of braces, black with hand-embroidered green ivy climbing up them – Gavin had come across them in town. Jonty had said ''Struth!' but Hester could tell he loved them. Giselle was not in good form. Once the braces had been handed over she announced she had a hangover and went upstairs to lie down. Rose was up there too, washing her hair, and Jonty, Jez and Daniel were watching England v. Sweden in the sitting room.

Hester sniffed the flowers. 'These are heavenly, thank you so much.'

'Nice, aren't they? There's a little florist near my office which specialises in hothouse plants – orchids, gardenias, those things – if you ever want anything like that for a special occasion, just let me know.'

'I will, definitely.' Hester noted, with a warm optimistic glow, that this offer seemed to be predicated on the idea of a shared future, and also, less happily, that it was Gavin who had bought the flowers, as well as the braces.

He lit a cigarette, and she put a Crown Derby coffee saucer on the windowsill next to him.

'Thanks – by the way, do you mind?'

'Not at all, there's too much cant about smoking.'

'Amen to that – come to think of it, haven't you delivered a broadside to that effect in your column?'

'Probably.' She put the table centre in place and stood back to admire it. 'You don't want to believe everything you read in the papers, but that one at least was for real. Giselle smokes, after all, and Daniel, although he imagines we don't know.'

'Actually,' said Gavin, stepping forward and adjusting a couple of the chincherinchis, 'Zelda's given up.'

Hester looked at him in disbelief. 'You're joking.'

'Scout's honour.' He grinned complacently.

'Well – I can't pretend I'm not delighted. What brought that on? I mean, forgive me for saying so, but it can't be your example.'

'Absolutely. I can take no credit whatsoever. I'm ruled by the blasted weed. It was her decision.'

Hester sat down at the table. 'How's she feeling now?'

'A bit rocky. She may have dispensed with one vice but she's making up for it with another.'

'Poor old Grizzle.'

'The third we won't mention.'

'Third?'

'Vice.' Gavin ground out what was left of his cigarette in the saucer and grinned at Hester. She felt obscurely flattered, but also embarrassed, as though she were pimping for her daughter. He was, she thought, a very confusing person.

Apparently unaware of her embarrassment, he said: 'The table looks nice. You have a flair for this sort of thing.'

'What sort of thing?'

'Creating the right ambience. All the little touches.'

'Oh, I don't know about that . . . I'm not the world's greatest cook so I have to make up the ground somewhere. I don't know how I've got the cheek to have you to dinner, a genuine expert.'

He smiled acknowledgement. 'The food's only a small part of entertaining.'

'That's what *I* say when we're here. When we're with your parents at Raglan Road I think the opposite. Your mother is the best cook we know. The best private cook, I mean, of course.'

'She can cook all right,' conceded Gavin. 'But she can't create,' he waved a hand, 'this.'

Hugely gratified, Hester picked up a fork, blew on it and rubbed it on the welt of her sweatshirt. 'Is the bedroom all right? Have you got everything you want?'

'More than all right, thanks. I have a nasty suspicion we've been allotted the honeymoon suite.'

'Not really, it's just that we haven't got round to decorating Giselle's room yet.'

'Not exactly *Homes and Gardens*, eh?'

'You could say that.'

'I can believe it.'

'Oh dear,' Hester looked anxious, 'your poor flat.'

He shook his head. 'That's not what I meant. I adore having Zelda there. What's a little mess in the great scheme of things?'

'In my experience the mess isn't usually all that little . . .' Hester was aware of being drawn more than was necessary on a subject which was no longer, after all, her responsibility.

'No, you're right there, your daughter's an expert. Do you remember, absolutely yonks ago, coming down to my parents' place for lunch with a whole crowd of women to listen to some talk or other?' Hester nodded stiffly. 'Remember the lunch got wrecked by one of the kids?' He levelled a forefinger at Hester. 'Your daughter.'

'No—!' She clutched her hair and groaned. 'God, that's *awful!* I had my suspicions at the time, but you said—'

'Ah.' Gavin lit another cigarette. 'She was very persuasive, even then.' He grinned at her through the smoke. 'But don't you dare tell her I told you.'

Rose tapped on the spare room door, and entered in response to Giselle's grunt. Her hair lay in a sleek, damp curtain down her back.

'Hallo . . .' She went over and sat down on the edge of the bed. Giselle was lying on her back, fully dressed but under the duvet, her arms crossed over her face. 'How are you feel-ing?'

'Like shit.'

'Do you fancy a cup of tea or something?'

Giselle shook her head.

Rose lay down across the bed on her side, nudging her sister's feet out of the way.

'It must have been a good party.'

'It was as boring as hell. A crowd of complete wankers all showing off about knowing the boss at Schmooze. It was get drunk or nothing . . .'

'I hope you showed off back – about knowing the boss. In the biblical sense.'

'Who gives a fuck?'

Rose sighed. 'Come on, Griz . . . How are you doing down there in the Smoke, anyway? I find it so hard to imagine – you and Gavin, and the job and everything.'

Giselle let her arms fall so they were folded over her chest. 'There's no "everything".'

'Sorry?'

'You're like Mum, you think this is some sort of big deal.'

'And it's not?' Rose adopted the studiedly casual tone of one who knows she could be the recipient of an exclusive.

'Not really.'

'You moved in with him, that's pretty big. And Gavin's—'

'A rising star, tell me about it.'

'God, Griz, you do sound jaundiced!'

This met with silence. Rose pressed on.

'A smart flat with every mod.con., a bloke who I've got to say is jolly attractive and a bit of a celebrity, and obviously for some obscure reason enslaved by you, and a new-reg. Cabriolet, what's the problem?'

Giselle turned her head and gave her sister a hard stare.

'Don't ask me to be grateful. I went down there because *I* wanted to.'

'You did, yes – good for you. I didn't mean—'

'I do that cruddy job so I won't be dependent on Gavin.'

'I really admire that.'

'Fine.'

Rose plucked at the duvet cover. 'Have you two had a row?'

'No.'

'Only you don't seem yourself—'

'You guessed!'

'Gavin's downstairs, and you're up here in an absolutely foul mood—'

'Look—' Giselle hauled herself up against the bed head. 'I didn't ask you in here, you wanted to come, you don't give a toss how I feel, you want to know all about "everything", and there's nothing to tell, okay?'

'Of course, I—'

'So why don't you clear off and go and flash your legs at Jez?'

'He's—'

'Or Gavin, he'd lap it up.'

Rose went briskly to the door. 'Now you're being childish.'

'I'm not, he likes blondes.'

Rose leaned back into the room. 'Dye yours, you've done it often enough.'

'Fuck off, Rose!'

'I will. Steady on—' Rose stepped aside hastily as Giselle blundered past at speed. 'Now where are you going?'

Her answer came as the lavatory door closed behind her sister, immediately followed by noisy and protracted retching. Rose withdrew until she heard Giselle stumble back to the spare room, and then held her breath as she went into the lavatory, flushed it once more, opened the window and made liberal use of the Spring Glade. Well, somebody had to.

Hester went into the sitting room. It was snug, the atmosphere both soporific and excitable in that way engendered by televised sport. Jez half-rose as she entered, and then sank down again as if embarrassed by his knee-jerk politeness.

'Coming to watch?' he asked.

'I shouldn't think so.'

'It's a rout,' grumbled Jonty, 'at the moment. We need to open up our game and move the ball about.'

Hester perched on the arm of the sofa next to him. 'Who's winning?'

'He just told you,' said Daniel, 'the Swedes.'

Gavin, who had followed Hester into the room, stood behind her, smoking. Jonty looked up at him.

'Want a seat, Gavin?'

He shook his head. 'No thanks, I'm not into team games.'

'How's Gr – Giselle?'

'Sleeping it off,' said Gavin. Daniel gave a derisive snort.

'Something you know all about,' said Jonty to Daniel without looking at him.

Jez moved to the front of his seat. Hester felt a surge of sympathy for him, an essentially nice, thoughtful young man who had not yet quite found his weight in relation to others in the household. And with whom, she suspected, Rose was beginning to get bored.

'Think I'll go and see what Rose is up to . . .'

He left the room with self-conscious stealth, and they heard him going up the stairs two at a time.

'Talk about donkeys!' exclaimed Daniel, pointing at the screen. 'Did you see that?'

'I fancy a walk,' said Gavin. 'Where are the nice walks round here?'

'There are lots, I'll show you.' Hester got up. 'I might even come too.'

Hester put on her moon boots, waxed jacket and tartan scarf and accompanied Gavin on a walk round Chuffington's ancient village boundary.

'Where's the black Labrador then?' asked Gavin.

She was startled. 'Which?'

'You know, the bounding black Labrador that goes with people like you, living in a house like that, in a village like this . . .'

'Actually,' said Hester, embarrassed for both of them, 'we had to have Gus put down.'

'I'm so sorry.'

'Don't be. That's dogs for you.' She smiled ruefully. 'You have them as puppies, you lavish care and attention on them, you teach them everything you know, and then they break your heart.'

The footpath circumvented fields, crossed streams and ditches, threaded through a couple of spinneys and here and there clipped the edges of the village itself. They met the vicar, Geoff Baines, and his younger daughter, and assorted other locals, both singly and in pairs. Most of them were accompanied by dogs, all of them greeted Hester.

Gavin looked impressed. 'Is there anyone you don't know in this village?'

'Not many, but it doesn't mean anything. Everyone knows everyone in a place this size.'

'I should find that claustrophobic.'

'Like I used to find London.'

'But at least there one has anonymity, which gives a degree of freedom.'

Hester clambered over a stile and hopped down the other side. 'It depends what you want to do.'

Gavin put his hand on the top bar and vaulted over. Hester wondered if he'd weighed up the chances of the vault going wrong. 'That's true. I bet there are times when the other locals wish they didn't live so close to a star columnist.'

She laughed. 'Possibly.'

'It doesn't worry you?'

'Not really.'

'What about the family?'

'They're used to it.' She cast him a quick glance. 'Why, what's Giselle been saying?'

'Nothing, nothing!' He raised his hands jokily. 'But I can't pretend I shan't be waiting for the moment when I appear.'

'Don't worry, I don't write about people for the sake of it. The idea has to come first.'

She thought she saw a split-second flash of disappointment. 'Thank God for that. It was my only reservation about becoming part of the Blake household.'

Hester felt she had been fed a cue, but she did not take it. There was a slipperiness in this conversation with Gavin and she was unsure of her footing. Instead she paused and took his arm to turn him a little. 'There you are – our best angle. That view hasn't changed in two hundred years. You can't even see a TV aerial.'

'To be honest it makes my blood run cold.'

'Towny.'

'I'd hate to live here – but no, it's great. Idyllic.'

They walked on. 'By the way,' Hester said hesitantly, 'I'm glad you feel you are becoming part of us.'

'How could I not?' He sprang in front of her and walked

backwards for a few steps, his arms spread wide to embrace the whole of Chuffington. 'How could I not, when I think the world of Zelda?'

Dinner that night was, for Hester, like the unwrapping of the book that morning. It should have been perfect, so its mere near-perfection made it terrible. The setting was inviting, the food simple but sumptuous, the chincherinchis fragrant and Jonty himself extravagantly appreciative. But nothing could save the company. The happy and harmonious group envisaged and longed-for by Hester was simply not available. Daniel was itching to go out to a party and, as soon as he'd hoovered up his syllabub with brandysnaps, did so. Rose looked exquisite and was generally vivacious, but cool with Jez, who became increasingly crestfallen. Gavin was ebullient, talking up a storm and letting his food go cold, then wolfing it down in seconds. He and Rose formed a kind of unholy alliance, being the life and soul and teasing Giselle about her self-inflicted malady. Hester cast her younger daughter agonised glances but received not so much as a flicker in return. She looked wonderful, in one of her eccentric black witch-dresses, hung with clunking jewellery that caught the candelight. But her face was taut and pale, and she was silent. This wasn't the sullen silence of rebellion, which would at least have denoted a familiar reaction, but a strange, grave emotional absence.

Unhappily, Hester thought: 'We have no training for this, no preparation, no warning. While we're deciding who we are, we become parents, and when we're wondering what to do when we grow up, our children become adults.'

Gavin felt amorous, ardently so. He was buoyed up by his day, and by the feeling that he had come through it with flying colours. He could not help imagining what his hosts might be saying about him – stuff like how well he fitted in, how good he was for Giselle, that this relationship could be the making of her . . . He leapt from the cold of the room into the warmth of the bed and the richly rounded landscape of Giselle's waiting body . . .

'Yes, I like him fine,' protested Jonty in a vehement whisper. 'But I'm bound to say I can't see any future in it.'

'Don't be such a Jonah.'

'I'm not. Brrr!' Jonty slipped beneath the duvet and tucked his cold feet between his wife's warm legs. 'It simply doesn't strike me as a union made in heaven.'

'If they care about each other, they'll change,' said Hester, feeling she was quoting someone though she couldn't remember who. 'They'll adapt.'

'You mean Grizzle will have to adapt.'

'Not necessarily. Both of them.'

Jonty peered down at her. 'Does he look to you like one of nature's adapters?'

She didn't answer. He kissed her hair. 'Anyway, I had a lovely birthday. Thanks.'

He picked up the book from his bedside table, opened it, and gazed distractedly at the first page.

Gavin nuzzled Giselle's back, and then put his arm around her, trying to pull her towards him. She resisted solidly.

'I don't want to, Gav.'

'You don't have to do anything. I'll do it all.'

'Ha ha.'

'I mean it.'

'No!' She was fierce.

'Okay!' He withdrew his arm, but still lay on his side, tracing patterns between her shoulder blades with his finger. 'Okay . . .' He traced for a minute or so, and then asked: 'What's the matter? Please tell me.'

'Not now.'

'Please, Zelda.'

'I don't want to.'

'Don't want, don't want!' he mimicked with a flash of anger, and then got it back under control. 'It's been a nice day, don't spoil it.'

'You seem to forget I've been feeling lousy.'

'Well, I'm sorry about that, but it's hardly my fault. Come on Zelda. . . don't let the sun go down on whatever it is.'

'I won't!' She moved her head slightly in his direction. 'It'll still be there tomorrow, believe me.'

'What will?' he asked.

CHAPTER TWELVE

It was the third week in November and Ann was spending a rare client-free afternoon writing Christmas cards. She had already sent the dozen or so overseas cards in time to catch the last surface mail posting, and had prioritised the remainder into bands. There were the long-standing but seldom-seen friends who required the famous Armitage round-robin to bring them up to date on the doings of the boys and the plans for the following year (many of these had gone with the overseas batch); there were valued old friends who were seen on a regular basis and most of whose cards would contain invitations to one of the two seasonal fork suppers to be held at Raglan Road in December (the Blakes were among these but now merited a dinner party as well); there were B-list friends and acquaintances awaiting, as it were, preferment; there were relations; and there were the miscellaneous clients, colleagues and contacts (including Katie Hogan, Josette, Mrs Ramilies, Vidyut and Ava Lawrence), any of whom might pop up in a different band (excluding that of relations) next year.

For years, Ann did not send Christmas cards. She was against them. She tolerated those sent to her and Byron on the grounds that the senders got something out of it. That was when it was awfully hard to find a card that was not either overtly religious, mawkishly sentimental or coyly humorous. Otherwise intelligent people did the strangest things. The Blakes, for instance, veered between *The Adoration of the Magi* one year and two squiffy robins the next.

Ann had elected to stay out of it. The Armitages prided themselves on an enlightened atheism, but she personally deplored many of the non-religious manifestations of the modern winter solstice celebrations and the self-serving aspect of sending charity cards.

But happily the captains of the card industry underwent a sea-change. They seemed at last to realise that there were many of Ann's persuasion out there, with A/B attitudes and commensurate spending power, who were not served by the available product. A new type of card appeared on the market, designer- rather than seasonally-led, and on recycled paper. A card one could send without feeling one had traduced oneself. Earthtrust produced some of the best of these, and Ann overcame her reservations about charity cards on the grounds that saving the planet was universally desirable whatever one's creed, colour, or socio-economic group, and that she was supporting an old friend. She was scrupulous.

Having completed the round-robin cards and those containing invitations, Ann set aside the remainder to be done fairly quickly next Sunday morning and turned her attention to Christmas itself.

While she had no truck with mumbo-jumbo about mangers and virgin births she conceded that there was intrinsic value in having a time set aside for the family to be together. So the Armitage boys had always had stockings, and presents round the tree and a traditional Christmas dinner (though Ann did prefer goose to turkey). In recent years she and Byron had sometimes chosen to go elsewhere for Christmas – a cottage in the Lake District, a small hotel in Bruges – but this year she had already decided that it would be enjoyable to be at home, and to have the whole family round the table, with perhaps one or two selected guests . . .

She had done most of her Christmas shopping. There were two essential prerequisites – a budget and a list. Window-shopping and impulse buying led, as night followed day, to wild extravagance and hopelessly unsuitable gifts. Ann put a lot of thought into her presents, and if money needed to be spent she would spend it, but the rightness of the gift was infinitely more important. One year she had given Sebastian a set of wind chimes and Julian a cashmere sweater. Both had been well received and neither son had commented on the disparity in cost.

The outstanding present remaining to be bought was Gavin's. She was as yet undecided whether it would be in order to give something to Giselle, or even (she experienced a little bubbling-up of hope) to both of them jointly. She could afford to put that on hold for the moment.

She straightened the piles of cards, placed her pen on top of the present list, and went down to the kitchen to make herself a cup of coffee. While the kettle was boiling she considered the likelihood or otherwise of Giselle accompanying Gavin to Christmas dinner at Raglan Road. There was always the possibility that he might be invited to Chuffington . . . or that they might each choose to stay with their own families . . . Or – she frowned as she tried to accommodate a new notion – they might go away together . . . Schmooze closed for five days at Christmas . . .

Would it, she wondered, pouring water on to grounds in a small earthenware jug, be pushy to invite them here? And if so, when? If she did so too soon the chances were that Gavin would claim he couldn't possibly think about Christmas at this stage: if she left it too late Hester might get in first—

Shocked, Ann stopped stirring with the wooden spoon. What was she thinking of? Had she really become so calculating, so unspontaneous, so devious, that she could regard herself as being in competition with Hester over something as essentially trivial as Christmas?

She poured her coffee through a strainer, and emptied the remaining sludge down the waste-disposal unit. Then she stood gazing down at the gently rotating surface of the coffee and forced herself to relax, bit by bit, to 'let it go' as she so often advised her clients to do. But even as she did so a balloon of something unpleasantly like panic began to swell inside her, and she fought to suppress it. Her heart thundered as she went to the freezer to take out something for supper.

Julian had landed himself a job at a posh little private crammer in Lancaster Gate. He made no bones about the fact that it was a cushy number, and Byron had wistfully to agree. His youngest son had only a modest facility for languages, but he was eminently personable. He had always *looked* like the sort of chap one would want to have in one's employ . . . Whereas Byron himself, with twice the brain and an infinitely more serious approach to teaching, had never really looked like that sort of chap . . .

He climbed down, warily and heavily, from the step-ladder and surveyed the wallpaper he'd just hung in Julian's Belvedere Road flat. It was an absolute bugger, art nouveau in flavour, with the sort of hectic pattern that would have been considered unliveable-with only a few years ago. Such were the inscrutable vagaries of taste. Byron was eternally grateful for his wife's good sense which had dictated the classic, high-quality, no-nonsense decor at Raglan Road, and for the handsome windfall which had funded it.

He sat down carefully on the steps, leaning forward and wedging his backside in between two of the slats. It was cold in the flat because Julian turned the heating off when he was out at work, and Byron didn't like to turn it on.

He'd had a hand in all the boys' flats – not heavy stuff, but decorating, putting up curtain fittings and shelves, sticking up tiles, that sort of thing. The boys themselves were competent but slapdash, whereas he prided himself on being a bit of a perfectionist. When he did something it stayed done. Like this wallpaper – he gazed round the room appraisingly. Julian had chafed at the length of time it had taken him, but it was a completely professional job. No matter how close someone stood to this, they wouldn't see the join.

There was the sound of the front door opening and closing and almost at once Julian appeared.

'Oh, great!'

'You like it?'

Julian walked to the middle of the room and turned around on the spot. He was dressed in an artfully collegiate style, with an argyll pullover, a herringbone tweed jacket and a long hand-knitted scarf.

'It's terrific. Thanks. Was it hell?'

'Hell-ish.'

'Sorry about that. I appreciate it.'

'My pleasure.'

'Christ!' Julian clasped himself. 'Aren't you cold?'

'No,' lied Byron, 'not particularly.'

'It's taters in here.' He went out to the thermostat in the hall and turned the dial. 'Won't take long to warm up. Fancy a cup of tea?'

'No thanks, I'll get back to Raglan Road.' Byron gave the bottom of the sash window a tug.

'By the way, this thing's jammed.'

'Forget it, I'm not bothered.'

'I'll pop over tomorrow and take a shufti.'

'Don't worry about it.'

'It ought to be done, it'll get worse with winter coming on.' Byron succeeded in raising it an inch.

'I won't want to open it in winter.'

Where his sons were concerned Byron was accustomed to treading a fine line between being of assistance and irritating the hell out of them.

'Fair enough.' He pushed the window back down. 'I'll leave you to it then.'

'Cheers.'

Byron put on his anorak. 'I'll clear that stuff up tomorrow.'

'No need, I'll do it.' This was no more than a token exchange since both father and son knew that Byron would indeed come back tomorrow, clear up the wallpapering gear and probably see to the window as well.

Byron also knew from experience exactly when to place his next question, and with what degree of casualness. He was almost at the door when he paused.

'I almost forgot – your mother said if you wanted to come over for supper there's plenty. You're more than welcome.'

'Thanks, but I've got a load of marking. Can I leave it open?'

'Of course.' Byron opened the door. 'Sevenish as usual, if you feel so inclined. Au revoir.'

'Bye.'

They both refrained from saying: 'See you later.'

Over supper, at which Sebastian was also present, Ann asked after Gavin.

'Does anyone know how he is? We haven't seen him for quite some little while, have we, Byron?'

Byron agreed that this was so.

Julian (who had found time to drop by) said: 'He's probably shattered, trying to keep Giselle happy.'

Ann frowned. 'She's not that difficult, surely?'

'That's not what he means,' said Byron.

'Not what—? Oh . . .!' Ann laughed sportingly. 'I see!'

Sebastian began scraping the crust of the *pommes dauphinoises* off the side of the dish with his fork. 'They were fighting like cats last time I went round there. You want my opinion, poor old Gav's pussy-whipped.'

'Seb, that is a disgusting expression,' reprimanded Ann playfully, and then assumed an expression of concern. 'When was that?'

'A few days ago. I could hear them at it as I came up the stairs.'

'But did you listen at the door?' asked Julian. 'That's what Mum wants to know.'

'I most certainly do not,' said Ann gravely. 'When you went in did you catch any hint of what the trouble was?'

'No,' said Sebastian. 'It was a routine domestic.'

'How were they otherwise?' asked Byron.

'He was in a filthy temper to begin with but he perked up.'

'What about young Giselle?'

'She went to bed and left us to it.'

Julian smirked. 'A proper little one-man arbitration service, aren't you?'

Ann had not taken her eyes off Sebastian. 'I do hope all is well.'

He leaned towards her. 'Not a darn thing you can do, Mommy dearest, if it isn't.'

'Sebastian's right,' said Byron, 'there isn't. And it's none of our business.'

'Quite so,' said Ann. 'All the same I should very much welcome it if you, Sebastian, and you, Julian, could keep your eyes and ears open. Forewarned is forearmed.'

Hearing this, Byron was filled with affectionate admiration. That phrase might have been his wife's motto.

Katie bumped into Hester Blake by the cook-chill cabinet in the supermarket.

'Hallo, Katie!' cried Hester in her so-there-you-are voice. 'Welcome to salmonella city.'

'It's an awful temptation when it's just for one,' explained Katie, before remembering that Hester herself was in the same place.

'It's only me and the old man tonight,' said Hester, also explaining, 'so I thought I'd get a few little treats.' She waved her hand over a basket which contained among other things fat black olives, smoked turkey, walnut oil and balsamic vinegar.

'Good idea,' said Katie, taking a vegetarian cheese crumble.

'How are you getting on? I've been meaning to come and call on you the last few times I've been in, but such is office life . . .'

'Fine. I'm enjoying it. All the partying's quite tiring, but I'm not complaining.'

'It would finish me,' said Hester. 'But then I've got twice the miles on the clock that you have.' She gave Katie a look of shrewd kindliness. 'You're looking well on it, I must say. Are you over that unpleasantness with Gavin Armitage?'

'Oh, absolutely,' lied Katie. 'To such an extent that I haven't even bothered looking out for a replacement – it's rather nice to be fancy-free for a while.'

'And no more of that guilt nonsense, I trust?'

'Not a trace.'

'Good for you,' said Hester, 'I'm delighted to hear it. Look, let's have a natter over a glass of something when I'm in next week, shall we?'

'That'd be nice.'

'It's arranged. Bye now, my love.'

'Bye.' Katie smiled. 'Enjoy the treats!'

'What?' Hester looked blank, then down at her basket. 'Oh, the treats! Yes, you bet . . .'

Hester didn't realise how relieved she was until she was out of earshot, and released a huge sigh. So at least Katie was definitely off the scene – it had been preying on her mind.

Mary looked up from reading the latest HB Page as she came in.

'It's a bit serious this,' she said. 'Are you going to change your image, because if so I'd like to know about it in advance.'

'Certainly not,' said Hester, opening the mini-fridge and putting the contents of the supermarket carrier inside. 'I *am* serious from time to time, you know that. Light-hearted doesn't have to mean lightweight.' She put her hand to her cheek. 'God, how pompous.'

'No, fair enough,' said Mary. 'And anyway, I didn't say I didn't like it. But it is different.'

'Good.'

'Let's hope the GBP feel the same.'

'I hate to say it, but *that* to the GBP.'

'For goodness' sake,' said Mary, as the internal phone rang, 'don't let our leader hear you talking like that. Hallo?' She covered the mouthpiece as she handed it over. 'Talk of the devil.'

'I find myself with a cancelled meeting late this afternoon,' said Robert. 'I wondered if you'd care for a drink, about six.'

Hester did some rapid calculations.

'Or will that completely foul up your return journey?' he added politely.

'Not at all. I'd like to.'

No matter how near the bone things seemed to be getting he always acknowledged her other life and its prior claim on her. And the minute he had done so it seemed she had been given the necessary permission to do what he suggested.

'I'm staying in town tonight,' he said, 'and I'd offer dinner, except that I know it's completely out of the question.'

'It might not be,' she said.

'It doesn't matter either way. Let's have that drink and you can let me know then.'

'Right.'

'By the by, Hetty, I liked this week's offering.'

'Did you?'

'You sound surprised.'

'No.'

'It was different. Thoughtful.'

'Thank you.'

'But don't do it all the time,' he warned, 'or your public might get worried.'

'The problem with getting older,' she had written, *'is that you don't. The body may sag, the skin may wrinkle, the hair may lose its lustre and the brain cells pop their clogs at the rate of thousands per minute but the heart – ah, the heart! – remains for ever eighteen. My guess is I'm not the first woman of a certain age you've heard this from. I bet your mother said it to you, just as her mother said it to her. But you don't believe it until you experience it for yourself. And the irony is that it's when your children grow up that the sensation is at its keenest. While you're wondering who you are you become parents, and while you're deciding what to do when you grow up your children become adults . . .'*

Gavin usually liked lunching with Della. For one thing she was smart, in every sense of the word, and reinforced his sense of being a mover and shaker. He had been pretty dubious about going into partnership with a woman, but Della understood that you had to give clever, creative people autonomy. Having put up a major tranche of the cash, she'd adopted the attitude of a benign den-mother. Today he craved her sympathy but shrank from being specific about the reason.

Ostensibly, these monthly lunches were *ad hoc* board meetings, a chance to sound out the office burbles, and to run new ideas up the flagpole away from the pressures of the brasserie. Gavin disliked in principle giving business to the competition, so they met in the only halfway decent wine bar within striking distance of Schmooze. It was tricked out in quasi-Somerset Maugham style, with palms in basket tubs, wicker chairs, and revolving fans overhead. In a nod to the season the management had this week added a fluffy white Christmas tree with pink and silver balls.

Della drank iced spritzer and drew on a single pre-prandial cheroot. Gavin drank house red and smoked incessantly. On this occasion they dispensed with the token business side of the meeting inside half an hour and by the time Della was toying with *fusilli carbonara,* Gavin was allowing his *moules provençales* to go cold as he inveighed against fate.

'I'm in crisis,' he explained tersely, but violently, in case she had missed the point. 'Professionally, financially and emotionally.'

'Really? Oh well, you're quite used to it,' Della reminded him.

'But that's how stress works, in a series of ascending peaks, with intermittent troughs, each a little shallower than the last. The troughs, or remission periods, are what prevent so many people from seeing that they are heading for a breakdown.'

'Is that what you think you're doing?'

'It *is* what I'm doing.'

'Well, Gavin,' said Della, spearing a pasta twist with one prong of her fork and darting it at him, 'you must get help. Because we need you.'

'I know that. I'm very well aware of that. Why do you think I'm first to arrive and last to leave, virtually every day?'

'Because you want to?' Della suggested.

'Because that place is my life.'

'Well, it doesn't go unappreciated.'

'I'm afraid I think it does. I get the distinct impression that some of our people have not grasped the implications of being involved in a ground-breaking enterprise of this kind in a ferociously competitive industry, in the teeth of a worldwide recession.'

'I'm sure they haven't.' She nudged his plate with one perfectly manicured hand. 'Eat. They're just glad to have jobs and anxious to hang on to them.'

Gavin frowned down at the plate, as if wondering what it was and how it had got there, and absent-mindedly dabbed ash from his cigarette on to the side.

Della caught the waiter's eye.

'Please could you replace this? There's been an accident.'

Gavin continued to scowl as the plate was removed. Della waved a hand back and forth in front of his face.

'Are you hearing me? Be sure to get the next one down you or you'll die of malnutrition before you have that breakdown.'

Gavin gave her a hard stare. 'You're not taking me seriously.'

'Wrong. I am. You're cracking up. You don't eat enough. You drink too much, you smoke too much, and you very probably do everything too much—'

'What's that supposed to mean?'

Della made a shrugging face. 'You live with a much younger woman.'

Gavin blenched. 'If you only knew how sick I am of the imputation that I am some sort of lecherous cradle-snatcher who can't stand the pace—'

'Goodness, did I say that?'

'My brothers, my father, you – it's pissing me off.'

'Sorry,' said Della cheerfully. 'Now, here's your replacement. Do yourself a favour and eat.'

Gavin put out his cigarette, in the ashtray this time, picked up a mussel and began prising at it viciously with half of its own shell.

'Let's accentuate the positive,' said Della. 'Business is good. You've got a great new relationship—'

'Hm.' Gavin discarded the recalcitrant mussel and began jabbing at another. Della ignored him.

'—and you have a supportive family who are always there for you.'

'Please!' Gavin had got the second mussel halfway to his mouth, but this was too much for him and he lowered it again. 'I wish to God they'd keep their noses out of my life.'

'Don't be churlish, Gavin,' reproved Della. 'There aren't that many families who manage to maintain contact these days. You're one of the lucky ones.'

'Lucky? If I haven't spoken to her for a couple of days my mother checks up on me, my father wouldn't notice if we never spoke again, one of my brothers is an over-indulged brat, the other's a smackhead, neither of them do a hand's turn worth the mention, and they feel free to turn up at all hours of the day and night, usually when they want something – Christ!'

'"Golly, Moses! that's why I'm a mess!"' sang Della cheerfully.

'Just don't run away with the idea that they're some sort of emotional prop,' snapped Gavin.

'Okay,' said Della.

'As for my great relationship,' he went on, 'you don't know the half of it.'

'I should hope not indeed.'

'Zelda and I may be sexually compatible,' allowed Gavin, with an emphasis which attracted a certain amount of covert attention at the tables nearby, 'but intellectually and emotionally we're poles apart.'

'Tricky,' Della agreed.

'Our relationship is no bed of roses. It takes a huge investment of effort, time and energy, of which time is in increasingly short supply and energy already stretched to capacity.'

Della picked up his fork and finally stuck a mussel into his mouth. She cocked her head and made a clicking, chin-up sound.

'Did I ever tell you you're my hero?' she said.

There was no foreshadowing of the falling-out between Giselle and Mr Paretska, although when she looked back on it she saw it had probably been inevitable. It was, if not her fault, then at least because of her; she conceded that without regret or remorse. She'd been near the end of her tether for some time.

Customer relations were the problem. Because of Mr Paretska's non-interventionist style, keeping the peace with him had been largely a case of turning up, getting on with the job and being seen to wash one's hands from time to time. But dealing with the public was another matter.

She had got by so far by tolerating them. She didn't exactly launch a charm offensive, but she stopped short of actual rudeness. And Mr Paretska, having overheard her talking to Ann a couple of times, was under the mistaken impression that she was forming profitable relationships with some of the more regular customers.

Such was very far from the case. They drove Giselle up the wall and round the bend. Their indecisiveness, their need to explain why each and every item was being purchased, their assumption that she knew the difference between two kinds of yoghurt, their habitual proffering of ten-pound notes when their purses and

pockets were jingling with change – all these things and many
more caused Giselle to simmer with rage. Added to which she
was feeling chronically tired at the moment, so her tolerance was
at an all-time low on the morning when Mrs Baumblatt came into
the shop.

Mrs Baumblatt was plump and permed and prinked and patho-
logically vivacious. She went in for miniaturisation, always asking
for 'a spot' of this and 'a tiny bit' of that, and 'a soupçon'
of the other, so that you wondered how on earth she got to
be like a beachball on legs until you remembered she came
in almost every day. She was always dressed up to the nines
and jingling with charms and chains and had a hairstyle like
the DNA models on Open University. To begin with, Giselle
had assumed that Mrs Baumblatt was on her way somewhere,
but she had long since realised that her elaborate toilette was
habitual – Mrs Baumblatt was born to shop. She got off on
it. You could tell by the brightness of her eyes and the hectic colour in her cheeks and the way she pressed a plump,
red-tipped forefinger against the glass of the chill cabinet as
she made her interminable selection. You could tell (it made
Giselle shudder to think of it) by the way her mouth filled with
saliva as she deliberated aloud. Her appearance in the shop had
for some weeks engendered in Giselle a voluptuous longing to
garotte her with one of her fine gold chains and batter her to
a pulp.

One of Mrs Baumblatt's most annoying habits was that of asking
a question, often repeating it if it wasn't answered immediately,
and then to begin speaking on a usually unconnected matter so
that she failed to hear the answer and had to ask again. Giselle
took an exquisite masochistic pleasure in counting the incidence
of this particular quirk. She even from time to time prompted it,
in order to feel her teeth itching.

No such prompting was necessary today. Mrs Baumblatt was
in top form. Like a child tweaking the whiskers of a cat which
it believes to be a soft toy, she tweaked Giselle's nerves. She
dithered prettily, even allowing another customer to go before
her while she made up her mind. She toyed with the idea of
Roquefort, and then Tôme de Savoie before finally deciding on
Dolcelatte; she spent a full five minutes moving things about in the
refrigerator before taking one plain goat's milk yoghurt; she asked

to sniff canisters of herbal tea 'just for fun' before finally having a quarter of her usual brand; she peppered her discourse with rhetorical questions, each succeeded by a 'hm?' to which Giselle then responded, only to find herself talking into a counterbast of mindless wittering.

'Now then,' said Mrs Baumblatt, surveying her little array of goods, 'tell me. I'm going to visit my dear old lady on Thursday and I want to take her a special little treat, she finds the food so difficult in that place, now what do you suggest? Only a tasty morsel of something, she has a very small appetite . . . what would you recommend?' Giselle hesitated, ostensibly thinking about it. 'Hm? What do you think?'

'Um, I—

'A little piece of the home-made date loaf, perhaps, with some of the organic honey.'

'Yes, or the natural—'

'Hm? What's that?'

'Forget it.'

'Sorry?' For the first time since coming into the shop Mrs Baumblatt looked directly at Giselle, but still with her winsome choosing smile in place. Giselle said nothing so she went back to the bread shelf.

'Mm, what a beautiful little saffron loaf—

'I said, forget it!'

'Mm?'

This was the point at which Mr Paretska, who had been drinking his coffee in the back room, appeared in the doorway behind the counter, unknown to Giselle.

'I said—'

'What's that?'

Mrs Baumblatt, still smiling and now holding aloft the saffron loaf, looked again at Giselle, something in whose expression finally alerted her.

'Did you say something?'

'Why don't you try listening, and then you'd know?'

Mrs Baumblatt turned to face Giselle fully, but with the smile still in place, unable to believe her ears.

'I beg your pardon?'

'I said try listening.'

'How dare you!'

'And try making a list so you can come in just once a week and give us all a break!'

Mrs Baumblatt goggled, speechless. Giselle took a single backward glance at her bridges and put them to the torch.

'You're too fat anyway. A couple of weeks on carrot juice is what you want. And if you want to give your old lady a lovely treat, why don't you stay at home?'

'Giselle,' said Mr Paretska, his voice as sour as organic apple juice. 'Wait for me at the back, will you?'

Giselle didn't wait for him. She went to the back, collected her leather jacket and her bag and walked out again through the shop. She did not simply ignore them, she was oblivious to them both. She was already, in her mind, gone.

She didn't go straight back to George Street, but walked blindly across the Bayswater Road, heedless of blaring horns and shouted imprecations, and went to the playground in Hyde Park. She found a bench and sat down, staring at the children scampering and squawking, their bright coats dissolved into seeping splodges of colour by her tears.

She felt sick, frightened, and absolutely alone.

'Aha,' said Jonty. 'A card from Ann and Byron and an invitation to dinner on Friday week.'

'Oh, God,' said Hester. 'It should be our turn.'

'What does it matter?'

'Politeness matters. We owe them.'

'Get away, Ann loves cooking. "Only the four of us," she says. That's what I like to hear. All the more for us.'

'I bet they'll have one of those fork suppers, too.'

'That is mentioned.'

'We'd better have a huge drinks in the New Year.'

'Stop angsting. I like Ann's dinners.'

Ann had made traditional French onion soup; carbonade of beef with shallots and oyster mushrooms, served with baby carrots, and creamed potatoes whipped into soft, featherlight peaks; and baked pears with ginger accompanied by home-made vanilla ice cream and freshly baked *langues de chat*.

'Winter food, but not Christmas,' she explained happily as they greeted it with gasps and tucked in with groans of surrender and delight. 'We'll all have had quite enough Christmas a few weeks from now.'

'Don't,' said Hester, 'I haven't even thought about it.'

'Actually,' corrected Jonty, 'she does little else, but acting on it's another thing.'

'Every year,' said Byron to Jonty, 'now that the family are grown up, I propose a moratorium on the giving of presents, but it never happens . . .'

As Jonty took up the refrain, Ann turned to Hester and spoke quietly.

'Shall you have a full house out there in Chuffington this year?'

'Well, Jonty's father will probably be coming, so we can enjoy our very own Crisis at Christmas. Other than that, us and the kids, or at least I haven't heard anything to the contrary . . .'

'Giselle will be joining you . . .?'

'I suppose so – now you come to mention it, I don't know. I suppose she and Gavin are a *ménage* of their own these days. They may have other plans. I haven't asked.'

'No more have I,' said Ann. 'I imagine they'll let us know in due course.'

'You and Byron will be here then?'

'We thought we would this year.'

'We intend having a party of some sort over the holiday, you must come.'

'We'd love that.' Ann placed her spoon and fork together and rested her chin lightly on her folded hands. 'I did send Gavin a fax to the effect that you would be here this evening if they wanted to drop in for coffee and a drink.'

'Really?' Hester felt a pang of pleasure and anxiety. 'We haven't seen them for three or four weeks and when I rang, Giselle scarcely gave me the time of day.'

'But Hester,' Ann reminded her, 'we do not become parents in order to be appreciated.'

'Just as well,' said Byron. 'Or there'd be one hell of a lot of disappointed people about.'

He and Ann began to wrangle good-naturedly. Hester thought about Giselle. She wanted to see her and to speak to her, but Raglan Road was not the context she would have chosen. Every instinct told her that Giselle was unhappy, but that only a statutory

period of shared silences, standoffs and eventual *rapprochement*
in a familiar setting would be likely to yield results. The prospect of second-guessing her daughter's frame of mind amid the
cross-currents of Ann's lively interpersonal skills, Gavin's verbal
fencing and Giselle's own natural obstructiveness filled her with
foreboding. She caught Jonty's eye and he gave her the suggestion
of a wink, but it failed to cheer her.

They turned up at a quarter past ten. Gavin let himself in with
his own key and they came through to the dining room in
silence. Everyone else also fell silent momentarily before Ann
took charge.

'Hallo strangers!' she cried. 'Gavin, pull up those chairs. Giselle,
my love, what would you like? Have you both had something
to eat?'

'I'm fine, thanks,' said Giselle. 'Hi,' she said to Hester, and moved
her head fractionally in Jonty's direction to take him in too. Hester
thought she looked anything but fine. She had lost more weight
and was very pale.

'What have you got?' asked Gavin.

'Wine, coffee, lots of food still.'

'Some wine and a plate of whatever there is would be nice,' he
said, adding pointedly, 'I haven't eaten yet tonight.'

'Dear me.' Ann pushed back her chair. 'Let's put that right
at once.'

'You could have eaten at the brasserie,' said Giselle. 'I don't know
why you don't.'

'I don't have time.'

'Or at the flat – you came back first.'

'I didn't fancy a processed cheese sandwich.'

'Sound like a married couple, don't they?' asked Byron of the
table in general.

'Have some pears with ice cream, Grizzle,' suggested Jonty,
'they're gorgeous.'

'No, thanks.'

Ann returned to the table with a glass of wine and a plate of
carbonade for Gavin.

'Giselle, are you sure? A cup of tea?'

'No thanks, as a matter of fact,' said Giselle all in one breath,
'I've got something to tell you.'

'We're all ears,' said Ann.

Gavin ate his food in a way that suggested he was only doing so in order not to throw it all at someone. He looked up briefly. 'There's bad news and bad news.'

'Shut up,' said Giselle.

Byron leaned towards Jonty. 'Another snifter?'

'Afterwards – it sounds as though I might need it.'

'Why not let us be the judge of what kind of news it is,' said Ann. 'Giselle?'

'Well, for one,' said Gavin, 'Zelda's got the sack.'

'Let me speak for myself, can't you?'

'Exactly,' said Ann.

'Oh, darling, no,' exclaimed Hester. 'What happened?'

'I was rude to a customer.'

'That's news?' enquired Jonty. 'You'll have to do better than that, Grizzle.'

Gavin swallowed a large mouthful of wine and lifted his glass towards her. 'She's about to, believe me.'

'Please, Gavin,' said Ann. 'Giselle?'

Giselle looked at Hester. Not waving but drowning.

'I'm pregnant.'

CHAPTER THIRTEEN

H ester gave a gasp and clutched her hair.
'How about that drink?' asked Byron.

'Don't mind if I do . . .' murmured Jonty.

'It's early days,' said Gavin briskly, as if daring anyone to make a big thing of it. 'Plenty of time to discuss the options.'

'And how do you feel about it, my dear?' asked Ann. Hester, still trying to gather together her response, saw her role being usurped before her eyes.

'Sick,' said Giselle. 'Literally.'

'Poor you,' agreed Ann.

'But, Grizzle,' said Hester, scrabbling for a toehold on this, to her, surreal conversation, 'what will you do?'

'I don't know.'

'An accident, I take it,' said Jonty in a voice in which atavistic outrage and acquired permissiveness were present in about equal parts.

'There was always a slight chance it might happen,' said Gavin. 'You know how these things are.'

Byron pulled an anxious face. 'Any chance we could postpone the details . . .?'

'Don't be stuffy, Byron,' said Ann.

Hester had never felt so helpless in her life. 'How far gone are you?'

'Four or five weeks.'

'Nothing you couldn't lose on the head of a pin,' said Gavin almost boisterously. Giselle turned slowly to look at him with an expression of bafflement.

'So it's due in . . .' Hester, close to tears, was quite unable to make the calculation.

'Late July or early August,' supplied Ann.

'I told you, Zelda,' said Gavin. 'They're all dying to be grand-parents.'

There was a general murmur of denial, and even some laughter with which Gavin, but not Giselle, joined in. The atmosphere lightened, warily.

Under cover of this shift Hester leaned across. 'Have you considered the implications, love?'

Giselle gave her a despairing look. 'For Christ's sake, Mum, what do you think I've been doing for the past four weeks?'

'Of course . . . I'm sorry.'

'One thing's certain,' said Ann to Hester. 'These two have some hard emotional work before them.'

Hester gave a slow, unemphatic nod, her eyes on Giselle's face.

'You mentioned options,' said Jonty, 'but you chose to make this announcement when we'd all be together. Are we to infer that you're going to go ahead?'

'It's on the cards.' Gavin gave Giselle's shoulders a squeeze. 'Isn't it, Zelda?'

'I don't know.' Hester noticed how wooden the girl looked in his encircling arm.

Jonty raised his eyebrows. 'Then you're being a bit precipitate, aren't you?'

'I don't think so,' said Gavin. 'We've talked it over. Exhaustively.'

'You have,' corrected Giselle. Gavin withdrew his arm.

'And what conclusions have you drawn?' asked Ann.

'That we're better placed than most in our position. We've got the flat, and the company's pretty buoyant – with a bit of luck, Zelda can find another job—'

'If I decide to look for one.'

'Well, sure—' there was a hint of testiness now in his voice. 'At any rate, the practicalities don't present that much of an obstacle.'

'Perhaps,' said Ann, 'they are not the most crucial issue.'

'Are you going to get married?' asked Byron.

'Byron, please.' Ann pursed her lips.

'Perfectly innocent question.'

'I don't know.' Gavin glanced at Giselle, whose face, Hester thought, appeared frozen. 'I'd like to think we haven't completely ruled it out.'

'Well, I'll be . . .'

'I don't know what to say . . .' Hester ran her fingers into her hair
and lowered her head for a moment, partly because she could no
longer bear to look at the two of them. When she did look up she
said, 'Can we assume that when some sort of definite game-plan
has emerged you'll let us know?'

'Of course,' said Gavin. Hester stared pointedly at Giselle, who
gave a nod so brief only a mother would have recognised it.

'I think,' said Ann, quietly and firmly, 'that now these two have
paid us the compliment of letting us in on their plans—'

'What plans?' asked Byron amiably.

'—their deliberations then, we should let them have the space and
time they need to complete those deliberations. It's good to know
that both of you,' she turned to Gavin and Giselle, 'realise that your
parents are there for you, and will give you all the support you need
in what may be a difficult time ahead. All we can say—' she looked
around to include the rest of them '—is that we are here, with such
expertise, energy and experience as we have accumulated, and at
your disposal.'

'We know,' said Gavin drily, 'but don't worry, we'll handle it.'

Hester glanced at Jonty. He looked pinched and preoccupied.
With a conscious effort she got up and went round the table to
Giselle, putting her arms round her and kissing her cheek which
in spite of its pallor was hot.

'Love you, darling,' she whispered, as Ann began tactfully to talk
to Gavin. 'Do let us know whatever we can do.'

She was rewarded by another minute inclination of the head.
Hester felt as if she might burst from suppressing such a storm
of mixed emotions – anger, anxiety, shock, joy and frustration.
She brushed Gavin's shoulder with her hand as she returned to
her seat. He acknowledged the gesture with a strenuously cheerful
grin. Which was more than could be said of Jonty, who was now
listening to Byron's analysis of the Melbourne Test with a stony
expression.

How strange we are, thought Hester. If this were France, or Italy,
or Ireland, there would be laughter, tears and shouts, everyone
would be acting out the drama with unambivalent gusto. But
here we are, the English middle-classes, curiously, even more
emotionally hampered by our formative 1960s years, quite unable
to express – or even to find – our reactions to this age-old situation.

So we are terribly polite. We allow one of our number to run a kind of committee meeting on our behalves. In trying to behave well we are curiously inappropriate. The men in particular, thought Hester, looking at them, are gauche and emotionally hog-tied. Giselle might be forgiven for thinking that her father simply was not interested in her condition, that he did not care. And, God knows, she needed to know that they both did.

Hester leaned forward, picking up on the conversation. 'It's the blood sugar,' she said. 'Morning sickness – it's low blood sugar. You want to eat small, dry snacks, little and often.'

'I've told her that,' said Gavin.

'Yes, you have,' said Giselle with undisguised sarcasm.

'But it's true,' Hester insisted. 'Keep a packet of plain biscuits at the side of the bed and have one as soon as you wake up, before you even have a cup of tea.'

'I hate to say it,' Ann delivered her casting vote, 'but Gavin and your mother are right. And low blood sugar also accounts for the tiredness you may be experiencing. You should cultivate a grazing mentality.'

'I'll try.'

'That said,' went on Ann with a cajoling tilt of the head, 'can I get you anything now?' She reached for the plate of *langues de chat* and proffered them. 'This sort of thing is absolutely ideal.'

'I really couldn't, thanks.'

Gavin took several and slipped them into his pocket. 'For later.'

Giselle pushed her chair back. 'Do you mind if we make tracks? I'm pooped.'

'My dear, of course not!' said Ann, rising. 'You get back to George Street and have a good night's sleep. Gavin, you look after her, won't you?'

Gavin favoured his mother with a look of such brutal coldness that Hester wondered she didn't freeze in her tracks, but she appeared not to have noticed.

'Please don't all get up,' he said, 'we'll see ourselves out.'

Again they grouped and re-grouped, kissing, shaking hands, embracing, murmuring, making no assumptions, gingerly negotiating this new minefield of uncertainties and imponderables. When Hester hugged Giselle, and whispered: 'Take care of yourself,' she felt the suggestion of an answering pat on her back. She felt like a rescue worker, straining for the least sign of life buried beneath the smoking rubble.

They sat down once more at the table and Byron offered more drinks, loudly and jovially, because Giselle and Gavin had not yet left the house. When they heard the front door close, Ann said:

'May I suggest we don't pick up at once on the topic closest to the forefront of all our minds? Our respective offspring have clearly not yet resolved all the problems connected with it, and it would be invidious for us, I think, to pre-judge the issue.'

'Quite a bombshell,' declared Byron.

'It's so strange,' Hester said, 'that they chose to tell us like this and yet they've not decided what to do. I do *hope*,' she added, feeling Ann's gaze upon her, 'that they have talked it through together. I got the impression they weren't exactly seeing eye to eye . . .'

'We should certainly feel flattered that they have taken us into their confidence at this early stage,' said Ann, agreeing with a point which Hester had not made.

Jonty ran his fingers back and forth along the edge of the table. 'I hope Grizzle is at least prepared to consider abortion.'

'Termination,' corrected Hester in a brittle voice. 'Why?'

'If I may say so,' interjected Ann, 'you are illustrating my point. Of course it is your daughter who has most at stake in this situation, but Gavin is also directly involved and not simply biologically. They have forged a relationship and must make these decisions for themselves. They are after all both over eighteen.'

'Not by that much, in Grizzle's case,' pointed out Jonty, coolly.

'Quite so,' Ann conceded. 'Nevertheless, she is a young woman – and one with a mind of her own. The two of them have seen fit to place the situation before us, but my understanding is that our opinions were not being elicited. It might therefore be best if we did not air them now, even amongst ourselves.'

'You may be right,' said Jonty with a perceptible emphasis on the second word.

'One thing's certain,' said Byron, 'whatever we think will make precious little difference to what happens in the long run.'

Hester felt suddenly exhausted. 'That's true.'

'So I take it we are agreed,' posited Ann quietly but firmly. 'A moratorium until we see what transpires. Shall we have coffee in the drawing room?'

*   *   *

The Blakes scarcely spoke until they were on the motorway, and then it was Jonty who broke the silence.

'Bloody hell. What a facer.' In spite of his words he sounded much more cheerful.

Hester, who was leaning back on the head-rest, gave a little moan. 'I keep telling myself it happens all the time, and these are the nineteen-nineties, and all of that . . . but it doesn't stop it being a shock.'

'You're not joking. I mean, can you see Grizzle looking after a baby?'

'No, but then half the women who have babies are people you could never imagine looking after them, and they cope – some of them brilliantly.'

Jonty shook his head. Hester stared out of the window.

After a moment she said: 'What upsets me is that she didn't come and tell us herself, on her own. It put us in an impossible position.'

'No worse than Ann and Byron, presumably.'

'Much worse than Ann and Byron! It's bound to affect us more directly, and we weren't even on our own territory—' Hester's voice wobbled and she put her hand to her mouth. She regained control, and went on: 'Frankly, my feelings were hurt . . . and there was so little I could do or say to help . . .'

Jonty patted her knee. 'I know. It's tough. But on reflection I'm quite heartened by the way they chose to do it. It does at least mean they see themselves as a unit even if they don't agree on everything. And that they respect our opinion. If Grizzle has definitely decided to go ahead, and I personally rather hope she'll have a change of heart, then at least it would appear that she's doing it with his support.'

'Yes . . .' Hester wiped her cheeks with her fingers, 'that's true. So she won't be on her own.'

'She won't be on her own anyway: she has us.'

'She looked awful.'

'She's feeling sick, Hes. You remember what it's like.'

'I know, but—'

'Ann had a point. Let's not talk about it any more until there's something definite to talk about.'

'And that's another thing,' Hester's voice swelled, 'I resent being told how to behave by Ann!'

'Yes—' Jonty glanced in the mirror and pulled the Range Rover into the outside lane— 'it was remarkable how we all stayed in character. You were emotional; I went on hold; Byron became fatuous; Ann's instinct is to organise, and that's what she did. It was no surprise. You know as well as I do she means nothing by it. It's just her way.'

'I don't care,' said Hester. 'It may be her way, but on this occasion she was bang out of order.'

Ann put her mug of herbal tea on the bedside table, and began to undress. Byron, who was already in bed, was reading an article in *The Economist*. Their bedroom was spacious and quiet. Byron did not look up from his reading as his wife moved about, hanging up her dress, placing her shoes on a rack, laying her tights and underwear over the back of a chair; and she in turn moved with the unhurried precision of someone engaged in a ritual, and who is not waited for. She was humming a tune to herself, but so quietly that only the faint sniffs and exhalations of her breath could be heard, and then only from time to time.

She put on her cotton nightdress, yoked and sprigged like a schoolgirl's, and went into the en suite bathroom to wash and clean her teeth. On returning she brushed her short hair vigorously, first with her head hanging upside down, then back into place without looking in a mirror, and then climbed into bed. She propped her pillows against the bedhead and picked up her herbal tea, but not her book, a mighty (over a thousand pages) saga of the Indian sub-continent which came garlanded with the plaudits of the critics and the recommendations of discerning friends.

She took a sip of the tea. Byron turned a page. His aura of tranquil concentration might have discouraged interruption from anyone other than his wife.

'Byron,' she said.

'Mm?'

'Might I ask you something?'

'Of course.' Byron lowered *The Economist* and gave her his full attention. 'Fire away.'

'I hope you think I did the right thing tonight.'

'When was that . . .?'

'In suggesting we postpone further discussion of Giselle's pregnancy until the young people are clear in their minds.'

'You know very well it suits me. I'd pay good money to avoid discussing pregnancy. Anybody's, at any time.'

'Now you're being facetious.'

'Never more serious, I promise you.'

'You understood my point, I hope – that we should not, as potential future grandparents, overstep our brief.'

Byron nodded. 'Quite.'

'I thought it was very brave of them to come as they did and face us all with the news.'

'Well—' Byron hesitated. 'Yes. I suppose it was.'

'And if only for that reason I felt very strongly that we should not be discussing them behind their backs the moment they left the house.'

'I don't know about that . . . it's axiomatic that when you leave a gathering those who are left talk about you.'

Ann looked stern. 'You will allow, I think, that this is a special case.'

'Yes, yes, of course.'

'And you agree with the line I took?'

'Yes.'

'We simply cannot risk muddying the waters at this delicate early stage.'

'Indeed not.'

Throughout this exchange Byron's hands had been resting, fingers laced, on the open pages of his magazine, and his eyes fixed on his wife's face.

Now Ann said: 'Thank you.'

'My pleasure,' he replied. And picking up the magazine, resumed his reading.

Ann in her turn left the Asian masterpiece undisturbed, finished her tea, switched off her lamp, and lay on her side, staring into the brown paisley of Byron's pyjamas, her mind racing.

'Shit . . .! Shit . . .! Shit!' cried Gavin.

'Oh bloody lovely shit . . .' he moaned, slipping sideways from Giselle and bringing her down with him so that they lay collapsed, both facing the same way. He licked the slick of cooling sweat off her shoulders and fondled her breasts, which were still more bountiful with the onset of pregnancy.

'God, you're so great,' he mumbled. In answer she took hold of one of his hands and lifted it to her mouth, giving the palm a little hot, nibbling kiss before returning it with deliberate sensuality to her breast. He sighed and snuggled into her.

'You're even sexier than usual since – at the moment.'

She moved her head in acknowledgement of the compliment.

'What do you reckon,' he went on. 'I think we can make a go of this baby caper . . .'

She gave a small shrug.

'I thought this evening went pretty well, considering. They appreciated us going there together and telling them. They're all busting for a grandchild. My mother would look after it any time. Your father was the one I was least sure about, but he was okay . . . And suddenly I feel the time is right. I believe I'm ready to have a child . . . hey, Zelda?' He hitched himself up on his elbow and rested his chin on her shoulder. 'Giselle?'

She was sound asleep.

Hester awoke in the small hours, suddenly, but with complete calmness and clarity. The realisation was growing in her, as small and still as Giselle's cluster of foetal cells – the realisation that she did not wish her daughter to have an abortion.

She wanted, more than anything, her grandchild to be born.

CHAPTER FOURTEEN

The following afternoon Gavin received a fax from his mother. It was timed, with her usual precision, 3.32 p.m., and was couched in the businesslike language designed not to cause embarrassment if read by his staff.

On the other hand Ann had reckoned without Bar, who regarded all fax messages as being in the public domain, and who slipped it in front of her employer as he talked on the phone, with a breezily whispered: 'Jump to it – it's from your mama.'

Gavin held the sheet between his finger and thumb and stared at it unseeingly while he finished his call. When he had put down the receiver, he focused on its contents.

'Dear Gavin, It was so nice to see you last night and to hear your news. If there is anything you would like to discuss it goes without saying that we are always available. We do, however, have perfect faith in your ability to make the right decision. As a point of information we shall also be at Raglan Road over Christmas. Give our best wishes to Giselle, Yours, M.'

Gavin studied this communication with a slight pucker of the brows. Ann was adept at sending many more messages than were at once apparent from the words on the paper. Gavin knew her well enough to appreciate that the mere act of sending a fax to Schmooze rather than contacting him at home was a message – it aligned him with her, family with family, like with like, and expressed a certain discreet solidarity. The invitation to discuss 'anything' was to him alone, and the friendly final reference to Giselle merely emphasised this. Also, the expressed belief that he would make 'the right decision' was a throwing down of the gauntlet – his mother had no doubt what that right decision might be, and was leaving the way open for him to check with her if he himself was uncertain. That they would be at Raglan Road for Christmas was probably the least weighted of her statements.

He took all this on board in less than thirty seconds, and then screwed up the sheet of paper and tossed it into the bin. Downstairs the brasserie still burbled profitably through the long gentle uplands of the afternoon. For the past three hours he had done what he did best superbly well – moved among his customers, spread the buzz, made them feel that this was the only place to be. An enchanting actress had told him this was how she imagined heaven – she was a bit drunk, as he was now, but she still pressed all the right buttons. At home, Giselle waited, sexy, and fecund. Gavin felt a profound satisfaction at finding himself for the moment at least in the position he relished most – that of the still point in a turning universe.

Giselle could picture her hormones. They were an angry crowd, heated and turbulent, clogging her system so that it was sluggish, churning up her stomach so that she felt sick, tiring her out with their constant and unreasonable demands, never satisfied and never still.

She took her mother's advice and kept a packet of rich tea biscuits by the bed. Gavin objected to this. He pointed out that he always brought her biscuits with her morning tea anyway. Giselle said that she liked to know they were there when she needed them. He said it was a messy habit. She countered that smoking in bed was dangerous on several counts, and the ashtray was messier than a few crumbs. He said she would encourage mice. She invoked Mensa. Gavin could not remember when Mensa had last caught anything. She said in that case it was time he learnt. He called her a slut. She called him an old woman. He stormed out. At lunchtime when she was in a hot bath the doorbell rang and it was the usual roses with a handwritten grovel. She left the roses in the kitchen sink, and the rich tea biscuits by the bed.

The biscuits helped, but there were still certain things which made her stomach contract and sent the bile shooting up her throat: coffee, anything frying, the sheepskin collar of Gavin's flying jacket and some scent he'd given her called *Rose du Matin*. (Her inability to wear it without gagging caused another altercation.) She wasn't often actually sick, but her violent retching occasionally produced a small amount of yellow liquid which scorched the inside of her mouth. Unpleasant though this was it was a relief to produce it, and she began to see it as a sort of message from within, the eruption of hot lava produced by the volcanic proceedings lower down.

No matter how Gavin liked to represent it, the pregnancy had indeed been an accident. She had not ordered her repeat prescription, he had nothing else in the flat. She had known almost at once. The sense of invasion, of being done unto, was strong and immediate. But in spite of the lava flow, and Gavin's mercurial bursts of enthusiasm and the painfully tolerant reaction of the olds, Giselle's father would have been pleased to know that she was still considering the options. Pregnancy had made her aware of her own body and its role in her destiny in a way that nothing else had ever done. Leaving Ark, moving in with Gavin, acquiring the job – none of these had had half the effect on her thinking as this one small physiological slip-up. And the more other people knew, the more she realised her power, and the power caused her to reflect.

Since being sacked by Mr Paretska she had made a friend, Chloe. She had met her once or twice during lunch hours while still working at Good and Healthy, when she used to take a bacon baguette and a 7-Up into the park. Chloe had a little boy of eighteen months, Carl, who with his café-au-lait skin and liquorice eyes was so beautiful that she had at first mistaken him for a girl. If Chloe was nearby Carl would stand and stare at Giselle, and she'd stare back, both of them impervious to Chloe's remonstrations that to stare was rude. Each knew instinctively that in this particular case it wasn't. Carl, who was not a bold or challenging child, stared out of curiosity and Giselle from a sort of dispassionate, almost scientific, interest. Here was the product of what was going on inside her, the consequence of all that churning and convulsing, the scorching yellow liquid and the enervating tiredness.

Chloe herself was not a factor to begin with. It was not until after Giselle was sacked, when the park ceased to be a mere gap in the day and became a way of using up time, that she leapt into focus.

The weeks before Christmas were cold. Carl's clothes became thicker and heavier until he was entirely covered in navy quilting except for his face, in which the eyes were still lustrous and penetrating. Giselle's clothing had not altered. She wore her jeans and leather jacket no matter what the temperature. Already the jeans, though not tight, were beginning to be uncomfortable, as though she needed more space in which to remain the same.

It was the day she'd done a bit of Christmas shopping that Chloe spoke to her.

'I'm sorry he always stares at you. I can't stop him doing it, he really likes you.'

Giselle tore herself away from Carl, who was standing in front of her holding a length of red twine on the end of which was a yellow and white telephone on wheels, with oscillating eyes. Chloe was on the next seat. She wore a cherry-red duffle coat and a knitted hat and gloves. She smiled when she caught Giselle's eye.

'I'm Chloe, Carl's Mum. I honestly think he'd take you home with him if he could.'

'It's okay, I don't mind.'

They both looked back at Carl, Chloe with affectionate amusement, Giselle with a new respect.

Chloe said: 'Ready for Christmas?'

Giselle had heard this question before, though never directed at her. She always wondered whether it meant ready in the organisational sense, or whether, in some more sinister way, it cast doubt on the subject's mental preparedness for the challenges and rigours of the season. Whichever, Giselle knew what the answer was.

'No.'

'At least you're honest.'

Giselle sensed that Chloe probably *was* ready for Christmas, but was forgiving, even admiring, of those who weren't. She nodded at Giselle's two carrier bags.

'Been getting some of the shopping done?'

'Some, yes.'

'You're so calm. If I haven't got the presents bought and wrapped by mid-December I go mad.'

Giselle could not imagine this. 'Why's that?'

'Because I'm a neurotic little housewife,' said Chloe, un-neurotically. She smiled once more at Carl. 'Look at him, he's transfixed. Whatever you've got I wish I could bottle it, hours of happy fun, better than the telly.'

'It's a soft job,' said Giselle, 'what's the going rate?'

Chloe laughed. 'You haven't got children?' Giselle shook her head. 'You love them to death but all the time they're squeezing the juice out of you. That's okay, that's how it's meant to be, you're the life-support systems, but it doesn't do anything for a girl's self-image. Do you work?'

'Until recently. I got the sack.'

'Ooh, you don't want to do that,' said Chloe, like Harry Enfield.

'It happens all the time. What about you?'

'I was a high-powered legal secretary.' She looked down at herself as if checking her arms and legs. 'Incredible, isn't it?'

'Will you be going back?'

'When he starts playgroup I'll start looking around. My old firm did say they'd keep the seat warm, but it's been over a year now, and with lots of bright young grads flooding the market every autumn, I have to be realistic.'

'Do you like being with him all the time?'

Chloe gave an infectious wheezing laugh. 'Not all the time, no, but that doesn't mean I don't love him to death.'

'You're not longing to get back to work.'

'I'd like to work again when he's a bit older, but I left because I wanted to bring him up.'

'He's lovely.' Giselle smiled at Carl who was suddenly bashful and ran to bury his face in Chloe's lap.

'He is, yes.' Chloe hoisted Carl up on to her knee and kissed his cheek. 'He's my friend, aren't you? We must go, it's getting chilly.'

She stood up and began putting Carl into his pushchair. The rack under the seat was loaded with shopping.

Giselle asked: 'Are you married?'

'You're joking.' Chloe gave another wheezing laugh. 'No, but Carl's dad and I do live together. He's Turkish Cypriot, that's where the exotic colouring comes from, a touch of the tar brush as my father never stops reminding me.'

Giselle looked thoughtful. 'You both wanted a baby, did you?'

Chloe stood behind the buggy, one hand on the handle, and stroked the top of Carl's head. 'Yes. Why don't you come back with us now and have a cuppa? We only live a few hundred yards away.'

Giselle felt she had been recalled to herself. 'No, thanks, I'd better get this lot back.'

'Another time then – it'd be nice to have a natter. I'll see you here another day, shall I?'

'Oh, sure.'

Chloe began to move, then stopped. 'I don't know your name.'

'Giselle.'

'I'll see you soon then.'

'Bye.'

Giselle watched as the two of them headed for the park gates on the Bayswater Road, Chloe with her brisk, slightly duck-footed walk and Carl hanging over the side of the buggy to take a last look at her as they left.

*   *   *

Mary lowered the phone and looked across at Hester. 'Your daughter's here.'

'What?'

'It's reception. Your daughter's come to see you.'

'Good God.' Hester pushed her chair back from the desk and clutched her hair. 'Which one?'

'How should I know?'

'Sorry.'

'Do you want me to ask?'

'No, no, of course not—'

'Shall I ask Janice to send her up or will you—?'

'No, tell her I'll go down.'

'Janice? Hester will come down right away.'

Giselle was in reception, in front of the corporate Christmas tree with its ambiguous red bows and white doves. She was dressed in her old style – black jeans, black boots, two T-shirts, black leather jacket and assorted thongs, chains, fringes and metal jewellery. She sat leaning forward, her forearms resting on her knees, tapping her fingers together restlessly. When she saw Hester she stood up.

Janice the receptionist smiled indulgently. 'There she is,' she said. Though she appeared to go back to her book, Hester was aware that this encounter with her daughter was being subjected to the closest scrutiny.

'Hallo, darling,' she said, 'what a lovely surprise.'

'Hi.'

Hester was alive to the kiss-or-not-to-kiss question, and today it was clearly a case of not. Giselle's head remained resolutely upright, and her hands were thrust into the back pockets of her jeans.

'It's so nice to see you,' said Hester again. 'What brought you this way?'

Giselle shrugged. 'I've got nothing much to do and I remembered this was the day you were in.'

'What a happy thought. Do you want to come upstairs and have a coffee or something?' Even as she spoke Hester thought of Katie, but fortunately Giselle shook her head.

'Can we go out for a bit?'

'Umm . . .' Hester rubbed her brow. 'I don't know, I don't see why not . . .'

'Oh go on,' said Janice, giving herself away, 'it'll all still be there when you get back.'

'That's what I'm afraid of.'

'Don't worry about it,' said Giselle stiffly, 'it doesn't matter.'

'No, I'd like to.' Hester reminded herself how rare an occurrence this was. 'Let me dash up and get my bag.'

Mary looked up as she rushed in. 'So which one is it?'

'Giselle – my younger one. She wants to have a talk so I'm going to pop out for half an hour.'

'Why don't you bring her up here? I'd love to meet her.'

'Exactly.' Hester pulled on her coat. 'That's why I'm not bringing her up.'

'Spoilsport.'

Downstairs in reception Giselle was still standing where Hester had left her.

'The pizza parlour's closest,' Janice was saying. 'Or if you're feeling grand you could stroll down to the Waldorf but it costs an arm and a leg.'

'Cheerio, Janice,' said Hester.

They went to the resolutely un-Christmassy pizza parlour. Hester would have preferred the Waldorf, but she was by no means sure whether a hotel of that kind might still have a dress code. They ordered coffees and Giselle had a Danish as well.

'So how are you feeling?' asked Hester. 'A bit less grotty?'

'A lot less.'

'How's Gavin?'

'Okay,' said Giselle without much interest.

'You and I ought to go and have lunch at Schmooze some time.'

'No, for goodness' sake. Things are confusing enough as it is.'

'All right.' Hester looked out of the window before trying again. 'Have you seen Byron and Ann recently?'

'Not for a couple of weeks.' Giselle spooned the froth from the top of her cappuccino and ate it, leaving a pale moustache of bubbles on her upper lip. Hester mentally scrabbled for some line of conversation which would not appear either intrusive or predicated on false assumptions.

'Actually,' said Giselle, 'there was something I wanted to ask you.'

Thank God for that, thought Hester. 'Fire away.'

'They've asked us to go to Raglan Road on Christmas Day.'

'That's nice, I should think you'll have a great time – I mean, if you're going to go. Do you want to?'

'I think we *are* going.'

'Good—'

'Gavin's not all that into Christmas, and they haven't been all together for ages, so he thought he ought really to make the effort.'

'Absolutely.'

'You don't mind?'

'We'll miss you, of course,' Hester trod carefully, 'but you know your father and me – we shan't be doing a head count and awarding Brownie points for attendance.'

'No . . . no.' Giselle fiddled with her rings. 'Anyway, I can't say I'm that keen but it looks like it's arranged.'

'I'm sure Ann and Byron will appreciate it,' said Hester, 'and they'll be marvellous hosts.' She watched Giselle's face. The cappuccino bubbles had evaporated, leaving a faint brown line. Hester suspected that some other announcement was waiting in the wings.

'I'm definitely going to have this baby,' said Giselle, as though it had been the subject under immediate discussion.

'You are.' With difficulty, Hester kept her tone neutral.

'Yes. I definitely want to.'

Hester was flooded with relief. 'Grizzle, that's wonderful – I can't tell you how pleased I am.'

Giselle looked at her suspiciously. 'Are you really?'

'Yes! I didn't want to say anything but I should have hated it if you'd had – if you'd done anything. I mean, it would have been your decision – yours and Gavin's—'

'Right the first time. Mine.'

'Primarily yours, but I realised after we saw you last time just how much I wanted you to have it. Oh, darling—' Hester half-rose, which was tricky in a banquette, and leaned across to kiss her. 'I'm *so pleased!*'

'What about Dad?'

'He was more worried about the practicalities and everything, but basically he'll want whatever you want.'

'Okay.' Giselle mopped up some pastry flakes with her fore-finger.

'And Gavin's pleased, too?'

'Yes.'

'He seemed it when you came round that night.'

'Yup.'

'Darling – everything is all right, isn't it? I mean you said before that there were a few storm clouds . . .'

'When is everything ever all right?'

'You know what I mean. He really is behind this decision of yours, is he?'

'So he says.'

Hester wasn't sure whether her question had been answered or not. She hated herself for probing; on the other hand she didn't know when she'd get another chance. 'You both of you feel ready to take this on?'

There was a split-second hesitation, not lost on Hester. 'Yes.'

'In that case, what can I say? I'm tickled pink. A granny! I may even dig out some knitting needles and attempt something extremely simple. It's so exciting!'

She was rewarded by the trace of a smile. 'I can't see you knitting.'

'Well there you go, there's a lot you don't know. I can knit. I knitted for you lot – especially Rose, because she was the first, and you. I'm not sure so much with Daniel.' She beamed. Giselle looked away. The conversation seemed to be at an end. 'Look, love, I ought to get back, but I'm so glad you dropped in. Do it again some time, soon. And make sure you come out and see us before Christmas so we can give you your presents – and how about Boxing Day?'

Giselle shrugged. 'Sounds cool.'

'Fine. Boxing Day then, both of you – of course. All three of you. And is it official? May I tell people?'

The smile peeped through again. 'Tell who you like.'

'Get away!' cried Mary. 'You little devil!'

'Tell me I look too young – please.'

'You do, but that's beside the point. All grandmothers look too young these days.'

'I never thought I'd find it so exciting. Not until they first mentioned it and there was still some uncertainty. Then I realised how much I didn't want her to have a termination.'

'Tell us a bit more then – what's the dad like?'

'Quite a bit older than her—'

'He can look after her then. Been married before?'

'Not as far as I know.'

'D'you think they'll get married?'

'I wouldn't dream of asking.'

'You're too polite,' said Mary. 'But I'll tell you one thing. There's a few column inches in this.'

Before going home Hester went into Mothercare and bought a navy and green hooded Babygro and a tiny baseball jacket with 'Junior Dodgers' across the back. The assistant smiled indulgently at her. She left the shop walking on air.

Everybody loves a lover, she thought, but they love an expectant grandmother even more.

'But Gavin,' said Giselle on Christmas Eve, 'I bought presents already.'

'You can always give them a little extra something – a sort of thank you for lunch type present. But I thought we'd give them something jointly this year.'

'Why?'

'Well – we're going there together, and the baby's on the way and so on. It seemed like a good idea, more streamlined. And economical.'

'It's not bloody economical when I've already been out and bought stuff! You never said you were going to do this! And you've spent a fortune.'

'Okay.' Gavin dropped the carrier bags on the bed and lifted his hands in the air. 'Sod it. Who gives a toss? We'll keep these. We'll give them what you bought if it'll make you happy.'

'What would make me happy is if you ever thought for one minute about what other people might be doing!'

They stood glaring at each other across the bed and the offending shopping. From the radio in the kitchen came the faint jangle of Christmas pop on LBC.

'You are such a big kid, Zelda. Put a lid on it, why don't you?'

'And you're Mr Sensible, I suppose?'

The doorbell rang. Gavin took the opportunity to stalk out. Giselle stood there, listening as he spoke on the intercom. She heard him press the button that opened the front door.

'It's a delivery,' he said, only just loud enough for her to hear.

She didn't answer.

After a moment he opened the door of the flat and she heard a heavy, laden tread on the stairs, and some bumping and scraping followed by a: 'Sign here, please.'

'Buy yourself a drink,' said Gavin. 'Happy Christmas.'

'Cheers, you too, mate. All the best.'

The flat door closed again. Curiosity got the better of Giselle. She went to the door of the bedroom.

'What is it?'

'Our present from the olds.' Gavin gave it a kick with the toe of his shoe. 'A sodding washing machine.'

CHAPTER FIFTEEN

THE HESTER BLAKE PAGE

So how was it for you? Christmas, I mean. All better now? Or are you still mentally shell-shocked and physically wrecked? Me too.

Since these days there's counselling available for just about everything from nailbiting to beekeeping, why-oh-why is there still none available for seasonal-survival disorder?

I could do it. I can tell you right now you have to go through all the necessary stages: dread . . . exhaustion . . . crazed optimism . . . mawkish sentimentality . . . homicidal fury . . . dyspeptic stupor . . . cold reality . . . and bleak depression. My guess is you're probably on the last, as the brown envelopes flutter home to roost and your dog disinters the turkey carcass from the one binbag which has managed to evade the erratic yuletide garbage collection.

Never mind. Even with the worst of the winter yet to come you can at least say, 'It's over for another year.' As your counsellor, I advise you to excise the infection as soon as it's decent to do so. Have no truck with all that sissy waiting-for-twelfth-night stuff. Once Boxing Day's out of the way throw everyone out of the house for an hour and rip down the lot – tree, streamers, cribs, candles, swags, swathes and all those tacky old glittery things that nobody likes but you're too mean to throw away. DO IT! When the rest of them get back I'll lay good odds they won't even notice. It's like when my husband shaved his beard off. People vaguely knew something was different, but what . . ? I say again, destroy the evidence, and it will be as though nothing had ever happened . . .

I did enjoy it though. Honest injun. Thanks for all your lovely cards and seasonal messages, they're so much appreciated. And just between ourselves, I'm starting the new year in an extra-optimistic frame of mind, because I'm going to be a granny!

Now <u>next</u> Christmas is going to be a real humdinger . . .

Apart from the last couple of sentences Hester had been at pains
to stick to generalities in her Christmas column. She refrained, for
once, from mentioning the excesses and shortcomings of individual
family members. Jonty's father escaped scot-free for his racist tirade
over Christmas lunch. She avoided any reference to the hostilities
which had accompanied the cold turkey on Boxing Day, when
Giselle had disappeared from the house for a full three hours,
leaving Gavin to play – and easily win – a tight-lipped game of
Trivial Pursuit (Baby-Boomers' version) with Rose and Daniel. The
veiled sniping between Jonty and Gavin on the subject of charity
was not covered. She could scarcely bear to recall, let alone to
write about, the two set, white faces, one facing ahead, the other
gazing out of the window as the red car departed for London. She
neglected to mention that she was rude to her father-in-law and had
to ring him up and eat humble pie after Jonty had taken him home.
She made light of the fact that after forty-eight hours of obligatory
family togetherness she had never felt more desolate.

Ann, taking a cursory glance at the Hester Blake Page before
consigning it to the recycling bin, noted its jovial tone with a
twinge of something dangerously like jealousy. Christmas Day at
Raglan Road had not been an unqualified success. Dinner, though
she said it herself, had been a triumph, but she sensed that for
those round her table it might as well have been pemmican and
hard tack. The washing machine was acknowledged with only the
briefest of thanks. Gavin was at his most verbosely overbearing,
Giselle was silent, and the two other boys left early, repulsed, she
suspected, by the daunting atmosphere of conflict. The pregnancy
was not referred to. In the afternoon Byron had fallen asleep, Gavin
read a report, and her attempts to initiate a dialogue with Giselle
fell on stony ground. When they left at six o'clock she had felt so
utterly drained that she went upstairs and lay on her bed, unable
even to face dealing with the leftovers. That evening she and Byron
ate lentil soup from a carton. She was dreadfully worried.

In the third week in February Daniel called on Ark at the Barlow.
He found him sitting with his feet on the table reading a local paper.

Dolly lay on her beanbag in the corner. She seemed dazed by the prevailing atmosphere of *ennui*, and managed only a token grumble as Daniel came in.

On seeing him Ark swung his feet down and brightened visibly. 'Have you come for your session?'

'No. Just a bit of a chat, really.'

'Make yourself at home.' Ark turned the sign on the door to CONSULTATION IN PROGRESS. 'How you doing?'

'Not bad.'

'Still got the job?'

'Yeah. I'm saving. I'm going round Europe in a couple of months.'

'Good on you. How long?'

'Till the money runs out.'

'Great.'

Ark took out his tin of makings and offered them to Daniel, who shook his head.

'I got my own.'

Ark began arranging the tobacco shreds delicately along the length of the paper.

'How's Zelda?'

'Pregnant.'

Ark looked up, still holding the paper steady. 'No shit.'

Daniel shook his head. 'End of July.'

Ark licked the paper, his eyes still on Daniel's face. As he rolled the cigarette between his finger and thumb he asked: 'Who's the father?'

'That twat Gavin.'

'They're together still, then?'

'Suppose so.'

Ark lowered his eyes and struck a match. The flame quivered very slightly. With the cigarette held between his lips he shook the match out and tossed it in the plastic bin.

'She's going ahead with it, is she?' Daniel nodded. 'You'll be an uncle.'

'Tell me about it.'

'I hope she's pleased.'

'I dunno,' said Daniel. 'They came out the day after Christmas, I haven't seen her since then. She seemed okay. You know.'

'What about him?'

'Yeah, well – full of the joys of spring, life and soul of the party type thing. Said he wanted to play special music for the foetus to ensure it was born in the right frame of mind.'

'Sounds okay,' said Ark charitably. 'I buy that.'

'Mum got drunk, it was total gross-out.'

'Good luck to her, I should think she needs it.'

'She's going mad about being a granny.'

'That's nice. What about the old man?'

Daniel shrugged. 'Taking it in his stride.' His brow furrowed as though something had just struck him for the first time. 'He doesn't like him much though.'

The two of them sat in reflective silence for a moment. Both of them knew what needed to be established, but it was excruciatingly difficult to achieve it.

'So what do you reckon . . ?' asked Ark cryptically.

'How do you mean?'

'About Zelda, and this guy.'

'What . . .'

'It's going all right.' This was a statement being used as a shock-absorber.

'She's having the baby.'

'She's still at his place down in London?'

'Yeah.'

'Right.' Ark stubbed out his cigarette. 'Give her my best when you see her.'

'Check.'

'Griz! I'm coming up to see the new David Hare at the National,' said Rose to Giselle over the phone. 'Can I cadge a bed for the night?' She could never have imagined that she would be asking to stay with her sister in her London flat.

'That'd be great,' said Giselle, who in her turn could never have imagined that the prospect of a visit from her sister would be the source of such undiluted pleasure.

'Will that be okay with Gavin?'

'It's none of his business,' said Giselle. 'See you later.'

It was not often that all three Armitage brothers got together outside the bounds of a family gathering. They were not close in any emotional sense, but linked by a visceral tribal awareness of their own particularity, and that the world was a touch tardy paying out the living it undoubtedly owed them.

Their meeting this evening at O'Hare's Bar, off Praed Street, was largely coincidental. Now that Byron had finished decorating, Julian was considering a housewarming party in Belvedere Road and had rung Gavin and Sebastian to check their availability, and in Gavin's case his willingness to contribute drink and lend his superior sound system. Gavin was dismissive of the party – he could not help feeling that the news of his impending fatherhood was not being treated with the respect and admiration it deserved. In accordance with his policy of only patronising the most unpromising watering holes, he suggested to Julian that he join him in O'Hare's, a favourite haunt of the London Irish, and bring Sebastian with him.

They convened at seven. Though Gavin had the shortest distance to come he was last to arrive. Schmooze was quiet, but he wanted it known just how hard it was for him to tear himself away. O'Hare's was typically crowded when he entered but he had no difficulty in spotting his brothers, whose luxuriant hair and comfortable clothing singled them out from the brilliantined stubble and rusty black suits of the other patrons.

He advanced on them with an air of unstoppable bonhomie.

'Hi there! Good of you guys to come. What are you having? Barman, a large Jack Daniels and two Bushmills, if you please. So. Jules. How about this thrash of yours then?'

'Bit of a housewarming,' said Julian warily. 'Nothing too grand.'

'Include me in,' said Sebastian. 'Gav, can I bum a fag off you?'

Gavin handed the JPs. The drinks arrived, and he raised his glass. 'Cheers. You can borrow the sound centre provided you collect it, and bring it back in the same condition.'

'Sure, no problem.'

'And how about a case of champagne?'

'No need to go mad. A couple of bottles of plonk is fine.'

'No, come on . . .' Gavin slapped Julian's shoulder. Sebastian watched with interest. 'Indulge me. After all, there's more than just your flat to celebrate, isn't there?'

'Oh yeah, you're going to be a daddy,' said Sebastian.

'It's official. Zelda had her first scan the other day. She brought home a photograph, bloody amazing.'

'He's going to show us,' warned Sebastian.

'I'm not,' said Gavin, 'because she carries it around with her. But you can see the head, arms, legs, spinal chord – it's there all right.'

'Any sign of a tadger?' asked Sebastian.

'Not as yet, but the next time should tell us whether it's a boy or a girl.'

Sebastian asked, with ill-concealed boredom: 'What do you favour?'

'A human being'll do me.'

'Statesmanlike answer,' approved Julian. 'Frankly, if it means a box of gigglewater I'm all for it.'

'How's things in the nest?' asked Sebastian. 'All koochy-koo and hunky-dory?'

'Pretty good,' said Gavin. 'Considering.'

'Considering nothing. When Patsy was up the spout she was like a rabbit on ginseng – insatiable.'

Gavin fought down, with reasonable success, any reaction to the information implicit here, but Julian wasn't proud.

'You bastard! You never said.'

'A, it was none of your business and B, you were putting yourself about in foreign parts at the time.'

'So what did she have?'

'She didn't. We dealt with it.'

Gavin had by now recovered sufficiently to offer a remark. 'I take it all this was when she was giving you a hard time?'

'She went ballistic.'

'Poor kid,' said Julian.

'Poor, my arse,' countered Sebastian. 'She didn't want the kid. She blamed me for the whole thing.'

'Totally unreasonably, I presume,' said Gavin with heavy irony. He was now rather enjoying taking the high moral ground in what was clearly a noisome swamp of deceit and depravity.

'I had a hand or whatever in it, naturally,' conceded Sebastian. 'We're not talking immaculate conception here. It's not even the first time Patsy's got herself knocked up.'

Gavin smiled at Julian. 'Note the defensive-reflexive case,"got herself" knocked up . . .?'

Sebastian shrugged. 'I don't know what you're so smug about. You weren't exactly overjoyed at the news to begin with, if my memory serves.'

'I had to step warily. I didn't know how Giselle would react. Or the parents, both sets.'

Julian chuckled. 'Oh yeah, I forgot about that. The old chums network. I don't know how you can stand lugging that weight of expectation around with you.'

'Get away,' said Sebastian. 'He loves it.'

'It's not part of the equation,' protested Gavin.

'Come on, it has to be!'

'Zelda and I will chart our own course and our respective families will have to accept that.'

'I see,' said Julian, exchanging glances with Sebastian. 'So it's "a plague on both your houses".'

Rose came in the late afternoon to drop off her case. She wore goofy patched dungarees and red baseball boots, but her face, hair and nails were gleaming and immaculate.

'Where's Jez?' asked Giselle as they sat at the kitchen table drinking tea.

'He's not with me. I'm meeting a friend who's at the Central School.'

'Oh.'

'You may as well know, we're not together any more.'

'Sorry.'

'Don't be.' Rose lifted her sleek curtain of hair off her neck and let it fall again with a little shake so that it fanned out over her shoulders. 'It was well and truly over.'

'Anybody else?'

'Not at the moment. My decision – I've got finals in a few months' time, and I want to get a first if I'm going to stand any chance of a job in the media. Plus,' she added pragmatically, 'I don't want to start anything now with a Uni bloke when we'll all be going our separate ways in the summer.' She sipped her tea and gazed levelly through the steam at Giselle. 'Honestly, Griz, I can recommend it.'

'I believe you.'

'So how are you?' The gaze became more penetrating. 'I just can't *believe* you're going to be a mum!'

'Nor me.'

'You're not showing at all.'

'I'm only coming up to four months. But I can't wear jeans.'

'You're looking great. Aren't you really excited?'

'I am, yeah.'

'What about Gavin? It's so romantic. Does he sit for hours waiting to feel it kicking?'

'It's not kicking yet – any day now though.'

'But is he thrilled? I bet he is.' Giselle made no comment. Rose gave another dig with her cattle-prod of enthusiasm. 'I bet he can't wait to be a father.'

'I wouldn't know.'

Rose's eyes narrowed as she shook her head in wonderment. 'You've changed so much . . . Do you feel different?'

Giselle considered this. 'Not different. More the same, if you get me. More like I always was but hadn't realised.'

'God!' Rose exclaimed. 'A genuine voyage of self-discovery – I never thought I'd come across one in captivity.'

She laughed, they both did. Giselle rocked her chair back.

'It's true – once you're hatching another human being you get a better idea of what it's all about – what you want for yourself, and for the baby, and why. You have to.'

'And what do you want?'

'I want the baby because I think I can bring her up well – what I think is well. It's the *only* job I've ever wanted to do, the only one I've really looked forward to. I want her to feel free, and be happy, and to know that I'm her friend.'

'If you could hear yourself – you sound like Miss World.'

'Can't be helped.'

'And that's what Gavin wants too, is it?'

Giselle shrugged. 'Who knows what Gavin wants?'

'Are we going to get something to eat?' asked Julian. 'What's on offer here?'

'Don't consider this menu unless you like hospital food as well,' warned Gavin. 'The pickled eggs here are straight out of *Alien 3*.'

'How about a curry?' suggested Sebastian.

'Nice one,' said Gavin. After three bourbons he had decided that the brasserie could survive without him for another couple of hours. 'Mind if I give Zelda a ring, see if she'd like to come?'

'Is curry wise for expectant females?'

'Come on, Jules, this is Zelda we're talking about – she's got a digestion like an office shredder.'

'I won't, thanks,' said Giselle. 'Rose is here for the night, remember?'

'But she's going to the theatre, surely.'

'She could be back by ten-thirty and if I'm not here she won't be able to get in.'

'You could leave a note.'

'No – look, I made the arrangement with Rose first, right?'

'It's not often I take an evening off from work.' Gavin sounded petulant.

'No,' replied Giselle. 'And when you do you're with your brothers and expect me to jump.'

'I simply thought you'd like to join us.'

'Sorry, can't. You carry on.'

Gavin put the phone down. Behind him, in the noisy crush of the bar, Sebastian and Julian would be looking his way, waiting. He kept his back to them for a full thirty seconds while he regained his composure.

'I think it's some kind of fundamental, hormonal thing, knitting,' said Hester in response to her husband's question. 'Pregnancy is a creative process, knitting's the same.'

'But it's not you that's pregnant this time.'

'The female line is particularly strong. I'm empathising.'

Jonty pressed the remote control in search of the snooker. 'Don't overdo it, will you?'

'What?'

'The empathising.'

'For heaven's sake—' Hester put down the knitting, keeping one forefinger on her place in the pattern. 'What is this, psychology for pleasure and profit? It may have escaped your attention but I am not exactly a possessive mother. To be honest, we're both so laid-back we're practically invisible. I think I ought to be allowed a little harmless knitting.'

'Keep your hair on. You're welcome.'

'Thank you.' Hester looked back at the pattern. 'Damn.'

'In these circumstances we have to be especially careful to maintain the differentials.'

'What the hell.' Hester dumped knitting and pattern to one side. 'What on earth do you mean?'

'I mean that our unmarried daughter is pregnant by a considerably older man.'

'Honestly, you make it sound like something out of a Victorian melodrama. Giselle is hardly Little Nell.'

'I'm only stating the bald facts.'

'I think it's all to the good. Anyone can see it's broadened her horizons.'

'Let's see,' Jonty lowered the sound on the already pin-drop silence of the Crucible Theatre. 'She's gone down there, lost a job and now she's pregnant.'

'So you see it as a chapter of disasters.'

'Nothing's ever black and white. But that is an interpretation that could be put on it. And it's received wisdom that pregnancy is very often the way out for girls who feel they've achieved nothing. They start a baby for vague reasons to do with their self-worth, and the need to find a purpose in life.'

Hester frowned in disbelief. 'You think that's what it is? They said it was an accident.'

'I'm merely calling to mind a particular line of argument about this sort of situation.'

'Okay, but surely now that the decision's made, and she's going to have it, the least we can do is treat it as a happy event.'

'Yes. You're right.'

'So?'

Jonty increased the volume a little, to thunderous applause. 'Calm down, Hes. You're right, we should be pleased for her and take a positive attitude. But we've also known Ann and Byron for years and we have to take that into account.'

'It's a plus, I'd have thought.'

'At the moment. But if anything – heaven forfend – if anything goes awry it could prove a complication. I'm only saying we should keep a little distance, as a fail-safe procedure.'

Hester shook her head in disbelief. 'You are *so* cautious. You are *so* careful.'

'Only watching our backs. Someone has to.'

'Okay, fine. You stand the dog-watch if that's what you want to do. But as far as I'm concerned if I want to knit leggings, I shall!'

Jonty pointed at the pile next to her. 'I hate to be a Jeremiah but it looks to me as though you've dropped a stitch.'

Rose got back first. When the doorbell went Giselle was lying on the green and white sofa with her head resting on the inflatable man's crotch, eating toffee crunch ice cream from the tub and reading a magazine. Before going to the door she pushed the magazine face-down beneath the sofa and replaced what was left of the ice cream in the freezer.

Rose, when she came in, was sparkly and garrulous, full of the play and how wonderful it had been. She hardly drew breath as Giselle made tea and led her back into the sitting room.

'. . . it makes me realise how long it is since I went to a really first-class production – the style and pace, the sheer *impact*, it was so exhilarating, Griz – you know, you and I ought to go to something some time, now that you're down in town. Oh, well, actually, I suppose you and Gavin would want to do that sort of thing tog—'

'You're right, you and I should,' said Giselle, flopping down once more on to the inflatable man. 'You'd have to choose though. You know me – uneducated thicko.'

'No problem, it'd be such fun—' Rose put her cup on the ground, spotted the corner of the magazine and pulled it out. 'Hey, what's this?'

'Something I picked up—'

'"Motherhood" – Grizzle!'

'I told you – I'm into it.'

'You really are, aren't you?' said Rose wonderingly, as if the truth of this had only now fully dawned on her.

'Yes. I really am.'

Rose riffled the pages, then dropped the magazine. 'Isn't it weird, how things turn out?'

'How do you mean?'

'I don't know . . . less than a year ago you were the prodigal daughter with the unsuitable bloke and the dodgy lifestyle, and I was Goody Two-Shoes at university with the nice young man . . . now look at us.'

'Things aren't that different.'

'God, they couldn't *be* more different. I'm still a student with lousy job prospects, and Jez is history. You're living with Gavin in this smashing flat, with a baby on the way and two entire families becoming dewy-eyed at the prospect.'

'It isn't quite the way you make it sound. I told you, I don't feel as though I've changed, I've just discovered what I want.'

'Yes!' Rose picked up the magazine and held it to one side of her face, beaming and pointing at the masthead: '"Motherhood"!'

When Gavin and Julian got back twenty minutes later it was impossible not to hear their loud progress from car to outer front door, and then across the hall and up the stairs. Their laughter had the self-congratulatory note of the just-drunk-enough. Rose opened the door to them.

"Struth,' said Julian. 'It's raining women.'

'Hi, Rose.' Gavin kissed her, and then added, with his arm still around her shoulders, 'this is Zelda's big sister, Rose.'

Julian inclined his head. '*Enchanté* . . .'

'Hallo,' said Rose. 'Nice evening?'

'Nice . . . was it nice . . ?' Gavin pondered. 'Jules, was it a nice evening?'

'Not particularly, that's why we're ratted.'

'Speak for yourself.' Gavin headed in the direction of the sitting room. 'Anyway, Rose's evening was unimpeachably nice, she's been to the National.'

Julian hovered. 'Is that right – what did you see?'

'The new David Hare,' said Rose.

'Christ. On a scale of one to ten, how preachy was it?'

'It was absolutely brilliant.'

'That's not an answer—' Julian saw that Rose was serious, and effected a lightning change of tack. '—no, actually I admire Hare's work. The National's taken a bit of a pasting lately, though. What did you think of the production?'

'It was superb.'

'That's good to know. I'm lamentably out of touch, I've been working in France for the past year.'

'Giselle said.'

'The place I was in was the social and cultural equivalent of Yeovil on a wet bank holiday.'

Rose laughed, and Julian joined in. The wake of the laughter was still on their faces as they entered the sitting room. Giselle sat in the corner of the sofa with her arms wrapped round her legs, leaning back on the inflatable man. Gavin sat as close to her as this position would allow, his right arm resting on Giselle's knees, the hand holding a cigarette. Rose pointed at it.

'You're not going to let him do that around the place, are you?'

'The woman is right,' added Julian. 'Passive smoking can damage the unborn child.'

Gavin transferred the cigarette to his other hand. 'Steady on. She was like an industrial chimney herself till the other day. Judge not lest ye be judged, eh Zelda?'

Giselle tweaked at the knee of her leggings. 'I'd prefer you didn't.'

'Ha ha!' crowed Julian. 'Ha-ha, ha-ha!'

'Dead right, Griz,' said Rose, 'you tell him.'

Gavin took a drag. 'There is nothing, absolutely nothing, half so sanctimonious as an ex-smoker.'

Julian consulted his watch. 'I'm going to summon a cab. Got a number, Gavin?'

'There's a couple of cards pinned on the board.'

'Cheers.'

'I'm going to make a cup of coffee,' said Rose, 'anyone else want one?'

Giselle shook her head.

'Sounds wonderful, but we ought to be offering you something,' said Gavin, shooting a pointed look at Giselle, 'you're the guest.'

'No I'm not, I'm Giselle's big sister, as you said, and I know where everything is. Milk and sugar?'

'Neither, thanks.'

'Coming up.' Rose got as far as the door and leaned back into the room. 'You stay here and promise to be good.'

When she'd gone, Gavin stubbed out his cigarette and folded his arms. 'What's the matter with you?'

'Nothing at all, but since the subject came up I would like it if you didn't smoke around us.'

'Us?'

'Me and the baby.'

'I see . . . I thought for a moment you were using the royal we.'

'No.'

'You don't seriously expect me to give up though, do you?'

'It's an idea.'

'An idea?' He looked at her in exaggerated disbelief. 'When I said that about ex-smokers I didn't mean you, but I'm beginning to wonder. Look, so you gave up. Well done. Great. Marvellous. Legion of Honour and VC. The baby will benefit no end. But all grown-up people know that this passive smoking business is a lot of holier-than-thou garbage.'

'It's proved to be harmful.'

'I beg your pardon?' Gavin fanned his hand back and forth in front of her eyes, which remained unblinking. 'Is it really you? I think you've been listening to too much Radio Four.'

'And anyway, I don't like it. I don't like the smell and it makes me feel sick.'

'Ah!' He was triumphant. '*Now* we come to it. This isn't about the baby at all, it's about Giselle Blake, the first woman in the history of the world to be pregnant.'

Out in the kitchen Julian put down the receiver for the third time. 'Still bloody engaged. I think I'll pack in teaching and start a minicab firm.'

'Did you want a coffee?' asked Rose, spoon hovering over the jar.

'No, thanks.'

'This is such a lovely kitchen,' she remarked. 'I won't say it's wasted on my sister, but I'm envious.'

'Gavin does all right. He makes out it's touch and go with that caff of his but he's coining it in.'

'He knows how to spend it,' said Rose, looking round admiringly. 'Where do you live?'

'Not far, Holland Park.'

'Nice. I suppose it's your own place?'

'Yes . . . Look, I'm having a party in a couple of weeks – a sort of housewarming. Would you like to come?'

Rose picked up the two mugs. 'It's sweet of you and it sounds fun, but I'm down in Bristol.'

Julian smiled and shrugged. 'You came up for David Hare.'

'He's a special case. And finals loom.'

'All work and no play . . . I went to Vienna the weekend before my finals.'

Gavin walked in and took his coffee from Rose's hand while addressing Julian. 'You still here?'

'Bloody line's permanently engaged.'

'I'll run you back, I'm going back to the brasserie.'

'You've had a skinful.'

'Don't you start,' snapped Gavin. 'What's all this guff you're giving Rose about your finals?'

'I'm trying to persuade her to come to the party. I told her she shouldn't overwork and make herself stale.'

'No,' Gavin turned to Rose. 'You mustn't. Very bad idea. Come and dance your socks off instead.'

Rose laughed, flicking her hair. 'I'll think about it.'

'Come on then,' said Gavin, 'do you want a lift or what?'

When they'd left Rose went through to the sitting room. Giselle was sitting exactly as before, with the lower part of her face pressed into her knees.

'Griz? Are you okay?'

She lifted her head. 'I'm fine.'

'I hope you gave Gavin what for about the smoking.'

'He knows what I think.'

'And is he going to mend his horrible, smelly, baby-damaging ways?'

Giselle stretched and gave a gaping yawn. 'I doubt it.'

A few days later Giselle accepted Chloe's repeated invitation and walked back from the park with her and Carl.

Chloe and Mehmet shared a small ground floor flat in a Sixties block in Parsifal Road, near the Porchester Baths. To give Chloe a break Giselle pushed the buggy out of the park, now sprinkled with crocuses shivering in the cold wind, and down Queensway. Every few yards Carl would twist his head round and give her a long, searching stare.

The flat when they got there was small and overfull. Released from the pushchair Carl ran into the kitchen ahead of them, climbed on to a chair and clamoured for food. Chloe made a chocolate spread sandwich and orange squash in a cup with a lid. She caught Giselle looking.

'Yes I know, nightmare, but it's because you're here and I want some peace and quiet.'

'It doesn't bother me.' Giselle watched the chocolate spread form an extra mouth, like a clown's, around Carl's real one. 'It's none of my business.'

'I'm actually rather fussy about diet,' said Chloe. 'I like cooking and I want Carl to eat properly and learn to enjoy decent food. But it's like books. You want your child to read good ones, but it'd be po-faced to deprive him of comics. Chocolate spread on white bread is edible comics – it's fun and does no harm as long as it's not all there is. Aaargh!' She shook her head rapidly. 'The modern mother gives vent to her usual torrent of self justification . . .'

Giselle found herself liking Chloe a lot. Maybe this was why she felt suddenly compelled to say: 'I'm expecting one in the summer.'

Chloe's eyebrows flew up. 'You're having a baby?'

'Yes.'

'Congratulations!' To Giselle's complete surprise Chloe kissed her warmly. 'That's marvellous.'

'Thanks.'

Chloe rinsed out a J-cloth under the hot tap and applied it vigorously to Carl's face as he squirmed from the table. 'Are you on your own?'

Giselle was taken aback by her directness. 'I don't know.'

Chloe gave her a shrewd look. 'I see. Well if the answer turns out to be yes I've got masses of things you can borrow – a Moses basket, clothes, cot bedding, a bouncy chair. You must say.'

'It's really good of you, thanks.'

'Where will you be living – round here still?'

Giselle hesitated. 'I don't know.'

'I hope so. That'd be nice. I love them when they're tiny, like squirmy little animals.' The sound of the television came from the other room. 'Oh Lord, never mind. He gets more quality time than any child has a right to expect, and I want to talk to you.'

'He's great. I'm longing to have a little kid like that.'

'D'you want a girl or a boy?'

'I don't mind. I imagine a girl, but I don't know why.' Giselle hadn't talked like this about the baby yet, it felt strange and frightening, as though she were doing something extraordinarily bold.

'You can find out, you know,' said Chloe. 'At your second scan.'

Giselle shook her head. 'I want a surprise.'

'What about the father, what does he think?' Chloe tactfully reached down a tin from the shelf as she spoke so as not to appear too interested.

'He'd quite like to know. He is,' added Giselle, 'a person who likes to know about things.'

Chloe put the tin on the table and pulled off the lid. 'Sticky bread?'

'Yes, please, it looks great.'

'It is great, and keeps for ever. I'll give you the recipe.' Chloe cut two slices. 'But he's looking forward to it,' she said matter-of-factly, taking a bite, 'that's the main thing.'

Giselle sensed in Chloe a sturdy integrity which would never betray a confidence, but she was not yet sure she wanted to confide. Confusion made her cautious. She took the implied question as a statement and responded with one of her own.

'You and Mehmet obviously got it together.'

'With difficulty,' said Chloe. 'Middle Eastern men aren't noted for their liberalism. But we do love each other, for what it's worth, and he's a wonderful father. My parents think the whole thing is the absolute end, which is a shame because I care about them and I don't like hurting their feelings, but this is my life, you know? The real thing, not a rehearsal, so I may as well get on with it.'

Giselle listened respectfully. If anything were needed to remind her of the truth of Rose's observation that she had changed, this was it. Chloe, with her un-cool clothes, and her sticky bread, and her toddler in his chain-store buggy, was someone to whom she would not have given the time of day a year ago. To the new Giselle Chloe seemed strong and independent and her situation, with all its anomalies and difficulties, a thing to be envied.

'You're so right,' she said. 'You have to go for it.'

Chloe grimaced, licking her fingers. 'I'm not sure many people would see me as having "gone for it" – after all, I gave up an interesting, well-paid job in order to bring up the baby of a chauvinistic foreigner. To put it baldly.' The front door opened and closed. 'And here he is.'

Without fully realising it Giselle had pictured a short, swarthy, portly man many years older than Chloe. She was consequently stunned by Mehmet, who was tall and lithe with the dark eyes and hair of a gypsy, the cruel moustache of a corsair and the velvety manner of a young Al Pacino. On being introduced he greeted Giselle with courtly, dispassionate formality, and then planted a long, open-lipped kiss on Chloe's forehead. Chloe's eyes closed for the duration of the kiss.

'I was just off,' said Giselle.

Chloe put out a hand to detain her. 'Don't do that, why? Stay for a bit. Mehmet's going to play with Carl, aren't you, presh?'

'I am.' Mehmet looked at Giselle to confirm this. 'When I get home early I like to mess around with my son.'

'He's lovely. And he's very like you.'

'Yes,' replied Mehmet contentedly. 'A handsome devil, like his father.'

'Let's hope he's as modest,' said Chloe.

Mehmet took a Coke out of the fridge and went into the sitting room. They heard the whoops and shrieks of delight as he entered.

Chloe pulled a rueful face. 'How can I compete with that?'

'Why should you?' asked Giselle. 'You must like it, though. To know they're so happy together, that they enjoy each other so much. You must feel you did the right thing.'

'No doubt of that,' said Chloe. 'No doubt of that at all.'

When Giselle left a few minutes later she glanced into the sitting room. The television was off. Mehmet was lying on the floor with his head on a cushion, Carl lay on his stomach on top of his father, his chin resting on his hands. The two of them were eyeballing each other at a distance of a few inches. The expression on both their faces was one of silent rapture.

It occurred to Giselle, as she trudged back to George Street in the fretful wind, that she had been afforded a glimpse of something ideal. It was rather awesome. But it was also dispiriting in that it showed how far short of ideal her own circumstances were. It would be dishonest to pretend, for the sake of peace, that this was otherwise. Honesty had become extremely important to Giselle of late, the more so because of Gavin, for whom it was a flexible, not to say dispensable commodity. It was not enough for her simply to appear to be doing the right thing: she had not discarded one disguise only to have another foisted on her.

It had to go. After all, conventional Chloe had risked disaffecting her parents, and for all she knew Mehmet's, but the world had not ended. She still had her old family as well as her new one, whatever the tensions. Giselle had a feeling that she was going to have to rock her own family boat – sink it, if necessary – in order to stay afloat herself. The prospect was not comfortable. Her heart was heavy as she opened the door of Gavin's dark, empty flat.

On Friday evening Jonty too got back to an empty house. The light on the answering machine winked at him.

'Sorry, darling,' said Hester, 'got tangled up in a meeting, and I'm going for a drink with the others till the rush dies down a bit. Carry on and grab something to eat. See you later.'

It was eight o'clock, and there was no prospect of even Daniel's company since he was working extra shifts at the supermarket in aid of his European trip. Jonty applauded the effort and commitment, though he did rather wish the work itself was of a more challenging nature. Also, there was no question of Daniel contributing to his keep. The work was there to subsidise leisure, and fun. Insignificant things such as food, clean clothes and a roof over his head were accepted free, as of divine right.

Jonty looked in the fridge. There was a piece of pizza wrapped in foil, a Pyrex dish containing goulash that would probably come up okay in the microwave, cheddar cheese, four eggs and some slightly past-it salad. He felt deeply sorry for himself. Like Mole returning to Mole End he saw himself as lonely and pathetic, lacking the warm nourishing framework of domestic support that was the prerogative of the securely married man.

He went upstairs and changed out of his suit, putting on a pair of threadbare cords and a navy guernsey. On his way back down he passed Giselle's room. It was tidy, and Daniel had painted it, for a consideration, a couple of weekends ago. The inside gleamed in all its empty, eery tidiness. It made the back of Jonty's throat ache to look at it. He hurried downstairs, picked up his keys and went out of the house and off in the direction of the pub.

Immediately, he missed Gus, the swing of the lead in his hands. It had been like an amputation that day when he'd got home to find Hester had done away with the dog: so dreadfully shocking and sudden, with no time to adjust. Where had she found the reserves of ruthlessness to do that? Maybe it was true that women, ruled by their biology, were more severely practical about life and death. He thrust his hands into his pockets. She should have told him.

The five-minute walk to the Axe and Compass took him past the church. Jonty was not a regular member of the congregation, though Hester generally got him there at Easter and Christmas. He had, however, been instrumental in setting up the Friends, who raised money to repair and restore the fabric of St Catherine's, and he had an atheist's sentimental affection for the building, rather as one might for a sweet but doddery distant relative whom one did not have to see too often.

For some months the church had been kept locked because of a deplorable wave of petty vandalism and pilfering. The iron gates were closed and padlocked every day except Sunday and at those times when a service was in progress. But this week, with a period of quiet behind it, the PCC had seen fit to restore the status quo. Without hurrying, as if he were simply making a detour through the churchyard, Jonty went up the path, resisted the urge to look sheepishly over his shoulder, and went in.

Too late, he realised there was a light on. He hovered near the door, not sure why he was here, and very much not wishing to meet anyone. The voice, when it came, made him jump.

'Jonty – good evening. I'd better announce myself or you'll get the fright of your life.'

'Hallo.' Jonty took a few more steps to the apex of the centre aisle, where the matting was worn and shiny. The vicar, Geoff Baines, was crouched near the north door with a screwdriver in his hand, changing the plug on the tea-urn.

'Hallo, Geoff.'

'I don't suppose the plug is the problem, but I thought I'd better eliminate the obvious suspects from my enquiries before we have to order another one of these damn things.'

'Trouble, eh . . .' said Jonty feebly and awkwardly.

Geoff glanced up, blowing at a lock of hair. 'Urns are always trouble. The tea-urn is the window of the parish's soul.'

'Well—' began Jonty.

'I haven't seen you for ages,' said Geoff, plugging in the urn and standing up. 'Or Hester come to that, which is more unusual. Last time I saw Hester,' he said teasingly, 'she was beating the bounds with a rather personable young man.'

'Really? Don't ask me. That woman has her own life.'

Geoff laughed agreeably. 'Family okay?'

'All well, yes. Daniel's off on his travels in a few weeks. Rose has got finals.'

'And Giselle?'

'She's down in London.'

'That's right, someone told me . . .' Geoff pushed the switch of the urn down with his toe. 'Eureka.' He flipped it up again. 'You and Hester must come round for a jar soon. Life's immeasurably better for us now that Camilla's started school. We feel we can enjoy a well-earned breather.' He pocketed the screwdriver and grinned at Jonty. 'Flipping kids. Still, yours have more or less all reached years of discretion now, haven't they?'

'Sort of,' agreed Jonty doubtfully. He felt the butterfly touch of

Geoff's slightly longer than necessary glance, and his throat ached again with the desire to unburden himself.

Geoff slapped his pockets and smiled briefly at him. 'I'll get the social secretary to call you. Apart from anything else I'm hoping your very wonderful and high-profile wife will be a steward at the fun run in May. If I get her involved it encourages the others . . .' He glanced around. 'Right. I'll leave you to turn the light off if you don't mind. Goodnight.'

He went. After the door, with its heavy *clunk*, had closed behind him, Jonty realised with a pang that he had been left alone, and never questioned. Discretion, he thought, might be the better part of valour, but in friendship it was sadly misplaced.

After half an hour at the pub, during which he consumed a baked potato with chilli and two halves of Dobbey's, and exchanged platitudes – as comforting as any religious litany – with Nick, the landlord, Jonty returned to The Old Clink.

He went in at the back door. Daniel was standing in the middle of the kitchen eating mini Shredded Wheats out of a mixing bowl. Beyond him, in the hall, a shadowy figure sat on the three-cornered chair.

'Hallo there,' said Jonty. He often these days felt slightly ill at ease with his son – the biological gap was narrowing. 'How were things at the workface?'

'Not bad. Y'know.'

'Mum here?'

'She rang. She said she'd be back around eleven-thirty.'

'Fine. Sorry I wasn't around, I fancied a jar at the pub.'

Daniel shrugged and put the bowl in the sink. Jonty peered at the figure in the hall, which looked vaguely familiar.

'Giselle's back,' said Daniel.

'I didn't know she was coming this weekend.'

'She's not. I'm telling you, she's back. Like back, back. As in staying.'

Daniel sloped off into the living room. From upstairs, now that he was listening for it, Jonty could hear the dim tom-tom beat of music. And in the hall the inflatable man, for it was he, gave a faint sigh, and slumped forward on to the floor.

CHAPTER SIXTEEN

'It may seem tedious,' said Byron to Josette, 'but for these essays it pays to give a bit more attention to things like planning and structure. It's not simply a question of retaining the information, but of putting forward and sustaining a coherent argument.'

'I know my written work isn't what it should be,' admitted Josette. 'I'm afraid it's going to let me down.'

'Not at all.' Byron was anxious to reassure her. 'It's a case of learning a few tricks. Easy as anything. I can teach you.'

They were sitting in the kitchen at Raglan Road, with the contents of Josette's folder spread out on the table. It was Saturday morning, and Ann had left to attend a seminar at the Maudsley. Mr We-We Sun had returned to Hong Kong a few weeks before, leaving behind him a shower of strange and unusable gifts and a faint but distinctive smell in the guest bedroom.

In spite of its educational nature a pleasant air of leisure attended their enterprise. Sunshine beamed in through the window. Byron had made fresh coffee and put a few of Ann's peanut butter cookies on a plate. Josette had discarded the pleated skirt and jumper she wore for work in favour of grey leggings and a plaid shirt.

Byron had rediscovered, if not a gift, then at least a distinct penchant for teaching. He found himself wondering whether perhaps it was adult education he should have been involved in for all those years. His attempts at enlightening the young had been a complete failure, but this with Josette was a most rewarding experience.

Byron needed the odd reward. Even his role in his own family was unclear. Ann was the powerhouse, and he was happy to let her fulfil the role to which her talents suited her. He liked to think he was more than a mere yes-man and a keeper of the peace – and yet it was hard to know what else he was. His undoubted practical capabilities went largely unnoticed and unappreciated and he could not help feeling that his lack of any outside status made him almost invisible to his sons. He remained baffled by them: their looks, which they certainly had not got from him, their attitudes which he supposed he must have helped to form, their ruthlessness and peculiar cold frivolity. He had meant it when he told Jonty he envied him his daughters. He would have loved a girl – but perhaps she would have been the same, you couldn't tell. Byron felt that he had much to give, but that no one wanted it. He was undervalued, but then he would have been the first to admit that he undervalued himself.

Josette did value Byron. He responded gratefully to this, and to her humility – a quality in short supply among Armitages – and her innate seriousness. She sought his advice keenly but paid him the compliment of not accepting it unconditionally. She scrutinised, questioned and considered all suggestions before acting on them. She possessed a lively, unspoilt intelligence which Byron appreciated. Indeed, it was one of the qualities which had first attracted him to Ann, thirty-odd years ago.

'I'm really grateful,' Josette had said. 'There were so many things I just didn't know how to do. I could have gone on making the same mistakes and got nowhere.'

'No, you couldn't,' Byron told her, 'because your tutor would, in time, have told you what I'm telling you now. It's all very basic stuff. But if I can help get you off to a good start then it's my pleasure to do so.'

She smiled her wise, appreciative smile. When she gave him that smile he knew that there were many things Josette could teach him, but they were sadly quite out of the question.

'You don't think Mrs Armitage minds, do you?' she asked one day and for a moment he had thought that she was touching on the unthinkable.

'Minds?' he repeated loudly, feeling his neck prickle.

'I did ask her for help before I started the course – but with you having done the same subject it hasn't really worked out like that.'

'Of course she doesn't mind.' Byron was swept by an emotion which he told himself was relief, but which felt perilously like disappointment. 'To be candid my wife is so busy and involved in so many things she's better off not taking on any more. Whereas I tend to have time on my hands.'

Josette nodded. The respect and discretion between them had not been ruptured. And, yes, Byron was relieved.

They'd spent another ten minutes or so considering the best approach to Josette's analysis of crime statistics among the under-eighteens when Byron heard the front door bang. He paused, pencil poised.

'Who's that, I wonder?'

'Mrs Armitage?'

'She's not due back till about six. I suppose it might be her, if she's forgotten something . . .' Heavy footsteps ran up the stairs and faded into the upper part of the house. 'That's not Ann.'

'One of your boys, perhaps?' suggested Josette. Byron glanced at her quickly. He had the feeling, less from what she said than from the way she said it, that Josette disapproved of his sons.

'It could be. I'd better go and check. Will you excuse me for a second?'

Byron got as far as the half-landing, panting rather – he was beginning to find the stairs at Raglan Road something of a trial – and called: 'Hallo? Who's up there?' The sound of his own voice embarrassed him. There was no reply. Rather than call again he trudged heavily up the next flight. He was standing with his hand on the newel post, catching his breath, when Gavin appeared from the direction of the top floor, dressed in a crumpled black suit and grey T-shirt, his curls in hectic disarray, his expression forbidding.

'Good Lord,' said Byron, 'what are you doing here?'

'Looking for a file I may have left here – I'm going back to the brasserie.'

'On a Saturday?'

'It's our busiest day, for Christ's sake.'

'What about Giselle?'

'What about her?'

Byron tried to sound jovial. 'I bet she takes a dim view of that.'

'I wouldn't know,' said Gavin, sweeping past his father and on down the stairs. 'She's back in Chuffington.'

There was no time to respond to this. The front door banged shut while Byron was still toiling down to the hall. By the time he reached the kitchen he had told himself that Gavin's remark was open to more than one interpretation and that there was no reason in the world why a young girl who was pregnant should not go and spend a weekend with her parents if her husband – sorry, partner – was working.

Josètte was running her finger down a row of figures, frowning slightly in concentration. Byron sat down at the table.

'Sorry about that. It was Gavin.'

She stopped her finger at a point near the bottom of the page, and tapped. 'No wonder. I've repeated a row.'

Byron looked. 'So you have. Well, that could explain a good deal.'

'It's just as well I'm not training to be an accountant.'

'Even accountants do it, and not always by accident, believe me.'

She ran a line through the superfluous row, and sat back with a little sigh. 'Sometimes I wonder if I'm up to the job.'

'Nonsense, of course you are. More coffee?' She shook her head. 'Do you want to call it a day? We've covered quite a lot.'

In answer she began to collect up her papers and slot them back into the folder. 'Yes. It's time I got home anyway. My daughter lays such a guilt trip on me about my studying.'

'You should worry.' Byron gave in to an overwhelming need to confide. 'We're going to be grandparents.'

'No!' Josette smiled, but her eyes moved over his face as if trying to gauge his mood and her reaction. 'Well, that's nothing to feel guilty about.'

'It's all a bit unorthodox. Gavin and the girl aren't married.'

'So who is these days?'

'I suppose so . . . but remember I come from a generation that still believes in a notional norm. It all seems so – unreliable.'

'There's nothing you can do, that's for sure. The girl's over eighteen?'

'Yes. Not by much.'

'Makes no difference. She's a woman,' said Josette. She shuffled her books together and placed them on top of the folder, and then rose and pushed her chair in. 'All you can do is sit back and enjoy it. You'll make a lovely grandpa.'

Byron feared that this was so. He suspected that the qualities which made him an ineffectual parent would be those most suited to grandparenthood.

'It's funny,' Josette went on, 'you hear about something once and suddenly you see it everywhere. I was only reading in the paper about what it's like when you're going to be a grandparent. It was Hester Blake, in her column, do you ever see that?' Byron shook his head. 'It was very good the way she put it, funny but sad. She said she'd never even thought about being a granny, but now it was going to happen it was the most important thing in her life.'

'Really?' Gloom seeped softly through Byron like ink on a blotter. 'Is that what she said?'

Hester got back from the hypermarket on Saturday to find Jonty giving the grass its first mow of the season – a displacement activity if ever there was one – and Giselle curled up in an armchair in the sitting room, looking at one of the weekend supplements. It was the first time Hester had seen her since Jonty had said she was back. She was still wearing her night things – a giant T-shirt splattered with the blueish stains of old hair dye, and black slouch socks. Hester wondered, rather unworthily, if these were the garments in which she graced Gavin's bed down in London.

'Hallo there!' she said with forced cheeriness.

'Hi.'

'I'll come and talk properly in a minute when I've got this stuff put away.'

Giselle didn't answer. For several minutes Hester toiled in and out through the front door with boxes of shopping, and for several more moved briskly about the house distributing her purchases to the fridge, kitchen cupboards, larder, utility room and bathrooms, according to type. Giselle did not move. Neither, Hester could not help noticing, did she turn a page.

Eventually, she went into the sitting room and plumped down on the sofa. 'Thank God that's over for another week. It was like the seventh circle of hell in that place today, it reminded me why I normally make it a rule not to go on Saturdays.'

Giselle moved her head slightly in acknowledgement of this remark.

Hester had noticed before how it was often those occasions when one's intentions were impeccable, and one wanted desperately to behave well, that one slid inexorably into the pattern one most wished to avoid. In a terrible assertion of the instinctive over the deliberate one heard one's voice saying things one would much rather it didn't say.

'So where's Gavin?' she asked, and knew that everything about this question – its tone, content and construction – was bound to antagonise.

Giselle mumbled something brief and inaudible.

'Sorry?'

'I said, where do you think?' said Giselle, still without looking up. 'In London.'

'I see. I only wondered why the two of you weren't here.'

Giselle lowered the paper with ostentatious patience. 'What is this? A Nazi interrogation?'

'There's no need to be childish, it was a perfectly innocent question.'

'If you don't want me to be childish, don't treat me like a child.'

'I wasn't, I simply asked where—'

'I *know* what you asked!' Giselle threw the paper on the floor. 'And I told you the answer!'

She folded her arms and turned her head away from Hester, glaring into space. An angry, expectant silence developed. Hester drew a deep breath.

'How are you anyway, darling? You look well.'

'I'm fine.'

'You don't look as if you've put on any weight.'

'I have, a bit.'

'What about clinics and things . . . have you booked in anywhere yet?'

There was another silence which Hester was unwisely tempted to fill. 'Only you really ought—'

'For Christ's sake, stop going on at me! I'm the one who's pregnant, right? I really want this baby and I'll do everything to make sure it's okay, including going to antenatal clinics, yeah?' Giselle thrust her hands into her hair and tugged, in a gesture exactly like her mother's. 'Look. I did go for a scan. I even got a photo, do you want to see?'

'I'd love to, thanks.'

'Fine.' Giselle spoke as if the production of the photograph would settle the matter and end the discussion. She got up and left the room. At the same moment Hester heard the kitchen door open and close and a second later Jonty put his head round the door, looking about with exaggerated delicacy.

'*Alles in Ordnung . . ?*'

'I don't know,' replied Hester in a grimly lowered voice. 'But she's gone to fetch a photo of her scan.'

Jonty entered the room. 'What does that imply?'

'Nothing. Except it's our first glimpse of our grandchild.'

'Oh, I see. Great.'

Giselle's stockinged feet flapped down the stairs and Jonty grabbed her as she entered and kissed her cheek.

'Come on then, Grizzle, show us your snapshot.'

Giselle handed it to him. Trying not to feel hurt Hester got up and went to look over her husband's shoulder. The photograph was reproduced twice on an A4 sheet of hospital notes. It resembled an underwater picture of the Loch Ness monster, an ill-focused assortment of shadows, blotches, dots and streaks upon which the radiologist had imposed a pattern by means of a white pencil. But on inspection, yes, there it was, the rounded mass of the head, the stippled curve of the spine, the half-furled shoots of arms and legs. Hester's eyes smarted with tears, and she felt Jonty's arm go round her, empathising.

'Oh . . . isn't that incredible? It's so complete.'

'Yup,' said Giselle abrasively, going back to her place on the sofa. 'It's all there all right.'

'I don't remember anything like this with ours,' said Jonty. 'Did we get pictures?'

'No, I only ever had a scan with Daniel, and there certainly weren't prints on offer.'

'Keep it if you like,' said Giselle offhandedly.

'Are you sure?' asked Hester. 'Don't you want it yourself?'

'Not really. I've got the original.'

'What about Gavin?'

'He's not fussed.'

'In that case, thank you.'

'I must return to my labours,' said Jonty. 'Nice to have you around, Griz; I expect this means I'll get a decent lunch for once.'

Hester gave him a withering look. When he'd gone, she said to Giselle: 'I'm sorry if I seemed to be interrogating. I'm a bit on edge.'

'Join the club.'

'You know you're welcome here any time at all, love. It's super to see you, and looking so well. And this—' she waved the scan sheet, 'is a huge thrill.'

'You're welcome.'

'Rose rang – she's finished with Jeremy.'

'I know.'

'She told me she'd stayed with you the other night. That was nice. Did she say much about the break-up then?'

'Not really.'

'So she wasn't too depressed?'

'You're joking.'

'Good.' Hester could not shake off the impression that there was something she was not being told. No matter how much a small inner voice reminded her that this was probably because Giselle did not want to tell her, the impression was irksome.

'If you want a lift back tomorrow night,' she said lightly, 'I expect it would be on the cards.'

'Thanks,' said Giselle, getting up and heading for the door, 'I'll bear it in mind.'

Giselle hurled herself face down on her bed. She had known exactly what she wanted to say and how she would say it. If only her mother had not come in and tried to hassle her she wouldn't have screwed up.

After a moment she rolled on to her back, sniffing, and scrubbed angrily at her tears. She'd have to find a way of keeping her cool, and getting the message across without a scene. She'd have to try again. It was so hard when she got back here to be anything but a child.

'*Oh* dear,' said Ann, when told of Gavin's visit. 'I know of no files. How did he look?'

'A bit wound up, but nothing out of the ordinary.'

'And he was going to the office, you say?'

'So he told me.'

Ann sighed. 'Pour me a glass of wine, would you Byron?' She sat composedly as he did so. 'I think in view of what he told you about Giselle he almost certainly wanted to talk.'

Byron poured himself a glass and joined his wife at the kitchen table. It was six-fifteen. Ann's briefcase stood on the floor by her chair and she still wore her grey Jaeger throw. He couldn't help thinking what a different atmosphere there was now from when he had sat here with Josette this morning.

'That certainly wasn't the impression he gave,' Byron said. 'He couldn't get away fast enough.'

'Hmm,' mused Ann. 'To be candid, that may have been because I was not around. Gavin would always be less likely to unburden himself to you.'

'I'm aware of that,' said Byron gloomily. 'But the opportunity was there if he'd wanted to take it.'

Ann placed her hands flat on the table on either side of her glass. 'I confess I'm a little concerned.'

Byron remembered Josette's comment. 'That's as may be, but there's nothing we can do.'

'I beg to differ. If, as I believe, Gavin actually came round this morning to talk to us, but did not do so for whatever reason, then we must assume our help is being sought.'

'In which case,' said Byron, 'he'll ask again.'

'It is not in the nature of the beast,' Ann pointed out, 'to ask at all.'

'But you said—'

'I said help was being sought, not asked for. A crucial difference.'

Byron changed tack. 'You know, there's a real danger of us overreacting here. They're not married. And even if they were there's no earthly reason for them to be in each other's pockets all the time, especially these days . . . I would expect that Giselle's gone back for a weekend at home to chat to Hester about whatever pregnant women chat to their mothers about.'

'I hadn't discounted that possibility.'

'Give one of the others a ring,' suggested Byron. 'Put them on the job. Time they did their fraternal duty.'

'I shall think about it,' said Ann.

'That's the spirit. And why don't we go out for supper?'

Ann stood up and removed her throw. 'For the very good reason that I have a chicken chasseur in the freezer, and wild rice and french beans to go with it.'

'Good-oh,' said Byron.

When the phone rang after supper, Daniel answered it. He was on his way out of the door to go first to the pub, then on to a party with the other lads. Jonty had switched on the Sean Connery film, and Hester was in the kitchen showing Giselle the coat and leggings she had knitted.

'Hallo,' said Daniel in his bored, ding-dong telephone voice. 'No. Yeah. Daniel, yeah. Oh, hi. Sure, I'll get her.'

He laid the receiver on the table next to the phone. Hester began automatically to move towards it, but he said to Giselle: 'It's for you.'

'Who is it?' she mouthed.

'Gavin's mum,' said Daniel aloud, leaving and banging the door behind him.

Giselle advanced on the phone and stared at it for a second as though it were an unstable substance before finally picking it up. Hester addressed herself with fanatical concentration to a knitting pattern.

'Hallo?'

'Giselle, it's Ann.'

'Oh, hallo.'

'I do apologise for importuning you at home, and on a Saturday evening, too, when you are doubtless snatching the opportunity for some woman-talk with your mama . . .'

'That's all right.'

'It's just that I think Gavin may be doing a Gavin, as we say in the family, and you are currently the person best qualified to throw some light on the matter.'

'What's he done?'

'Nothing specific as yet, but I'm accustomed to heed the signs. I myself have been out all day, but apparently he stormed into Raglan Road mid-morning on some very flimsy pretext, scarcely gave his father the time of day, and stormed out again. It's quite clear from the reports Byron has given me that he wanted to offload emotional baggage of some sort but thought better of it when he found that I was out. And a moment ago when I was talking to Sebastian on another matter, he said that he'd dropped by at George Street and been told to bleep off in no uncertain terms. Of course, I realise that you would have been first in the line of fire had you not been weekending with your people.'

'Probably.'

'So, really, all I ask is your advice. Do you have any idea why he's going up in smoke? And do you think it would be helpful or unhelpful if I were to give him a ring and, say, offer a spot of lunch tomorrow?'

'Do whatever you like,' said Giselle. 'You're his mum.'

'But you, my dear, are his partner.' Ann allowed a small hiatus to elapse, which Giselle did not fill. 'And the last thing I want is to step outside my brief.'

'I'm sure he'd like Sunday lunch.'

'In that case it will do no harm to extend an invitation, and I will do so.'

'Good idea.'

'It's probably nothing that a few slices of rare roast beef can't cure!' added Ann, quite gaily. 'And now, tell me, it's remiss of me not to have asked right away, how are you? Is the pregnancy progressing to plan?'

'As far as I know.'

'I'm very glad you're taking a breather out there in Chuffington. An expectant mum needs a little TLC from time to time and I do know how difficult my son can be.'

'Yes . . . well.'

'But then which of us isn't from time to time?' added Ann, again pausing briefly but in vain for Giselle's assent. 'I only hope when you get home tomorrow that he won't still be spitting tacks and undo all the good of your weekend away.'

Giselle's voice became, if possible, even smaller. 'Let's hope not.'

'Listen, I mustn't take up any more of your time. Will you give my love to your parents and tell them we must all get together soon?'

'Yes, I will.'

'And perhaps you'll drop in on Raglan Road in the next couple of weeks and tell me what you'd like me to make for the new arrival?'

'Yes.'

'Goodbye, my dear.'

'Bye.'

Giselle returned to the kitchen. Hester looked up after a second or two, as if dragging herself away from her scrutiny of tiny garments.

'How's Ann?'

'All right. She said you must all get together soon.'

'Yes, we must have them out here, we're down several fixtures at the moment.' Hester riffled through a few more pages of the pattern book. From beneath her lashes she could make out Giselle's hands fiddling with her rings.

'Any other news?'

'Gavin's tossed a wobbler.'

'Really?' Hester hoped her agitation could not be detected through her smokescreen of lavish unconcern. 'What on earth about?'

'What do you think?'

'I've no idea.'

'Me being here.'

Hester put the pattern down. 'I suppose it's perfectly natural he should want you there with him.'

'I don't see why,' said Giselle, 'when he's at that bloody restaurant most of the time, and when he is around we do nothing else but row.'

'Is that why you're here?'

'I'm bored with his temper tantrums,' went on Giselle, which Hester took to mean 'yes'. 'He's full of shit.'

'Oh well,' said Hester with a calm she was very far from feeling. 'A few rows aren't the end of the world. They're only to be expected in the situation you two are in. Things'll calm down. I'm glad you felt able to come out here and take a break.'

'It isn't a break!'

'What?' said Hester, who had heard perfectly well.

'It's not just a break. I don't want to be with him.'

Jonty had arrived in the kitchen. 'What's the poor blighter done wrong?'

'How long have you got?' snapped Giselle.

Jonty shook one hand as though he'd burned his fingers. 'Phew.' Hester gave him a warning look.

'So what exactly are you saying?' she asked.

'I'd have thought she made it pretty clear,' said Jonty. 'She's sick of the sight of him and she wants out.'

'But that's not on, is it?' said Hester, looking from Jonty, who was looking at Giselle, to Giselle herself, who was glaring at her feet. 'There's a baby on the way.'

'Exactly,' said Giselle.

'A baby changes everything.'

'Exactly!'

'Look, love,' said Hester carefully, 'we've been extremely for-bearing so far about all this—'

'What do you mean, forbearing?' Giselle's voice was squeaky with outrage. 'You said you were pleased!'

'We did, and we are, Grizzle.' Jonty sat down at the table between them. 'But a baby is heavy manners. You can't simply abandon ship when the going gets rough.'

'I'm not abandoning anything. I *know* a baby's heavy manners. I *know* a baby changes everything. That's why I want to be here and not there.'

'What,' said Hester, ignoring Jonty's stifled shushings, 'so things get a little messy with Gavin and you cut him out of the equation?'

'I never said that. I'm not cutting him out of anything.' Giselle leaned forward with her brow on her hand and began scratching the surface of the table with a dinner knife. 'I said where I wanted to be. And you,' she pointed at first one, then the other of them with the knife, 'said I was welcome.'

Hester reached out automatically and removed the knife. 'You are. You know we're always here for you, and this is your home, but you made a decision to go and live with Gavin and then another decision to go ahead and have this baby. A decision, I might add, which you were in no position to make unilaterally—'

'What's that when it's at home?'

Jonty laid a hand on Giselle's shoulder but she jerked away. 'It simply means that you should consider your situation. You're not some thirtysomething career woman with a highly organised life-plan which includes single parenthood and very possibly a nanny. You've thrown in your lot with Gavin. It would be massively irresponsible simply to announce you're bored with the set-up and want out. Apart from anything else, what about your financial status? You no longer have a job, and if you leave Gavin you're completely dependent on us.'

'No I'm not, I've got my giro.'

'There's more to independence than collecting state benefit.'

'So you're going to chuck me out, are you?' asked Giselle. Her face had the set, unyielding look which in childhood had presaged tears.

'Please,' said Jonty patiently, 'that's not fair. You know that isn't what I was getting at.'

'What we are saying,' said Hester, 'is that you no longer have the luxury of simply deciding where you want to be at any given moment. You are having a baby. Gavin is the baby's father. The two of you should be together for the baby's sake.'

Giselle dropped her head on the table and spoke from that position. 'I don't think so.'

Jonty placed his hand on her back and this time wasn't shaken off. 'There's nothing so outlandish about it, Grizzle.'

'You don't understand.'

'We do,' said Hester, who found to her dismay that she did not. 'We honestly do, darling.'

Giselle shook her head, rolling it back and forth on the table top.

Jonty said, 'Anyone fancy a drink?'

Another roll of the head. 'Yes, please,' said Hester. 'A splash of Amaretto would be nice.'

'You got it.' Jonty went to fetch the bottle from the dining room. Hester sat wretchedly, gazing at the top of her daughter's head. As Jonty returned, Giselle sat up. The tears Hester had imagined were not there. She was dry-eyed and composed.

'I think I'll go down the pub.'

'All right . . .' Jonty brandished the bottle. 'Sure you won't have one here with us before you go?'

'No, thanks.' She got up, unhooked her leather jacket from the back of the chair and slipped into it. Hester noticed with a pang the marked swell below the elastic waistband of her leggings.

'Watch out,' said Jonty, 'you'll probably find Daniel and the rat-pack still there, deciding where to get wrecked for the rest of the night.'

'I don't mind.' She turned her collar up and stuck her hands in the pockets of her jacket, thumbs jutting out like the Artful Dodger. 'I'd like to stick around for a few days, okay? To chill out, get my head straight. If that's no problem.'

Hester and Jonty shook their heads eagerly. 'No problem,' they said.

It was half past two in the morning when Hester was woken by the sound of a car pulling up outside. She hadn't been sleeping well after wrangling unhappily with Jonty till after midnight about the Giselle situation, and her first reaction on hearing the car was that it was Giselle returning. She experienced first relief, then a gradual resurgence of anxiety. She lay tensely, her forehead resting on the warm, deeply imperturbable mass of Jonty's sleeping back, her eyes wide open, gazing into the darkness below the duvet line.

Two minutes passed in utter silence. No car door banged, no latch clicked, no house door opened. Hester got out of bed and drew aside the curtain on the front window. A car was parked at an angle, the front wheels slewed towards the house as though the driver had only narrowly prevented himself from executing a ram-raid on the front door. There was no-one about and from up here it was impossible to tell whether there was anyone in the car.

Hester looked back at Jonty. He had not stirred. His breathing was deep and distant. She put on her dressing gown and slippers and went out on to the landing. With a small shock she saw that Daniel was back – in her agitation about Giselle she had forgotten all about him. His pale bare shoulders were turned towards the bedroom door; his breathing was noisier than Jonty's, ruffled by recent debauch. As Hester drew the door to she smelt the familiar warm, foetid whiff of booze and fags and unwashed clothes. If Daniel was here, then Giselle probably was too – her door was closed.

She went down into the hall. Nervously, she did not turn on the light because she did not wish to advertise her presence. Instead she went into the dining room, whose front window faced the drive, and peered out. From this angle it was possible to ascertain that the car was not a taxi, that it did look familiar, and that there appeared to be someone in the driver's seat. She squinted furiously but the outside light was not on and she could make out nothing more.

Slowly she opened the front door and advanced towards the car, stooping a little to look inside and to suggest to whoever was there that they should identify themselves.

Gavin was bent forward over the steering wheel, his head resting on his hands which were clasped at the top of the wheel. This attitude was strikingly similar to Giselle's at the kitchen table earlier in the evening. Hester tapped on the car window with the knuckle of her forefinger. As she did so Gavin's shoulders heaved and shuddered, and he gave vent to a rasping sob.

Dismayed, Hester opened the door and laid a hand on his back. 'Gavin . . ? Gavin, my dear, what on earth's the matter?'

He lifted his head and gazed pitifully at her. His hair looked greasy and was scraped back off a face haggard with tiredness. Her dismay increased.

'I'm so sorry, Hester. I should never have done this to you . . .'

Hester's brain flittered momentarily here and there, collecting and collating clues.

'Done what?'

'Turned up at this hour of the night. I tend to forget, working the hours I do . . . I know what a damn fool way it is to behave . . .' He pinched the top of his nose between finger and thumb and shook his head in despair. 'I wasn't even going to knock on the door, I promise you . . .'

'To drive out all this way and then not knock *would* have been a waste of time,' said Hester, sounding more bracing than she felt. 'Look, it's freezing out here, do you want to come in?'

He looked beseechingly at her once more. 'Are you sure you don't mind?'

'Of course I don't mind, you're in an awful state and I'm extremely chilly.'

'Bless you . . .'

He climbed unsteadily out of the car and followed her, shoulders hunched and arms folded, to the front door. Unfortunately, the door had closed behind Hester and she had to spend an embarrassing few minutes making her way round to the back of the house, and feeling under the clay chimney flowerpots for the spare key. Gavin did not accompany her and when she'd let herself into the kitchen and opened the front door for him, he was shuffling impatiently from foot to foot on the front step, smoking a cigarette.

'Sorry,' she said *sotto voce*, 'I can never remember which pot the key's under. Come in.'

'Thanks.'

Hester closed the door very quietly and motioned him into the kitchen. He followed and stood in the middle of the floor, snatching and puffing agitatedly at his cigarette. Hester watched him warily.

'Are you all right?'

He opened his mouth to speak, then closed it abruptly and shook his head.

'I'm sorry,' she said, 'silly question. Shall I get Giselle?'

He looked at her sharply. 'She is here then?'

'Yes. She came back last night – sorry, Friday night.'

'What did she say?'

Hester gazed down at her slippers. 'Not a lot, really. She feels she needed to come back for a while. A natural nervousness about the baby, I expect.'

'I doubt it. Christ . . !' Gavin sat down at the table and pressed the heels of his hands into his eyes. 'We had such a bloody awful row . . .'

Hester feared he was going to cry again and stepped in hastily to prevent it. 'The two of you are bound to be a bit up and down with all you've got on your plate. I'm sure it's not the end of the world. Let me go and wake her – I know she'll want to talk to you when she knows you're here—'

'Don't bet on it,' he said bitterly. 'She won't. And anyway, I don't want to disturb her.'

'Why don't you spend the night then? The spare room's made up. Things are bound to look a bit less bleak in the morning and you and she can talk things over in the cool light of day when you've both had a rest.'

Gavin got up, scraping his chair on the tiles, and strode to the sink, dropping his cigarette end down the waste disposal and running the tap. He then turned to Hester and without warning lowered his head on to her shoulder, racked with sobs.

She was touched, and appalled. Nervously she put her arms round him and stroked his trembling back. His hair had the warm, sweaty smell she associated with sick children. She was not at all sure what the right thing was to do. He was like a child in need of comfort, but she was uneasy when Giselle, whose place it should have been to comfort him, was upstairs asleep.

'Now come on,' she said. 'Don't let's make a drama out of a crisis.'

'Then you concede it is a crisis?' He raised his head, and gave her a curiously accusing look.

'No, I concede no such thing.' Hester stepped back. 'It's an expression. Don't be so touchy.'

'Touchy? *Touchy?*' He threw his hands up and turned away from her. 'Your daughter's expecting our child, she's walked out on me and you accuse me of being *touchy*?'

'I didn't accuse you of anything.' Hester was suddenly attuned to the phrase 'a no-win situation'. 'I just think we should all calm down. Would you like a drink?'

'No, I would not. Thank you.'

'Do you mind if I do?'

'Hester – it's your house.' The politeness was etched with sarcasm.

Gavin lit another cigarette and swung back and forth in the middle of the kitchen as she made herself a black coffee and added a shot of Christmas cake brandy from the cupboard.

She took a couple of sips and felt stronger. 'As a matter of fact your mother called earlier.'

'Good God.'

'She rang to speak to Giselle. I think she was concerned about you.'

'For concerned, read interfering.'

Hester was torn between a certain sympathy with Ann, and a weaselly pleasure in having her own most private opinion endorsed.

'That's quite unjust, and you know it. And, I might add, she was sufficiently tactful to consult Giselle first.'

'Tokenism,' said Gavin.

'Not at all.'

'So what did Giselle have to say on the subject of my dramas and crises? Did she put in her four penn'orth? Did everyone have their say?'

'I'm not going on with this conversation if that's your attitude,' announced Hester. She put down her mug. 'I'm not sure we should be having it anyway. I'm going to wake Giselle.'

As she left the room she saw Gavin put his head in his hands. His cigarette was no more than a stub. She couldn't help thinking that he'd burn his hair if he wasn't careful.

On the landing she met Jonty, emerging from their bedroom and tying his dressing gown. He'd got it on lopsided, so that one of the front corners hung well below his knees and the other barely protected his modesty.

'What the devil's going on? Who's downstairs?'

'Gavin . . .!' she whispered. 'In a state. I'm going to root out Giselle.'

'Is that wise?'

'Well, what the hell else can I do? He refuses to be calmed by me, Ann's getting a bad press, I've suggested he spend the night but he's not having that either—'

'Okay, okay.' Jonty lifted his hands. 'I get the picture. Do you want me to go down and perform some manly function or other?'

'Go down by all means, but don't expect to get much change.'

'At this hour of the morning my expectations are absolutely nil, I assure you.' Jonty smiled at Hester and she was granted a fleeting, brilliant insight into what made them tick, and why they were still together. It was both a comfort, and strangely confusing.

'That's as maybe,' she said. She gestured at him. 'But if you intend being taken seriously, do something about that dressing gown.'

When he'd gone she went over to Giselle's door, and knocked very lightly. As anticipated, there was no response. She knocked again, this time with one hand already turning the handle.

Giselle was not there. Only the inflatable man lay prone on the bed, flaccid, faceless and discarded.

'So, Gavin!' said Jonty, entering the kitchen. 'What brings you out here at this hour of the morning?'

Gavin glared at him. 'Your daughter.'

Jonty had the unwelcome sensation of being dictated to in his own house. 'Yes, I gather the course of true love is a touch bumpy at present.'

'You could say that.'

'These are difficult times. Grizzle's but young—'

'She is, if I may say so, a grown woman,' said Gavin, sounding exactly like his mother.

'Biologically, perhaps, but—'

'I'm growing a little tired of having her lack of years used as an excuse for everything from domestic squalor to total fucking irresponsibility.'

Jonty felt the repressed anger explode inside him with a muffled boom.

'That'll do, if you don't mind.'

'Excuse me for being so frank, Jonty, but your daughter is bad news.'

'There is ample reason,' said Jonty thinly, 'for her to say the same thing about you.'

'Oh yes?' Gavin lit another cigarette, making Jonty wish that he had overruled Hester and enforced a no-smoking rule at The Old Clink. 'It may have escaped your attention but I have driven fifty-odd miles at dead of night, after an exceptionally draining day, in a last-ditch attempt to make some sense of this situation.'

'Really?' The anger was now thudding wildly about inside Jonty. 'Then may I suggest you get back in the car and drive straight back again, because nothing you've said to me persuades me that your presence here will be anything but profoundly unhelpful.'

The front door slammed. Jonty was still standing in the centre of the kitchen, his legs shaking slightly, when Hester came in. She looked worried, then startled.

'She's not there – where is he?'

Jonty sat down at the table and rubbed his face wearily. 'He's not here either. Sorry.'

At 10 a.m. Ark and Giselle waited on the pavement for the cab he'd ordered for her. He had given her some money towards it as well. Dolly sat next to them, patient in her muzzle.

'Thanks for listening,' said Giselle.

'I'm glad you felt you could come, Zelda. You know how I feel about you.'

'Yeah . . .' She gave him a slightly hangdog smile, and glanced at her watch. 'You don't have to hang around.'

He shrugged. 'We got nowhere else to go but the park, eh, Doll?'

The minicab came round the corner at a slow, speculative pace, then spotted them and drew up bustlingly alongside.

Ark opened the door. 'She wants Chuffington,' he said.

'Somebody has to,' replied the driver. 'That one of them pit bulls?'

'She's registered,' said Ark. He leant in through the back door to speak to Giselle. 'Remember Zelda, this is your life. Yours and the baby's. You don't have to do anything you don't want.'

'Don't worry,' she said. 'I'm not going to.'

Jonty and Hester were sitting bleary-eyed at the kitchen table when the minicab pulled up outside. Hester got up so quickly her chair fell back with a bang.

'That's got to be her!'

'Probably, but Hes—'

Hester had opened the front door. 'It is! How can she do this to us?'

'Hes!' Jonty raised his voice. 'That's paranoid. She hasn't done anything to us.'

'She doesn't think about anyone but herself, and never has!'

'Yes she does – don't jump down her throat. *Don't.*'

The minicab drew away and Giselle stood there, not moving.

'Sorry I didn't call or anything.'

'We were out of our minds with worry!'

'No we weren't.' Jonty joined his wife. 'We assumed you were okay since you hadn't been in touch. No news is good news.'

Giselle stuck her hands in her jacket pockets. Jonty thought she looked particularly splendid. He put his hand on the back of Hester's neck and rubbed his thumb softly beneath her hair.

'Gavin was here,' said Hester. Jonty could feel her agitation, like a current, making the delicate bones in her neck vibrate. 'And he *was* out of his mind with worry.'

'God . . .' Giselle glanced up at the windows. 'Is he still around?'

'No, I tried to persuade him,' explained Hester, 'but he wouldn't.' Jonty was too tired to correct this impression. 'He's gone back to London.'

'In time to get his Sunday lunch at Raglan Road, then,' observed Giselle. 'Look, can I be straight with you?'

'We very much wish you would,' said Jonty. 'Come on in.'

'I will in a tick, but I'd rather say this out here.'

'Why, for goodness' sake?' asked Hester.

'Because outdoors keeps things in proportion.'

'You're right,' said Jonty. So why, he wondered, do I not like the sound of that?

'The thing is,' said Giselle, 'I want this baby.'

'We know. You said. And we're glad.'

'But I don't want Gavin.'

They stared back at her.

'Did you hear me?' she asked, not aggressively but earnestly. 'I want the baby, but not Gavin. It's never going to work, there's nothing between us any more, there was never much – it would be a disaster.'

Now she walked towards the house and Hester and Jonty fell back to admit her and watched, with the door still open, as she started up the stairs.

She paused.

'I know you don't like it,' she said. 'And no-one else will either.

And I'm ready to take all the flak. But none of it will change my mind. So don't say I haven't been honest with you. I'm going to have a bath.'

'Turn on the boiler switch,' murmured Hester. 'Your father will want one too.'

CHAPTER SEVENTEEN

7 Raglan Road
London W11

May 5th

Dear Hester,

How are you? I dare say your thoughts will be very much with Daniel on the continent and with Rose as she takes her finals . . . Children! If we had but an inkling of half the worry they would bring us, would we be quite so susceptible to the twinkle in the male eye?

How is Giselle? It seems strange to think that our – and your – first grandchild is already a viable human being and could in theory be born at any time. It must be an even more fascinating experience for you as Giselle's mother. I believe, though I have no experience of it myself, there is something almost mystical about the continuance of the female line. Does she know yet what sex the baby is, or does she prefer to look forward to a surprise on the day? I'm almost glad that no such information was available when I was expecting – I might not have felt so sanguine if I'd realised how much heartache, as well as how much joy, my tribe of boys would cause!

It is probably no bad thing that Giselle is taking this, as it were, sabbatical, to get back in touch with her own familial roots. Gavin very naturally feels bereft, and patience was never his strongest suit, but I have impressed upon him the advisability of allowing Giselle her space at this delicate stage. That they have a shared future is now beyond question, and the exercise of a little forbearance now may pay dividends in terms of mutual respect and affection in the years to come.

I realise that I may be laying myself open to charges of interference, but with the futures of two – no, three – young people at stake I feel justified in making this next request, as one old friend to another. Could you prevail upon Giselle to adopt a slightly less intransigent position with Gavin when he gets in touch with her, whether by fax, letter, or phone? As I hope I've already made clear I would uphold the right of any young woman in her condition to seek privacy and space, but Gavin, as a prospective first-time father, has concerns and anxieties of his own, only one of which is his feeling for Giselle herself. He too deserves consideration, and perhaps more sensitive treatment than he is at present receiving.

If you find it strange that I should be interceding on behalf of a man who is, after all, over thirty, I would only say that no matter how old your children, you never cease to be their mother. I should also add that Gavin has no idea I am making these representations, and would doubtless be horrified if he knew.

I understand there was a small altercation between Gavin and Jonty. I should like you to know that Byron and I regard this as perfectly understandable, and harbour no hard feelings. We have persuaded Gavin, with rather more difficulty, to take the same view. After all, your home is your private place and there is no reason in the world why you should be subjected to the emotional excesses of a young man of very uncertain temperament, no matter what the provocation.

Please give my warmest regards to Giselle, tell her I should like to see her or hear from her at any time. And let us hope that she and Gavin, the soon-to-be-parents of our eagerly awaited grandchild, will be back together in the very near future. We hope too to see you and Jonty before the baby is born.

                                Yours,
                                Ann

Fax transmission from Hester Blake

TO: *Gavin*
FROM: *Giselle*
DATE:
TIME:
NO. OF PAGES INCLUDING THIS ONE:

Can't you see that you're only making things worse for both of us by going on and on like this? It's over between us, as far as I'm concerned. I don't want to see you at the moment. I don't want to see anybody. When I'm ready I'll let you know. Till then take no for an answer, why don't you. G.

7 Raglan Road
London W11

May 12th

Dearest Gavin,

I didn't like to fax your place of work on this subject, nor did I want to get my head bitten off, so I'm popping this through your letter box on my way to pick up our new PG from Heathrow. By the by, she is Sonja Mann, Gustafsson Professor of Old Norse Semantics at Trondheim, a very interesting woman. She is unlikely to be taking dinner out during her first week, so do feel free to drop round for supper any evening – I'm sure you would find it stimulating, and it might help to take your mind off the present, and I'm sure temporary, difficulties with Giselle.

I did indeed suggest to Hester that she have a word with Giselle, and was as persuasive (I hope) as it was appropriate to be. We can only assume that Giselle is, for the moment, deaf to all entreaties. This is very painful for you, I know, but it would probably be in your best interests to stand back for a while. Giselle is very young and, even if she does not admit as much, fearful for the future. I am optimistic that she will come round, so try to be patient, however hard that may be.

Remember, Gavin, that I am doing all I can to help. I do not want or expect gratitude, but I should prefer not to be used as an emotional football in a situation which is not, after all, of my making. Take care,

Love, M.

23A Belvedere Road
London W11

May 17th

Dear Rose,

   So great to see you at the party the other night, and looking <u>amazing.</u>
I'm only sorry my brother was such a sod – it would have been better if
he hadn't turned up at all, instead of coming and being such a bastard,
probably just to see if his blasted sound centre was okay! It's hardly your
fault if your sister's giving him a hard time. I thought you handled it
brilliantly. I've already told him what I think about him getting shit-faced
at my party without bringing so much as a bottle of Vimto, let alone the
much-hyped case of champagne!

   I'm going to be down in the Bristol area this weekend – okay if I contact
you? Perhaps we could take in something at the Old Vic, if that's what
you'd like, have dinner, whatever. If I don't hear from you between now
and Friday, I'll assume we're on and give you a bell on Friday night when
I arrive.

   Hoping very much to see you soon,

                                   Julian

21/5/93

Darling,

I feel rather foolish writing to my own daughter in my own house, but sometimes it's easier to formulate one's thoughts on paper, and I don't want to be endlessly banging on at you about things.

I'm sorry you found that letter from Ann. She means well, I'm sure. You must never think that Dad and I are not on your side, or don't want what you want. But we wouldn't be doing you or the baby any favours if we didn't urge you to give your relationship with Gavin your very best shot. No matter how hard it is now, you must try to see things long term. You certainly <u>did</u> care for Gavin – even if, as you say, the feelings were always stronger on his side – and the arrival of a baby changes everything. You and he will be parents, willy-nilly, but whether you'll be a family or not is in your hands. This is grown-up time, darling. You can't simply run away, and it would be wrong of us if we gave you that impression. We're a support system, and possibly a safety net, but not a feather bed. You must think of what's going to be best for the baby and be very, very responsible.

That said, it's your life and we can't, and wouldn't want to, live it for you. I hope today's appointment at the clinic went well and the queue wasn't too bad – I remember what a drag that used to be! Tell me all about it this evening.

> *Love you lots,*
> *Mum*

41 Parsifal
20.5.93

Dear Giselle,

Good to talk to you on the phone – I was feeling particularly jaded with all things maternal, and hearing you reminded me of how exciting it is to be pregnant. I imagine the last thing you want to do is come tooling down into the Smoke in the merry month of May, when I imagine the country must be absolute heaven, <u>but</u>– I have sorted out some things for you. Obviously, some of them are a bit bulky – bouncy chair, babywalker, bath and so on – so you'll need to come and collect them by car. Will that be possible? If not, I might be able to find someone who's driving out your way in the next few weeks . . . but then we won't have a chance to natter. Carl often mentions your 'piggy-ring', by which I think he means the one in your nose – how does it feel to be a seminal influence? Anyway, give me a buzz and we'll sort out the handover – it would be lovely to see you.

Tons of luck, by the way,

Chloe

LEONARD ARKWRIGHT
REIKI MASTER

Tuesday

My dear Zelda,

  *No matter what you say, I feel a bit iffy about calling you at home. I'd
be prepared to bet your parents want you to make a go of it with this
Gavin guy, and you can't really blame them.*

  *I wanted to let you know that when Daniel dropped in one time in the
winter he bought a session off me. He was only being kind because he was
coining it in at the superstore and things weren't too brisk here. What I
mean to say is, he's never going to use it, so why don't you? Reiki's great
for expectant mothers, and the foetus, too. Don't bother with the receipt,
I know Dan's away. Just turn up, Wednesday or Saturday,*

Ark

SCHMOOZE INC.
33 *Clipstone Place, London*

Katie Hogan
Orde's Diary
The Post
Monckton House
High Holborn

· May 25th

Dear Katie,

A blast from the past . . . I happened to pick up a copy of the Post at my parents' place, and saw your name on that little piece about the Geldofs. You must be doing well if you're getting bylines – but then I never doubted that you would. How is the world treating you otherwise? Life, love, men? It would be nice to have a drink, or perhaps dinner, some time, and do some catching up, as long as you can guarantee no sixteen-stone admirer with fists like sledgehammers, waiting to defend your honour . . .

I have to warn you I probably shan't be brilliant company. I've been dealt more emotional body-blows in the past few months than Chris Eubank's sparring partner . . . it's very hard to see a way through the woods at the moment . . . But that's my problem. It would be lovely to see you, Katie, and to hear your account of the Street of Shame.

Fax or phone, you know where I am,

Gavin

St Catherine's Vicarage
Church Street
Chuffington
31/5/93

Dear Hester,

Good to see you and Jonty on Sunday. Ruth says she appreciated your note – so few people bother these days. A propos our brief exchange as you left, this is to let you know that the Fun Run is on 15th June, over the usual route. We have made one slight alteration in the Dibbs Cross area in view of what happened there last year. But if, as you say, you are happy to be a steward on the corner of Ickford Road and the B1253 we will send you a map for info. Perhaps I could also give prior warning of the Garden Fête, here, on July 31st – there is a move afoot to ask you to open it, on the grounds that the prophet has been for too long without honour etc.

Just one more thing, on Ruth's behalf – she's a member of the B&PW and has received an enquiry about you from the secretary of a branch in Suffolk. Naturally, she doesn't want to hand out your address or number without consulting you, so she wonders if it's all right to do so? This woman apparently heard you speak at the South-East conference and was mightily struck.

Hope that the family are all very well, especially Giselle – she looks wonderful.

Sorry about all the favours!

Yours,
Geoff

Fax transmission
7 Raglan Road
London W11

URGENT, PRIVATE AND CONFIDENTIAL

TO: *Hester Blake, Post Editorial*
FROM: *Ann Armitage*
DATE: *June 6th*
TIME: *4 p.m.*
NUMBER OF PAGES INCLUDING THIS ONE: *One*

My dear Hester,
   My concern over the situation is deepening. Is there a chance you could call in at Raglan Road after work for a pow-wow? If I hear nothing I shall expect you at 6-ish.

                              Ann

Somewhere Spanish
June

Eat your hearts out, this is the business. Got a bit of a result in Cordoba, washing up in a Col. Sanders, but my 501s nicked at the hostel, so YWSYLS. Hope you're all okay, is the baby born yet, can't remember when it's due, see you soon, D.

Memo:

Dear Robert,

   I'm afraid I shan't be able to make our proposed meeting this evening, due to pressing family matters. However, I'll be in the office on the usual days next week and hope we can reinstate it then. So looking forward to it – and many apologies for any inconvenience caused – H.

Apt. 231, East 29th St, New York, NY 101

June 8th

Sweet Sebastian,

Summer's hit this city with a vengeance and you could fry an egg on my windowsill . . . my pot of home-grown basil (no head inside, I promise) is all shrivelled up, so my dreams of fresh pesto are fading fast. Not so, my other dreams . . . At the end of the semester I'm heading for my wooden house in Connecticut to recoup, recharge and re-create . . . it will be open house, as always . . . only qualifications for guests are good looks, golden hair and an English sense of humour . . .

Call me, collect, to confirm (no option offered).

Ava X

The Old Clink, Chuffington, Nr Forbridge, Essex

June 10th

Dear Ann,

I've thought a lot about what you said the other evening, and have discussed it with Jonty, as I imagine you have with Byron. I am writing to you, rather than calling, because I find it easier to assemble my thoughts alone, and on paper – the family will tell you that I'm a terror for knee-jerk verbal reactions which I later regret . . . That's not to say that I didn't agree with much of what you said. In an ideal world two people expecting a baby <u>would</u> be together and be looking forward to a shared future as a family. But these are the far-from-ideal and all-too-real nineties and though we may be, as you put it, concerned parents and future grandparents we aren't and should not be Thought Police. Excuse the cliché but we can't live their lives for them, much as we might like to do so. I think it would be both unwise and unhelpful to try and form some sort of wrinklies' committee to run things.

Also – and this needs bringing out in the open – I'm sure you feel, as we do, that in the final analysis our roles as parents are paramount. In other words, if Gavin and Giselle do not (God forbid) find a way of settling their differences, we must support Giselle, wholly and unconditionally. This doesn't mean that we should be in any way antagonistic to Gavin, but that our prime consideration must be Giselle's, and her baby's, peace and security. We <u>very</u> much hope that everything will work out and I have, as I told you, urged Giselle in this direction. But – and again I mention this because you, as a valued friend, deserve better than flannel – she strikes me as a girl who has made her decision and is more than prepared to live with the consequences.

We are fond of Gavin, and are desperately sorry if he is as distraught as you say. He is very welcome here, but we must respect Giselle's wishes, so it must now be at her invitation, or with her agreement, only.

Gosh, looking back over this, how stern I sound! I repeat, we hope more than anything that there will be a happy outcome, but feel that we, and you and Byron, have to take a back seat or we may do more harm than good.

Perhaps we could all meet up on neutral ground some time soon – do you fancy the new Ayckbourn? A good laugh at the expense of middle-class angst might be just what the doctor ordered . . !

Love to you both, from us both,

Hester

15/6/93

Dear Mr Armitage,

I had the enclosed report from my tutor, and couldn't resist showing it to you. I'd never have reached this standard without you and all the trouble you've taken, so this is to say a big thank you. Most important of all, I'm really enjoying the course, even the written work which I knew I was going to find difficult. Thanks for everything.

I look forward to our next session,

Josette

Post Editorial Fax transmission

TO: *Gavin Armitage, Schmooze Inc.*
FROM: *Katie Hogan*
DATE: *June 16th*
TIME: *1 pm*
NO. OF PAGES INCLUDING THIS ONE: *One*

Dear Gavin,
   Lovely to hear from you, sorry to hear you're having a bad time. This job's like yours, it involves a lot of evenings out, but I'll give you a ring at home, probably at the weekend. Look forward to seeing you soon – chin up – Katie.

By the way, I spotted your press release floating round editorial, and I'm hoping to do a piece on your annus mirabilis . . .

The Old Clink, Chuffington, Nr Forbridge, Essex

June 20th

Dear Chloe,

Thanks ever so much for all the stuff. I don't think I realised quite how much there was till Mum and I were unloading it this end. I actually think Mum was a bit down because she wouldn't be able to go out and buy all those things new, but she couldn't get over how kind you were. Also, it made everything seem very real and very close. It made me think, I could have the baby any day, and even if it arrives on time it won't be long. You're right about the clinic, I have met some other single mums there, and one or two of them are nice, so I'll probably keep up with them. But don't let's lose touch. I need all the friends I can get just now, there's a lot of flak flying about because of my decision to go it alone. My mum and dad have been great but they're still having a bit of a dig about making it work with Gavin. They're wasting their time – he doesn't want us, he just doesn't want everyone to see he's lost out. Sad, only I'm not sorry for him. You're lucky with Mehmet, even if he is a chauvinist. Give Carl a big kiss from me and tell him he can come and see the baby when it's born.

Thanks again for everything,

Love,

Giselle

High priority
Contact Giselle—(baby book?)
Ditto Gavin
Blakes

Other
Josette
Sebastian—US finance
Julian's carpet—remind Byron
Group AGM—stand down
Reduce workload

7 Raglan Road
London W11

June 22nd

Dear Jonty,

   Thanks for lunch. It was particularly appreciated on this occasion, since the water temperature vis à vis my son and your daughter seems to be rising dangerously. I took to heart what you said on the subject, but Ann is a tiger in defence of her young and I can't promise she will take the same view. Perhaps you and I will be able to stick together, and keep our heads while all round us and so forth . . .

   Life gets teedjus, don't it?

                        Yours,
                        Byron

PS Did you catch that amazing last wicket stand at Lord's? Must be old age, but nothing does my morale so much good these days as seeing a couple of young England players throwing the bat at everything in sight.

7 *Raglan Road*
London W11

June 25th

My dear Giselle,

   How are you? Since we have heard nothing directly, Byron and I are assuming that our future grandchild is doing well, and all set for imminent arrival. Will you be having a hospital or home confinement? And if the former, where do you plan to return to afterwards? Naturally, I have spoken to Gavin on these matters, but he appears now to have been totally excluded, and doubt cast on the legitimacy of his interest and involvement.

   I make no apologies for asking you to reconsider your abrupt decision to distance yourself from the father of your child. So far as Byron and I can tell Gavin, in spite of a killing workload and an always-mercurial temperament, has welcomed the idea of the baby that you and he are expecting, and was making plans for its arrival. I do not believe that you have acted maliciously, but thoughtlessly, and I would point out once more what I suspect you do not fully realise, which is how deeply damaging your actions are.

   Giselle — for the sake of Gavin, and the long-standing relationship between your parents and ourselves, and for the child so eagerly awaited by so many — think again. To do so will mean that we can all look forward to the baby's arrival with the unalloyed joy which should accompany such an event.

   The alternatives are too distressing to contemplate. Please think again,
                    Yours,
                         Ann

Tuesday

Ark – came round about that free session, but you weren't in. Please call me at home, no one will mind. I feel as if I'm going completely mad – G.

The Old Clink, Chuffington, Nr Forbridge, Essex

June 28th

Dear Geoff,
   What can I say? I'm so dreadfully sorry about my no-show at the Fun Run. I gather it was a huge success and very profitable anyway, but that doesn't excuse my non-appearance. I have written to Dodie Pye to thank her for standing in at such short notice. In my defence I can only say that Jonty and I have been completely overwhelmed by events recently, and it's taken a real effort of will just to keep the show on the road, let alone do our bit in other respects. In view of this, I'm afraid I shall also have to say 'no' to the Fête. I simply don't feel I could do it justice in my present frame of mind, but I don't want to leave you in the lurch, so I've taken the liberty of writing to a dear friend, the radio quiz queen Lorna Beckinsale, who is an absolute delight and brilliant at that sort of thing. She owes me a favour, so I'm fairly confident she will accept. Tell Ruth I don't mind my name going forward to the B&PW, on the assumption that things can only get better!
   Again, many, many apologies for being such a broken reed. I'll let you know as soon as I hear from Lorna.
                     Yours,
                     Hester B.

SCHMOOZE INC.
Fax transmission
from Gavin Armitage

TO:
FROM:
DATE:
TIME:
NO. OF PAGES INCLUDING THIS ONE:

B I T C H!

*Bitch bitch bitch bitch bitch bitch bitch bitch bitch bitch bitch bitch
bitch bitch*

THE HESTER BLAKE PAGE

. . . *a quick update on the expectant-grandparent front; I know you're dying to know. I accompanied my daughter to an antenatal clinic, and it's all so different now. Comfortable seats, a crèche, staff who smile, nice ladies dispensing refreshments, and free leaflets on everything from bowel movements to benefits. And yet, you know, I couldn't help feeling a pang of nostalgia for the bad old days. Do you remember, girls? The peeling lino on the floor, the carbolic green paint on the walls, the small hard chairs, the six-foot nurse with BO and a moustache. Ah me.*

Mind you, there's one thing that hasn't changed – the Mid-Flow Sample. How well I understood the expression on my daughter's face as she was handed a tiny bottle with a narrow neck and told to "let a bit go, catch a bit, and let the rest go". It's an exercise which could only have been devised by a man. Many and varied are the wonders of the female anatomy, but a reliable directional facility is not one of them . . .

July 2nd
Milan

Pissing with rain here for days, went to see Inter play yesterday and they got stuffed. Muffer caught something itchy in Rimini, but it hasn't got to me yet, wise move. Am I an uncle? – Dan.

CHAPTER EIGHTEEN

The kitchens of Schmooze, usually a clanging, hissing, clamorous ferment of activity, were eerily quiet. Ewan, his sous-chef Kurt and commis-chefs Jason and Shane, leaned silent and still against the work counters, surrounded by the gleaming copper and steel of their trade, like young Pharaohs interred with their possessions. Ewan inhaled with slow truculence on a proscribed Marlboro. The extractor fan hummed. It was intensely hot. With nothing to combat it, spicy whiffs of Ranjit's mutton dansak had infiltrated from next door to add to the tropical atmosphere.

It was a Monday with no scheduled meeting, but reliable sources in the shape of Bar and Della indicated that Gavin was on his way in, in a towering rage over a dip in business, customary at this time of year. The denizens of kitchen, brasserie and office were bracing themselves to withstand the flak, an ordeal that was becoming something of a habit. It was common knowledge that GA had personal problems, and he had never been one to keep his private and professional lives separate. During his short-lived association with a black American *chanteuse* the place had been turned into a twenty-four-hour photo opportunity, good for business if not for staff relations. When his drink-drive case came up before Marylebone magistrates he exacted a heavy toll in deeply wounded waiters, and an astronomical telephone bill. The latest relationship had seemed at first to be a steadying influence (in itself so unprecedented as to be suspicious) but was now apparently driving him to the uttermost edge of health and sanity. Ewan was moved to ask how you could tell, since these far-flung reaches were where GA seemed to spend most of his time, but there was no avoiding the fact that he was in a vile humour. Tangential remarks from Gavin himself implied strongly that the girl in question was too demanding and possessive, and that the relationship had become one-sided as she obsessively sought a commitment he felt unable to give.

Whatever, it was a bummer. Ewan in particular was fed to the back teeth with the histrionics, the sulks, the unpredictable and unwarranted criticism of himself and the other kitchen staff, the playing to the gallery in the brasserie . . . He had left a secure, well-paid hotel job in Norwich to join Schmooze with its attendant risks at the outset because it was his ambition to create first-rate affordable food in unsnobbish surroundings. Instead, he found himself relegated to a peripheral part in the Gavin Armitage floor-show.

The door opened and Bar entered hurriedly, glancing back over her shoulder as though being pursued by gunmen.

'Cave, everybody, he's on his way and there's smoke coming out of his ears.'

'This is bloody ridiculous,' growled Ewan. 'Who does he think he is, Jesus God A'mighty?'

'Probably,' Bar nodded. 'That or Lucifer. He's got the hairdo for a fallen angel.'

'Curlylocks, him and his fuckin' image! I tell you,' snarled Ewan, stabbing his cigarette in the direction of the door, 'he can stuff his fuckin' delusions of grandeur. I don't have to put up wi' em. None of us do. He wants tellin'. He needs us. He's bloody lucky to have us. It's us made him the face in the papers. He's nae more than a bit of money and a waggonload of bull-shit!'

'Sssh! He might hear you.'

'It's about bloody time he did!'

'What, and make it all twice as bad for the rest of us?' demanded Bar. The younger chefs turned their backs on the door, red-eared with apprehension, and began unloading the market boxes. 'Look, he's been in the worst mood in the history of the world for weeks. If I wasn't the warm and wonderful human being that I am I should long since have told him to stick his spreadsheets where the sun don't shine. But I haven't, because if I do he'll burst into tears on my shoulder and then mosey on down here and sack everything with a pulse!'

Ewan dropped his fag-end down the waste-disposal. 'It's fucking preposterous. I'm tellin' him.'

Della entered, cool and immaculate in a cream Nicole Farhi suit and a cloud of Paloma Picasso.

'Morning, all.'

'Where is the toe-rag? I'm tellin' him.'

'Sure you are,' said Della. 'He's just sent the window-cleaner packing and he's having a pop at Mikhail about his jewellery.'

'Arsehole!'

'It doesn't mean anything,' soothed Della. 'He's in a bit of a state at present but it'll blow over, it always does. Just sit tight and weather it.'

'I've had it up to here wi' weatherin' it—'

The brasserie door flew open and Gavin burst in. If Bar had appeared to be on the run from gunmen, her employer looked like a deranged axe-murderer who had just caught up with his prey. His face was distorted with fury, his eyes huge, his knuckles white where he held the bookings file clutched to his chest. His appearance brought home to them all the absolute impossibility of rational argument. This storm had its origins elsewhere and they were mere lightning conductors. Before closing, the doors swung to and fro a couple of times behind his back, revealing the cluster of pale, resentful faces he had just left. The red-eared underlings continued to unpack fruit and veg, robotic with anxiety.

'Here he is,' said Della smoothly, moving towards the cafetière on the hot plate. 'Shall I be mother?'

'Let me,' said Bar. 'I know how everyone has it.'

'Forget it,' said Gavin. 'This isn't a social occasion.'

'Too friggin' right,' growled Ewan.

'Never mind,' Bar frowned pointedly at Ewan as she began putting cups on saucers,'we could all use a coffee. Especially you, Mr Armitage, sir. You look like the wrath of God.'

'He does,' agreed Della. 'You work too hard. Chill out, Brains.' She patted a stool. 'Have a coffee.'

It might have worked. Beverages and sympathy, dispensed with a certain bracing solicitude, had occasionally been successful in the past. The young chefs glanced over their shoulders in trepidation. For a split second Gavin's mood hung in the balance, and they all, with the exception of Ewan, maintained expressions of affable neutrality as though posing for a team photograph.

'Forget it, Della.' Gavin slammed the stool back in against the edge of the table. 'I'm sorry, but I haven't the time. And neither have any of you,' he added in the direction of Bar, who stopped setting out cups and turned to face him.

Della glanced at her watch. 'Will this take long? Only I've got an early lunch and it'd be nice to go knowing that we're all one big happy family again.'

'Don't hold your breath!' He threw the bookings file down on the worktop with such force that it slid off and landed open on the floor, the pages slewed and crumpled. Bar bent down to pick it up.

'Leave it.'

She straightened up again.

'Big fairy . . .' muttered Ewan.

Gavin nudged the file with his toe as though it were a dead rat. 'Do you know what this is?' he asked, and continued at once over their preparatory intakes of breath: 'I'll tell you. It's a catalogue of fudge, failure and total fuck-up. It shows bookings down by five per cent over the next six weeks, and the reason?' He jabbed his finger at each of them as though pressing a series of doorbells. 'You! And that palsied shower out there, who wouldn't know decent service if they woke up in bed with it! You think I'm being hard on you?' He stared round at them. Della examined her nails. Bar opened her mouth to speak. 'Uh-uh. I'm sorry, Della, but we're too sodding tolerant. I never at any stage said that working here would be a bed of roses. It was going to be tough, and get tougher. I don't expect total commitment, I demand it. I *don't* expect to carry a bunch of people with a piss-poor work rate and the motivation of gerbils!'

'Right,' said Ewan with low, gravelly emphasis. 'And I don't expect to take seven kinds o' shit from a great girl's blouse who can't keep his woman in line.'

The young chefs gaped. Della and Bar exchanged a wild look. The staring face of a spy appeared in the round glass of the swing door.

'I beg your pardon?' Gavin's voice shook. 'Did you say something? I'm not sure I heard.'

'Oh, you heard all right.' Ewan's voice carried the accumulated menace of several generations of Glaswegian hard men. He stepped forward, placing one large foot squarely on the bookings file as he did so. 'You heard, twinkletoes. So now you can get the fuck off our backs and start looking for a new chef.' As he spoke he laid the tip of one large finger in the centre of Gavin's chest and withdrew it only after administering a light push which made him rock back on his heels.

In the horrified silence which followed Ewan lit another Marlboro, took his jacket from the back of the door and slung it over his shoulder, and left in the direction of the brasserie. As he passed Gavin he leaned towards him and uttered the chilling words:

'I . . . know . . . you.'

One of the chefs made a sound perilously like a stifled laugh, but it went unnoticed because at the same moment Gavin folded abruptly on to the stool and slumped forward on the worktop, his head cradled between his biceps, his fingers laced at the back of his neck. His shoulders rose and fell with a shudder.

'Get on, please,' said Della, and then inclined her head to Bar's. 'I'll rush along and try a bit of cheque-book diplomacy. You take him upstairs.'

She hurried away. Bar picked up the bookings file from the floor and hooked the other arm beneath Gavin's, exerting a firm, friendly upward pressure.

'Come along. That's enough tired teddies. Let's go.'

As she escorted her employer from the room the young chefs' ears turned redder than ever, this time with suppressed hilarity.

'So your son is not coming?' enquired Professor Sonja Mann, surveying Ann's braised ox tongue with Cumberland sauce, red cabbage and baby new potatoes glazed with butter and sprinkled with fresh chopped parsley. 'Again?'

'Apparently not,' said Byron.

'He operates in an extremely high-pressure field,' said Ann in a level voice, scraping the carving knife back and forth on the steel. 'We're used to his irregularities. I'm only sorry he can't be here. I know how keen he is to meet you.'

'Don't apologise!' cried Sonja. 'There will be all the more for us.'

It took a lot to put Byron off his food but the current shenanigans and the presence of Sonja Mann had almost done it. He hated unpleasantness, it made him quite literally feel ill. He had great admiration for his wife's ability to remain calm and in control in situations which made his stomach churn. She had always handled the boys' ups and downs in what, to him, was a masterly fashion. He only hoped she could do the same this time. It was all most unfortunate. Worse than unfortunate.

He watched dully as Sonja dribbled sauce over meat, cabbage

and potatoes, ending with a fine flourish to create a subsidiary pool at the edge of the plate. She passed the sauce to Ann, keeping up a running commentary on the excellence of the Armitages' hospitality and what they might expect if they were to pay her the honour of a return visit in Trondheim. Sonja was very fat, and ate with a gusto which even Byron, who liked a trencher-man, found slightly repellent. When someone that size ate that amount with such enthusiasm one had the worrying sensation of watching them swell before one's eyes, bulging and ballooning with each piled and dripping forkful. It was like harbouring a monstrous parasitic organism which might burst and engulf the whole house and its occupants in a thick lava of exploded sub-cutaneous lard. He thought nostalgically of the trim and moderate Mr We-We Sun.

'I will give him some!' said Sonja now, wielding the sauce boat over Byron's plate with a moist chuckle.

'Thank you.' The raisins plopping down in the sauce looked, to his jaundiced eye, like dead insects, the tongue too much like tongue. To dispel this impression he began despondently to cut it into pieces.

'Your Sebastian,' said Sonja, making it sound like a foreign car or exotic breed of dog. 'Has he gone to the States?'

'Not yet,' Ann replied, 'there are one or two fiscal matters still to be finalised.'

'Fiscal . . .?' queried Sonja.

'Money,' Byron told her.

'Aha. Money!' Sonja bridled and shook her head with its great swaying mass of beige curls. She then with the utmost deliberation put a forkful of tongue and potato into her mouth and chomped appreciatively, but with an expression which indicated she had more to add on the subject. Ann and Byron waited patiently.

'Money!' she repeated when she had finally seen off the mouthful. 'It is the root of all evil.' She leaned slightly forward, head tilted to the side, to accommodate the newly freighted fork.

Byron had been vaguely hoping for something original, especially after that build-up. He could tell from his wife's politely frowning face that she had been doing the same. One had to remind oneself that English was not Sonja's first language, nor even her second.

'Not quite,' said Ann. 'Not all.'

Dinner clanked and clinked and sploshed on its way. Byron felt

half-dead with fatigue and depression and a kind of boredom that
was new to him. He wanted Sonja, with her massive rotating jaws
and dimpled knuckles, out of the way so he could be half-dead in
peace. The effort of putting up with her at all was simply too much
for him. He was guiltily aware of leaving Ann to field a further
half-hour's worth of trudging observations and leaden clichés. She
was so good at it – always able to salvage some value or interest
from even the most pedestrian conversation.

Just as she was about to dish up the pudding the phone rang.
The kitchen wall-phone was at Ann's end of the table – Gavin
would have called it consumer-driven design – and she duly
answered it.

'Excuse me one moment, Sonja. Hallo? Oh, hallo my dear . . .'

Sonja turned to Byron and mouthed, 'Gavin.' Byron nodded
wearily.

'It doesn't matter at all,' said Ann. 'Though we've missed you,
naturally. Sonja is looking forward to meeting you.' She smiled at
Sonja while listening to Gavin. 'What . . .? Yes . . . yes . . . I'm so
sorry about that . . . I know . . . I understand . . . I *do* . . .' During
this last exchange Ann turned slightly away and lowered her voice
discreetly. Byron recognised a request for greater privacy. He
pushed his chair back.

'I'll go and get the afters,' he said.

'I can do something,' asserted Sonja.

'No, please, it won't take a moment.'

'Saying all these terrible things is not going to help,' Ann was
saying in the low, even tone she kept for the direst emergencies.
As he walked past Byron could hear the staccato crackle of his son's
voice on the other end of the line, rising, falling slightly and then
rising still further.

'What I would like to do,' murmured Ann, 'is to continue this
conversation a little later when we've finished dinner, so that I can
give it my full and undivided attention—'

Byron, taking a covered dish and a cream jug out of the fridge,
heard the fusillade of near-hysterical outrage that greeted this
suggestion. He returned to the table with a measured tread, placed
the dish in front of Ann's place, took the pudding bowls from the
sideboard and put them on her place mat with the serving spoon
alongside and the cream in front of Sonja. He then went back to his
place and sat down.

'We'll wait a mo, if that's all right . . .' he suggested. Sonja lifted the cover on the dish, took a girlish peep and rolled her eyes in delight.

'Gavin—' Ann said. Her voice rose a fraction. 'Gavin, that is not what I meant, as you must know perfectly well. Gavin—!'

Byron heard the muted hum of the dialling tone and then the soft click as she replaced the receiver. She paused for a second before turning. As she took her place there was the merest hint of a flush across her cheekbones. She looked younger, prettier, and more vulnerable, than Byron had seen her in ages. If Sonja had not been there he would have gone over and put his arms round her. As things were it was left to Sonja to restart the conversation.

'All is well with Gavin?'

The hesitation was so slight that only an experienced Ann-watcher would have noticed it, but Byron was experienced. 'Oh yes. In essence. He is his own worst enemy sometimes – are you familiar with that expression?'

Sonja did not bother to answer because Ann had removed the cover from the serving dish.

'But this looks superb!' rhapsodised Sonja. 'Absolutely – ' words failed her ' – mm!'

'*Petites tartelettes de pâté sucré avec des fruits d'été*,' explained Ann.

'They do look nice,' agreed Byron. He was filled with tender feeling for his wife. 'You really have excelled yourself.'

'Not really,' said Ann, with no more than an eggshell-crack in her voice. 'I walked to the *pâtisserie* and bought them.'

A little later, when Sonja had gone to her room to write letters and they were clearing the table together, Byron did at last manage to put his arm about Ann's shoulders as she transferred the remaining *tartelettes* to a smaller dish and covered them with tinfoil.

'Let me finish off here,' he suggested gently, 'if you want to go and speak to Gavin.'

She shook her head. Her hands stopped tucking and pinching the tinfoil around the edges of the dish. 'He'll be in the brasserie. He won't want to be dragged to the phone.'

'Go on. He only needs calming down. You're good at that.'

She shook her head once more, took her hands from the dish and laid them flat on the work surface. Byron was appalled by

the realisation that his wife was crying. And worse still, that
to acknowledge the fact by comforting her would only make
things worse.

Hester and Jonty were taking a walk in St James's Park at lunchtime.
For them to meet in town at all was sufficiently unusual for Hester
to comment on the fact as they watched the ducks sculling briskly
across the lake, cruising for crusts.

'It's hardly surprising,' said Jonty, 'since you're only in town
once a week and you tend to want to see other people on that
day. Perfectly natural.'

'Possibly.' Hester had dark glasses on and he couldn't read her
expression. A group of girls rose from a seat a few yards away and
Hester went over and sat down. As Jonty joined her she turned her
head away slightly, as though to look at him directly might put her
off her stroke. In the lavish sunshine, with a background drone of
traffic and a counterpoint of idle conversation and splashing ducks'
wings, she had created her own small cell of unease. He sat down,
but at the other end of the seat, not intruding.

'It's nice to be doing it now, anyway,' he said. 'And what a day.
If it stays like this over the weekend I'll crack open the Pimm's.'

'Ann rang me up this morning,' Hester said. 'At the office.'

'Oh yes.'

'You know she wrote to Giselle.'

'No.'

'No, I didn't either until Ann told me.'

'What about? I mean, what did she write to Grizzle about?'

'*What about?*' Hester removed her dark glasses and looked at him
in disbelief. 'For goodness' sake!'

'I know, I know,' said Jonty patiently, 'but what line was she
taking?'

'She thinks Giselle is being completely selfish and unreasonable.
"Sociopathic" was one of the words she used.'

'Meretricious bullshit!'

'She wants us to exert our parental influence to make her change
her mind.'

'I was under the impression we'd already done that, or tried
to.'

'We have. And I have explained to Ann once why we're not
prepared to do it again.'

'So what's the problem?'

'Everything!' Hester's voice rose, and then fell again. 'It's all such a mess.'

'Only if we let it be one, which it will if we start trying to orchestrate things. We may or may not approve of what Giselle is doing, but we've said our piece, and if she's still adamant then she has to know that we are completely on her side.'

'Even if we're not?'

'But we *are*. If you want the plain unvarnished truth I can't say I'm that enamoured of our Gavin.'

'No.' Hester shot him a rueful look. 'But Ann kept saying how distraught he is—'

'That's not our problem.'

'Isn't it?'

'No. Look, Hes, we've been down this road before. Misplaced twinges of conscience will only make things more difficult. If you must bring conscience into it think how horrified you would be if we pressured Giselle into something she didn't want to do and it all went wrong.' He put out his hand and laid it firmly on his wife's warm, bare forearm. 'Hm?'

She continued to search his face for a second, and then brushed his hand with hers.

'I know you're right. I suppose I simply want everything to be rosy. Especially on a day like this . . . And Ann's call got me all stirred up . . . These people are our friends, Jonty – where's it all going to end?'

'There's no point in even thinking about it,' he said, with a confidence he was very far from feeling. 'Simplify. Clarify. Our daughter is having a baby, which she wants very much. She no longer has any feelings for the father. That does not mean to say the father cannot retain a long-term involvement with the child. We have put in place what checks and balances we can, and now we very naturally and properly support our daughter in what she wants to do.' He stood up and held out his hand to Hester. 'Finish.'

She rose, rather slowly and stiffly, not taking his hand, but he reached out and clasped it anyway, tucking it into the crook of his arm.

'Don't worry,' he said. 'We will do the right thing.'

*   *   *

At the edge of the park Hester stopped.

'May I get something off my chest?'

In his own chest Jonty felt his heart suddenly trip, and scramble to right itself. 'Of course.'

'In her call Ann said – or implied – that this situation might be the only thing keeping us together.'

'What?'

'She said it was something she saw often in her work. Married couples using their children's problems as glue. She suggested we were going through a rocky patch.'

'Ann has absolutely no *right*—'

'Jonty, shut up. You said that about my wanting to see other people on the day I was in London.'

'Yes.'

She had replaced her dark glasses when they began walking, but now she took them off. She looked tired under her tan. 'I want to tell you something.'

'But do I want to hear it? Jesus Christ!' He exploded. 'Sod Ann and her meddling!'

'It's not so dreadful.'

'Then it's not important.'

'It's important to me. Especially with all that's going on, and the baby due.'

'If you're up for confessing, Hes, that's fine but don't let Ann dictate to you. She's way out of line.'

'It's not even a confession.' Her seriousness unnerved him. 'More an admission.'

'You *don't* have to tell me.'

'But I want to.'

'I mean,' he said more gently, regaining control, 'that you don't have to tell me, because I know.'

She shook her head. 'You can't possibly.' She gave a dismayed laugh. 'There's nothing to know!'

'I know *you*, Hes.' He said it in all humility. It was tough not to allow her her moment of honesty, but he wasn't going to let Ann have the satisfaction. He waved an arm to attract a taxi, and then looked down at her steadily.

'By the way, it was a superb book.'

Giselle had left a message on Gavin's answering machine to say she was coming, but his expression as he opened the door to her was one of intense impatience and irritation.

'What's all this about then? You know I work on a Saturday.'

She produced a piece of paper from the pocket of her dungarees. 'This is what it's about.'

'Okay, so I was out of order.' He flopped down on the sofa and used a still-smoking butt from the ashtray to light a fresh cigarette. 'I was angry.'

'Don't you dare send stuff like that to me again. Especially at home.'

He blew out a sharp stream of smoke. 'What's the matter, you don't want your parents to know how things are?'

'They know how things are.'

'They don't know the half of it.'

'What's that supposed to mean?'

'The way you've treated me, Giselle – it beggars belief.'

'Does it?' She was towering over him. 'You think you're such a catch that no one could possibly give you up? Dream on, Gavin.'

'You used me!' He poked his cigarette at her pregnant bulk, which was at eye-level as she stood before him. 'You exploited me!'

'Christ, any moment now you're going to say I threw you away like an old glove.'

'No, I won't. For the simple reason that it won't be so easy to throw me away. Running back to your parents in their safe little backwater won't save you. I'm a part of your life now, and you'd better not forget it.'

'Correction.' Giselle walked to the windowsill, behind him, and sat down on it. 'You can be part of the baby's life if that's what you want. Not mine. Not ever.'

'I think you'll find,' he said, not turning, 'that the two go together.'

'Don't tell me what I'll find.'

'The thought of you bringing up a baby—' Gavin shook his head with insulting incredulity. 'But then I suppose your mother will supervise your every move.'

'I shan't be living there.'

'Oh?' Gavin twisted round, one arm on the back of the sofa. 'And where will you be living? The YWCA?'

'It's none of your business.'

'Excuse me, but it's very much my business where my child is to live. And I shall be taking the closest possible interest.'

'Don't bet on it!' Giselle got up, snatched the lighted cigarette from him and ground it into the carpet with her foot. 'You smug, hypocritical bastard! Your child! *Your child*—?'

'I realise there's no guarantee of paternity without a blood test—'

Giselle hit him in the chest hard, with the heel of her hand, so that he lurched back with a grunting exhalation. He took a second to recover, with bowed head, and then smiled up at her complacently.

'Temper.'

'All you want is something else for your CV! That's all you ever wanted, trophies! Well I'm no trophy—'

'Too right.'

'And neither's my baby!'

She towered over him, trembling with fury.

'I'm sorry, am I interrupting something?'

They had neither of them heard Ann's key in the lock. Now she stood, set-faced, in the living room doorway.

'No,' said Gavin, his face averted sulkily.

'Giselle?'

'I was just leaving.'

'Please—' Ann laid a restraining hand on her arm as she walked past in the direction of the door. 'It is I who should go.'

'Don't bother. I'm out of here.'

'The very last thing I want is to terminate any discussion between the two of you—'

'It was no discussion,' said Gavin in a flat, bitter voice.

'—no matter how heated,' concluded Ann. She glanced at Gavin censoriously and followed Giselle into the hall. 'Giselle – please. Any exchange, all communication, can only be valuable. Do stay. Thrash this thing out. Speak your minds freely to one another—'

'We have, believe me.'

'Then don't let it end there, for your baby's sake. I can't tell you how pleased I am that you have reopened negotiations—'

'Shut up!' Giselle was so close to Ann that she saw a spot of her own saliva land on the older woman's cheek. 'I only came here to tell your toe-rag of a son not to send me abusive faxes to my home! I need him like a fish needs a fucking bicycle! Believe it, and butt out!'

The door, slammed in Ann's face, seemed to ripple in the backwash of anger as Giselle's footsteps receded down the stairs.

With great effort she collected herself and went back into the living room. Gavin stood with his hands in his pockets, looking out of the window. She hesitated before going over to him, but still did not touch him. Instead she stood at his side and they watched as Giselle strode, her *embonpoint* huge and purposeful, down the street.

'I'm afraid,' murmured Gavin, 'that girl is unbalanced.'

'She was certainly enraged – what has been going on?'

Gavin gave a deep, wrenching sigh. 'I tried. I really tried. She turned up here spoiling for a fight. I did everything I could – conceded that our relationship was over, tried to discuss the baby's future, it was hopeless. She attacked me, nearly burned the place down—' he indicated the cigarette butt on the carpet. 'Perfectly in character.' He paused, and then added reflectively: 'You know she was the one who wrecked your lunch party that time?'

'Lunch party . . .' Ann's brow furrowed. 'I'm sorry, Gavin, you've lost me.'

'That pro-abortion thing you had. Years ago.'

'Oh, that . . .' Ann's expression registered recollection, then bafflement. 'You're saying that was Giselle? But she was only a child . . .'

Gavin turned away from the window and from her. 'Once a wrecker, always a wrecker.'

'I'm afraid,' Ann concluded, in a regretful voice, 'that I am becoming inclined to agree.'

'You've got a visitor,' said Jen to Jonty when he got back to the Earthtrust offices.

It was the last thing he wanted to hear. 'Who?'

'I don't know. Not business, I think. Linda will tell you.'

Jonty didn't bother asking Linda. He had a premonition which was born out the moment he entered his office.

'Hallo, Byron.'

'Do excuse this intrusion . . .' Byron made as if to rise, then stopped himself and squirmed uneasily in his seat.

Jonty was annoyed. 'Not at all.' He went to his desk and slung his jacket over the back of the chair. Sitting down, he picked up a pen and began twiddling it rapidly between his fingers.

Byron looked round the room. 'So this is where the planet is saved.'

'Not really.'

'Where the resources are raised, at any rate . . .' Byron smiled disarmingly. 'I must say, after all these years, it is somewhat discombobulating seeing you in your work surroundings.'

'You think?'

'Yes. Though, God knows, it would have been worse when you were with the wicked admen—'

'Look, Byron, normally I'd offer you a coffee but on this occasion I am a bit pushed.'

'I know. I know.' Byron's change of expression showed just how much of an effort the smile had been. His face seemed to settle into folds of anxiety that had been there for ever. 'You know that I've never done this before, and I'm not a creature of impulse. I wouldn't be here if I didn't think it was important.'

'No. I'm sure.'

'At least here is, so to speak, neutral ground.'

'You could have rung,' said Jonty, and then immediately wished he hadn't. The furrows on Byron's face deepened.

'I could, yes, but I felt the need to speak to you face to face. And the girl said you'd be back . . .'

'Okay.' Jonty laid down the pen. 'I'm sorry.' He wasn't, but he knew he should be. 'Would you like that coffee?'

'No, no, for goodness' sake. I'll get right to the point. Is there anything we can do to avert this disaster between Giselle and Gavin?'

It was only what he'd been expecting, but it still made his heart sink. He looked coldly at Byron and replied with brutal directness.

'I doubt it.'

'I realise that you and Hes, in fact all of us, have been doing our best, but it seems to have had no effect—'

'Perhaps that tells us something about what can or can't be achieved by intervening.'

'Maybe . . .' Byron stuck doggedly to his theme, 'but I don't think we should simply allow them to take this course without trying every means at our disposal to dissuade them.'

'Them?' Jonty raised his eyebrows and linked his hands behind his head. At that moment he actually loathed Byron, not least for making him loathe himself. 'Them? I think you ought not to be mealy-mouthed about this, Byron. It's Giselle you're talking about.'

'I never said any—'

'Isn't it? It's Giselle.'

Byron looked wretched. 'Since you insist, Giselle is the one who seems to have decided to go her own way.'

'But there you are, you said it. She has decided. She's made up her mind in spite of being bombarded with advice from every side – some might say because of it.'

'You think she's simply being perverse? Surely not.'

'Of course not, I'm simply pointing out that interventions at this stage are useless. They've fallen out of love. It happens all the time.'

'So I understand.' Jonty thought he detected something uncharacteristically insinuating in Byron's tone. 'But they no longer enjoy the luxury of being able to fall out of love, as you put it. Not with this baby's future at stake.'

'Don't let's get melodramatic about this,' said Jonty snappishly. 'The baby's future is not "at stake", as you put it. The baby will have a future. Whether or not that includes our daughter and your son being together is neither here nor there—'

'Forgive me.' A pale aureole had appeared around Byron's lips. Jonty realised with astonishment that he was angry. 'But I do find that assertion quite extraordinary.'

'I can't think why.'

'You would if you'd seen the distress being caused in my family by your daughter's – I won't call it cruelty—'

'No, don't.'

'—let's say irresponsibility—'

'No, don't let's. Your wife has already seen fit to refer to Giselle as sociopathic, whatever that may mean, and frankly I'm brassed off with all this high-handed and misdirected name-calling.'

Byron looked coldly astonished. 'I don't think you've quite understood me. Gavin has been summarily and arbitrarily rejected. Ann, who is not some sort of silly weeping woman, is more upset than I've ever seen her. And yet you and Hester appear quite content to wash your hands of the whole thing.'

'God, Byron—!' Jonty looked away, eyes closed and lips compressed. At this moment Linda tapped on the door and put her head round enquiringly.

'Can I get anyone a coffee? Kettle's on.'

'No, thanks!' Jonty raised his hand, palm outwards, in such a way that she withdrew hurriedly. He continued in a tense, lowered voice. 'We are not washing our hands, as you put it, of anything. It's been no bed of roses out our way either. You forget that our daughter's nineteen. She has no qualifications, no independent means of support, and she is expecting a baby by a considerably older man with whom she is not, for whatever reason, living. Nor likely to be. It is a worry, Byron. A great worry. I have so far forborne to play anything remotely like the heavy father with regard to your son's role in all of this, but if pushed I may well do so, and with what most would see as complete justification.'

They glared at one another, their eyes not quite meeting. The hair on Jonty's neck and forearms bristled in spite of the heat. He realised with something shockingly like pride that his hackles were up; he was horripilating. And this at a man whom he had often secretly thought of as poor old Byron.

'I see.' Byron's mouth was now circled by a white ring. 'Well, thank you, Jonty. I'm sorry to have disturbed you.'

He got up. Jonty did the same, pushing his chair back with his legs but remaining behind the desk.

'That's all right.'

'At least we now know where we all stand.'

'Our relative positions haven't changed, Byron.' Jonty used the cold, brisk tone he reserved for the very worst polluters. 'But since you ask I owe it to you to be honest.'

Byron went to the door. He looked thin, stooped and old, but his expression as he looked back at Jonty flashed with contempt.

'Please,' he said. 'No more.'

'So where are you off to?' asked Sebastian. He was doing several things at once: talking to his younger brother on the phone, lighting a spliff, and managing to keep one arm so positioned that he did not disturb the girl who was asleep on his right shoulder. He accomplished the lighting operation and sank back on the pillow, shaking the match and shying it in the general direction of the window. The girl gave a small groan.

'What?' said Sebastian, in response to Gavin's query. 'Mind your
own business. And anyway you're a fine one to talk—' he held the
receiver away from his ear for a second, '—yeah, yeah, I know. I
know, okay? You're a hero. Give Katie my love, right? Cheers.'

He replaced the receiver on the phone which was on the floor
by the bed. The girl, with a grumpy expression, lurched on to her
other side and he took the opportunity to withdraw his arm from
beneath her head. She had a thick, slightly matted mane of frizzy
hair which, along with her beestung lips and hooded eyes, lent
her the passing resemblance to Kim Basinger which had initially
attracted Sebastian. But she smelt a bit and had the morals of a
mink.

Free of her, he slipped out of bed, pulled on his briefs, and carried
the phone out of the bedroom, closing the door behind him. In the
kitchen he put the kettle on as a pretext, should one be needed,
and sat down with his feet up on the table. He drew deeply on
the spliff. It was hot, and the woman next door was out in her
garden, weeding her border with fussy tweaks. If she looked up,
as she generally did, she would see him. He scratched his crotch
luxuriously as he dialled.

'Hi, Pats, it's me. Look, there's something I ought to tell you . . .'

The sun beat fiercely on Ann's back. She wanted to get up and draw
the curtain, but it would have been extremely bad practice to do
so when a client was in full flow, as Mrs Jameson most certainly
was at present. Mrs Jameson was convinced she was a terrible and
damaging parent. Ann was quite sure this was true, but not for
the reasons the client imagined. Sometimes she resented the ethos
which dictated that a counsellor should not, in fact, counsel, but
merely listen constructively. It was frustrating to have to sit and
wait patiently until the client reached her own – generally faulty
– conclusion.

Mrs Jameson brimmed and quivered with tears. The box of tissues
stood ever-ready on the sofa, the top one fluffed out invitingly like
an advertising picture. The afternoon sun beat through the window.
Ann maintained a calm façade, but the heat and Mrs Jameson were
beginning to take their toll. A thread of sweat crawled down
her back beneath her cream blouse. Her hands, which had been
loosely laced on her lap, were clenched stickily together. She was
experiencing all the early symptoms of migraine.

'. . . what I find so dreadful,' said Mrs Jameson, 'so terrible, is that those things can never be undone, that I shall be remembered as bad-tempered and neglectful, when I actually believe I love my children more than most—'

'Oh?' said Ann. 'What makes you think that?'

'I know it,' quavered Mrs Jameson, still not alerted to anything unusual in her counsellor's manner. 'When I speak to my friends, to other women, I realise that they had their children as some sort of rite of passage, something that happened to them rather than from a real desire to see an individual develop and grow—'

'And you were different? Is that what you're saying?'

'Yes. My children were my *life.*'

'So what went wrong?'

A flicker of anxiety disturbed Mrs Jameson's luxurious tears. 'How do you mean?'

'You say they *were* your life, so presumably they're not now.'

'Well . . . as I said . . . they're teenagers now . . . I'm on my own, I find it hard to cope, we have these awful rows—'

'But you expect them to understand your difficulties?'

'I don't necessarily *expect* them to, but I would like—'

'In that case why aren't you speaking not to me, but to them?'

'I have tried, but it isn't easy.'

'Whoever said being a parent was easy?'

'I know . . .!' sobbed Mrs Jameson. 'You're not warned, and nothing can prepare you for it—'

'And yet,' pointed out Ann, her voice deathly quiet, 'many people with, if I may say so, a mere fraction of your natural and acquired advantages understand that, and make a surprisingly good job of it.'

Mrs Jameson's jaw dropped. One of her nostrils, Ann noticed with distaste, was about to run. 'I know that.'

'Then go forth,' said Ann, 'and do thou likewise.' She stood up and opened the drawing room door, moving as she did so from the broiling heat into pleasant, calming shade. 'There's nothing for you here.'

'But surely,' said Mrs Jameson, 'you—'

'Out!' cried Ann. 'Out!'

Following the hugely successful press reception at Schmooze, Gavin drove Katie back to Fulham and walked with her to her front door.

Even at eleven o'clock it wasn't fully dark, and the amber of the London skyline faded into a warm flannel grey in which the stars were beginning to come out, one or two at a time.

'It's been a great evening,' she said. 'I'm so glad I was able to come.'

He squeezed her arm. 'Me too.'

'Quite apart from the fact that you deserve a really good piece, and I'm going to write it, it's made me realise how much I'd have hated not to see you again.'

'Oh, Katie—' He pulled her against him and clasped her tightly, burying his face in her soft scented hair. Her hands stroked his shoulders and her voice made sounds of tender concern into his neck. 'Katie . . .'

'Come up,' she murmured. He could feel how warm and yielding, how almost-there she was. 'Come up for a little while. Jackie's out.'

'No,' he whispered. 'Not this time. But hold me for a minute, Katie. Hold me very tight . . .'

Giselle couldn't sleep. She suspected, although she didn't know, that she was not the only occupant of The Old Clink who was wakeful, and for that reason she walked quietly past her parents' room on her way downstairs.

She went through the kitchen and out of the french window into the garden. The night was as soft and sweet as warm milk, the grass threading coolly between her toes and the flowers like pale, composed faces watching her. Faces for once without a point of view, benignly acquiescent. She walked some way from the house and then leaned back against one of the stooped apple trees, her hands clasped beneath her stomach. In bed, the baby had been surging and kicking restlessly, but now that she had moved it lay heavy and tranquil inside her. The head was engaged, it bore down on her sleep-relaxed muscles with a gravid, friendly force. Gazing back at the house she thought: everything's about to change. The simple, irrefutable truth of this embraced and held her. She was at peace.

In the house Hester had heard Giselle go out, and prayed urgent, fractured prayers for a host of blessings to soothe her daughter in the warm night garden.

CHAPTER NINETEEN

A ll through the second half of July the sun shone. Day followed perfect day like a string of pearls, each with the soft luminous polish that such days have in England where they have scarcity value. In Chuffington, most humble and hearty thanks were given by the godly and the ungodly alike – the Garden Fête, the school sports, the children's pet show, and the church flower festival all had a record turnout and correspondingly large profits, and the givers of innumerable weddings, christenings, Pimm's parties, barbecues, fork lunches, flannel dances and strawberry teas also had cause to praise the benison of the Almighty.

For a second week it dawned clear and golden, and a third. Hardworking souls who had stared from train and office windows all week, philosophically preparing themselves for the wet weekend dictated by sod's law, were rewarded by unbroken sunshine. The air filled with the drone of mowers and strimmers, the splash of paddling pools, the chirrups and yells of children in back gardens, the dusty roar of combines heading for an early harvest, the subversive twang of boxed music and the leisurely clop of ponies disinclined to trot. At church services the doors were left wide open to admit, along with the torrent of sunshine, the occasional bird or butterfly which fluttered, frantic and pretty, about the place until Geoff decreed a pause during which it could be rescued or shooed back into the churchyard. The congregation, admittedly not large, sang up with particular gusto, knowing that they could be heard by passers-by.

It was the same story nationwide. TV weathermen in shirtsleeves proudly displayed charts of the British Isles scattered with nothing but little yellow suns and the occasional puffy white cloud, like a field of buttercups and daisies. In towns, frowsty old pubs with windows that had been closed for years moved tables and chairs out on to the pavements, and people made use of every inch of outdoor space on roofs and balconies, in parks, car parks and playgrounds, and on the steps of public buildings, on walls and trees and municipal statues.

The Chuffington cricket XI were enjoying a tremendous season, due in no small part to the form of Jonty Blake who was throwing the bat about with the fire and aggression of a man half his age.

Number 7 Raglan Road, with its high ceilings and calm, well-ordered spaces, was a pleasantly cool house. Its south-facing garden basked in sunshine from mid-morning till as late as eight in the evening at this time of year, but the house itself retained a certain dignified reticence, retiring from the frivolity of summer behind curtains which Ann prudently kept drawn during the heat of the day, in the continental manner. Not for the Armitages the red shoulders, peeling noses and heat-and-drink headaches of their less circumspect compatriots. Ann had accustomed her family to behave like the natives of hot countries, and treat the sun with respect and moderation. She and Byron took breakfast outside, and then waited until the cool of the evening to take a long glass of chilled kir royale on the lawn.

On this particular Friday evening they did so in the company of their sons, because Sebastian was due to depart for the States the following day. As well as the jug of kir, Ann had provided chilled mango and passionfruit juice and a selection of bite-size choux buns and pastry *bâteaux* with savoury fillings.

In spite of everything, Ann was keenly aware of the need for fairness, and to give time and attention where it was due. This, she made clear in many small ways, was Sebastian's evening, and no matter what Gavin's emotional turmoil, or indeed their own, nothing must be allowed to hijack the occasion. She had even made a point of ascertaining that Sonja was out at a faculty cheese and wine before extending the invitation.

'Byron,' she said, when all the boys were present and glasses had been charged. 'I think a toast is in order.'

'Of course,' agreed Byron. He lifted his own glass. 'Sebastian – to New York, and all points west.'

'Seb – to opportunity!' echoed Ann, giving Sebastian a fond smile. He and Julian were looking sleek and satisfied, which made Gavin's gaunt appearance all the more painful. Even she, who loved his curls, could see that his hair was too long, and his eyes were bloodshot. He also had dirty cuffs – she suspected that the washing machine had not yet been plumbed in.

'So come on,' said Julian, 'tell us exactly what the plan is, I'm not clear.'

'Nor me,' said Sebastian, who had long since learned the disarming trick of admitting as much of the truth as possible in order to prevent people guessing the whole. 'But I've always wanted to write, and these crazy friends are offering three months' free board, maybe more, in upstate New York, for me to give it a go, with the use of the college library and anything else that takes my fancy.'

'I bet,' said Julian. 'Anything – or anyone?'

Ann laughed convivially. 'Please. What Sebastian does in his spare time is his own affair, I think.'

'Who are these friends?' enquired Byron. 'Anyone we know?'

'No,' said Sebastian. 'Friends of friends, not close.'

'If you want computer facilities at any time,' said Gavin, breaking a long silence in a low, attention-grabbing voice, 'I can give you the number of the best brain in Manhattan.'

'Cheers,' said Sebastian. 'You never know.'

Julian made a face. 'We can guess. Does this best brain have a sister?'

'It might be a woman in the first place,' put in Ann.

'Thank you,' said Gavin.

'Not at all.'

'Your mother,' said Byron, enjoying this rare moment of family harmony, 'combats sexism and prejudice wherever it is to be found.'

'No, I'm going to write,' declared Sebastian, topping up his glass and taking a clutch of choux buns which he held cupped in the palm of his hand. 'Let's face it, if I don't give it my best shot while I've got the opportunity I could spend my whole life wondering, what if.'

'Absolutely right,' agreed Ann. 'And don't worry about the flat, Josette and I will pop in and give it a once-over and thereafter it should only need keeping an eye on.'

'You ought to sub-let,' suggested Julian, 'make a few bucks.'

'Excuse me, but I'm not sure that's such a good idea.' Ann was pensive. 'You never know when you might want to return at short notice, and this way we can keep the flat shipshape.'

Sebastian lifted an eyebrow at Julian. 'Got someone in mind?'

'No, just a thought . . .'

Sebastian turned to Gavin and gave his leg a push with his foot. 'Let me know what occurs, won't you. You'll be a dad by the time I get back.'

Gavin glowered. Ann said, judiciously: 'That is a fact, but whether it will be a cause for celebration or not remains to be seen.'

'I'll be celebrating,' said Julian. 'It's not every day I become an uncle. And there's something I ought to tell you.'

'Get on with it then,' Byron urged. 'It would take an awful lot to surprise your mother and me just now.'

'I'm seeing Giselle's sister.'

'I did warn him,' growled Gavin, 'but he wouldn't listen.'

Byron sighed heavily. Ann took a sip of kir and fixed a gimlet gaze on her youngest son.

'I do hope,' she said softly, 'that you realise on what dangerous ground you are treading.'

'Spare me the melodrama, Mum. Rose is great. I'd really like this to last. That's why we've made a particular point of not coming here together, or going up to Chuffington. It's nothing to do with anyone else. The only reason I told you is because Rose and I will be wetting the baby's head whether anyone else likes it or not.'

Gavin grunted morosely. 'Feel free. You'll probably wind up seeing more of my child than I will.'

'Don't be foolish, Gavin,' said Ann. 'You have a moral right to be a father to that baby.'

'Maybe,' ventured Byron, 'Giselle should be wooed instead of fought.'

They all stared at him.

'It was only a suggestion.'

'*My* suggestion,' said Ann, 'is that we return to the matter in hand, which is to wish Sebastian good luck and success on his trip to the States.'

'Excuse me,' Gavin rose and shrugged on his jacket, 'I think we've done that. I must go.' He held out his hand to his brother. 'All the best. If you can't be good be careful.'

Ann half-rose, but Byron laid a restraining hand on her shoulder. 'I'll see Gavin out.'

He had some difficulty keeping pace with his son and was panting by the time they reached the front door.

'Gavin . . .'

Gavin stood with one hand on the door knob in an attitude of ill-restrained impatience.

'I meant what I said,' persisted Byron. 'Perhaps we've all been too ready to let this situation become confrontational.'

'And who, if I may ask, is responsible for starting the confrontation?'

'I don't know, it's not my place to—'

'For Christ's sake, Dad, of course you know! Giselle Blake used me to get herself knocked up and then waltzed back to Essex to three square meals a day and a place at the top of the housing list! What do you mean, you don't know?'

This tirade was wasted on Byron, but for one word. It was so long since any of his sons, let alone Gavin, had addressed him as Dad, that it was like a shot of something right into the vein. As Gavin glared at him, white-faced, he was reminded of all those occasions, donkey's years ago, when he'd taken this spiky, embattled, hysterical little boy on to his knee and calmed him with stories and drawings while Ann, quivering with contained exhaustion, clattered saucepans in the kitchen.

'I'm on your side, old man,' he said gently. 'But there's more than one way to skin a cat.'

Gavin opened the door and delivered his parting shot framed against the leafy sunlight of Raglan Road.

'I'm not crawling on my belly for that little bitch. If she wants me she can bloody well ask.'

Byron did not return at once to the garden. He sat down on the stairs and massaged his eye sockets. How in hell had it come to this? Their life had always been ordered: Ann had ordered it. Any misgivings he himself had had were always balanced by the certainty that Ann could manage things, and they would remain within her control. Now it seemed some insidious poison had infiltrated that life and was contaminating everything it touched. Worst of all, thought Byron, it had brought with it something he had never thought to have: enemies.

The door opened, wide and bright.

'Good evening!' cried Sonja. 'Alone and palely lingering?'
Byron did not bother to correct her.

Because of the sun making the curtains glow, and a seething
nervous energy which rarely let him be these days, Jonty woke
early that Saturday. In spite of the window being open the
bedroom was hot and the duvet felt heavy and sticky. He kicked
it away from his legs and rolled towards Hester. There was not the
slightest response. She slept like the dead at the moment, rushing
into unconsciousness with a desperation which Jonty recognised as
the flip side of his own hyperactivity. His moment's eagerness was
doused. He got up.

It was six-thirty. Jonty padded about in his Ralph Lauren shorts –
a present from Hester – drawing the downstairs curtains. The views
thus revealed – his own garden, the front drive, the cabbagey trees,
stubby chimneys, conical spire and cream- and pink-washed walls
of Chuffington, had a shining, untarnished beauty in the early sun.
He experienced a warm, revelatory sense of the importance of the
work of Earthtrust.

In the kitchen he made tea, and took Hester's upstairs. All that
was visible of his wife was a reddened cheek and a night-jumbled
fuzz of fair hair.

'Tea,' he said, and set the mug down on the beside table. She
didn't stir.

Downstairs again he opened the french window and stepped out
for a minute on to the rough, mossy bricks of the patio. The ants who
had colonised the layer of sharp stand beneath the bricks – it should
have been mixed with dry cement – sent envoys to investigate; he
could feel the minute, sharp pinpricks of interest on his bare feet.
Jonty often told Hester she was too sensitive about the ants, what
harm did they do for goodness' sake? But now he cursed, hopped,
smacked at the soles of his feet and jumped back into the kitchen.

They had heard nothing from the Armitages since his excruciating
exchange with Byron three weeks ago. Whether anything had passed between Giselle and Gavin he did not know and was not going
to enquire. Pregnancy had lent his errant daughter a womanliness
which Jonty found slightly intimidating. Her swaying full-breasted
figure had a kind of timeless dignity which quelled doubt and
silenced argument. Jonty remembered no such grandeur connected
with Hester's pregnancies. But then, he had been involved in

those in the most intimate way, always sharing though perhaps marginally less enthralled with each successive one. He had entered his wife's pregnant body, explored and examined it, made it his business to know. Giselle's separateness became more evident with each day that brought her closer to her confinement, a fortnight away. The layers of fat and fluid which protected the foetus seemed also to set apart the mother. Jonty kept saying to himself: 'My child is expecting a child', because it was so extraordinary.

'Hallo, Dad.'

Suddenly she was there in the kitchen, leaning to select an apple from the fruit bowl, her face utterly impassive as though she was slightly ashamed of having spoken to him at all.

'Hi there. You're up early.'

She sat down on the step of the french window and bit into the apple.

'Watch out for ants,' warned Jonty. 'They're out in force.'

'If the bastards get in my pants they could wind up getting more than they bargained for,' said Giselle.

'I was thinking of your feet.' She seemed not to hear him. 'Sleep all right?' he asked.

She shook her head. 'No, but then I don't at the moment. The baby's on the go half the night, and my brain won't stop working.'

'I'm the same,' agreed Jonty. 'I think I must be out in sympathy.'

She cast him a look of affectionate scorn. 'Steady on, who's having this baby?'

He gave a short laugh and watched her in silence as she finished the apple with big, noisy bites and vigorous munching, her eyes closed against the sun. Then she threw the core on to the grass. 'Go, ants,' she ordered. 'Fetch!'

It was a typical, soppy, woman's throw, all effort and no knack, which for some reason comforted Jonty. Emboldened he said: 'May I ask you something?'

'Sure.'

'Do you want anyone to be with you – when you have the baby?'

'Not particularly. Should I?'

'Not at all. Only I know – if you do want some company, moral support, whatever, I know your mother would be glad to provide it.'

'Do you think so?'

'But she doesn't want to be pushy about it.'

'Mum can come along if she wants to.'

Jonty had the feeling his suggestion was being given a wrong emphasis.

'It's a case of what *you* want, Grizzle.'

She shrugged. She didn't see it. Jonty remembered Giselle's own birth, the most difficult of the three because she had been lying face up and had to turn with painful slowness before making her final appearance. He had been present at all his children's births – enthusiastic, a bit fearful, keen to help but all too dismayingly aware of his ultimate uselessness. He remembered that after the closeness and intimacy of the preceding nine months Hester had gone to some separate female place to make this journey on her own. Not all the antenatal classes, nor the books, nor the kindly, encouraging advice from the medical staff could alter the fact that he was an adjunct and not a participant. Then when the baby was born – in Giselle's case, nine pounds with a shock of black hair – Hester came back to him, sticky, bruised and exhausted but with a look in her eyes which he would never forget, and together they welcomed the new arrival. Thinking about it now, he realised that he had never talked about this to another man: never quietly and privately compared his own experience with that of a fellow father. He and Hester both laughed at people who kept slides of the afterbirth, and forced their friends to watch videos of the Great Miracle of Life, but Jonty would have liked to know how another chap felt.

Giselle stood up, reaching her arms forward as she did so to act as a balance.

'Nice day,' he said. 'Got any plans?'

'I thought I'd go into town,' she said. 'Have a look round the shops . . . see what thin people are wearing.'

'Want a lift?'

'Sure.' Once again she made it sound as if she were indulging him.

As she passed him to go upstairs she added, without actually looking at him:

'I might tell Gavin – when I start to have it.'

Jonty made a couple of slices of granary toast with Marmite and ate hungrily. He heard a bath being run upstairs, and the sound of Giselle's heavy footsteps across the landing, the door closing. Going up to get dressed, he found Hester sitting on Giselle's bed, gazing through the open door so that her eyes met his when he reached the top of the stairs. With her face still rather puffy, her hair up in an elastic band, and her legs tanned below the hem of her outsize T-shirt she looked ludicrously young to be almost a grandmother. Jonty went and sat next to her and at once she put her arms round him.

'Thanks for the tea.'

'It must have been cold. You were out of it.'

'You were too early.'

'Want another?'

She shook her head and pulled away from him as though taking a grip on herself.

'What brings you in here?' he asked.

'Foolishness,' she said briefly.

'I'm sure not.' He looked around the room, as he knew she must have been doing. The baby stuff was in place – the things Chloe had given Giselle, plus bits and pieces which Hester had not been able to resist buying new. The Moses basket was made up with a yellow stretch undersheet, a white shawl and a patchwork blanket. A red PVC toy box held teddies, rattles and other paraphernalia – tubs of wipes, powder and cream, a changing mat, a bucket with a lid. A mobile of wooden dolphins and seahorses covered in blue and white marbled paper hung from the ceiling over the basket, turning gently. Around this oasis of fragrant newness the room remained steadfastly, messily Giselle's. The inflatable man, patched with a puncture kit, sat in the corner gazing fixedly towards them.

'I hope to God,' said Hester, 'that it's all going to work out.'

'I don't know what you mean by that. And neither, I suspect, do you.'

'That Giselle will be happy – and the baby will be all right—'

'Grizzle seems in pretty good shape to me. And there's no reason why the baby shouldn't be fine, is there? You two are the ones who talk about it. I thought the reports were good.'

'I feel bad about the Armitages,' said Hester, not listening.

'Wallowing won't help.'

'It's as though we've slammed the door in their faces. Ann and Byron – two of our oldest friends.'

'We've done no such thing. If any door-slamming went on, Giselle did it, for reasons of her own. She's entitled. We've been down this road before, Hes.'

'Perhaps I ought to get in touch with Ann, what do you think?'

'After what she said to you?' Jonty looked astonished, then shook his head. 'But sure, get in touch with her whenever you like, it's a free country.'

'You know what I mean – to try again – '

'I think that would be a mistake. We have to let Giselle make the running for the present. What do they call it in your paper? Tough love.'

'It's too awful . . .' She grabbed at her hair, but because it was tied back she only succeeded in dislodging a few strands, and making her eyes water.

'Let me tell you something,' said Jonty. 'Something which may or may not come off, and may or may not be helpful.' He hesitated.

'Yes?'

'Grizzle's thinking of telling Gavin when she goes into labour – so he can be there.'

'No!'

'She just said so when she was downstairs with me.'

'You think she meant it?'

'I think she's seriously considering it.'

Jonty was astonished at how cheered Hester seemed to be by this small development. Her face was alight with hope.

'Do you think she might even be – you know – thinking again?'

'I've no idea.' Jonty got up. 'Come on, she won't appreciate us hanging around in here when she comes out of the bath. I said I'd give her a lift into town.'

Hester rose and he put his arm round her as they left the room. On the floor near the door stood a battered grey flight bag – Giselle's hospital case, ready packed. They both noticed it, but found it too poignant to mention.

Jonty and Giselle had left for town, and Hester was about to get in the bath when the phone rang.

'Mum, it's me.'

'Rose, hallo darling – how's it going?'

'Fine, great – the weather's brilliant.'

'And here.'

'It's so amazing not to have to work. We've all been lying about and drinking too much. I've put on weight since finals, but I've got a positively continental tan.'

'You can afford the weight, love. Anyway, I'm glad you're enjoying yourself, you deserve it. Any news . . .?'

Hester realised from her daughter's laugh that her stab at casualness had been unsuccessful.

'Mum, you're hopeless. Jez is off the scene. *Finito*. But I have not been beastly to him, and in fact he's taken up with another woman who seems to be helping him get over his devastation with complete success.'

'I wasn't asking about him, I was asking about you,' protested Hester vainly.

'Sure, sure, sure. Well, I'm fine. A bit strapped for cash – I'm going to look out for some sort of job, however menial, before the milk round starts or I won't be able to get away this summer.'

'Do you want me to ask around this end?'

'That's kind, but no thanks . . . as a matter of fact I was thinking of finding something in town.'

'Down there, you mean – Bristol?'

'No, London.'

'Oh, right.' A separate agenda was becoming apparent, but Hester could not yet see enough of it to discern its nature. 'Good idea. Where will you live?'

'Actually, I've got an offer of a place.'

'Really? Look before you leap, won't you love, London rents are in a different league to the ones you're used to down there.'

'It'll be okay, it's a sort of loan-cum-share – dirt cheap.'

'Lucky girl. Rosie . . .'

'Mm?'

'It's all above board, isn't it? All properly organised and beyond reproach?'

Rose gave a honk of laughter. 'Mum . . . It'll be absolutely ideal, and it'll mean I'm on the spot for my interviews. As a matter of fact it's where I'm calling from now. I came up for the weekend to take a look.'

'That's sensible,' said Hester, 'but do check the small print.'

'There is something I ought to mention,' said Rose. 'I should really have told you before, but I keep forgetting – settle down, I heard the sharp intake of breath – it's just that I'm going out with Julian Armitage.'

Hester took this in.

'Mum?'

'I'm still here.'

'We've been seeing each other for a couple of months.'

'I see.'

'That's all. I hope it doesn't complicate matters, there's no reason why it should.'

'No.'

'You don't sound very sure.' Rose's tone turned threatening.

'Darling, it's none of my business who you go out with.'

'Stock response.'

'Well, what do you want me to say?' Hester's voice rose. 'That I'm thrilled to bits and it's exactly what I always wanted?'

'A year ago that's exactly what you would have said!'

'Rosie, this is silly, a year ago we wouldn't have been yelling at each other over the phone like this.'

'No,' agreed Rose caustically, 'we wouldn't. What a difference a year makes. And we all know who we've got to thank for it!'

She rang off, leaving Hester standing there with the receiver buzzing in her hand. She replaced it slowly. Her knees were shaking and her throat was constricted.

In the bath she stopped crying, it never seemed to go with hot water and bubbles. Rose was still run-down from finals, she told herself, and understandably touchy about the situation. It would blow over. And who knows, there was always the faint possibility that the liaison with Julian Armitage might be helpful.

The phone rang for the second time when she was getting dressed. She sat down on the edge of the bed in her shorts, towelling her hair with her free hand.

'Is that—' the caller began, and was instantly cut off.

Hester pulled on a singlet and was debating whether she could, at her age, go bra-less with impunity, when the phone rang again.

'Hallo?'

'Mum?'

'Daniel?'

'How's it going?'

'Fine.'

'I've only got—'

'Reverse charges!' Hester bellowed.

Daniel took her advice.

'Third time lucky,' he said cheerfully when she'd agreed to pay
for the call.

'Where are you?'

'Holland. We're coming back.'

'When?'

'Now – like in, what, twenty minutes, right.'

'Twenty minutes . . .?'

'Ferry leaves in twenty minutes, right.'

'To where?'

'Where – hang on.' There was an offstage exchange with Muffer.
'Harwich.'

'That's a long crossing.'

'Few hours, yeah. Tea time it gets in.' Daniel's itinerary, like his
life, was mapped out in meals.

'How are you getting back from Harwich?' Hester went through
the motions of asking, though she already knew the answer.

'We wondered if you or Dad were on for a lift. Only Muffer and
me're potless.'

'Oh all right, seeing as how the wanderer returns and all that.'

'Smart. Look, we gotta go, can you check the time?'

'Don't worry. See you later.'

'Safe.'

This conversation, in spite of the obvious logistical problems
it raised, cheered Hester up. Daniel's was a fortunate personal-
ity, propelled by a genial and uncomplicated self-interest which
absolved everyone around him of the need for subtlety. You either
could or would, could not or would not provide that for which
he was currently asking, and whichever it was one was neither
swamped with gratitude nor shrivelled with resentment. Hester
dried her hair, put on a bra, and went downstairs feeling that her
status as a normal parent was at least partly restored.

'I'm sorry I couldn't fit you in this morning,' said Ark. 'You should
have given me a bell.'

'It's okay,' replied Giselle. 'I told you, I didn't come as a
patient—'

'Client.'

'I came to see you.'

'Suits me.'

They were sitting at a green metal table in the courtyard of the Red Cow in Forbridge. On top of the table were two pint glasses, one containing Dobbey's, the other a ginger beer shandy. Beneath the table lay Dolly, slit-eyed and panting in the warm shade.

'You've got plenty of clients these days, then,' said Giselle.

'Yeah. Word gets round. The Barlow's offered me another half day in September if I want it, and the way things are going I may be able to take them up on it.'

'Let me know if you need any help. I'd be glad to, if you don't mind me bringing the baby along.'

'Sure, I'll bear it in mind. Baby's no problem.'

'It'd have to be cash.'

'Naturally.' Ark flapped unhurriedly at a wasp which was hovering over their glasses. 'So you told them what was what, did you?'

'Yes.'

'How'd they take it?'

'All right – they didn't have much option, really. I feel a bit – you know, they've been friends with his parents for years and years—'

'That's their problem, not yours.'

'But it kind of puts them on the spot. If they accept what I want to do then that means they're against his family. There isn't any in-between.'

'That's what parents are for, isn't it? It's written in the contract.'

'I suppose so . . .'

''Course it is.' Ark leaned across the table and laid his hand on her stomach. 'You'll find the same.'

She took his hand and held it tightly in both of hers, giving him a smile that was slightly skewed by anxiety.

'Sooner than you think,' she said. 'I'm in labour.'

Ann's voice was a light, businesslike patter down the line.

'Who is this, please?'

'Katie – Katie Hogan.'

Ann did not break stride. 'Katie, my dear, that was a nice little piece you wrote about the brasserie – my cleaning woman showed me.'

'Thank you.'

'Is Gavin there?'

'Er – I think so—'

'Then would you please ask him to come to the phone?'

'Yes – I'll see, um – hang on a moment.' Katie let the receiver hang and went to the bathroom. She knocked quietly and tried the door.

'Come.'

She put her head round. Gavin was lying back amid fragrant floes of bilberry bath essence, reading an Asterix book.

'Sorry to interrupt, it's your mother on the phone.'

'Shit. Tell her I'll call her back, will you?'

'I'll try.'

Katie returned to the phone. 'Ann, he's in the bath, do you think he could—'

'I'm afraid on this occasion I must ask him to come and speak to me. It's extremely urgent. I was a little surprised to discover he wasn't at work, I've been trying there for some time, but the answering machine's been on. Do you think you could persuade him,' said Ann with wounding condescension, 'to pop a towel round his middle and come and have a brief word?'

Katie, smarting, relayed the message. Gavin hauled himself out of the bath with the worst possible grace and went to the phone.

'Couldn't it have waited five minutes?'

'I'm afraid not.'

'A message, then. I could have called you back—'

'Gavin, someone called Leonard Arkwright called me from the hospital in Chelmsford. He, too, has been unable to contact you. You will understand the impossibility of my leaving a message with Katie when I tell you that Giselle is in labour. Your child is about to be born.'

There was a short silence during which Gavin could hear the cooling water dripping from his body on to the kitchen floor.

'Gavin? Are you still there?'

'Yeah. So what am I supposed to do about this?'

'Gavin!' Even Ann's rigorously maintained calm was jolted by shock. 'You should be *there*.'

Gavin gave a sneering laugh. 'You're joking. Me? I'm just the father. Surplus to requirements. Not wanted on voyage.'

'Self-pity is unattractive at the best of times, and singularly misplaced at this moment, Gavin. You are, as you rightly point out, the father of this child, and you are finally being offered an opportunity to behave as such—'

'By whom?'

'Giselle herself asked this friend to call on her behalf—'

'Listen, Mother dear, that's no friend. You know who this Arkwright is? He's the sad old seventies throwback she was going out with when she met me.'

'I'm not interested, Gavin!' Ann's voice sharpened, but it was a mere blip, and at once levelled out again. 'I am interested only in the future of your child, our grandchild. Please make some appropriate excuse to Katie, get dressed and get up to Forbridge immediately.'

'It's a complete—'

'*Immediately*, Gavin.'

'Don't tell me what to do!' Gavin's perturbation prevented him from noticing Katie's discreet departure from the flat. 'This is my life we're discussing here!'

'Only in part,' responded Ann crisply. 'More importantly, it is the life of the baby about to be born. I understand it may not be easy. You have every right to be in emotional uproar. Your father and I will be round to pick you up and drive you to the hospital in—' there was a split-second pause while she looked at her watch. Gavin tried unsuccessfully to interrupt but she overrode him incisively: 'Fifteen minutes.'

Having slammed the phone down, Gavin stood for a moment in his silent, empty flat, boiling with irritation. But as he stumped rebelliously to the bedroom to get dressed, he was swept by a heady excitement. This, after all, was it. The real thing. Quintessential human drama – and he, Gavin, was centre stage. Whatever the outcome his behaviour and responses would be the focus of every eye.

He rubbed his hair vigorously and then, naked but for the towel draped round his neck, opened his wardrobe and considered what to wear.

'That was nice,' said Hester as she and Jonty emerged from the dining room of the Tickled Trout, a pleasant pub they'd stumbled across en route to Harwich. 'Though it does feel a bit like bunking off.'

'That's what's nice about it,' agreed Jonty.

'Do you think I should ring home—?'

'No.'

'—to check Giselle's all right?'

'She will be. She is. And it's hardly as if we're sneaking across the Channel to some unknown destination. We're going to pick up Daniel. A more blameless activity would be hard to imagine,'

'What if she—'

'She knows what to do. Her case is packed, a unit of crack obstetric troops awaits her. And anyway, she still has two weeks to go and first babies are notoriously late.'

'That's true,' said Hester.

Jonty unlocked the Range Rover and they climbed in.

'If we let this situation rule our lives at this stage,' he said, reversing with a flourish, 'we'll never get out from under.'

They turned out of the pub car park and headed eastward, sped on their way by *The Eagles' Greatest Hits*.

'You didn't have to do this,' said Rose to Julian as they joined the M11 northbound carriageway. 'I wasn't hinting.'

'I know that. It's my pleasure, pussycat. Besides—' he jerked his head at the driver of a Bedford van, 'it's high time I came out of the closet and introduced myself to your parents.'

Rose flashed a smile at the mortified van driver. 'I hated ending on a sour note with Mum. And I didn't really mean to blame Giselle for anything. She can't help it. Disasters fly to her side like iron filings to a magnet.'

'My brother certainly blames her,' said Julian. 'In fact he does little else at the moment.'

'Don't let's talk about it, please,' begged Rose. 'I want to have a nice peaceful afternoon in the garden, watching you charm the parents.'

Julian glanced at her for slightly longer than was judicious when cruising at ninety in the fast lane.

'You're an old-fashioned little thing at heart, aren't you?'

She turned her head away, smiling. 'Keep your eyes on the road.'

The midwife had introduced herself as Hazel. She was a laconic black Brummy with a husband named Brian, three children of her own, and several thousand deliveries to her credit.

'I'm with you for the duration, girl,' she told Giselle. 'But that won't be too long, I'm here to tell you.'

'I bloody hope not!' gasped Giselle.

'Only another couple of centimetres to go,' intoned Hazel soothingly. 'This is a super-efficient mechanism you got here.'

The contraction ebbed. 'Fuck me, I wouldn't want a dodgy one . . .'

Ark nodded at the pain-relieving device attached to the small of her back. 'That thing work?'

'I wouldn't know, would I?' snapped Giselle. 'I don't know how much more agonising it would be without it, and I'm not about to find out!'

'Take it easy,' said Ark, 'I only asked.'

Hazel was busy with her trolley, like a tea lady. 'You two went to antenatal classes?'

'I tried one,' said Giselle. 'That was enough.'

'Now, now, that's not the attitude,' reprimanded Hazel placidly. 'Only you seem to be breathing nicely.'

'Yes, well, I've been practising that all my life, haven't I?'

'You should have done a bit of Reiki, Zelda, like I suggested,' said Ark, who was leaning on the basin in the corner. 'It's relaxation for the soul.'

'For Christ's sake, don't you ever stop advertising—? God – ah—!' Giselle embarked on an escalating series of long, wailing breaths as another contraction began its slow dawn.

'Reiki, I've heard of that,' said Hazel. 'There was something about it on Channel Four a few months back.'

'That's right,' said Ark, gratified, taking Giselle's hand and raising his voice slightly above the din. 'That was Kevin McDiarmid, one of the most senior Reiki masters in the country. I trained with him.'

'I'm not like everyone you'll meet around here,' Hazel told him. 'I got a lot of time for alternative medicine, the holistic approach and so on. My husband was half-dead with back trouble until he learnt self-hypnosis, then—'

'Will you shut up?' yelled Giselle. 'I need something! I'm in agony! I want gas and air, an epidural, whatever you've got! *Now*—!'

'Let's just let this one die down, shall we?' suggested Hazel. 'And then I'm going to give you another internal, see how things are going.'

'I don't want any more hands up my fanny!'

'Because it's my opinion, sweetheart, that this baby's going to be with us very soon now.'

'I want something for the pain, you black bitch, and I want it now!'

'Darling, you can have whatever you want, you know that, but you're doing so well it's not necessary, believe me. A couple more contractions and you going to be ready to push this baby out.'

'Push . . .!' Giselle closed her eyes. 'I couldn't push a door shut . . .'

'Let's take a little look while things are quiet,' said Hazel, 'shall we? 'Cos they won't be quiet that much longer, that I can tell you.'

Ark retreated. 'I'm going for a fag.'

'No smoking in the building,' Hazel reminded him absently, pulling on rubber gloves.

The internal was deferred by another contraction, under cover of which Ark left the room. Giselle swore, Hazel applauded, and a cursory examination confirmed that the final stage was imminent.

'You're about fully dilated, darling. If your partner's too long having his cigarette he's going to miss this birth.'

'He's not my partner,' said Giselle snappishly. 'Worse luck.'

'Well whatever he is, he's a nice, kind man,' commented Hazel, applying the foetal heart monitor to Giselle's stomach. 'We see all sorts in here, and in my opinion you could do a lot worse than that one.'

The rapid, watery thundering of the baby's heart filled the room.

'You want my opinion—' said Hazel.

'I don't!' snapped Giselle.

'—this is a little girl.'

'Shit!' Giselle embarked, furious, on another contraction.

'That's my lady,' said Hazel. 'You're working well.'

'I don't believe this,' said Rose. 'All this way on a Saturday afternoon and they have the nerve to be out.'

'I love your house,' said Julian, patrolling. 'Have you seen that old Joseph Losey movie, *Accident*?'

'No . . . Hang on, a note . . .'

She read briefly, hand to her cheek, as Julian looked at pictures in the dining room.

'Oh, no, I don't believe it! Jules—'

'What?' Julian's voice drifted from the next room.

Rose hurried to join him. 'Giselle's gone in to have her baby! She came back to collect her case and found nobody here. I suppose the parents must be with her by now. What should we do?'

Julian shrugged. 'Let's drink tea. That's what people do on TV when they're waiting for babies.'

'Stuff tea!' said Rose. 'Let's go!'

She was about to close the door when the phone rang and she snatched it up.

'Mum!' gasped Rose, 'thank God you rang!'

'I knew we shouldn't have gone swanning off so close to the date . . .!' said Hester distractedly. 'Jonty, can you please, *please* put your foot down, does nobody but me have any sense of urgency about this?'

'I don't get it,' said Daniel, pushing the sleeping Muffer off his shoulder so that he flopped against the window. 'She's okay, isn't she? I mean, she's gone to the hospital, they'll look after her, right?'

'Right,' agreed Jonty. 'Darling, you're behaving as if this is some sort of life-threatening crisis instead of one of the most natural, common and basic processes in the world.'

'You haven't a clue, have you?' wailed Hester.

Jonty looked aggrieved. 'Yes, I have! I was there, remember? For all three. I showed up and never faltered.'

'Yes!' Hester sounded triumphant and exasperated at the same time. 'Exactly. You showed up – but there's no knowing whether Gavin will – always assuming she had time to tell him at all – she could be there on her own!'

'I doubt it,' said Jonty. 'If memory serves me aright it's a job to get a moment to oneself on these occasions.'

Daniel leaned forward. 'Mind if we have some music? Not the "Beagles".' He removed a tape from the still-insensible Muffer's personal stereo and leaned over to stick it in the machine. 'Tell you what,' he added as the car filled with outraged Afro-American rap, 'I'm gagging to see a baby born.'

'If they wanted to improve the Health Service in some really practical way,' reflected Byron, drawing to a halt and gazing mournfully through each window in turn, 'they could do something to ease the parking problem.'

'One thing's certain,' said Ann from the back seat, 'there's no sense in the three of us circling round and round out here. I suggest you drop Gavin and me at the main entrance, and join us when you've found somewhere.'

'Very well.'

Byron prepared to rejoin the slip road which would return him once more to the main entrance of the maternity unit. Ann placed a hand on Gavin's shoulder.

'How are you, darling?'

'How do you think?'

'Have you eaten at all today?' He shook his head. Ann did the same. 'Not good news. Labour can be a long, tedious business. Once you're installed with Giselle I'll find the hospital shop and buy you a baguette.'

'I can't promise to eat it.'

'You can try,' admonished his mother. She waved at his smoke. 'And you must put that out, it won't be allowed anywhere inside.'

'All the more reason for me to finish it, then,' said Gavin truculently, as Byron pulled up by the glass doors.

'See you later,' said Byron glumly. 'How much later is anybody's guess.'

'Just keep reminding yourself,' said Ann gaily, 'you could be a grandfather when you next see us.'

They got out and Ann watched Byron drive away at a snail's pace between the glittering, tight-packed ranks of cars. The heat was intense. Against the hospital wall, and again between the broad pavement and the road, straggly shrubs rose gamely from thin, gritty soil.

'I wouldn't advise throwing that cigarette end away out here, Gavin,' said Ann. 'You could start a fire in these temperatures.'

'"Single father wastes maternity wing".' Gavin was acid. 'Not a bad idea. Someone else has had a bloody good try—' He nudged a still-smoking butt with the toe of his shoe. 'Wacky baccy, too – on a hospital doorstep, can you credit it?'

'Darling . . .' said Ann in a voice of tender reproach, 'you've got odd socks on.'

'Have I?'

'And I haven't seen this old black pullover in years – for excellent reasons,' she added, tweaking a loose thread at Gavin's elbow.

'Yes, well,' said Gavin. stubbing out his cigarette on the inside of a metal litter bin, 'I wasn't thinking, was I? One doesn't, when rushing to be present at a birth . . . Shall we?'

Shaking her head in affectionate despair, but flushed with excitement, Ann followed her son.

The straining groans which had sounded faint and far-off from outside in the corridor burst noisily over Ark as he re-entered the delivery room. Hazel, holding Giselle's hand, and with one of Giselle's feet braced against her hip, beckoned him vigorously and shouted:

'Nicely in time to make yourself useful, friend. Hold her like I'm doing, will you?'

'You took your time!' yelled Giselle. 'Don't just stand there – get a fucking hold of me!'

Her face was blotched and streaked with effort, her hair plastered to her skull with sweat, her nostrils dilated. Ark smiled at her in fond and tender admiration. 'Take it easy, Zelda,' he advised unhurriedly. During the strenuous bedlam of another contraction he copied Hazel's stance and grip. 'There we go. Ready for the off.'

'Baby's coming round the corner all right,' said Hazel contentedly. 'We can see that head crowning, darling – she's got the blackest hair you ever saw. Now we want a big, big push with the next one, okay . . ?'

A sign in the corridor of the delivery ward announced: PARTNERS ONLY BEYOND THIS POINT.

'I should like to come along and ascertain Giselle's whereabouts,' said Ann, leading the way. 'Unless—' she hesitated. 'Perhaps you'd rather I didn't.'

Gavin muttered something which ended in the words 'care less'. This Ann took as an endorsement and together they continued to the desk.

'No, not at all,' said the duty nurse, smiling broadly. 'You don't want to take any notice of that old notice, we're very relaxed in Phoebe Ward.'

'Good,' said Ann, glancing with disfavour at a sticker on the

wall behind the desk which proclaimed: 'Nurses Do It In Squelchy
Soles.'

'You are . . ?' asked the nurse, glancing up prettily at Gavin.

'Gavin Armitage. I'm Giselle Blake's partner. Baby's father.'

The girl looked momentarily puzzled. 'Fine. She's in Room
Four.'

'Good luck, darling.' Ann would have kissed her son, but he
moved away so swiftly that she was left making a little jerky,
truncated movement which she converted into a pushing-up of
her cuffs.

The nurse smiled on. Young though she was, she'd seen a lot in
her time. 'Did you have awful trouble parking?'

'It's completely inadequate.' Ann was at home with this topic. 'As
far as I know my husband's still orbiting the building in search of
a space.'

'In that case,' said the nurse, 'perhaps you'd like to sign the
hospital users' petition.'

'Certainly,' said Ann. 'It would be my pleasure.'

'So, darling,' said Hazel, 'how does it feel to be a mum?'

Giselle had thought a lot about how she might feel when her
baby was born. She had prepared herself for a violent eruption of
emotion, or exhausted indifference, or even, perhaps, despondency.
The reality was quite other than all of these – a calm, warm sense of
recognition, of certainty and rightness. Her nine-pound daughter,
dark-haired and firm-featured, lay in her arms with a demanding
confidence which made Giselle want to shout for joy, and laugh
for pleasure. She felt vindicated and complete. A peaceful energy
surged through her.

'Brilliant,' she whispered. 'It feels brilliant.'

Gavin went into Room Four. Giselle was sitting up on the bed,
holding a peach cellular-wool bundle from which a small head of
black hair protruded. Beyond her the midwife was carrying out
assorted postnatal rites – washing things, throwing things away,
tidying things . . . She looked up only briefly as he entered. Giselle
did not look up at all. Her hair was slicked back off her face, and
she radiated a solidly rooted composure which Gavin had not been
expecting. He hesitated. The midwife gave a brief, businesslike nod
in Giselle's direction. He advanced to the bedside.

'Hallo, Zelda.'

'Hi.'

Her tone was neutral, preoccupied. Gavin wasn't even sure she had noticed who it was that had spoken to her. He thought that probably he should embrace Giselle, speak extravagant endearments, even weep a few manly tears, but for once he could manage none of these things. The situation demanded a bare, unadorned strength of feeling which evaded him. He was at a loss. He touched the baby's head with his finger. It was like a warm eggshell scattered with down.

'What—?' he began to ask.

'A girl.'

He sat down on the edge of the bed. Giselle had still not looked at him, her eyes remained intently on her daughter's face. From this angle Gavin could see that the baby's eyes were also open.

'We didn't have any names for girls,' he ventured lamely.

'I did.'

'We had a few more ideas for boys.'

'I'm calling her Fay.'

A spurt of anger penetrated Gavin's state of passive shock. 'Fay . . . Yes, okay, I don't mind, let's call her Fay then.' Giselle did not reply. 'May I hold her?'

She shook her head. 'Not yet.'

His face turned hot. 'She is my daughter too.'

'I never said she wasn't.'

'Please.' Gavin's jaw tightened with the effort of saying it. 'Please let me.'

'In a minute.'

Hazel, on her way to the basin, laid a motherly hand on his waist, and spoke into his ear. 'Let them be for a little while. Mum has to do her staring first.'

Gavin smarted, but Giselle seemed not to have heard. The room was very quiet. The gurgle and splash of the tap, the click of the pedal bin, the rustle of paper and the sibilant sound of Hazel's crêpe soles only emphasised the hush.

'How did it go?' he asked.

'Sorry?'

'How was it – the labour?'

Now, for the first time, she looked up at him. He had forgotten how fierce her stare could be beneath the Jack Nicholson eyebrows. 'You wouldn't understand.'

'Now come on,' said Hazel from her corner. 'Excuse me for eavesdropping but we had a nice natural childbirth here this afternoon. This lady was a star.'

'I see,' said Gavin. 'Glad to hear it.'

The door opened and Ark appeared.

'Where's that tea?' said Hazel. 'I'll pop along and chase it up.'

Ark waited till she had gone and the door had swung shut behind her.

'Hey,' he said, 'you made it.'

Gavin stared at him with cold surprise. 'What are you doing here?'

Ark raised his hands. 'No worries, I'm gone.'

'Don't,' said Giselle. 'She's gone to hurry the tea.'

'No, no, I'm hitting the road now you've arrived, man.' Ark nodded towards Fay. 'She's beautiful. Congratulations.'

'Thanks.' Gavin stood up, hands in pockets. For the first time he regretted the choice of clothes which placed him, even in relation to Ark, at a slight sartorial disadvantage.

'You've got odd socks on,' said Giselle.

'Have I?'

'What do you expect, Zelda,' said Ark, going to the bedside and touching her cheek in gentle reproof, 'when the guy's rushed out from London to be here?'

'If he'd rushed he'd have been here sooner.'

'You haven't answered my question,' said Gavin, whose eyes had not left Ark's face. 'What are you doing here?'

'Only filling in till you arrived. I couldn't reach you earlier; Zelda gave me your mother's number in the end, did she tell you?'

'So, let me get this straight,' went on Gavin, 'you've been here all the time?'

'Yeah.'

'I mean here. In this room. Not just in the hospital building.'

'Sure.'

'Ark was brilliant,' said Giselle. 'You wouldn't believe the shit he took from me.'

'Yes,' said Gavin, 'I would.'

'I did as I was told,' explained Ark. He smiled at Gavin. 'It's not for wimps, I'm telling you.'

'Let me get this straight. You're saying you were here, with Zelda—'

'Don't call me that.'

'You were *here*,' Gavin's voice rose insistently, 'when my daughter was born?'

'As it happened. Thought I'd better make myself useful.'

'Right. Fine. So you've been useful. Now you can sod off.'

Giselle glared at him. 'Don't speak to Ark like that.'

'It's cool,' said Ark, 'like I said, I was going anyway. See you around.'

He almost collided with Hazel coming the other way with the tea.

'I never knew a birth like this one for comings and goings,' she remarked. 'Who's for a cuppa?'

Unsuspecting, but always courteous, Ann wished Ark 'good afternoon' as he walked past. A delivery ward these days was, she observed, a very much more free and easy place than it had been at the time of her own confinements. Whether the change was entirely for the better she remained to be convinced. The nurse behind the desk looked across at her with an understanding expression.

'Hard being patient, isn't it?'

'When you get to my age, my dear,' replied Ann, who did not like being patronised, 'it comes quite easily.'

'Was that your son you brought in?'

'Yes.'

'You must be dying to go and see your new grandchild.'

Ann's cheeks flushed warmly. 'The baby has arrived?'

'Sure, about ten minutes before you got here. Why don't you go and knock on the door and take a peep now they've had some time to themselves?'

'Thank you,' said Ann. 'Perhaps I shall.'

At the same time as Ark was running down the stairs Rose, Julian, Hester, Jonty, Daniel and Muffer came up in the lift.

'Of course!' said the nurse, in response to Hester's hectic enquiry. 'All family?'

'Yes,' said Hester.

'Not guilty,' said Muffer.

'Carry on,' said the nurse. 'Room Four.'

Muffer collapsed on a padded banquette. Almost at once his head fell back, his eyelids drooped and his mouth hung open.

'Chicken shit!' jeered Daniel. 'Gutted.'

'Gavin!' said Hester, dizzy with euphoria and relief. 'I'm so glad you were here!'

'He wasn't,' said Giselle.

Ann said sternly: 'We did the best we could, my dear.'

'I am not your dear.'

'She's the most beautiful baby in the history of the world,' exclaimed Rose, who was holding Fay, 'isn't she, Jules?'

'Looks good to me.'

'What a result,' said Daniel. 'Give us her here a tick.'

'I'm glad it all went well, Grizzle,' said Jonty. 'You are clever.' There was a lump the size of a golf ball in his throat which he struggled to control. Whatever the justification he did not wish to cry in front of Gavin, whose hostile stare he could feel boring into him from across the room.

'Ark was brilliant. I couldn't have done it without him.'

'I beg to disagree,' said Ann.

'He had no business being here!' Gavin was white. 'And he bloody knew it!'

'Where is he?' asked Hester, gazing round.

'Gavin told him to go,' said Giselle. 'So he went.'

'I think,' said Ann, 'that was the proper course of action. This is after all a family occasion.'

'No it's not,' said Giselle. 'What do you mean? Fay's my baby, I had her. It's got nothing whatever to do with your family.' She glanced at Hester. 'Sorry, Mum.'

Gavin gave a snort of scorn and derision. His mother gazed unblinkingly at Giselle. Julian looked at the floor.

'I think,' said Jonty, putting his arm round his wife's shoulders, 'that we should all try to calm down, for Fay's sake.'

'For once I agree,' said Gavin, 'Now, Zelda—'

'How many times do I have to tell you not to call me that? That's Ark's name for me. Don't say it!'

Hazel popped her head in. 'Brave and calm, doctor's orders. I'm going to organise some more tea.'

By the time Byron had parked the car, on a patch of waste ground labelled 'Overspill', about a five-minute walk form the maternity wing, he was perspiring freely and his temper was worsening by the minute. The walk itself, in broiling heat and in constant danger of being mown down by ambulances, laundry vans, and people he assumed to be doctors driving like bank robbers, did nothing to improve his frame of mind.

He prayed, as he rose in the lift to Phoebe Ward, that it would all be in the bag and he would find a tranquil scene.

As Byron approached the desk he bade good afternoon to the barely-conscious Muffer, reflecting as he did so that it must be a sign of advancing decrepitude when expectant fathers looked ever younger.

'Baby's born,' the nurse told him. 'Are you family?'

'Well actually, yes,' said Byron, relaxing a little. 'So I suppose that must mean I'm a grandfather.'

'Lovely. In you go then. Room Four. They're all there.'

Outside Room Four Byron was conscious of a faint hubbub. Through the glass panel on the door he made out a large group, including Ann, Gavin and Jonty. As he pushed the door open the hubbub subsided and he was met by a wall of faces, still wearing the hostile expressions they had worn for one another.

'Hallo,' he said. 'I gather I'm a grandpa.'

Gavin, his face taut, brushed past him without a word. Ann, following, was at his side in an instant, her hand like a vice on his arm.

'Come along Byron,' she said. 'We're going.'

On the way down he asked helplessly: 'I don't understand it – where the devil did they leave that damn great thing of theirs?'

The answer was provided when they emerged into the dazzling sunshine to see the Range Rover parked near the door, with two wheels on the pavement and the other two on a double yellow line.

It wasn't fair, thought Byron. But then, what in this life was?

CHAPTER TWENTY

'Great knock on Sunday,' said Geoff to Jonty in the saloon bar of the Axe and Compass. 'You're seeing it like a football this season.'

'My swansong in all probability,' replied Jonty modestly.

'Nonsense.' Geoff chuckled, then looked serious. 'Jonty – I've been wanting to ask you something.'

'Fire away.'

'I wonder whether your outfit might be interested in a scheme the diocese is supporting to preserve the ancient green spaces – village greens, churchyards, glebes, that type of thing.'

Jonty felt his shoulders relax with relief. Once, a lifetime ago, he had longed to confide in Geoff. Now the thought of the conversation getting personal filled him with dread. 'It's a terrifically laudable idea,' he conceded carefully, 'but I'll be straight with you, it's a bit parochial for us.'

'Oh, literally parochial,' agreed Geoff. 'And none the worse for that.'

'No. But Earthtrust, as its name suggests, has a global emphasis. I'm looking at it from your point of view, and I can't help feeling that some organisation with a more specifically British remit would be more use to you.'

'The thing is,' said Geoff, 'you're a local figure. That counts for a lot, as you know.'

Jonty liked Geoff. He took a long draught of his Dobbey's while weighing his words. 'I don't believe it counts for as much as it did. It's possible to overdo these local connections, don't you think? People get sick of seeing the same old faces, and the impact is lost.'

'Can't agree,' said Geoff sturdily. His great asset as a parish priest was a calm and kindly tenacity. 'Not in the case of yourself, or Hes for that matter. You're perceived as being both high-profile and genuinely committed on the local community level.'

'It's kind of you to say so.'

'Not kind at all, it's a fact, and one I'd like to use to diocesan advantage if I can,' said Geoff with disarming candour. 'Can we at least leave it on the table? There's a few weeks before the inaugural meeting, and the scheme proper won't begin till next summer.'

'Okay.' Jonty was tired, and the thing simply didn't seem sufficiently important to make a stand over. 'Leave it there for the present.'

'Good man,' said Geoff. 'Now how about the other half?'

Jonty took his time walking back to The Old Clink. The late-August evening was mellow, but that was not the reason he was dawdling. He was dragging his heels.

He rather regretted his indecisive response to Geoff's request, not least because it had seemed like a capitulation to flattery. He didn't awfully like himself at the moment. He was not the man he wanted to be, or had always thought he was. He was whacked, certainly; the lack of a holiday this year was catching up with both him and Hester, but tiredness didn't usually make him this tetchy and unreliable (it certainly hadn't affected his strokeplay, he reflected wrily). It was as if his tolerance to the demands of others, no matter how legitimate, was at an all-time low. Which was not a good thing in the charity field, let alone that of personal relationships. And that brought him to another thing, which was the present tenor of family life.

Jonty had always had a sound, if liberal, attachment to hearth and home. He loved his wife, and was devoted to his children – even if it was hard sometimes to like them – and he took a very real pleasure in his surroundings which, in spite of Hester's moans, suited him perfectly. He realised now, though it had not been a conscious process at the time, that a year ago he had anticipated a new phase, in which he and Hester would have the house to themselves, where they would decide on holidays and jaunts without reference to the plans of their offspring, and where conjugal rights might be enjoyed at any time without fear of interruption or being thought disgusting.

This dream had not been realised. Daniel was at home, unemployed and becoming, as far as Jonty could see, less employable by the minute. Rose had only managed a 2:2 and was living in London with another member of the Armitage clan, waitressing at, of all places, The Old Hat, and conspicuously failing to fulfil her potential. And Giselle and Fay were with them until other accommodation became available. The Blake household, never notable for its neatness, was now a tip. Jonty, looking back, tried to remember whether his own children when small had been the source of such colossal and intransigent mess. He supposed they must have been, but the difference was that he had been a part of it all, entirely bound up and immersed in it, a participant and not a spectator. Now, the mess was happening to him, at a stage in his life when he was least prepared to withstand it. Plastic bags full of disposable nappies (often inadequately sealed) lay on the floor by the kitchen pedal bin. Tiny damp clothes were strewn, dripping, along the radiators. A pram and portable car seat occupied the centre of the hall, the former often with mud-caked wheels, for August had been wet. An intercom ensured that no matter where one fled, Fay's tyrannical importunings could be heard, well able to drown Jeremy Paxman in full flow, and even, on a bad night, Ben Elton. The bath in the early morning was invariably occupied by another, plastic bath half-full of cool water, large quantities of which would have found its way on to the floor . . . Mrs Carson was openly mutinous.

In the midst of all this turmoil Giselle breastfed tranquilly, sublimely content. She was unwavering in her assumption of lone parenthood. She no longer seemed to bear either Gavin or his family the slightest ill-will, but simply to have dismissed them from her mind. On the few occasions when Gavin had turned up, demanding to see the infant daughter who was doubtless being ruined by her mother and conditions at The Old Clink, Giselle handed Fay over, and reclaimed her with a dreamy air which sent him away in even higher dudgeon than when he'd arrived. Ann and Byron had so far been conspicuous by their absence, and even Julian no longer accompanied Rose when she came home.

Jonty didn't know whether to admire Giselle's composure, or be appalled by it. With the onset of pregnancy his younger daughter had become a different person before his very eyes.

Or perhaps qualities which had always been present came suddenly and powerfully to the fore. He could remember Hester during what the medics called the perinatal period, especially after Rose – emotionally charged, insecure, alternately weepy and elated, hyperactive and exhausted. Giselle presented none of these symptoms. Admittedly, she had little else to do but look after Fay, but her striking calm could not be accounted for merely by lack of domestic responsibilities.

Hester, on the other hand, was far from calm. As well as being passionately attached to Fay, she was riven by a deep seam of anguish about their position *vis-à-vis* the Armitages. Jonty was experiencing the strain of having to appear more confident than he was in order to reassure his wife. A certain resilience and spontaneity was ebbing from their relationship, leaving it dry and brittle. The supple interwoven fibres which formed the dense (and Jonty had always thought unbreachable) mesh of their shared life were beginning to split and separate. Bit by bit, steady and insidious, the rot was setting in, and Jonty felt helpless in the face of it.

He was seriously considering getting another puppy.

Giselle sat on her bed, leaning back on the bedhead with Fay in her arms. Her window was open on to the soft, damp summer evening, and a vase of white daisies stood on the sill. Fay was feeding, but occasionally she would open one eye and fix her mother with a piercing look. This made Giselle laugh. 'You're a hard woman, Fay Blake,' she whispered. It was what Ark used to say to her, and she had wondered sometimes recently if it were true. But she knew she wasn't. What she was now was not hard, but strong. She saw things for what they were. Gavin had had his chance, and blown it. He was angry, but in time the anger would burn away, and she and Fay would still be there if he was interested.

'Till then, young lady,' she said in quite a normal voice, not caring if she could be heard, 'it's you and me against the world.'

Hester and Robert sat in the bar of Gerards Hotel. The bar was on the top floor and afforded a magnificent view of central London looking south towards the Thames. The décor was cosmopolitan comfy, a bit art deco, a bit country house, but not enough of anything to delight or offend, designed merely to soothe. In the corner of the bar stood a white piano at which a man in a black polo-neck played selections from Porter and Berlin. In the restaurant beyond, a few scattered couples at green-robed tables were attended by bored, gliding waiters.

'Naff,' agreed Hester, 'but restful.'

'And secluded. Besides which, I have to confess to a sneaking liking for this kind of piano playing.'

'Me too. Nice tunes.'

They sat for a moment, listening. The pianist at once threw himself into a bouncy Sixties medley.

'He must have heard us,' said Hester ruefully.

Robert gave a short, absent smile. Another silence spread between them like a stain on a tablecloth, while the greatest hits of Gerry, Freddy and Billy J. provided the worst possible background for what she wanted to say.

'How is your grandchild?' asked Robert with the slightly stately courtesy which had shaken the resolve of better women than Hester.

'Adorable. Sweet. Eight weeks old now.'

'Is she really? A positive veteran. It seems like only the other day she was born.'

'For us it's hard to imagine what life was like without her.'

Robert smiled again, patient and correct. Hester was aware that on this occasion, and at her invitation, he was making time for her. Her agitation was not helped by the fact that she was at present particularly susceptible to Robert's restrained charm. His gently enquiring gaze made her hot and confused. Just when she most wished to appear worldly-wise she was feeling like a very silly woman.

'If you expect I'm wondering why you asked me here,' he said, 'you're absolutely right.'

He had placed his finger unerringly on the pressure point. She laughed, embarrassed but charmed because he understood her so well.

'I'm sorry . . . does it all seem so contrived?'

'Not contrived, but I was left in no doubt that I'd been summoned.'

'You're right, there is something I want to say.'

'Hetty, I am at your disposal.'

'It's a little hard to know how to approach it.'

'If I were you,' he said, 'I should cut to the chase.'

'Yes.' She placed her glass on the table between them and laced her fingers together. 'I will then. My instinct tells me we should stop having these – meetings.'

Robert raised his eyebrows. 'You make them sound like assignations.'

She flinched under a hammer-blow of disappointment. 'If I do, then perhaps that's because they are beginning to feel like that. We've known each other a long time, Robert—'

'Indeed.'

'—and I believe we like and admire each other and enjoy each other's company.'

'True.'

'But surely it's not only me that's aware of something else – something more?' Hester's tongue felt huge and heavy, like a dead thing in her mouth. 'Perhaps I simply have to come clean and admit that for me, it is. More.'

He spread one hand gracefully. 'I'm flattered.'

'Don't be,' she snapped, 'I'm at a dangerous age.'

'In that case I stand rebuked.'

'And don't take that line either, Robert, I deserve better from you than that. We both know that it would only take *that* much—' she placed her finger and thumb tips close together, '—to make us more than good friends. I don't take it at all lightly. And I don't take Jonty and my family lightly either, especially since Fay was born. I'm a grandmother, for goodness' sake.'

'I've always assumed grandmothers to be sentient human beings,' said Robert mildly.

'They are. I am. All the more reason why I would be happier if our relationship reverted to being purely professional.'

Robert offered a thoughtful silence. He used pauses, thought Hester, like chess moves.

'Has it not occurred to you, Hetty, that this outpouring is likely to produce quite the opposite effect?'

The blood rushed to Hester's stomach, then her face.

'No,' she admitted, 'it hadn't occurred to me.'

It was one of those moments of startling disclosure, when a landscape is revealed completely other than the one you thought you were passing through. As a child being driven to family holidays in Devon Hester could remember gazing out of the car window, looking out for the distant hills of Exmoor, and finally, thrillingly, spotting them on the horizon, only to discover a minute or two later that they were not hills but banks of low grey cloud. Now, in an abrupt shift in perspective, she saw that she might have been wrong all along about Robert.

She fixed her eyes on a tall glass office block beyond the window, reminding herself that there were people all around who were living their lives, sustaining shocks, bearing pain, many of them in all probability suffering a far greater degree of humiliation than she was at this moment.

Robert said: 'I mention it because I think you might be throwing the baby out with the bath water, if that isn't an inapposite metaphor . . . I value our time together and, as you say you do as well, why should we forego it for fear of something which exists entirely in the imagination?'

He was kind enough not to say that it was her imagination in which the 'something' existed, but his delicacy was more wounding than bluntness. She had no way of countering it.

He went on gently: 'I can only speak for myself, Hetty, but I should be sadder than I can say if we were not able to go on enjoying one another's society. Who's going to make me laugh, and blow away the cobwebs, and put things into perspective, if not you?'

'I don't know.'

'You have a very special place in my life. You are, if I may say so,' he added, and suddenly she knew what was coming, 'a very special lady.'

He had said it. She closed her eyes. It was the final indignity. The one thing she had never, ever, suspected Robert of being was corny.

'Hetty . . .? Did you hear me?'

'Yes.'

'I mean it. Very special.'

'Thank you.'

'I'm merely protecting my own interests by pointing out that you're attempting to head off a danger which is not there.'

'Yes, I understand that.'

'So, may I look forward to more of our pleasurable times together . . .?'

'No.' She got up. She could tell from his face that he either thought he had misheard or had not taken it in, for he still wore the same look of friendly hopefulness. 'No, I don't think so.'

His brow furrowed. She wondered how she had ever found him fascinating.

'Where are you going in such a hurry?'

'Home.'

He leaned back in his chair. Tactics. She remained standing.

He said: 'You'd do much better to leave it half an hour. You'll only stew in traffic.'

'I don't mind.'

'Sit down and have another drink—' She flinched as his hand touched hers and he withdrew it at once. 'Don't let the sun go down on it.'

She looked down at him. 'Please, Robert. I am not wrathful. I'm not anything that you would understand. But I do want to go home.'

'Very well.' He rose and did up the button on his jacket. She could almost see him moving into another mode, another phase. This was this, and it was over, and many other things awaited him. He held out his hand. 'Au revoir, Hetty.'

'Goodnight.'

'May I walk you back to your car?'

'No thank you.'

'In that case I'll stay and have another – catch a cab to the Garrick when the rush has died down.'

'Have a good evening.'

He shrugged. 'It will be perfectly routine, I imagine.'

As Hester walked away she saw him sit down, unbutton his jacket once more, and magic a waiter to his side. She knew that already he was thinking about something else.

It was seven o'clock and still hot. The roaring breath of the traffic, its stench and glare, and the heat thrown back from concrete, metal and glass shattered her fragile composure. She hurried, almost stumbling back to the car with the tears oozing over her cheeks beneath her dark glasses. She had reached Hendon before she noticed she had a parking ticket.

Jonty got back to find Giselle upstairs feeding Fay, and Daniel lying on the sofa watching a video of Spike Lee's *Do the Right Thing* for the umpteenth time. Jonty came in and stood behind him, taking

in the funny hairstyles and scatological dialogue which, in spite of
repeated exposure to the genre, he still found slightly threatening.

'Mum rang,' said Daniel, without taking his eyes off the screen.

'Oh yes?'

'She says sorry but she's held up.'

'I see.'

Daniel twisted his head to look up at him. 'Downer, yeah?'

One morning a few days later Byron was doing some maintenance
jobs at Gavin's flat. He had not been asked by Gavin, but
instructed by Ann, who took the view that a sense of order
and serenity could to some extent be aided by the replacement
of washers, tightening of window latches and repointing of tiles.
Byron, who no longer knew what was for the best, was more than
willing to undertake these tasks if they would make the slightest
difference to the fury and turmoil that was currently rampaging
unchecked through their lives.

The jobs at George Street were nothing to the ones he had just
completed at Sebastian's place. He had decided not to bother Ann
with the details of those. After all, it had been his idea that he
get the work done before she and Josette spring-cleaned, and
she had enough on her plate at the moment without worrying
about blocked drains, smoking light fittings and dodgy substances along with mouse droppings in the kitchen cupboards.
He preferred to acquiesce in his wife's view of their sons, and
had practised a lifelong discretion with regard to the boys and
their doings.

One particular discovery had overshadowed all others in Sebastian's
flat. As soon as he'd arrived with his tool kit on the first morning
Byron had been almost overpowered by the nauseating, fishy smell
of advanced putrescence. He left the front door wide and stumbled,
gagging, to the nearest window. Having opened all of them he
returned to the hall to find the woman from downstaris hovering
on the landing.

'I was going to contact someone,' she said, 'I reckon something's
died in there.'

'There was nothing to die,' said Byron, breathing through his
mouth. 'It's not as if my son kept any pets or anything.'

'That little black girl's been in a couple of times,' said the
neighbour, 'but she never seemed to notice anything.'

'Oh well,' said Byron, 'I'm going to be in and out for the next few days; I daresay something'll come to light.'

It had, but only by chance. He was replacing a cracked floorboard in the bedroom. The smell seemed particularly strong in here, though that might have been due to the continuing fine weather, and Byron had a damp hankie tied round his mouth and nose, as well as the window wide open, top and bottom. He half-thought he might be about to stumble on the source of the smell beneath the floor and was entertaining a ghastly Nielson-like picture of human remains, when he noticed the curtains. They were a wide purple and black stripe, a fabric chosen by Sebastian in Whiteley's and made up by Ann on her electric sewing machine. From his vantage point on the floor Byron could see the hem, which appeared to have a dark stain running along it. He assumed this to be the result of Sebastian's smoking and the none-too-clean windowsill, but a closer inspection revealed the stain to be brownish and damp. Lifting the hem to give it an exploratory sniff Byron was nearly asphyxiated by the stench, and also aware of an unpleasant squelchiness inside the material. With some trepidation he took his lino-knife and made a two-inch incision in the fold of the hem. A handful of dark matter plopped to the ground. Byron dropped the curtain and jumped backwards. When, rather shamefacedly, he bent over for a closer look he saw that the stuff was some sort of offal, mercifully not human – chicken livers, or kidneys. Having refreshed his hankie mask with a splash of Sebastian's old aftershave from the bathroom, Byron painstakingly unpicked the rest of the hem to reveal more of these gruesome titbits and, for good measure, some prawns. This, he thought respectfully, was monkey business of a high order.

Byron put the offal and prawns into a plastic bag and placed the bag, tied tightly at the top, in the dustbin. Then he took down the curtain, sponged the hem with soapy water and put it by the front door to be dropped off at the dry cleaners on the way home. His next task was to check the rest of the curtains in the flat. It was during the carrying out of this check – which revealed no further horrors – that he discovered the note. It was pinned to the inside of the lavatory door, at eye-level of anyone sitting on the seat.

'*Just for once Shitface,*' it said, '*there's a worse stink on the* other *side of this door. I hope they tear the place down. Suffer, you bastard.*'

Byron had filed this development with all those other things which came under the heading 'Don't Tell Ann'. He was seriously worried about her at the moment. She had taken the whole Gavin/Giselle business very hard. Not only was she cut to the quick by what she saw as the Blakes' cavalier disregard for their long-standing friendship, but she was suffering for Gavin, too. Rather more than Gavin himself, in Byron's opinion. And she was making the whole thing a thousand times worse for herself by her ingrained habit of control. Ever since he had first met Ann, Byron had admired her self-discipline. He had from time to time been less sure about her determination – from the best of intentions – to order the lives of those around her, but there could be no doubting her organisational abilities and her singleness of purpose in finding solutions to the myriad problems thrown up by family life. Now, in the situation in which they found themselves, her self-control seemed less of an asset. It was not simply that she was placing an intolerable strain on herself by suppressing so much tumultuous and conflicting emotion, but that she placed a strain on him by not allowing him to recognise it. A stubborn and in Byron's view idiotic pride precluded any show of understanding, let alone sympathy. He felt baffled and rudderless. This aridity seemed so unnecessary when the circumstances, no matter how unwelcome, might have brought them closer together. He couldn't pretend any very great distress about being separated for the moment from his first grandchild. He had never even seen the baby, and a secret chauvinistic quirk told him that she wouldn't be of much interest for several years yet. But Ann was cut up, and he wasn't going to say or do anything that would make things worse.

He was rather embarrassed handing over the curtains at the dry cleaners. He had rolled them up as tightly as possible, with the hems innermost, and stuffed them into a binbag, but needless to say the assistant dragged them out and shook them open, releasing the disgusting smell.

'Dear oh dear!' she cried, grimacing, and stuffing them back in the bag, 'what's the matter with those? It's like the revenge of the bodysnatchers in there!'

'I know,' said Byron helplessly, knowing the truth wouldn't be believed but congenitally unable to think up a convincing lie, either. 'We were the victims of a particularly offensive practical joke.'

'Offensive, you said it.'

'I hope there's something you can do with them.'

'I really couldn't say,' declared the assistant superciliously, 'someone'll have to take a good look.'

Smarting with embarrassment, Byron had left.

At George Street the jobs to be done weren't in the same league as those in Sebastian's flat and he anticipated no nasty shocks. He let himself in at about 11 a.m., made himself a mug of coffee and started on the tiles behind the kitchen sink to the accompaniment of the second half of *Woman's Hour*, followed by *Eurofile*, and *You and Yours*. Scraping and pasting away he learnt more than he'd ever wanted to know about toxic shock syndrome, Belgian farm subsidies and NIMBY disputes.

At twelve-thirty, as he ate Ann's excellent liver sausage and coleslaw sandwiches, washed down with Evian water, the front door opened and he experienced the involuntary tensing of the muscles which preceded any exchange with Gavin, particularly at the present time. He stared out of the kitchen window with a fixity designed to show how untroubled he was, and braced himself to withstand squalls.

'Oh – hallo.'

It was Katie. Byron could not have been more surprised. In fact for a moment, on hearing her voice, he thought it was Gavin fooling around. When he did finally take in who it was his curiosity was temporarily swamped by relief.

'Katie – you're the last person I expected to see.'

'Really? Ditto.'

'Of course. I do apologise.' Byron had always liked Katie whom one could tell at a glance was that old-fashioned thing, a well-brought-up girl. 'I'm doing a few small maintenance jobs about the place. I let myself in with my own key. I'll probably be about for a day or two.'

'How very kind of you.'

'Not at all, it's what fathers are for. Were you expecting to find Gavin? Because if so I'm afraid he's not here. Out at the cutting edge of catering as usual.'

'I know. I had to come back for – um – something . . .' Katie looked embarrassed as she realised she had said more than she intended.

'Oh, yes – fine – carry on. Sorry if I gave you a fright!' said Byron, the soul of discretion.

She reappeared after a couple of minutes, holding aloft a small blue bottle. 'Contact lens solution. I'm reporting on a celebrity birthday bash this evening and I'd be lost without it.'

'Anyone I'd know?' asked Byron. 'The bash? Bearing in mind I lead a very sheltered life.'

'Ludo Linklater. The gentleman jump-jockey?'

'Um . . . no, sorry. I'm not much of a racing man.'

'You don't have to be. The accent in his case is on the jump.'

'Good heavens.'

'They say he's ridden five hundred winners and any number of complete dogs – he's not fussy.'

Byron smiled faintly. It was clear that Katie was moving in different circles since last he met her. When she'd left he began work once more, reflecting that here was another development about which it would be best not to tell his wife.

Ann was finding Sonja a high trial. It was the first time she had reached this point with a lodger, and she blamed herself, naturally. Her morale at present was dangerously low: she had even been turning away clients. To remain on top of the situation she had to maintain complete mastery of her private feelings, and in order to do this it had been necessary to relieve herself of some of her outside responsibilities. Family matters were paramount with Ann, first, last and always.

Sonja (her London secondment unfortunately extended until Christmas) was quite the wrong person to have around during this acutely difficult time. Her elephantine humour, her clunkingly imperfect English, her size, her tactlessness, her gargantuan appetite – Ann could go on. Just when she felt an almost desperate desire to be alone, to collect her thoughts and marshal her forces, Sonja was there, suggesting outings, expecting meals, trying to cheer them both up. Worst of all had been a recent occasion when Gavin came round, spoiling for a scene, only to be greeted by Sonja with shrieks of delight. Ann would never forget the look on his face as she burbled on, and the lacerating rudeness of his responses. Not that he'd had any effect, Sonja's hide was proof against even Gavin's verbal barbs, especially in a foreign language.

The end of August was Ann's least favourite time of year. Under normal circumstances there was no way she would have allowed such a whimsical consideration to affect her spirits, but this year these dreary, tail-end days of summer increased her suffocating sense of helplessness. There was much she could, and would have done had Gavin been halfway willing to co-operate. She had conducted research into possible mediation, financial arrangements, even, heaven forfend, legal solutions. But at present his sense of outrage and injured pride (which, in deepest secret, she suspected was far stronger than any paternal feeling) made practical measures out of the question. Daily, Ann prayed to a God whom she hoped took a lenient view of the petitions of agnostics, that Gavin would calm down and come round sufficiently to listen to reason. In the interim all she could do was assume the role of fall guy. The fact that she had had no further contact with her new granddaughter since the day of her birth was an internal wound that gave her constant covert pain. But she didn't speak of it because she did not want Gavin to think for one moment that her desire to help was based on self-interest.

This afternoon she had decided to prepare some food for the freezer. Cooking was a therapy for Ann. She had always used the preparation and consumption of meals as a means of expressing her devotion to and interest in her family. The long maple dining table at Raglan Road had been a kind of altar, a place where the most sacred and intimate rites of family life took place – discussions, negotiations, confrontations and reconciliations. It was in the kitchen, rather than the bedroom, that she and Byron had plotted and charted the course of their long marriage.

Today she was going to make ratatouille, while the ingredients were still more or less in season in the shops. This was low-effort but satisfying cookery. She liked the brilliant colours and subtly varying textures of the different vegetables, the chopping and slicing with her sharp French knife, the intoxicating aroma of the frying garlic, the luscious amalgamation of onions, red and green peppers, aubergines, courgettes and tomatoes so that they gradually lost their separateness and became a deliciously rich, olive-and-terracotta stew. Classic FM, apparently attuned to her mood, played *Songs of the Auvergne*. Her spirit unclenched a fraction. She lost herself.

She didn't hear Sonja approaching until she was the other side of the work surface, exclaiming in delight: 'Ann! What a perfectly gorgeous smell! What are you making here?'

'Ratatouille,' replied Ann, wiping a hand on her apron and turning the volume down slightly on the radio.

'That is one of my big favourites. We are going to have some for dinner? I shall buy some *ciabatta* to accompany it.'

'No,' said Ann, cutting a Spanish onion into longitudinal segments prior to chopping it across the grain, 'we aren't having it for supper. I am stocking the freezer.'

Sonja leaned folded arms on the worktop, and rested her mighty bosom on her arms. Her nose was only inches from Ann's rapidly pecking knife blade.

'Can't you keep a little on one side for us to have as a side dish . . .?' She snatched a piece of red pepper from the edge of the board and munched it with noisy relish.

'Please don't do that,' said Ann, turning the onion, still held together like a chocolate orange.

'But you're so cruel,' complained Sonja with monstrous winsomeness, 'to feed the freezer and not the people!'

Ann laid down both onion and knife and stood holding the edges of the board, staring at the brightly coloured chunks of vegetable.

'Sonja, would you please go away?'

Sonja laughed. 'I'm putting you off – I know. The problem is, I am in love with your cooking!'

'Thank you. Would you mind leaving me alone to get on with it?'

'One more little bite—' Sonja's plump forefinger and thumb hovered over the peppers.

'I'd much rather you didn't.'

'A tiny one . . .?' Sonja pleaded in a wheedling, childish voice.

'No. Please.' Ann grasped the knife handle once more. 'I want to get on.'

'Too late!' Sonja popped a piece into her mouth.

Ann began to tremble uncontrollably. The knife blade made a scribbling sound on the board. The expression on Sonja's face told her that she looked as strange as she felt. To her rapidly escalating anger was added shame and dismay that she had let herself go to such an extent.

However, it achieved the desired effect. Sonja backed off warily. 'I'm sorry, I shall leave you in peace.'

She withdrew. With an effort, Ann steadied the knife and began once more to slice the onion. With the second stroke she inflicted a deep cut on the top of her forefinger. The onion and the chopping board were spattered with red. Ann's earlier trembling now became the deep, seismic shivering of shock. She turned on the cold tap and held her throbbing finger beneath it. Bright gouts of blood continued to well, unabated, to be dashed away by the water.

It was as she stood at the sink that Josette came in at the back door. She carried a gift-wrapped package. This time Ann did hear her, and saw who it was, but could summon no particular reaction. The icy water kept thrumming down on her hand, and she was shuddering.

'Mrs Armitage . . .?' Josette, naturally more delicate than Sonja, came no closer, but tilted her head solicitously, trying to see Ann's face. 'Are you all right?'

'I cut my finger.'

'Shall I run upstairs and get a plaster?'

'Thank you.'

While Josette was upstairs Ann turned the tap off. She held her finger aloft, but it continued to bleed freely, dripping on her clothes and on the floor. When Josette returned she allowed her to take charge, drying the cut, applying antiseptic cream and several strips of Elastoplast.

'Keep holding it up for the moment, won't you,' advised Josette. 'Now sit down. What about this?' she turned the heat off beneath the pan of olive oil. 'There you go. Would you like me to make a drink?'

Ann shook her head. 'No, thank you.'

'Maybe I'll put the kettle on anyway.'

Josette filled and switched on the kettle and then laid the gaily striped package on the table in front of Ann. 'I only came in to drop this off for Mr Armitage.'

'He's not in.'

'Please would you pass it on for me?'

'Yes.'

'It's a little present,' explained Josette, 'to thank him for all the help he's been giving me. I don't know what I'd have done without him.'

'Good,' said Ann. 'I'll tell him.'

'It's a book of essays,' went on Josette. 'I hope he finds it interesting. You might like it too, Mrs Armitage. The title caught my eye right away. It's called *The Ties That Bind* – it's about family relationships.'

For some time after Josette had gone Ann sat with her elbow on the table, forefinger held aloft, staring dully at the package. Then she got up, steadying herself for a second because she felt rather faint. When her head had stopped swimming she took the frying pan off the stove and put it in the sink. Then she scraped all the chopped vegetables into the rubbish bin, and threw Josette's package in on top of them before letting the lid drop.

'Womantalk' was a day-long workshop on the subject of communication, by, for and concerning women. Hester was the final speaker – 'the cherry on the top, so to speak,' the organiser had gushed, 'all you have to do is get up there and enjoy yourself' – but she had misgivings about the premise. While she would have been the first to say that every woman doing her chosen work should concede she was a feminist, she didn't terribly care for the herding of large topics into particular lobbies. Also, she was tired and depressed and was suffering from a crisis of confidence, none of which was going to help her to sparkle on the platform.

She had managed to fend off the genial pressure to attend for the full day, but had agreed to arrive in time to speak at four o'clock, and stay for tea afterwards. 'Or I'm sure we could rustle up a glass of wine for our distinguished guest . . .' the organiser assured her. It wasn't the first time that Hester, as the representative of Fleet Street, had been taken for someone who could not face so much as a ginger nut without a serious drink to wash it down.

The venue for 'Womantalk' was a distinguished but slightly faded women's club in Chelsea. The club had a proud history of struggle and eccentricity; its entrance hall was hung with portraits of stately, thoughtful women without a shred of vanity and hairstyles to match. The staff were motherly and rough-spoken, giving the unmistakable impression that they believed their lot to be the collecting of coats and serving of sandwiches to their intellectual betters. In this slightly down-at-heel, sisterly sanctum the massed black leggings, plaid workshirts, Issey Miyake waistcoats and razor-sharp haircuts of the two hundred delegates sat strangely. Such a multiplicity of messages were buzzing back and forth between the dark panels of the lecture theatre and soaring aloft to wheel among its metal-shaded, hanging striplights that Hester was unsure how to pitch her speech. Should she attune it to her surroundings, with a ringing sense of history and shared destiny . . . or to her audience, with many modern saws and instances and a sharp post-feminist perspective . . . or plump for the no-contest option and be entirely frivolous?

She took her place on the platform during the applause for the previous speaker, still undecided what line she would take, or even what her opening gambit would be. The distinguished academic sitting next to her leaned sideways.

'Don't suppose you suffer from nerves at all.'

'I do, actually,' whispered Hester. 'You can't perform without them.'

'You look cool as a cucumber,' the academic told her.

It was only a crumb of comfort but enough to stiffen Hester's spine. As she stood up her opening remark swam up over the horizon in the nick of time like the cavalry in an old western. And though she wasn't at her best, the subsequent stages of her speech did the same, presenting themselves seconds before she uttered them. She had their attention, the laughs came, there were no *longueurs*, but when the final burst of warm, appreciative applause came, on the very dot of her appointed time, she sat down with a sense only of relief, and her palms were sweating.

Tea was a noisy buffet served in the club's large, dim lounge. Hester stood in a corner with the organiser, earlier speaker and other members of the platform party, consuming tea, sandwiches and little cakes with the mindless gusto of relief. She was tired. Her feet were hot and swollen and she had the beginnings of a tension headache. These were circumstances in which she would formerly have longed to return home. The Old Clink had always been a paradigm of all that was relaxed, comforting, easy, tolerant – where no judgements were made and all was acceptance. The fluid emotional shorthand of married life let so much lie, and took so much on trust. Now that ease and fluidity were missing, she was dismayed to realise that with the thought of home came the uncomfortable nibble of anxiety.

'. . . the perfect ending to the day,' the organiser was saying fulsomely. 'There really is nothing like humour for putting things in perspective.'

'I'm glad you were pleased,' said Hester. 'It was a very receptive audience.'

The organiser beamed, she too was relieved. 'I can honestly say that this has been our most successful day yet. There can't be a woman here who's going away without some food for thought . . .'

She continued in this vein, her view warmly endorsed by those around her, but Hester could no longer hear them.

She had seen Ann was in the centre of the room. She was talking to a striking Bangladeshi doctor in a peacock-blue sari. Next to this brilliant figure Ann looked small and drab. She was as usual neat, too conservative to be elegant, but too classic to be dowdy. Her hair was slightly longer than it had been when Hester had last seen her in the hospital, in need of cutting. She was listening to the Asian woman with her customary intense concentration. Hester could not imagine from what reserves of self-control she summoned this concentration when she knew that Hester was in the same room – when she had only just been listening, in fact, to her speech. As Hester watched she lifted her left hand to her hair, as if self-conscious about it, and Hester noticed a thick covering of sticking plaster on the top joint of her index finger. The plaster was grubby. For some reason Hester found this quite unbearably poignant.

'Excuse me . . .' she said, and walked quickly from the room.

In the cloakroom she went into a cubicle and sat down on the closed lavatory seat with her head in her hands. Through the not-quite-closed zip on her shoulder bag she could see the red sou'wester of the Paddington Bear she had bought for Fay at Hamley's. Darling, vulnerable, imperious Fay – the source, if not the cause of all the trouble . . . Hester knew that only she herself could fully appreciate what Ann must be going through. She had not thought it possible to love her grandchild as much as she had loved her own children as babies, but she did, and it was a helpless, unconditional love, tortured by fears and frustration, unchecked by the small tyranny of maternal practicalities.

A loud, desperate sob escaped her just as someone else entered the cloakroom. She caught her breath, her eyes and throat bulging with tears. The thought that the other person might be Ann filled her with panic. But then she caught a whiff of the sort of scent Ann would never dream of using, and took a long, wavering breath. She dragged several feet of toilet paper off the roll and wiped the black stains off her cheeks. Then she stood up, pressed the lever and emerged. The other woman, young and sassy in a skirt that was not much more than a wide belt, and cork platform soles, flashed her a friendly smile.

'Thanks for the talk. I'm afraid I loathe your paper and everything it stands for, but you were great in there.'

'Thank you.'

Hester was used to this type of barbed compliment, and had learned how to accept it. She came out into the dingy corridor feeling a little better. She had to separate things out, as Jonty was always advising. The situation in which they found themselves was not of their making, nor of their choosing. But given the state of affairs between Giselle and Gavin it was probably inevitable. The important person in all this was Fay, who must be cherished and protected at all costs. And of course Giselle, who as Fay's mother and their daughter deserved their loving and wholehearted support.

She was mentally intoning these much-rehearsed statements when she saw Ann coming down the corridor towards her.

It was a long corridor, and there was no-one else in it at this moment. Every step brought them closer together. Ann was holding herself very upright, her step was quick and firm, there was no way that she could avoid seeing her. Hester glanced to either side. There was one door, marked 'Private'. Short of embarking on an elaborate and entirely unconvincing charade of having forgotten something, there was nothing she could do to avoid a confrontation. But need it be a confrontation? Suddenly she remembered the grubby sticking plaster.

She would do it. She would speak to Ann, and break this wheel of misery to which they'd all so wrong-headedly, self-righteously, bound themselves.

Gavin lay on the sofa with his head on Katie's lap. She stroked his hair gently.

'I'm sorry,' he said, 'if I'm being a bore . . .'

'You're not,' said Katie. 'Not for a moment. You must talk about it, let it all out. I'll listen.'

'You were always too good for me.' Gavin put up a hand to

cradle her cheek and smiled a sweetly rueful smile. Katie was quite overwhelmed with pity for this bruised and damaged man who had turned to her for help.

'I'll always be here,' she whispered. He closed his eyes and she continued to stroke his tousled hair, prepared to be endlessly, lovingly patient.

What she found so astonishing was that Hester Blake, whom she had liked so much, and who had been so kind to her, could have been instrumental in doing something so – so *cruel* (there was no other word for it) to a man whose only crime was falling in love with her daughter.

A small part of Katie's soft and generous heart tightened, and grew hard. Gavin, his face resting on her lap, smiled as he drifted into sleep.

Giselle sat in the garden of The Old Clink, beneath one of the apple trees. She sat cross-legged on a cushion, with another between her back and the trunk of the tree. She was feeding Fay. The answering machine was on, Daniel was out and the garden, in all its ripe summer superabundance, hummed richly in the late afternoon sunshine. Windfalls lay scattered on the ground and occasionally another would drop with a gentle thud into the unmown grass.

Ark, with Dolly on her lead, came round the side of the house and crossed the grass to her side. He dropped the lead and Dolly sank down, spreadeagled and panting.

Giselle smiled up at him, through his shadow, before he sat down next to her, his back also against the tree. With his finger he touched first Fay's hand, then the smooth and fruitful curve of Giselle's breast.

They didn't speak. There was no need. They were content.

Hester and Ann drew level with one another. For a fraction of a second their eyes met with a violent, stifled shock. Hester's heart thundered.

Then, without a word having been spoken, they passed each other by.

Other best selling Warner titles available by mail:

☐	The Flowers of the Field	Sarah Harrison	£6.99
☐	A Flower That's Free	Sarah Harrison	£6.99
☐	Hot Breath	Sarah Harrison	£4.99
☐	An Imperfect Lady	Sarah Harrison	£6.99
☐	The Forests of the Night	Sarah Harrison	£4.99
☐	Foreign Parts	Sarah Harrison	£4.99
☐	Be An Angel	Sarah Harrison	£6.99

The prices shown above are correct at time of going to press, however the publishers reserve the right to increase prices on covers from those previously advertised, without further notice.

WARNER BOOKS

WARNER BOOKS
Cash Sales Department, P.O. Box 11, Falmouth, Cornwall, TR10 9EN
Tel: +44 (0) 1326 372400, Fax: +44 (0) 1326 374888
Email: books@barni.avel.co.uk.

POST AND PACKING:
Payments can be made as follows: cheque, postal order (payable to Warner Books) or by credit cards. Do not send cash or currency.

All U.K. Orders   **FREE OF CHARGE**
E.E.C. & Overseas   25% of order value

Name (Block Letters) _____

Address _____

_____

Post/zip code: _____

☐ Please keep me in touch with future Warner publications

☐ I enclose my remittance £_____

☐ I wish to pay by Visa/Access/Mastercard/Eurocard

Card Expiry Date

_____